"The enduring theme of family loyalty ennobles the Harte family saga and raises it to a heartwarming crescendo that longtime fans will appreciate. Now readers will relish it as well."

—BookPage

EMMA'S SECRET

"Readers who loved *A Woman of Substance* will enjoy *Emma's Secret*."

—*Denver Post*

"In her nineteenth novel, the grande dame of mass-market fiction revisits her first heroine—the indomitable Emma Harte."

—*New York Daily News*

"So many of us turn to novels like Barbara Taylor Bradford's latest, *Emma's Secret,* for our daily dose of amour."

—*Woman's Day* magazine

"Promises to tantalize, mesmerize, and titillate readers of all ages. It has all the Bradford touches: strong and swift plot, hints of secrets about to be revealed . . . spellbinding . . . destined to fly off booksellers' racks and be passed around many book clubs. It is a darn good read."

—*Roanoke Times*

"It will be . . . appreciated by those with an irresistible desire to follow the further adventures of the Harte clan."

—*Publishers Weekly*

"Bradford's characters are so real, readers clamor to know them better."

—*USA Today Weekend* magazine

"[An] original story with new energy. Emma Harte is one of those characters whom we never want to leave behind, and thank goodness Bradford has brought her back to us with a story worthy of this truly remarkable woman."

—*Romantic Times BOOKreviews*, "Top Pick"

TO BE THE BEST

"A novel for everyone . . . A satisfying, lushly detailed saga."
—*Rave Reviews*

"A compulsive read."
—*Daily Mail* (London)

"Will keep you up till all hours reading just one more chapter before you can bear to turn out the bedside light."
—*Prima* magazine

ACT OF WILL

"A master storyteller and character builder, Ms. Bradford again crafts another reader-holder novel . . . *Act of Will* is another winner."
—*Pittsburgh Press*

"Pure gold—certain to be a runaway bestseller."
—*Cosmopolitan*

"This novel continues the Bradford tradition of spirited romances peopled with memorable, self-made women . . . fetching."
—*Booklist*

HOLD THE DREAM

"Readers who shared the trials and tribulations and successes of the indomitable Emma Harte in *A Woman of Substance* will find this sequel equally engrossing. Attractive, intelligent, and capable, Paula McGill Fairley proves a worthy successor to her grandmother's domain."
—*Booklist*

"Another instant bestseller. The men and women are all gorgeous, rich, well-dressed. There are luxurious descriptions in this perfect page-turner."
—*Philadelphia Inquirer*

"A deeply involving story of women of power and wealth and sub-stance."

—*Publishers Weekly*

"Fascinating."

—*Houston Chronicle*

"A sweeping saga full of passion and intrigue . . . a gripping read."

—*Hello!* magazine

"A vibrantly characterized leading lady and a glimpse at the daz-zling world of the rich and powerful. A richly woven tale."

—*Working Woman*

"Barbara Taylor Bradford is the storyteller of substance."

—*The Times* (London)

VOICE OF THE HEART

"*Voice of the Heart* is the sort of book I cannot resist, indeed, I pray to find."

—*The Washington Times Magazine*

"It really keeps you turning the pages, wondering just why it is that two beautiful women who were once great friends are now sworn enemies."

—*Daily Express* (UK)

"A rare treat. We guarantee you will laugh and cry with the char-acters and that you won't be able to put it down."

—*The Literary Guild* magazine

A WOMAN OF SUBSTANCE

also by barbara taylor bradford

THE EMMA HARTE SAGA

OTHERS

the
ravenscar
dynasty

barbara taylor
bradford

St. Martin's Paperbacks

This is a work of fiction. All of the characters, organizations, and events portrayed in this novel are either products of the author's imagination or are used fictitiously.

THE RAVENSCAR DYNASTY

Copyright © 2006 by Beaji Enterprises.

ISBN: 0-312-94877-8
EAN: 978-0-312-94877-1

Printed in the United States of America

St. Martin's Press hardcover edition / January 2007
St. Martin's Paperbacks International edition / April 2007

St. Martin's Paperbacks are published by St. Martin's Press, 175 Fifth Avenue, New York, NY 10010.

10 9 8 7 6 5 4 3 2 1

For my husband, Robert Bradford,
who has lived with these characters for over
twenty-six years,
and has never lost patience with them or with me.
With my love.

author's note

This is a modern novel, told in the modern vernacular and set in the early part of the twentieth century. However, I have to a certain extent based my protagonist, Edward Deravenel, on the English medieval king Edward IV. Born Edward Plantagenet, the Earl of March, he was the eldest son of the mighty Duke of York and his Duchess. Edward's father was a prince of the blood and a royal duke, head of the royal House of York, rightful heir to the throne of England.

When Edward's father was killed in the Battle of Sandal Castle in Wakefield, Yorkshire, in 1460, during the Wars of the Roses, Edward assumed his father's hereditary title and became Duke of York. He continued his father's fight to win back the throne from his cousin Henry VI, Duke of Lancaster. He was aided in this struggle by his cousin Richard Neville, the Earl of Warwick, known later in history as the Kingmaker.

The throne of England had been usurped by the House of Lancaster some sixty years earlier, and it was in 1461 that Edward Plantagenet took that throne back when he defeated Henry VI and became king.

Aside from "borrowing" the exceptional good looks of Edward Plantagenet, and his height of six feet four, unusual for those times, I have used some aspects of his character and personality in the depiction of Edward Deravenel. Significant events in the life of the medieval king are used in modern form as the basis, in part, of Edward Deravenel's story.

New York, June 2006

contents

part one

❧

powerful
allies

edward and neville

Princely to behold, of body mighty, strong and clean made.

SIR THOMAS MORE

Yet there was magnanimity in him, and if he is not quite a tragic protagonist, he is a memorable human being. He refused to admit that there were disadvantages he could not overcome and defeats from which he could not recover, and he had the courage, and vanity, to press his game to the end.

PAUL MURRAY KENDALL

Their relationship, like their division of authority, was amiable and undefined.

PAUL MURRAY KENDALL

one

YORKSHIRE 1904

Edward Deravenel galloped ahead at great speed, leaving his brothers behind, rapidly gaining the advantage. He urged his white stallion forward, oblivious to the icy weather, the lash of the wind on his face.

At one moment, half turning in the saddle, glancing behind him, Edward laughed out loud, his hilarity filling the air as he waved to his brothers: George, endeavoring to catch up, his face grim in its determination . . . Richard, struggling even farther behind, yet laughing and waving back. But then he was the youngest, and much less competitive, the baby of the family, and Edward's particular favorite.

For a split second Edward considered slowing down and allowing Richard to win this impromptu race, which had come about spontaneously a short while before, then instantly changed his mind.

George would inevitably contrive to finish first, by pushing Richard out of the way in his overriding desire to be the winner. Somehow he always managed to do this, no matter what the circumstances. And this Edward could not permit. He strived to make certain Richard was never humiliated, never diminished by George, who was older than Richard by three years and frequently endeavored to lord it over the younger boy.

Edward continued at a gentler pace along the narrow

path, glancing to his left as he did. The cliffs fell steeply to
the rocks and the beach; six hundred feet below him, the
North Sea roared under the gusting wind, resembled polished steel in the January sunlight.

The waves frothed and churned against the jagged rock for-
mations, while above him kittiwakes, graceful and buoyant in
flight, squawked stridently as they wheeled and turned against
the pale sky. Hundreds of these beautiful white gulls with
black-tipped wings made their homes on the cliff faces, and as
a child he had watched them nesting through his binoculars.

He shivered involuntarily as the sudden remembrance of
a tragedy of long ago hit him most forcibly. A man in his father's employ, who had been bird-watching, had plunged to
his death from this very spot. Now, instinctively, Edward
veered away from the precarious cliffs, headed in the direction of the dirt road which led across the moors and was
much safer terrain.

This morning the moorland was dun-colored and
patched with slabs of frozen snow, and there was no question in Edward's mind that he much preferred riding up
here when the weather was more benign, the air even balmy
and filled with the scent of wildflowers, and the northern
summer light dazzling.

Edward mentally chastised himself for taking his brothers
out on this winter day. He had realized, rather late, that it was
far too bitter, especially for Richard, who tended to catch
colds so easily. He dared not contemplate his mother's ire if
the boy fell sick because of this ill-conceived outing. Swinging his head, Edward saw that the boys had again slowed and
were obviously fatigued by the long ride. He must spur them
on, get them home without delay. He shouted, "Come on,
chaps! Let's get a move on!" And he set off at a brisk canter.
Once or twice he glanced behind him, pleased that his brothers had heeded his words and were cantering hard on his
heels. Within minutes, to his profound relief, their ancestral
home was in his direct line of vision.

Ravenscar, the beautiful old manor house where the Deravenels had lived for centuries, stood on high ground, set back from the sea, and dominated the surrounding landscape. Dark green trees, ancient, tall, and stately, formed a semicircle around it on three sides, and these were backed by high stone walls; the fourth wall was a natural one—the North Sea. This stretched into infinity below the tiered gardens and sloping lawns that ended at the edge of the precipitous cliffs.

As Edward drew closer, he could easily make out the crenellation along the line of the roof, smoke curling up from the chimneys, and the many mullioned windows glittering in the sunlight. Within seconds he was bringing his horse to a slow trot, riding through the black iron gates and up the long, tree-lined drive. This ended with some abruptness in a small, circular courtyard covered with gravel and with a sundial in its center.

The house was built of a local, pale-colored stone that had mellowed to a soft golden beige with the passing of the centuries. It typified Tudor architecture with its recesses and bays, gables and battlements, and many windows of differing sizes. Ravenscar was one of those grand houses from the past, and it had a lovely symmetry and a charm all its own. To Edward there was a sense of timelessness about it, a quality of serenity and peace dwelling in its gently flowing facade, and he understood why his forebears had always cherished and cared for this treasure.

The Deravenels had lived in their house by the sea since 1578, the year it was finished. Before then, for many centuries, the family had occupied the fortified castle that had stood on the edge of the cliffs; a ruin now, it was nonetheless a well-maintained ruin. This stronghold had been built in 1070 by the founding father of the dynasty, one Guy de Ravenel, a young knight from Falaise, liege man of William, Duke of Normandy.

Duke William had invaded England in 1066, claiming his

right to the English throne through his cousin the deceased monarch Edward the Confessor, who had promised that the throne would be his one day. But for political convenience, Edward had reneged on that promise and passed over William in favor of his wife's brother, Harold, bequeathing the throne to the man who became, briefly, Harold II. Believing his claim to be absolutely legitimate, William had crossed the English Channel with the six knights who were his trusted childhood friends and a large army. He defeated Harold at the Battle of Hastings and was proclaimed William the Conqueror and crowned on Christmas Day of 1066.

A few years later, William had dispatched Guy de Ravenel to the north to act as his marshal. Based in Yorkshire, Guy had followed William's orders, had kept the peace, by force when necessary, built defenses and forts, and ensured the north's loyalty to the Norman king. And Guy had been enriched by William because of his staunch loyalty and unparalleled success.

Ever since that time, some 835 years ago, descendants of Guy de Ravenel had lived on this long stretch of coastline known as Ravenscar high above the North Sea. Nearby was the ancient seaport and spa of Scarborough; a little farther along the expansive stretch of coast was a picturesque fishing village with the quaint name of Robin Hood's Bay. Both dated back to Roman times.

Edward rode out of the courtyard and around to the back of the house, heading for the stable block. He clattered into the cobbled yard, his brothers following behind him, and jumped off his horse with his usual vitality and energy. As he hurried over to his youngest brother, he greeted the stable lads cheerfully; a moment later he was reaching up for the eight-year-old Richard, exclaiming, "Let me help you down, Dick!"

Richard shook his head vehemently. "I can manage, Ned. I truly can," the boy protested, stealing a surreptitious look at George through the corner of his eye. He knew only too well that his brother would tease him unmercifully if Ned helped him to dismount.

But Ned paid not the slightest attention to Richard; he put his strong arms around the boy, determined to lift him out of the saddle. Richard sighed. Accepting that he now had no choice, he slipped his riding boots out of the stirrups and reluctantly slid into his brother's enfolding arms.

For a split second, Edward held Richard close to his chest, and then he put him down on the cobblestones, noting that the youngster's narrow face was pinched with cold and drained of color. My fault, he chided himself, regretting even more his thoughtlessness.

"Thank you, Ned," Richard murmured, staring up into his oldest brother's face through his steady, slate-blue eyes. Edward was six feet four, broad of chest, very strong and athletic. His brilliant eyes were as blue as the speedwells that grew in the summer meadows, and his thick hair was a stunning burnished red-gold. To Richard, and to every woman who met him, Edward Deravenel was the handsomest man alive, and in addition, he had a warm, outgoing personality. He was affable, inordinately friendly, and blessed with a beguiling charm that captivated everyone. Richard loved him more than anyone else in the family, was completely devoted to him, and he would be all of Edward's life, and even after that.

"Inside the house as fast as you can," Edward cried, giving Richard an affectionate push toward the side door, which led to the mudroom. "And you, too, George, my lad. No dawdling around this morning."

The two boys did his bidding, and as Edward followed them at a quick pace, he called out to one of the stable lads, "The horses have been ridden hard this morning, Ernie. They need your very best rubdown, and put the heavy wool blankets on them before you give them water and feed."

"Aye, Master Edward," Ernie shouted back, glancing at him. He and the other stable lad took the reins of the three horses and led them toward the stables and tack room.

Once Edward and his brothers entered the mudroom, they felt the warmth of the house surrounding them. Shedding their black-and-white checked caps and thick woolen Inverness capes, they scraped their riding boots free from dirt. A moment later they all went down the corridor at the back of the house, heading toward the Long Hall at its center.

"I shall ask Cook to make us a small snack and hot tea," Edward informed his brothers, an arm on each of their shoulders. "Perhaps she'll be able to rustle up some of those delicious Cornish pasties of hers."

"Oooh, I hope so," George exclaimed and added, "and sausage rolls as well. I'm very hungry."

"And what about you?" Edward asked, glancing down at Richard. "Aren't *you* ravenous?"

"I will enjoy the hot tea," Richard answered, smiling up at his brother. "But I'm not really very hungry, Ned."

"We'll see about that when you smell some of Cook's tidbits. You know how they make your mouth water," Edward said and shepherded his brothers into the Morning Room.

The boys raced over to the fire roaring in the grate and stood warming their hands, glad to be thawing out. After doing exactly the same thing, Edward swung around and went back to the door, explaining, "I'm going to have a word with Cook. I'll be back in a few minutes." Closing the door behind him, he left them to their own devices. Edward hoped George wouldn't tease Richard; he so often did. He was a bit of a bully, and Richard had not yet learned how to go into verbal combat.

Mrs. Latham glanced up expectantly when the door to her kitchen opened. Instantly she broke into laughter. "Why, good mornin', Master Edward!"

"Hello, Mrs. Latham," he responded in his usual polite manner, giving her one of his most beguiling smiles. "I know how busy you are on Tuesdays, but would it be possible for you to make a large pot of tea and something to eat for us? The boys are famished after their ride on the cliffs."

"By gum, I bet they are!" She wiped her big, capable hands on a tea towel and strode across to the long oak table standing in the middle of the huge kitchen. "I've just been baking a few things—" She broke off, waved a hand in front of her morning's work, and added, "Pork pies, fish cakes, Cornish pasties, sausage rolls, and savory tarts. Take a look, and take your pick, Master Edward."

"How splendid," he said, grinning at her. "A veritable feast, Cook. But then you're the best in the world. No one has your skill in the kitchen, no one."

"Oh, get along with yer, sir. It's a real flatterer yer are." This was said with a hint of pride at his compliment. Straightening her back, she added, "I knows yer all like the Cornish pasties, and Master George is ever so fond of my sausage rolls. I'll get a tray ready for yer, sir, and send young Polly with it in a tick, once I've made the pot of tea. Does that suit, Master Edward?"

"It does indeed, Cook, and I can't wait to sample some of this fare, it smells delicious. Thank you so much, I do appreciate it." Once more he gave her the benefit of his warm smile and inclined his head.

"My pleasure," she called after him, watching him walk over to the door.

Swinging his head, he grinned at her, waved, and was gone.

Mrs. Latham stared at the door for a moment, her eyes filled with admiration. Edward Deravenel was blessed with the most pleasant nature as well as those staggering good looks. She couldn't help wondering how many hearts he would break. Scores, no doubt. At eighteen he already had women falling at his feet. Spoil him, that they will, she thought, clucking to herself as she turned to the ovens. Aye, they'll spoil him rotten, give him whatever he wants, and that's not always a good thing for a man. No, it's not. I've seen many a toff like him ruined by women, more's the pity.

She swung around as the door opened again and muttered, "There yer are, young Polly. I was just wondering where yer'd got to—" She broke off and clucked again. "Bump in ter Master Edward, did yer, lass?"

The parlor maid nodded and blushed. "He's ever so nice ter me, Cook."

Mrs. Latham shook her head and sighed but made no further reference to Edward. Instead she continued, "Set a large tray, please, Polly. I'm preparing a mornin' snack for Master Edward and his brothers. When it's ready, yer can take it ter the Morning Room."

"Yes, Cook."

Edward made his way back to the Morning Room and his brothers. He was lost in thought, contemplating his return to university. Today was Tuesday, January the fifth; in two days he would travel to London and go up to Oxford that weekend. He was looking forward to returning and especially pleased that he would be reunited with his best friend and boon companion of many years, Will Hasling, who was also an undergraduate.

His attention suddenly became focused on the end of the corridor. He had just caught a fleeting glimpse of a dark skirt and jacket, a froth of white at the neck, a well-coiffed blond head. And then there had been the click of a door closing.

He hurried forward, passing the Morning Room and not stopping until he reached the room at the end of the corridor. Pausing at the door which had just closed, he listened intently. There were no voices, only the sound of someone moving around, the rustle of papers. Tapping lightly on the door, he did not wait to be summoned. He simply walked in.

The woman in the room stared at him, obviously startled.

Edward closed the door, leaned against it. "Hello, Alice."

The woman took a deep breath, then exhaled. After a moment she inclined her head, stared at him, but said not one word.

Stepping forward, he took hold of her arm just as she

started to move around the desk, wanting to put it between them. Pulling her closer, he leaned forward and murmured, "Alice, my dear, you didn't come to see me last night. I was devastated . . ."

"Please," she whispered, "let go of me. Your mother might walk in at any moment. Please, Master Edward."

"Not *Master Edward*. Surely you mean Ned. . . . That's what you whispered to me in the dark last week."

She looked up into the handsome face, was momentarily blinded by the vivid blue eyes, and closed her own.

Edward was instantly alarmed. "What is it, Alice?" he asked in concern. "Are you ill?"

She opened her eyes, shook her head. "No, no, I am not ill. But I can't see you anymore. I'm afraid of . . . what might happen to me if we were to continue our . . . intimacy."

"Oh, Alice, darling, don't be frightened—"

"And then there's your mother to consider," she cut in, her eyes darting to the door. "You know she would dismiss me at once if she found out about our liaison. And I do need this position . . ." Her voice trailed off, and she swallowed hard.

Looking down into her pretty face, Edward saw the tears glistening in her hazel eyes, and he noticed the fear and anxiety gripping her. He nodded. "Yes, I'm afraid you are correct, Alice." He studied her for a moment. If she had been from the working class, or even a woman of his own class, he would have pressed his suit, certain that there would be no serious repercussions. But Alice Morgan was from the middle class, and very vulnerable. She was the widow of a local doctor with a small child to support, and she did indeed need this position as his mother's secretary. So, because he had a kind heart, he let go of her arm and stepped back.

A rueful smile touched his lips, and he let out a small sigh. "I won't trouble you any further, Alice," he said in a very low voice. "Everything you have said is true. And I don't wish to cause you any difficulties."

Leaning forward, she touched his cheek with one finger,

and then she swiftly edged around the desk and stood looking at him.

"Thank you," she said in a voice as low as his had been.
"Thank you for being such a gentleman."

He left without glancing at her again, and as he closed the
door behind him, he did not hear her say, "It's not because I
don't want you . . . I do. But I know you're the kind of man
who can't help but break a woman's heart."

two

Cecily Deravenel, matriarch of the family, was aware that her eldest son had followed Alice into the office. She had been walking along the minstrels' gallery above the Long Hall when she had seen first one and then the other enter the room.

Neither Alice nor Edward had noticed her, and she had continued on her way, heading for the wide, curving staircase which led to the ground floor. As she was descending, Edward had suddenly come out into the corridor and rushed into the Morning Room, closing the door sharply behind him.

Once again, Cecily's presence had gone unnoticed, and this pleased her. She had no wish to confront her eldest son regarding his interest in the young widow whom she employed.

Cecily had always been a good judge of character, and she knew Alice Morgan very well. She trusted her to handle the situation with practicality, decorum, and the utmost discretion, since she was a proper young woman. Fully understanding that this was a passing fancy on Edward's part, if it was anything at all, Cecily was nonetheless relieved that he would be going to London on Thursday, and then back to Oxford. She knew how much her son loved university life, and his studies would absorb him completely, as they always had. Also, his absence would bring the matter of Alice to a close, if it had not been terminated by one of them a few minutes before. At Oxford he would be safe.

She sighed. Edward could be wild, even reckless at times, acting without considered thought. And women of all ages found him irresistible. It had long ago occurred to Cecily that temptation was always in his way; in fact, poor Edward was stumbling over temptation, far more than the average man. It would take a saint to resist everything thrown in *his* face, she muttered to herself as she stepped into the Long Hall.

Cecily was a tall and regal woman in her mid-forties, handsome and graceful. She was usually dressed in fashionable clothes, even when she was here at Ravenscar. This morning she was wearing a navy blue wool day suit with a long skirt slightly flared from the calf, and a matching tailored jacket over a white cambric blouse with a high neck and frilled jabot. The jacket was short; it ended at her narrow waist and was cut in the style of the moment, with puffed sleeves, which became tight from elbow to wrist.

Cecily's hair was one of her loveliest features, a glossy chestnut color, which she wore upswept with a mass of curls falling to the front, just above her smooth, wide brow. This style was the latest and most fashionable because every woman in England was copying Queen Alexandra. Ever since Queen Victoria's son Albert Edward had ascended to the throne as Edward VII, his queen had become the arbiter of fashion, style, and taste. Edward's long-suffering wife, a Danish princess by birth, was much admired by the public as well as those in the top echelons of society.

When Cecily was living at Ravenscar, she wore little or no jewelry, unless there were houseguests or she and her husband were entertaining members of the local gentry. Today was no exception. Her choices were simple: small pearl earrings, her gold wedding ring, and a fob watch on the lapel of her jacket.

Now Cecily looked at the watch and laughed inwardly.

The small hand was just moving onto eleven. Her husband forever teased her, insisted that he could set his pocket watch by her, and in this assertion he was absolutely correct. She was the most punctual of women, and every morning at precisely this hour she set out on her tour of the downstairs rooms at Ravenscar.

What had begun when she was a young bride had turned into a daily ritual when she was in residence here. She needed to be certain that all the rooms in this grand old house were warm and comfortable, that everything was in order, with not one thing out of place.

Over twenty-six years ago, when she had come to Ravenscar as Richard Deravenel's wife and the new mistress of the manor, she had been startled, then saddened to find this Tudor jewel, glorious in its architecture and design, so uninviting. The rooms themselves were of fine proportions, with many windows that flooded the interiors with that lovely, crystalline northern light. But they were icy cold. Even in summer the cold penetrated the thick stone walls, and because of the nearness of the North Sea, there was a feeling of dampness in the rooms that faced the water, especially in the wet weather.

Richard had explained to her that the house was basically only suffering from neglect, that its bones were good, as was its structure. His widowed mother had grown parsimonious in her old age. She had closed off most of the house since her children lived in London, and had occupied a suite of rooms which were easy and cheap to keep heated.

When walking through it that day long ago, Cecily had quickly discovered that the warmest place was the huge kitchen, along with the small rooms which adjoined it. It was in these rooms that the cook and staff lived, because of the heat that emanated from the kitchen fire and ovens. All the other rooms were covered in dust sheets, closed off to the world.

Richard, trusting his young wife's judgment, had told her

to do what she wanted. Within a week of her arrival, she had
made sweeping changes. Every room was thoroughly
cleaned, as was every window; the walls were repainted, the
wood floors polished. Fires were soon blazing in every
hearth, and great quantities of wood were chopped, the logs
stored in the cellars so that fires could burn throughout the
year if necessary.

In London, Cecily purchased beautiful Turkey carpets
and the finest Persian and Oriental rugs, as well as beautiful
velvets, brocades, and other luxuriant fabrics in rich jewel
colors. The rugs went down on the hardwood floors, the fabrics were cut and sewn into handsome draperies for the
many windows, furniture was polished and reupholstered if
necessary. Because she had fine taste, a sense of style, and a
good eye, within a few months Ravenscar had been brought
back to life.

In a certain sense, none of this had happened by accident.
Cecily Watkins Deravenel, as the daughter of a titan of industry who had made an immense fortune in the industrial
revolution of the Victorian Age, was accustomed to homes
of great splendor. She had grown up in a world of stunning
beauty, amidst priceless objects of art, sculpture, great paintings, and fine furniture as well as almost overwhelming luxury. And so it was these elements which Cecily sought to
introduce at Ravenscar, because she herself loved them and
was comfortable with them. She succeeded, although only in
part in the beginning, because it took a great deal of effort
and time to collect unique and beautiful artifacts. Only now,
after twenty-five years of painstaking work, had she finally
accomplished what she had set out to do.

One of Cecily's latest innovations had been the introduc-
tion of electric light throughout Ravenscar. Gone at long last
were the gas lamps, replaced with shimmering crystal chandeliers and bronze wall sconces which bathed the rooms in a
refulgent glow during the day as well as at night.

Today, as she walked down the Long Hall, Cecily noticed

damp patches near a line of windows facing the sea. She made a mental note to point them out to the handyman. Entering the corridor off the hall, she opened doors to different rooms, checking the fires, the state of the furniture, and the general appearance. Sometimes she went inside, straightened a floor-length cloth or corrected the way a curtain fell. Her eyes, always keen, sought the slightest imperfections.

Half an hour later, Cecily found herself standing outside the Morning Room, debating whether to go in. Finally making up her mind, she turned the knob.

Three heads swung to face the door as she stepped inside . . . three of her four sons, three of her seven children. She had borne twelve babies, but only seven had lived.

George, at eleven, was more irrepressible than ever and, as usual, failed to hide his feelings. He was grinning at her now, his face open and revealing, as it always was. He came to see her constantly, to confide, even to admit his misdeeds and mistakes, but also to carry tales, and frequently she thought he had a touch of envy, perhaps even treachery, in his nature. But this morning he looked positively angelic; with hair the color of wheat, he was the blondest of all her children.

There was quite a startling contrast between him and his brother Richard. There *he* was, sitting next to his adored Ned, his face so very grave, and now he offered her a solemn sort of smile, a sad smile for a little boy of eight. How steady his gray-blue eyes were; such a serious child, so dedicated in everything he did, her Richard. For a split second she wanted to ruffle his black hair, but she knew he would not appreciate that, because he would think she was babying him. He was the darkest in coloring of all her children, like her, and he had inherited some of her traits, her stoicism and her stubbornness particularly.

Finally, Cecily's blue-gray eyes came to rest on her eldest son. Edward, too, was smiling at her, a loving smile. His eyes were so vividly blue they startled her, but then they had since his childhood. His red-gold hair, inherited from his Normandy forebears, resembled a polished helmet, and as his smile grew wider and his white teeth flashed, she thought of those women who fell all over him; yet he was so young, not even nineteen . . .

For a long time she had believed that Edward's inherent wildness did not negate his other qualities, especially his natural ability in so many areas. And he *was* very able. She never underestimated him, although his father occasionally did. Even so, Richard was fully aware, just as she was, that in Ned, family loyalty was bred in the bone. Family came first for him; she knew it always would. She relied on it, in fact.

Cecily stopped ruminating about the three boys present, thought for a moment of her second son, Edmund, gone to Italy with his father several days ago. Edmund, who was seventeen, seemed the most responsible of her sons, and he had begged to accompany his father on this business trip. He had his feet firmly planted on the ground and was very much his own man. It was his two elder sisters whom Edmund most resembled, at least in coloring; they all had light brown hair, hair which her daughter, Meg, now in her fifteenth year characterized disparagingly as *mousy*. Meg was blond but not quite as blond as George.

Edward said, "Please come and join us, Mother, won't you? We've been having a snack. Would you like to partake of something . . . a cup of tea perhaps? Should I ring for Polly?"

"No, no, but thank you, Ned," she replied, walking to the sofa. As she seated herself, George jumped up and rushed across the room, fell onto the sofa next to her, and leaned against his mother possessively. Automatically, she put her arm around him protectively. Years later she would remember this gesture from his childhood and wonder why she had done it so often. Had she somehow had a premonition that he would one day need protecting?

Ned ventured, "I wonder, Mother, if you know when you plan to return to town?"

"In a week. I told your father we would all be waiting at the Mayfair house when he returned from Italy. Of course, you yourself will be at Oxford by then." She glanced down at George, lolling against her, and then across at Richard before adding to Edward, "Mr. Pennington will be joining us at the end of the month. He will tutor the boys as he did last year when we were in London. And Perdita Willis has been engaged as governess, to tutor Meg. Where is she, by the way? Have any of you seen your sister since breakfast?"

Ned and Richard shook their heads, but George murmured, "I saw her going up to the attics."

"When was that?" Cecily asked swiftly.

"I can't remember the exact time, Mother."

"Force yourself," she said, a little sharply for her.

"Oh, about an hour ago," he muttered.

"I wonder why she was going up there." Cecily frowned.

"Oh, Heavens, Mother! I think *I* know why," Edward announced. "She told me her friend Lillian Jameson is being given a spring ball for her sixteenth birthday. Meg said she was going to look in those trunks—" Edward broke off, glanced at the door, which had opened to admit his sister.

"There you are, darling!" Cecily exclaimed, moving toward Margaret. "I was just wondering aloud where you were, and Ned said you'd probably gone to look in those old trunks."

"Yes, I did, Mama," Meg answered, gliding into the room; she was as graceful as her mother, and she looked pretty this morning in a red wool dress, black stockings, and black shoes. Cecily knew Meg was blossoming into a very pretty girl indeed, and smiling at her youngest daughter, she murmured, "You didn't mention that Lady Jameson is giving a spring ball for Lillian's birthday."

"It's not actually definite yet, Mother. The invitations

haven't gone out. They won't for weeks and weeks. If it happens at all. Well, you see . . . Lillian is *hoping,* and so am I. It would be rather fun, don't you think?"

"Are boys going to be invited?" George asked, sitting up straighter, staring at her intently.

Meg laughed, shaking her head. "You're incorrigible, George, truly incorrigible. Imagine you thinking *you* could be invited."

"Why not? I'm a Deravenel. We're invited everywhere."

"The likes of Papa, not you," Meg said with cool authority. "You're too young to go to cotillions, dances, that sort of thing."

"No I'm not, am I, Mother?" He gave her an appealing look.

"Well, George, perhaps . . . at this moment, let's say. By the spring you'll be a little older," Cecily replied quietly, wanting to mollify him.

"There, you see, Margaret! Our mother says because I'll be older by spring I could go. I'll think about it, and maybe I will come after all. . . . I shall give it considered thought, as Papa always says."

Edward chuckled. "I hope you'll ensure I get an invitation, Meg," he teased, winking at his sister, wanting to make light of all this since George looked sulky.

She laughed and nodded. "Of course I will. And if you come, you'll be the envy of every other man there."

His eyes narrowed. "Why?"

"Because all the young women will be falling at your feet," George announced. "Everybody says you're a lady-killer."

"That's enough, George," Cecily cut in, although she spoke mildly. "None of that type of vulgarity here, if you please." Turning to Meg, she asked, "Well, did you find anything interesting in the trunks?"

"Oh, yes, Mama, I *did,* some wonderful frocks, all beautifully packed away in cotton bags. They're like new. Will you come and look?"

"I'll be happy to," Cecily answered, taking her daughter's arm. Laughing, the two of them went out together.

The attics at Ravenscar ran the length of the house under the eaves. Since she was such a stickler for cleanliness and order, Cecily had them cleaned and dusted once a month. And her talent for organization meant easy access to the chests, boxes, and trunks which were stacked there.

Earlier, Meg had taken out several gowns and laid them across a sofa which had been covered in a dustcloth. The gowns were made of a featherweight silk, since they had been designed to wear over bouffant underskirts, or hoop skirts, which had been so prevalent in the middle of the Victorian era.

Meg ran over to the sofa, picked up one made of pale green silk, and held it against her. "I thought this color would suit me. What do you think, Mama?"

Cecily stood studying her daughter for a moment. Then she nodded. "I must agree; it's a pretty color and perfect for you. I am sure we can have several of them remodeled to fit you. Madame Henrietta is such a good dressmaker, and innovative, she'll create more up-to-date designs." Cecily handed another gown to Margaret. "Let me see how this shade looks; it's such a lovely blue, it reminds me of cornflowers."

"And Ned's eyes," Meg murmured as she took the dress, held it in front of her.

"Ah, yes, that is true," Cecily acknowledged, Ned's eyes indeed. They were close, Edward and Margaret, with only a few years' difference in their ages. Meg, like Richard, adored her eldest brother. And Ned had kept a watchful eye on her since childhood. In turn, it was Meg who took charge of her younger brothers, mothering them when Cecily was away.

"The blue is enchanting," Cecily now exclaimed, liking the way the color enhanced Meg's gray eyes. "We shall take the green and blue to London with us next week, and before we leave, do go through the other trunks, perhaps you'll find several more which can be remade."

"Oh, how kind, Mama, thank you so much." Margaret stepped closer to her mother and hugged her, the silk frock crushed between them.

Cecily, who was not a particularly demonstrative person, began to laugh. "It's my pleasure, but Margaret, my dear, you're ruining the dress."

Meg let go of her mother at once and shook the frock out. "I don't think any real harm has been done," she murmured, scrutinizing it with some intensity.

"I agree." With her head slightly tilted, Cecily studied her daughter, realizing once again how pretty she had become, with her flowing, fair hair and those large, transparent gray eyes, which were so beguiling. Instantly Cecily's thoughts zeroed in on the girl's marriage prospects. Meg would grow into a lovely young woman, that was a given. And she would make just as good a marriage as Cecily's two eldest daughters, Anne and Eliza, had done.

"I shall speak to Lady Jameson next week when we return to town, Meg, to ascertain what her plans are. It has suddenly occurred to me that perhaps your father and I should consider giving you a small afternoon tea dance later this year, to celebrate your fifteenth birthday."

"Oh, Mama, that would be wonderful!" Meg was startled by this suggestion, which was so unexpected, but the smile on her face revealed her genuine pleasure at the idea.

Cecily had also startled herself. She normally spent days in deliberation about things such as this. She wondered if she had made an error in bringing up the idea but immediately decided she could not backtrack now without upsetting her daughter. She would talk to Richard next week, but she was certain he would make no objection. He had always been quite content to leave such matters—the raising of their children, the running of their homes—to her. *Richard.* Such a good man. So devoted to his family, a wonderful father. The best husband any woman could ever have. She could not wait for him to come home. Her life was empty without him by her side.

She hadn't really wanted him to go to Italy, but he had felt obligated to do so. There was some sort of problem at the marble quarries they owned in Carrara, and as the assistant managing director of the Deravenel Company, he agreed with Henry Deravenel Grant, the chairman, that he was the best person to investigate the situation. And so off he had gone with Edmund, who had never been to Italy.

Her brother, Rick, and her nephew Thomas went along to keep her husband and son company; Richard and Rick had been close friends for many years, enjoyed each other's company and traveling together. Also, Rick hoped to buy some paintings and sculpture in Florence; he was remodeling his town house in London. He was something of a connoisseur, and he had said to her only two weeks ago that the thought of Florence made his mouth water.

Rick and she had been close since childhood, and after their father's death, it was Rick who had taken over the family business. Philip Watkins had been one of the greatest magnates in industry, but Rick had surpassed him a thousandfold; today he was one of the richest men in the country, and because of his genius for business, her own inheritance had increased. This was a great relief to Cecily. Richard was always at odds with Deravenels over money, even though the company really belonged to him. At least he should have been running it, not Harry Grant. Like all the Lancashire Deravenel Grants, Harry was incompetent when it came to finance. And Harry's French wife, Margot, was a woman riddled with ambition and greed who managed Harry like a puppet master. *She* probably is running Deravenels, Cecily now thought, and more's the pity.

"Shall we take the frocks downstairs, Mama?" Meg asked, interrupting her thoughts.

"Oh, yes, of course, let us do that, my dear." Cecily

looked at her fob watch and exclaimed, "Good Heavens, it's almost time for lunch." But as they went downstairs, her mind returned to the Grants; they were never far from her thoughts. Henry Grant's father had always cut her husband out, cheated him, and the hatred between them had escalated over the years. Now, Margot Grant was making things even more intolerable. There was going to be another battle between Richard and Henry, of that she was convinced.

three

There's a sea fret coming up," Richard said, swiveling on the window seat in Edward's bedroom and looking at his brother. "I can't see any of the fishing cobles out there, Ned; it's thick like a fog."

"Well, it really is a fog in a sense," Edward responded. "A fret usually comes up when cold winds blow in from the sea over the warmer land, in summer, as well as winter," Edward explained, glancing up from the box of books he was packing. "And there wouldn't be any fishermen out this afternoon, you know. Tonight perhaps, if the fog lifts, Little Fish."

Richard grinned. He loved this name Edward had given him years ago; sometimes Ned even called him Tiddler, which also meant "little fish," and this pleased him. Having nicknames bestowed by his oldest brother made him feel very special indeed. "I'll be glad to go to London next week," Richard said, introducing another subject. "Even though I have to work hard because Mr. Pennington is coming back to be our tutor."

Edward caught something odd in his voice and asked, "Don't you like it here at Ravenscar?" He frowned and then gave Richard a piercing look. "Perhaps it's too cold for you here in winter. On the other hand, I enjoyed winters at Ravenscar when I was young. There's always so much to do."

"Yes. I love it here, Ned, but I like London because *you're* not so far away. . . . I mean you're at Oxford and I get to see you more when I'm in London."

Touched by his brother's expression of his love and need, and pleased that he could articulate it so well, Edward put down the leather-bound book he was holding and walked across to sit on the window seat next to the boy. Placing an arm around his brother's narrow shoulders to give him a quick hug, he said softly, "I'll miss you, too, old chap, very much. You're quite correct, Oxford *is* much closer to London than it is to Yorkshire. And listen, I'll come up to town often, so we can spend some time together. Would you like that?"

Richard's face filled with pleasure, and his slate-blue eyes shone. "Do you promise me, Ned?"

"I do, Dick, I do promise you."

The eight-year-old visibly relaxed, his body growing slack as he leaned against Edward, fully at ease with him as he had been since his toddler days. "Things are not the same when you're not at home. . . . I do miss you so."

"I know how you feel, I miss you, too, Tiddler, but I'm not all that far away. Perhaps I could write to you occasionally."

"Oh, Ned, would you? How wonderful to have a real letter from you every week."

Edward began to chuckle. "I didn't say *every week*. But look here, Dick, it's not as if you're a boy alone when I'm at university. Meg is around, and you have George. Also, Edmund will be at home with you."

"Yes, I know," Richard answered in an uncertain voice. "I love Edmund, but he's so busy, and sometimes he seems a bit . . . impatient."

"I know he's a very busy fellow indeed." Edward laughed and added, "Doing what I don't know. But George is all right with you, isn't he?"

"Oh, yes."

Glancing at his little brother swiftly, Edward asked,

"Does George bully you too much? Tell me the truth, I don't want you to lie to me."

Richard stared at his brother askance and exclaimed, "I never lie, and I wouldn't fib to *you*. George *doesn't* bully me."

"I'm glad to hear it, but I do recognize that he can become overzealous, shall we say, about certain things."

"I can defend myself." There was a sudden flash of pride, a defiant tilt to Richard's dark head.

"I know you can. After all, I taught you." Edward gave him a light punch on the arm and stood up. He glanced out of the window, noticed how the sea mist was now obscuring everything; even the battlements at the bottom of the garden had been obliterated.

Turning, Ned strode back to the table where the large box stood. He put in another volume and checked it off on his list.

Richard, watching him, asked, "Will Edmund go to Oxford one day?"

"I expect so, and George, too, and you yourself, Dickie boy. When you're old enough. That's what Papa wants, that we all should be Oxford educated. Does that suit? Would you like to go? To be an undergraduate?"

"Oh, yes, I really would. Why does everyone call it the city of the shining spires?"

"Because there are many churches and buildings with spires, and they look beautiful in the light."

"It's very old, isn't it? Meg told me it was."

"It is indeed. Oxford dates back to the twelfth century, and it's the site of a castle, an abbey, a royal palace, and the university."

"Can I come and visit you one day, Ned? *Please.* I would like to see everything at Oxford. Will you take me to see everything?"

"Of course, old chap, and especially the Bodleian, that's *my* favorite."

"What is it, Ned, the Bodleian?"

"A library, a very lovely and very ancient library. It dates back to 1602."

"Oh, I'd love to see it! Meg told me that in the Civil War, Oxford was the Royalist capital, and that it was *besieged* by Cromwell's parliamentarians but it wasn't hurt by them."

"That's correct." There was a knock on the door, and Edward exclaimed, "Come in."

The door opened, and Jessup, the butler, entered, inclining his head. "Master Edward, please excuse me."

"Yes, Jessup?"

"Your mother wishes to speak with you. She's awaiting you in the library."

"Thank you, Jessup. You may tell her I shall be down in a few minutes."

"Mrs. Deravenel did ask me to say that it was a matter of some urgency, Master Edward."

"Very well. Then I shall come right away."

The room wasn't quite right. There was something curiously *wrong* about it. Edward hesitated in the doorway, not wishing to enter.

It was far too dark. It wasn't like his mother not to have the electric lights blazing; she loved sunshine and brightness. Only two small lamps were turned on in the vast room, even though it was late afternoon and gloomy as dusk descended. The shadow-filled room seemed oddly off-kilter. He felt a sense of desolation, even foreboding.

Opening the door wider, he went inside. In the dim light he could make out his mother standing next to a high-backed wing chair at the far end; behind her, wrapped in shadow, a figure stood staring out of the window, his back to the room.

Slowly Edward approached his mother, his mind racing, every one of his senses alerted to trouble. Fear, he decided, fear is present here, and the hackles rose on the back of his neck at this unexpected and irrational thought.

Taking a deep breath, he murmured, "You wanted to see me, Mother."

She said nothing.

Stepping over to the fireplace, Edward switched on a lamp standing on a small occasional table, then turned to his mother. He noticed how dark her eyes were and huge in her face, and they were filled with apprehension.

He stared at her more intently, waiting. Now he realized her face was without expression; it looked as if it had been carved from stone. She was very pale, all the color had drained away.

"What has happened? What is it?" he pressed, his voice rising an octave and filling with urgency.

A shudder rippled through her, and Cecily gripped the back of the chair, her knuckles gleaming whitely in the faint glow from the lamp.

Edward felt that fear spreading from her to him, and he asked again, *"What's wrong?"*

In a rush of words, she said in a low, tense voice, "It's your father . . . there's been an accident. A fire. Your father . . . and Edmund." She stopped, choked up, finished bleakly, "They're both dead." Her voice broke on the last sentence, but she managed to keep a hold on her emotions. In a wavering voice, she said, "My brother and your cousin Thomas . . . they, too, were killed in the fire."

Edward gaped at her. He found it hard to take in what she was saying.

The figure near the window turned around and walked forward. Immediately Edward realized it was his cousin Neville Watkins, eldest son of Rick and brother of young Thomas. "*I* brought the bad news, Ned," Neville announced, his voice thick with emotion. The cousins clasped hands for a moment, and Neville exclaimed, "It was I who brought death and sorrow here!"

Edward shook his head vehemently. "No! It's just not possible," he cried. "Not my father. Not Edmund. Not Uncle

Rick and Tom. It simply can't be, not our family gone like that in the blink of an eye."

Cecily's heart clenched at the sight of Edward's pale and stricken face, the tears welling in his eyes. Although she shared his overwhelming pain and sorrow, his utter disbelief that this tragedy had occurred, at this moment she thought only of her son. "How can I comfort you?" she asked, shaking her head helplessly. Tears began to seep out of her eyes, slid down her cheeks unchecked.

Edward did not respond. She knew he was in shock, just as she was herself.

It was at that moment that Cecily Deravenel uttered the words Edward would remember for the rest of his life. "Oh, Ned, Ned, has no one ever told you that life is catastrophic?"

For a long moment he was transfixed, staring at her, and then he swung around and rushed out of the library without saying a word. All he knew was that he had to escape this death-laden room. He had the desperate need to be alone in his terrible grief.

Edward half stumbled across the Long Hall, making for the double doors that led to the garden. Once he was outside, he fled down the paved path, through the tiered gardens, past the lawns, until he arrived at the ruined battlements of the old stronghold on the promontory at the edge of the cliffs.

The sea fret had lifted. It had begun to snow, and the tiny crystalline flakes stuck to his face, his burnished hair. In his anguish, he barely noticed.

He stood in the small, round enclosure which had once been a watchtower looking out over the North Sea, and although the roof had been gone for centuries, the walls gave him some protection from the wind and the sleet.

He pressed his face against the cold stones, his mind in a turmoil. How could they be dead? His father, his brother, his uncle, and his cousin. It didn't seem possible. And it certainly didn't make sense. How had they all died together?

Where had they been? When had it happened? Tragedy had struck not once but four times.

Papa is dead. And Edmund. Only seventeen . . . my lovely brother, so full of promise for the future. And Tom, Cousin Tom, with whom he had grown up. And Uncle Rick, the only other senior member of their closely knit families on whom everyone depended. They had all been constant, loyal to one another on every level.

Papa and Edmund. Oh, God, no. His throat closed, and tears flooded his eyes as grief finally engulfed him.

A bit later he heard a step on the cold stones, felt a warm cloak go over him and a comforting arm slip around his shoulders. "Weep, grieve, let it come out, Ned," Neville Watkins murmured against his ear. "As I did last night."

Within moments the two cousins went inside and stood conferring in the Long Hall. "When did you receive the news?" Edward asked. "And who was it that contacted you?"

"Aubrey Masters from Deravenels," Neville answered. "He telephoned me last night, as soon as he heard what happened in Carrara. He thought it better that Aunt Cecily and you and the children were told in person by me, rather than receiving a telephone call from him or a telegram. Much too impersonal, he said. And I told him he had done the right thing." Neville's face was deathly white and taut as he continued. "However, I had to come to grips with my own grief and my mother's distress before coming over to Ravenscar. I left Ripon as soon as I was up to it today, and came by carriage this afternoon. I hope you don't think I delayed too long."

"Neville, of course I don't! You're as grief-stricken about your father and brother as I am about mine."

"We must go to Florence," Neville now said. "And then to Carrara, Ned. We have to arrange for their bodies to be brought home for proper burial in Yorkshire. And we must do some detective work whilst we are there."

Edward did not respond for a split second, and then he murmured, "You obviously don't think it was an accident. You mentioned revenge . . ." His voice trailed off, and his eyes locked with Neville's. They shared a knowing look.

"No, I don't think it was an accident. I am relatively certain it was entirely planned."

"You're suggesting murder, aren't you?"

"Indeed I am, Cousin."

"My father was the actual target, is that what you are intimating?"

"Yes, I am, Ned."

Edward did not speak as he sifted this information through his brain. Finally he asked, "Where was the fire?"

"At a hotel our fathers and brothers were lodging in; other people were killed, too, by the way. I suppose you might call those deaths collateral damage."

"Oh, my God, how terrible. Do you believe Henry Grant is behind it?"

"Not Harry personally," Neville answered, looking reflective. "In my opinion he's a doddering fool. However, I consider that French wife of his capable of dealing in murder as well as in business. And so are his henchmen. They're a dangerous lot."

"What did you mean by revenge, Neville?"

"Just that. We must avenge the deaths of your father and mine and our brothers. I truly believe your father was killed because he has been making too much of a fuss lately about his role at Deravenels. He's been persistently reminding the current management that he is the one who should be chairman, and that the Lancashire Deravenel Grants are the usurpers, who grabbed the top job and took control of the company years ago. It happens to be the truth, but none of them like to hear it. And so they targeted your father. That's the long and short of it, in my opinion. You must do something about this, Ned, and I am here to help you. I shall support you all the way, and I shall protect your back at all times."

Edward nodded. "Thank you, Cousin, thank you. We shall make our plans later, but now I feel I have to go to my mother, and then we must give the other children this tragic news."

four

Cecily Deravenel was known for her stoicism and iron-willed self-control, but both had vanished. Edward became acutely aware of this when he found his mother in her private suite upstairs. After knocking on the door, he had walked in without waiting for her assent, knowing instinctively that she needed his comforting presence.

His mother was seated on a love seat close to the fire in the small parlor which adjoined her bedroom, staring into the flames. When she turned her head, he saw her ravaged face, the despair enveloping her like a caul. Her grief was so apparent he forgot his own for a moment and hurried to her, alarm touching his face.

Sitting down next to her on the love seat, he put his arms around her and drew her close to him. Cecily resisted, out of habit really, but only for a split second; then she collapsed against him, holding on to him, weeping as if her heart was breaking. And it was, he was certain of that.

Edward had never had trouble understanding this regal woman who appeared so aloof to many. He had been privy to her true self since his childhood, and he knew how gentle and loving her heart was, how deeply she loved his father, and him, and her other children. She had never been anything but an understanding wife and mother, and she was sympathetic, sensitive to everyone's needs, a constant and loyal ally to her family. And she was ready to help anyone in need, especially those who worked on the estate; they adored her, called her an angel.

His mother cherished her brother and depended on him in so many ways. Aside from their strong relationship as siblings, Rick handled her financial affairs and managed the fortune which had been left to her by their father.

Now the two most important mature men in her life had been ripped away from her. Her life had changed so abruptly, so unexpectedly it took one's breath away; all of their lives had changed, in fact; nothing would ever be the same again.

Neville Watkins had become head of the Watkins family; and Edward himself was suddenly head of the Deravenel clan, Yorkshire branch. What this actually meant troubled him enormously: total responsibility for the family, for everything their father had taken care of all his life, plus their stake in the Deravenel Company. Ned was not sure how he would manage to juggle all this being at university.

Neville was thirty-two, married, with two small daughters, a seasoned man of the world and a brilliant businessman held in high regard by his peers, while Ned was still considered a boy by most. Nonetheless, he and Neville Watkins would have to pick up the pieces and endeavor to bring all of their lives back to normal as soon as possible. Ned was fully aware that this would take time. There was a mourning period to get through, and many adjustments to be made. He also accepted that he had a lot to learn, and very rapidly. A balancing act, he thought. It will be a balancing act on a tightrope.

And he must keep a cool head at all times. That was a given. There was now only one person he could trust, aside from his mother, and that was Neville Watkins. His cousin and he were bound together as never before, and Ned knew he needed Neville, needed his guidance and support if he was going to succeed . . .

His mother's voice broke into his thoughts. "I'm so sorry, Ned, for giving in to my grief in this way. However, I'm afraid I really can't help it. Do forgive me."

"Mother, there's nothing at all to forgive!" he exclaimed, looking into her tearstained face, taking out a handkerchief and gently dabbing her wet cheeks. "It's vital to permit your grief to come out. It's a natural thing to grieve, you know. And it's *necessary* if one is to come to terms with it. People who push grief inside become ill."

"Yes, you're correct," she responded. "We have difficult times ahead, but we must find a way to keep going, lead normal lives if we can. I have the children to think about. They are going to need me, Ned, and they will certainly need you, too, although I think *you* are truly going to have your hands full with other things."

Nodding, Edward stood up. "We ought to go and speak to them, if you're feeling a little better. We don't want one of the servants to blurt out the news accidentally—"

"They know, Ned. I've already spoken to them," Cecily cut in. "Naturally, they have taken it badly. I came in here a few moments ago in an effort to pull myself together. And yes, we had better go and reassure them that everything will be all right, that we are both here for them."

"Are you sure you're up to it now?" he asked, eyeing her.

Cecily's voice quavered slightly as she answered, "I believe so, yes, Ned. I *must* come with you; it is vitally important for their well-being."

He gave her his hand; she took it and rose. Together they left the room and slowly climbed the stairs to the nursery floor.

The moment he saw his mother, George leapt up and rushed to her, flinging himself against her body so hard she staggered slightly. He wrapped his arms around her. "Oh, Mama, why did it happen? Why? Why?" he wailed, tears filling his blue-green eyes. *"Why?"* he demanded in a louder voice, his young face full of grief and anger intermingled. "I want to know why Papa and Edmund are not coming back. *Please tell me, Mama.*"

"If I knew, I would of course tell you, George," Cecily softly responded, holding the boy closer and glancing down at him, her heart full. She smoothed her hand over his blond hair and went on. "None of us quite understand yet what happened, George. Ned is going to find out if he can, and then he will tell us."

Swiveling his head to face his brother, George asked a little plaintively, "You will, won't you, Ned?"

"I will indeed. . . . As soon as I know, you'll be the next." Edward drew closer to his mother and brother and put his arms around them both, holding them close to him for a few moments. Suddenly he became aware of Meg standing near the window sobbing; George's volubility and Meg's weeping only served to make him conscious of Richard's absolute quietness. The youngest of his siblings was huddled in a chair at the far end of the room, his face the color of bleached bone, the light gray eyes almost black in the dimming light of late afternoon. The boy looked so sorrowing Edward felt heartsick.

Edward hurried across to Richard. "Don't be afraid, Dick," he murmured softly, leaning down to the boy. "I'll look after you."

Richard nodded and struggled to his feet. Gazing up at his adored Ned, he whispered, "I want to know everything, like George. I want to know about Papa and Edmund." Tears came into his eyes, and he said in a trembling voice that was almost inaudible, "I said Edmund could be impatient. . . . I wish I hadn't said *that*."

"I understand, but it's all right, Dick, really it is." Reaching out, Edward pulled the youngster into his arms and held him tightly, stroking his dark head. "I will keep you safe. Always."

"You do promise?" the boy whispered.

"I do promise. And you must try to be brave and help Mama."

"I will, Ned. I promise, too." He hesitated and then asked, "Are you going to Italy?"

"Yes, I have to, and Cousin Neville is coming with me. We'll find out everything, and then I'll tell you."

"You will come back, won't you, Ned?" Richard asked, his voice tremulous, his eyes suddenly awash with tears.

"Of course I'll come back. . . . Ravenscar is my home, and you're here, aren't you? I shall always come back to you, Little Fish."

Richard nodded and glanced at Meg. "She's been crying a long time."

"I shall go to her at once, perhaps I can console her."

A moment later Edward was holding his sister in his arms, trying to soothe her. Meg wept against his shoulder for a while, and then slowly her shoulders stopped heaving and the sobs lessened. When she lifted her hands to her face and wiped away the tears with her fingertips, Edward saw at once the anguish in her eyes. The whole family had been bludgeoned by the tragic news Neville had brought. They would be a long time recovering.

Edward said quietly, tilting his sister's face to his, "Our mother needs you, Meggie darling. You must endeavor to be strong for her, help her with George, and especially with Richard, who suffers in silence, as you well know."

Meg could only nod, not trusting herself to say a word. She had been extremely close to her father and Edmund. She felt she had grown old in a few minutes.

After a while, taking more deep breaths, she said, "How long will you be gone?"

Edward shook his head, his eyes suddenly bleak. "I don't honestly know. A week, perhaps two. I just don't know how long it will take to—" He broke off abruptly. He had been about to wonder aloud how long it would take to bring the bodies back to Ravenscar. And then he had realized he simply could not mouth those words.

◆ ◆ ◆

Edward could not sleep, and he was not in the least surprised. All manner of troubling thoughts jostled for prominence in his mind, each of them more dire than the last, and he did not seem able to focus on any problem in particular.

When he had come up to his room, an hour or two ago, he had believed that in its quiet and peacefulness he would be able to sort everything out, but this had not happened. And sleep had remained elusive as his mind raced and raced.

Sighing, he tossed back the bedclothes and got up. After putting on his thick woolen dressing gown, he padded over to the fireplace and threw two more logs onto the grate. Instantly, sparks flew up the chimney, the fresh logs began to crackle, and in the burst of firelight he saw that the carriage clock on the mantel read one-thirty. He was surprised how late it was.

Edward stepped into his slippers, pulled a wing chair closer to the fire, and sat down. This day had been the worst of his life. His mother and the other children had sat at the dining table with him and Neville, not touching their food. None of them had eaten, actually, and not much conversation had taken place either. Each and every one of them was too shattered by the tragedy that had so decimated their family, and Neville's as well.

Eventually his mother had shepherded the children up to their rooms; she had returned a short while later and invited Neville and himself to join her in her sitting room just off the Long Hall. They had dutifully followed her, glancing at each other questioningly.

Within minutes Jessup had brought them a tray of brandy balloons and a decanter of Cognac, placed it on a side table, and departed. Ned and Neville had been the only ones to pour drinks for themselves; his mother had declined, as she usually did.

Once the three of them were settled in front of the fire, Cecily had seemed reflective for a short while, and then she had looked at Ned intently. "I know you and Neville must go to Italy," she had begun and then hesitated. "I just want to caution you to be scrupulously careful. Pay attention, and don't leave anything to chance."

They had both promised her they would be on their guard at all times and would look out for each other.

Nodding her understanding, Cecily had then told them in a low, subdued voice, "There are powers at work here we know nothing about, and we must all be very, very cautious."

"What do you mean, Mother?" Edward had swiftly asked, frowning.

"I can't give you a proper explanation, I simply have this instinctive feeling of . . . *danger.*"

"I never ignore a woman's intuition," Neville had murmured. "It is usually infallible."

Cecily had gone on: "And you, Ned, will have to go to work at Deravenels as soon as possible when you return."

Startled, he had gaped at her. "Am I not to return to Oxford then?" he had asked.

"No, you cannot. Your father is dead. You are, by the rules of primogeniture, his heir. So you must now go to work at Deravenels. *That* is the *family* rule. . . . When the heir of a Deravenel is over sixteen or reaches sixteen, he must take his deceased father's place. Obviously, not in the same capacity, somewhere a little way down the ladder. But the heir *must* go into the company. It has always been that way."

"I understand. Now that you've mentioned it, I do recall Father explaining about this old family rule several years ago."

Neville had then volunteered, "And remember what I said earlier, Ned, I will help you any way I can." All Edward could do was nod.

His mother had turned to face Neville. "When do you plan to leave Ravenscar?" she had asked, somewhat abruptly.

"Tomorrow morning. My carriage will take us to York,

and we will then proceed to London on the afternoon train."
His cousin had paused for a moment, taken a swallow of the
brandy, and finished. "Once in London I shall make plans
for us to leave for the Continent on Friday or Saturday."

"I would appreciate it, Neville, if you would stay in touch
with me, and you, too, Edward."

They had both promised they would.

Then his mother had pushed herself to her feet, and they
had also risen politely as she walked to the door. Here she
had turned her head, said, very softly, "I must go and make
certain that the children are resting quietly. . . . There have
been far too many tears today, and so much heartbreak."

Left alone, Edward and his cousin had talked for a while
longer, mostly about their travel plans, and then they had
gone upstairs for the night. Now Edward stared into the
flames, thinking about his father's death.

Murder. Edward turned the word over and over in his
mind. Neville truly believed that deadly factions within the
Deravenel Company had hired an assassin, or assassins, to
kill his father. However, Edward knew that Neville had no
hard evidence; it was pure supposition, tied to what Neville
called "my gut instinct."

Edward was well aware that his father had been **grumbling** about the way the company was run for a number of
years, and of late his voice had become more insistent. His
father's chief target was Henry Deravenel Grant, who was
descended from the Lancashire line of the House of Deravenel. Henry was chairman of the board and his father's
cousin. "An absentee landlord," his father had called him,
along with a number of other choice names. But would
Henry's adherents resort to murder? Edward wondered.
They could have quite easily rendered Richard Deravenel
useless by restricting his power in the company. Or they
could have forced him into retirement.

Sitting back, closing his eyes, Edward pondered on these
matters for a long time, but he did not have any answers. What

was more, additional questions flew into his head, and all of them were unanswerable as well. One question in particular stood out. *Why* had his father gone to look into problems at the marble quarries in Carrara? Surely that was a job for Aubrey Masters, head of the Mining Division. And why had Edmund, Uncle Rick, and Thomas been killed if his father was the target? He was truly baffled, and it struck him that he would remain in a state of bafflement until he arrived at Carrara and started asking questions of the local authorities, as well as the manager of their quarries. Only then might he gain a better understanding of the fire, its cause, and the manner in which his family had died.

As he continued to gaze into the roaring flames, Edward remembered that he had not looked in his father's desk. He had meant to do so earlier, but he had become so distracted by the children's sorrow and need for him, it had slipped his mind. He hurried out of his bedroom, along the corridor, and down the wide staircase.

Within seconds he was turning on the lights in his father's spacious study and striding over to the desk positioned near the window. He knew exactly where the key was; some time ago his father had shown him the hiding place. "Just in case you ever need to get into my desk when I'm not here," he had explained.

Kneeling down in front of the mahogany Georgian partners desk, Edward pushed his head and shoulders into the space between the sets of drawers and reached his hand toward the back for the key. It hung on a hook on the section of the desk just beyond the knee space.

Carefully, Edward searched each drawer. His father had been meticulous, and everything was neatly placed. But he came up with nothing of any importance. There were no notes, no records, no diaries, and no files on anything to do with his father's work or the Deravenel Company. Everything was innocuous, personal, of little consequence.

Feeling frustrated, Edward let his eyes roam around the

study, thinking of his father and how much he had loved this room. Every piece of furniture in it he had chosen and placed; Edward noted his father's collection of ancient coins, the many photographs of the family in silver frames, and his treasured books. The Moroccan-bound volumes were carefully arranged in low shelves placed against one of the long walls.

And then there were the portraits . . . the paintings of so many Deravenels, from long ago to the present. Guy de Ravenel, founder of their dynasty, his likeness somewhat faded now in the extremely old painting. And there was the recently completed portrait of his father, commissioned by his mother and hung there by her only a few weeks ago. As he stared at his father's image, a lump came into Edward's throat. He swallowed hard, pushing back the incipient tears. How he would miss him.

His eyes continued on, focused on another wall, and he spotted a couple of Deravenel Turners from Wales, along with portraits of the Deravenel Grants from Lancashire. The Grants might spell trouble, but certainly the Turners were relatively docile, and there were not many of them left, only two, or so he believed. That line had dribbled down to nothing. Well, that was how his father had put it . . .

A rustling sound followed by a faint cough brought Edward's eyes to the door. He was startled to see Richard standing there, bundled up in his woolen dressing gown, staring at him. "What on earth are you doing up at this hour, Little Fish? It's the middle of the night!" Instantly Edward was hurrying across the room to his small brother. Leading him over to the fireplace, he sat down, brought Richard close to him.

"I couldn't sleep. I went to your bedroom, Ned, but you weren't there." Looking into his face intently, Richard frowned and asked, "You *will* come back, won't you?"

"I certainly will. I promised, didn't I?"

"Yes. But you see, well, Ned, I don't think George and I are old enough to look after Mama and Meg . . . but you are. So you *have* to come home."

"I understand what you're saying. Don't you worry. Once I've done my business in Italy, I'll be back. But you know, Dick, I have a feeling that the two of you *could* keep an eye on things for me. Or should I say four eyes?"

Richard forced a smile, but his eyes were sad. "I suppose so."

Funny how his eyes look more blue than gray at times, Edward thought. Then they become the color of wet slate, and sometimes they even turn black. They reflected his moods, Edward supposed. "Come along, old chap, let's go upstairs," he suggested. "It's time we both went to sleep, don't you think?"

Richard simply nodded. Taking hold of his brother's hand, he allowed himself to be led out of the study, across the Long Hall and up the wide staircase. It was only when they came to the first-floor landing that Richard tugged on Edward's hand. "Could I sleep with you tonight, Ned? Like I did when I was really, really little and afraid of the dark?"

"It will be my very great pleasure to share my bed with you," Ned exclaimed, smiling down at the eight-year-old, understanding that Richard needed to feel safe and secure tonight.

Edward found himself the recipient of a wide and happy smile from his youngest brother, and it touched his heart most profoundly.

five

LONDON

Will Hasling stood waiting at the barrier at King's Cross Station, stamping his feet to keep warm and huddling deeper into his long winter overcoat. This was made of gray merino wool and had a raccoon fur collar; the coat was slender and elegant, made him look taller than his five feet nine, and added to the twenty-two-year-old's air of prosperity.

A pleasant-looking young man, with a warm, expansive smile, hazel eyes, and light brown hair, Will hailed from a family of landed gentry in Leicestershire. His father was a landowner of considerable importance, with a stately home on hundreds of acres; the local squire and justice of the peace as well, he was something of a bon vivant. His son, too, enjoyed good food and drink, but unlike his father, he did not find rural life appealing. Hunting, shooting, and fishing held no interest for him.

After graduating Oxford, Will fully intended to live in London, where he hoped to work in the City, possibly as a broker on the London Stock Exchange. He loved London, especially these days. He found it glittering, glamorous, and exciting, *the* place to be. In the three years that he had been king, Edward VII had become even more popular than he was as Prince of Wales; everyone in the country adored him, from the aristocracy to the working classes.

Will, like the entire nation, had mourned Queen Victoria's passing, but he also felt the shared sense of relief, and expectation, now that Edward was on the throne. People were happy that the king had moved the monarchy back to London. He had lit the lights, thrown open the doors of Buckingham Palace, welcomed his friends inside, and the dancing had begun. It seemed to Will, and his cohorts, that after the constraints and repression of Victorian England, a new era had begun—a time of jollity, gaiety, freedom, and expressiveness. And he for one couldn't wait to sample all these excitements and pleasures.

Stamping his feet again, he moved around, trying to combat the icy weather. There was a fog on this Wednesday evening, a fog Will hoped would not turn into one of those dreadful pea soupers. There had been quite a few of those of late, and they blighted London, made the streets difficult to maneuver, whether on foot or in a hansom cab.

Will glanced around as he waited, amazed to see the station so busy, but then the majority of L.N.E.R. trains from the north and the northeast arrived here, most of them during the early evening. He decided it was a normal mix of people waiting here tonight. There were a number of women, accompanied by either a woman friend or a man, hovering close to him at the barrier. Plain-looking women in long, dark coats and cloche hats, obviously from the middle class. As his eyes roamed, he spotted a lot of bowlers and a few homburg hats but no flat caps . . . funny how one could distinguish a class by its headgear, he thought. Not many toffs or working-class men amongst the bustle, he realized, mostly chaps from the middle class, just like the women.

Adjusting the silk scarf wrapped around his neck, Will began to walk up and down, his thoughts turning to Edward Deravenel. His closest friend, indeed the man he considered his best friend. He was deeply concerned about him and had been since he had visited the Deravenel town house in Charles Street in Mayfair earlier that day.

His intention had been to ascertain when Edward was arriving from Yorkshire, wishing to plan their journey to Oxford together. Mr. Swinton, the butler, had answered the door, and Will had known at once, as Swinton invited him to come inside, that something was horribly wrong. A dour expression had ringed the butler's face, and a mournful feeling permeated the house. After greeting him, Swinton had confided the terrible news.

Will had been stunned, so much so that Swinton had asked him if he would care to partake of a glass of brandy. He had declined and then asked for more details. But Swinton had merely added that Mr. Edward had telephoned that morning to announce his arrival in the early evening. He and his cousin would be on the afternoon train from York. And then Mr. Edward had broken the sorrowful news.

When Will had inquired how Mr. Deravenel Senior and Mr. Edmund had died, the butler had explained, "It was in a fire in Italy. Mr. Watkins Senior and his son Thomas were traveling with them, and they were also killed. A great tragedy for the two families, sir," the butler had finished, looking on the verge of tears. Further shocked and appalled, Will had offered his condolences to the butler, who had been in the family's employ since boyhood, being the son of an old family retainer.

Will had eventually taken his leave, and placed his calling card on the silver salver on the hall table as he went out. Feeling upset and worried, he had walked back to his rooms at Albany, his senses positively reeling as he had strode down past Shepherd's Market, through Berkeley Square, and into Piccadilly, where Albany was located.

During his walk, he had made up his mind to go to King's Cross to meet the York train in case Edward needed him. And of course he would. To lose a father, brother, uncle, and cousin in one fell swoop was incomprehensible, and Will knew that, if such a catastrophe had happened to him, he would need his best friend and all the help he could get.

For Will, the rest of the day had been miserable. He had paced his rooms, left his food untouched. He had sat staring into the fire for hours, filled with sadness for his friend and wondering how to console him in his loss. Now Will heard a train hooting. Moving closer to the barrier, he peered ahead and was somewhat relieved when he overheard a man standing nearby tell his companion, "That's the York train pulling in now."

Train whistles blowing. Smoke, steam, fog mingling. Doors slamming. Hustle and bustle. Porters pushing luggage carts. Crowds hurrying along the platform. So much activity, so many people, Will thought, craning his neck, scanning the crowd for Edward Deravenel and Neville Watkins. Within a few minutes, the crowds were dissipating, and suddenly Will spotted them walking together along the platform, followed by a porter with their luggage. He instantly made the decision to stay put. He was standing just behind the barrier, and certainly Edward would spot him immediately.

Naturally, it was hard to miss Edward Deravenel. He was so handsome, so tall, he stood out in any crowd. And there was no mistaking Edward's cousin. Neville had always had a taste for fine clothes and was attired in the latest and most stylish fashions on all occasions. His reputation as a bit of a dandy had stood for years; there were even those who referred to him as the Edwardian Beau Brummell, making reference to the Regency dandy of that name.

Tonight Neville wore a black homburg hat, in the jaunty style favored by King Edward, and a black overcoat with an astrakhan collar. It had obviously been impeccably tailored in one of Savile Row's best establishments.

Although he was not as tall as his cousin, Neville was a striking man, and he held himself regally, walked as if he owned the world. In a sense, he probably did, now that his father was dead. He would inherit the many companies which his grandfather had left to Rick Watkins, and which Rick had run most successfully. But Neville was a prosperous man in his own right; his fortune came from his own efforts, plus, there was the fortune his heiress wife, Anne, had brought as her dowry. Will knew that Neville Watkins was considered one of the most important magnates in England, and now he would be the richest by far.

People standing in front of Will hurried off to greet the travelers they were meeting, and Will found himself looking straight down the emptying platform. Edward caught sight of him, and a smile glanced across his handsome face.

Will waved and went to the gate, clasped Edward's hand as he came through. Neville nodded, thrust out his own hand, and when the greetings were over, the three men moved toward the street entrance.

"Good of you to come, Will. I suppose you've spoken to Swinton?" Edward asked, raising an eyebrow.

Will nodded. "I went to the Mayfair house today to find out when you were returning from Yorkshire. Swinton told me the news. Ned, I'm so very, very sorry. This is such a terrible tragedy . . ."

"Yes," Ned said laconically.

Turning to Neville, Will went on. "Please accept my condolences, Neville. I know you're as heartsick as Ned."

"Thank you, Will," Neville responded a little brusquely and cleared his throat. "Did you come in a hansom?"

"Yes, I did. The driver's waiting for me."

"My carriage will be outside. Would you care to ride with us, or do you prefer to make use of the cab which brought you?"

"I'd like to come with you and Ned, naturally," Will answered. "I'll pay the driver off; he'll be happy to pick up another fare here."

By this time they had reached the exit, where several private carriages were waiting along with a number of hansom cabs. Will glanced around until he found the one he had come in; he hurried over to pay the driver while Neville and Edward showed the porter where to put their luggage. Within a very short while the men were seated in Neville's elegant carriage, heading for the Deravenels' town house in Charles Street.

After making desultory conversation for a few minutes, all three men fell silent almost simultaneously. Will, who was sitting opposite Edward and Neville, realized that both of them had drifted into their own thoughts. And with good reason, Will decided. Several times he was on the verge of saying something, then bit back the words. Their expressions were sorrowful. Edward, who was usually garrulous and filled with vivacity, was positively somber; Neville's face bore no expression at all, except for his eyes. And they were cold, pale blue ice.

Will finally leaned back against the padded seat of the carriage, lost in his own mental meanderings. He noticed that the fog had deepened but was not yet so thick that the driver couldn't make his way. He closed his eyes, drifting, the only sound the clatter of the horses' hooves on the road.

A little later Will opened his eyes and saw that Edward was studying him intently. Edward said, "I hope, Will, that you will join me for a light supper, and you, too, Neville?"

Before Will could say a word, Neville shook his head. "I do believe I should get back to Chelsea. I must attend to our travel plans, but thank you, Edward."

Edward glanced at Will. "And what about you, my friend?"

"Of course I'll dine with you, Ned, and I'll help you any way I can."

six

Edward and Will sat in front of the fire in the small parlor of the Mayfair town house, each nursing a balloon filled with Cognac. Edward was recounting everything he knew about the tragic deaths of his family, and when he finished, he added, "However, Neville believes they were murdered."

Will, who had been listening attentively, sat bolt upright. He gaped at Edward and then exclaimed, "*Murder,* by God, Ned, that's preposterous—" Will cut himself off abruptly. Leaning forward, he fixed his eyes on Edward intently and in a quieter voice, added, "Perhaps it's not so preposterous, after all. There has been bad blood between your father and his cousin Henry Grant for years. Is that what Neville is suggesting? That Henry Grant had your father killed because he feared your father, feared that he would endeavor to take over Deravenels?"

Edward nodded. "That's the gist of it, yes, Will. But of course Neville doesn't mean Henry but his cohorts, and he doesn't have anything concrete to go on as of this moment. It's what he calls a gut feeling. You know very well that Neville is a masterful businessman, and he has great psychological insight." Edward sighed. "He's convinced he is right, perhaps he is . . . I just don't know. So we are going to Italy to investigate. Maybe we will find something, maybe we won't. Once we've finished checking the facts, we will bring the bodies back for burial. We plan to leave for Florence on Friday, actually, by way of Paris."

"Where *was* the fire in Florence?" Will asked, wondering why he had not read about it in *The Times*. After all, Florence was the greatest Renaissance city in the world, and a fire anywhere there would be bound to make news.

"It wasn't in Florence, Will. The fire was in Carrara, in the hotel where they were staying. My father had gone to Carrara to look into a problem with our marble quarries. Edmund had begged to go with Father because he'd never been to Italy, and Uncle Rick and Thomas asked if they might accompany them, because my uncle was eager to buy sculpture and art for his house. Naturally, Florence was a very tempting place to visit."

"I understand," Will answered, then hesitated for a moment, looking down into the amber liquid in his glass, his expression thoughtful. After a split second, he asked, "Could I come with you and Neville? I think I might be of some help, and if you don't think I can do anything special for you, do remember I can give you moral support. I'm very good at that, don't you know."

A smile flitted across Edward's mouth and was instantly gone. He glanced across at his good friend, his expression suddenly quizzical. "What about Oxford? Your studies? We were supposed to go back there this coming weekend, you and I."

"That's absolutely true. But isn't this an emergency?" Not waiting for an answer, Will continued. "We could return together in a few weeks, when this problem has been resolved."

"I won't be going back to university, Will. This is it for me, I'm afraid. My mother informed me yesterday that I must take my father's place at Deravenels. That's the family rule."

Will looked crestfallen. "So you won't be coming back ever? Is that what you mean, Ned?"

"I do. And of course I do regret that. On the other hand, there is nothing *I* can do about it, since that rule has been in existence for several hundred years. Don't forget, the Deravenel Company was founded by my ancestor Guy de Ravenel once he'd settled in Yorkshire after the Norman Conquest. He started importing wines and exporting raw wool, spun wool, and woolen goods."

"It's amazing when you think about it, Ned. Over eight hundred years of trading." Will shook his head. "Few companies are that old."

"Yes, you're right. But it didn't really come into its own until the fifteenth century, when Deravenels began trading all over the world, importing and exporting everything under the sun. And we still do. I suppose we are the largest trading company in existence today, and I know my father felt he had entitlement to it."

"I've never really understood the bad blood between members of your family. What is it all about?"

"It's actually fairly simple, Will. Sixty years ago, Henry Grant's grandfather deposed one of our cousins, who was running Deravenels. He did this by putting out bad stories about the man's private life, along with harmful allegations about his business abilities. In fact, he made our cousin look incompetent and reckless. Because our cousin had no children, his direct heir was a second cousin, Roger Morton Deravenel. However, this man died, and so it was Roger's son Edmund who was next in line. But he was only seven."

"Henry Grant's grandfather just grabbed the top position because one man was weak, another had just died, and the next in line was too young to run Deravenels," Will interjected. "What an opportunity that was. *Irresistible.*"

"That's true, and suddenly the Lancashire Deravenel Grants were in control, having pushed the Yorkshire Deravenels—in other words, *us*—out. Not long after this, our cousin who had been shoved out died in mysterious circumstances, so there was no opposition left. Henry Grant's grandfather was tough and ruthless, and that's the reason our side of the family has been in second position at Deravenels all these years. But it truly should be ours."

"Cousins fighting cousins," Will muttered.

"A family feud of long standing. But we do try to be civil with each other . . . at least my father did. I don't know that I can be."

Will half smiled, then asked, "Well, what do you say, old chap? May I join you on this trip to Florence?"

"If you are inclined to do so, why not? I am quite certain that Neville will appreciate your presence, as indeed I will."

After Will had gone home, Edward hurried up to his father's study on the next floor. He went in, snapped on the electric light, and recoiled slightly. The room had a faint odor of the cigars his father had enjoyed, mingled with the bay rum aftershave lotion he had always favored.

In his mind's eye, Edward saw his father sitting behind the large Georgian desk at the far end of the room, smiling across at him, and a lump came into his throat as a rush of emotion swamped him. He had loved his father, admired him, and he would miss him inordinately.

For a moment Edward thought of walking out, going up to his bedroom, then instantly he changed his mind. He would have to become accustomed to these flashes of overwhelming feeling, the vivid memories, and face them squarely. His father was dead, just as Edmund was, and nothing would bring them back. However, the remembered past and their lives existed inside him, so there was really no death in his lexicon. These two men lived on in his heart, and for as long as he was alive they would be alive, too, part of *him* forever.

He walked over to the desk, went around its bulk, and sat down in the comfortable black leather chair. He knew at once that he would find nothing of any importance here, because all of the drawers had keys in their locks. Nothing to hide, nothing to find, Edward thought as he opened the top middle drawer. It contained only a few items, none of any importance, and as he went through each drawer, he discovered the same thing.

Closing the last drawer, Edward sat back in the chair, sighing. He wondered what he had been looking for. He had no idea really, but he had thought that somewhere there might be a piece of revealing evidence about Henry Grant and the men who surrounded him, or his French wife.

Glancing around the room, Ned saw it more objectively than ever before. He had always liked its warmth and handsome overtones: the deep red-flocked wallpaper, the large, comfortable sofa covered in a matching red velvet fabric, the worn black leather armchairs near the fireplace, the wall of leather-bound books. Despite the prevalence in most homes of that tabletop clutter of the recent Victorian era, there was a paucity of it here. His father had never cared for bric-a-brac, but then neither did his mother. As in his father's private abode at Ravenscar, there were numerous silver-framed photographs of himself, his siblings, plus several of his mother. And that was the extent of it, except for a silver cigarette box and, over on the long side table, a humidor for his father's favorite Cuban cigars.

It was *his* room now. At least it was his if Edward wished to make use of it, courtesy of his mother. The town house belonged to her; it had never been his father's property, but had come to his mother from her father, the industrialist. Until his grandfather's death, they had lived in a much, much smaller house in Chelsea, one which had been passed down from his other grandfather, Charles Deravenel, to his father. It was a nice house, and relatively comfortable, but extremely modest in comparison with this one. And, of course, it was his mother's inheritance that paid for its upkeep, and for the maintenance of Ravenscar as well. Edward wasn't sure why his father had always been short of money and embarrassed by his impecunious situation. But no doubt *he* would find out soon enough.

On the train to London, Neville had suggested they both go to the company tomorrow to question Aubrey Masters and to have a look around. "It won't do any harm," Neville had said. "And it's only natural that we would want to go over there together, since our fathers and brothers died together."

Ned had immediately seen the sense in this suggestion, and Neville had offered to pick him up at ten o'clock. The Deravenel Company had large offices in the Strand, "which," Neville had pointed out, "is the place you'll have to occupy for the rest of your life. But at the top of the heap, if I have anything to do with it."

Edward knew that Neville was a brilliant strategist, with money to burn. Whatever else happened, he was secure in the knowledge that Neville Watkins, cousin, friend, and mentor, would get to the bottom of the tragedy which had taken place in Italy. But he had no idea how Neville proposed to put him at the top of the heap in the Deravenel Company. That would take a miracle.

Once again, sleep eluded Edward. At eleven o'clock he got out of bed, went into the adjoining bathroom, and splashed cold water on his face. He stood for a moment, staring at himself in the looking glass. He appeared tired, with faint, dark shadows under his eyes, but other than that there were no real signs of the grief he had suffered since learning of the family tragedy. In fact, he looked like himself, a strapping young man in the bloom of youth. He returned to his bedroom, dressed in fresh linen, took a dark suit from his wardrobe, put it on, then filled his pockets with small change, keys, his money wallet, and the gold watch his grandfather Watkins had left him in his will.

Ten minutes later, bundled up in a dark overcoat and scarf, he went to the butler's pantry. "I'm afraid I must go out on an errand," Edward said, adding, "And please don't wait up for me, Swinton, there is no need for that."

"Whatever you wish, sir," Swinton replied, his face unreadable.

Edward inclined his head politely and returned to the front hall. Within seconds he was on the pavement hailing a hansom cab. He climbed in as the driver was saying, "Evenin', Guv, where can I be taking you?"

Edward gave an address in Belsize Park, told the driver he was required to wait, then sat back against the seat. The cab began to move forward, and Edward asked himself why he was going to see Lily Overton tonight of all nights. He had learned of his father's death, his brother's death, and those of his two close relatives only the day before. Four of the family gone, and here he was going to see a woman he knew would give him a certain kind of solace. But it was not her sexual solace he sought tonight. It was solace of another kind he craved. He needed to be comforted and soothed; he hoped she would be able to ease his heartache. One thing he knew for certain was that she would be alone; Lily was not a prostitute. She was yet another widow he knew, older than Alice at Ravenscar, and well provided for, having been married to a successful solicitor.

Edward had acquired a liking for older women when he was seduced at the age of thirteen by the wife of the choirmaster at a Scarborough church. A woman who had instructed him in the pleasurable art of sex in a cave on the beach at Ravenscar, just below the ruined stronghold built by his ancestor Guy de Ravenel. She had been twenty-five and a beautiful blond with silver-gray eyes. Lily Overton was thirty-two and just as beautiful as Tabitha had been, another blond-haired temptress who held him in her thrall. He closed his eyes and thought of both women; they intermingled in his mind, and he felt the thrill of unexpected sexual arousal.

A short time later the hansom cab jolting to a stop made Edward sit up with a start; glancing out the window, he saw that they had arrived at the small house where Lily Overton lived.

Opening the door, he jumped out and said to the driver, "Wait a moment, please."

"I understands, Guv," the cabbie said.

The house was in darkness, but Edward noticed the glimmer of a candle flame in an upstairs window. Lifting the brass knocker, he banged hard on the door.

Lily did not appear. Once more he lifted the knocker, but before he used it again her voice said, from behind the door, "Who's there?" She sounded alarmed, and he knew he must reassure her at once, using a code they had devised together.

"Lily? It's me, Ned. Your brother-in-law. I've come to see my brother. Is he at home?"

"Come to the window," she replied in a low voice, "so that I can see you, be certain it *is* my brother-in-law outside at this hour."

Stepping over to the window, Edward waited for her to peep through the lace curtains. Once she had done so, he moved back to the front door; within a second Lily was unlocking it. Before he stepped into the house, he called over his shoulder to the driver of the cab, "Please wait for me. I won't be too long."

"Righto, Guv'nor," came the reply, followed by a quiet chuckle.

Once he was inside the house, Lily locked the front door and turned to Edward, her light green eyes questioning, her expression puzzled.

He had always sent notes by messenger, asking if he could visit her, and she had responded using the same messenger, either declining or acquiescing to his request. It was usually the latter. His unannounced arrival tonight had surprised her. He said quickly, "Excuse me, Lily, for coming to see you without prior warning, and at this very late hour. I hope I have not inconvenienced you."

"No, not at all. Perhaps I misunderstood the letter you posted from Yorkshire. . . . I was expecting you on Friday . . . before you went back to Oxford the next day."

"I did plan that. But I returned to London earlier than I expected, this evening, in fact, and I had such a need to see you, to be in your company, if only for a short while, I just had to come here."

He had spoken softly, and there was a seriousness about him tonight which was unusual. She suddenly wondered what was wrong. Lily Overton was not a stupid woman by anybody's standards, and she detected an unfamiliar sadness in Edward; sorrow dulled his brilliant blue eyes, and his demeanor was uncharacteristically quiet, reflective almost.

Since their first meeting last year, she had found him irresistible and readily succumbed to his charms. Even though he was far too young for her, she cared about him deeply, and he was the only man who had ever satisfied her sexually. Instinctively understanding he needed comforting, she put a hand on his arm and said gently, "Hang up your coat and scarf, and let us go to the sitting room upstairs, where we can talk for a while. I was reading there when you arrived, and there's a lovely fire."

Edward nodded, put his coat in the closet, and followed her up the staircase into her private haven. He liked this small but charming room, with its dark rose colored walls, rose damask sofa and chairs, and moss green carpet. Rose velvet draperies banished the foggy winter's night from sight, and the room was warm and inviting, as he remembered.

"May I turn down the gaslights?" Edward asked. "It's rather bright in here."

"Of course," Lily answered, adding, "And could you please throw another log on the fire while I pour you a glass of your favorite Cognac?"

He smiled at her, added logs to the grate, and reaching up, lowered the gaslights on either side of the mirror above the mantelpiece; instantly the room was more restful, intimate.

Walking over to the sofa, Edward sat down. He leaned back against the needlepoint pillows, hoping he could relax here; his nerves were taut, and he had developed a raging headache. But Lily had never failed to have a soothing effect on him.

Within the space of a few minutes, she was handing him the balloon of brandy and seating herself next to him. Studying him intently through her narrowed eyes, Lily said finally, "I *know* there's something wrong." When he was silent, she asked, "Would you care to talk to me about it, Edward?"

For a moment he did not answer, and then he said in a subdued voice, "There has been a terrible tragedy in my family. We are all devastated, Lily, grief-stricken—" He broke off, shook his head, as if he still disbelieved what he was about to say. And then slowly, speaking in that same low monotone, he told her about his father and brother, uncle and cousin, their sudden deaths in the fire at Carrara.

Lily was stunned. She sat staring at him through tearful eyes, and it took her a moment or two to find the right words to respond to his unimaginably awful news. But at last she said, "Oh, Ned, Ned darling, I'm so very sorry. It is heartbreaking for you and your family, I understand that . . . a great tragedy, catastrophic. Words are such cold comfort at a time like this, words are just . . . *hopeless*." She blinked back her tears and went on in a quavering voice. "How can I help you? Is there anything I can do to comfort you?"

Ned sighed, shook his head. "Not really . . . just being here with you is enough. You have always been so kind and loving—" His voice trailed off, and he took a swallow of the Cognac, put the glass back on the side table. When he turned his face to hers, he looked at her carefully. "Thank you for being . . . well, for being you. So understanding, so compassionate."

Lily took his hand in hers, brought it to her lips, moved closer to him. Placing his hand in her lap, she stroked it. After a few minutes of mutual silence, she murmured, "Do you want to be with me? To stay here tonight?"

"I really can't," he answered swiftly, frowning. "I am meeting my cousin very early tomorrow morning, so I must leave here soon. I haven't slept at all since we received the news."

"I understand." She paused, then remarked quietly, leaning into him, "You are so *tense,* overwrought, Ned. At least let me give you a massage before you go. You know how much my massages help you to relax."

Now it was his turn to hesitate. After a moment of thought, he said, "I'll stay for an hour, Lily, if that's all right with you."

"Whatever you want, darling."

seven

Lily Overton was a wise woman, and over the years she had acquired a degree of sophistication and worldliness. She had been married and widowed twice. Her first husband had been a surgeon, and her second a solicitor who was head of his own law firm; both men had left her their considerable wealth. She was a widow well placed. During her marriage to Oscar Overton she had met people from all walks of life, and she had benefited enormously from this exposure. It was because of her insight and bright intelligence that she had rapidly come to understand Edward Deravenel.

Their initial encounter had been a year ago, and Lily found herself thinking about that evening now, reliving it as she waited for him to return to the sitting room after going down to speak to the cabdriver.

Last January she had been invited to a small dinner party at the Kensington home of her dear friend Vicky Forth, the newly married sister of Will Hasling. Will had arrived with his best friend, Edward Deravenel, and it had been patently obvious to Lily that Edward was drawn to her the moment he set eyes on her. He had gravitated to her at once and remained glued to her side until they had gone in for dinner, not saying much but focused on her to the exclusion of all else.

Much to her surprise, she had been filled with genuine disappointment when she found herself seated between Will and a middle-aged banker with a walrus mustache and a slight lisp. A moment later, she had smiled with delight as Edward was shown to the chair opposite her. His brilliant blue eyes had barely left her face throughout dinner; they had greedily devoured her as he left his food untouched. His interest in his female dinner partners on either side had been vague, only meeting the standards of courtesy. His concentration had again been focused entirely on her, and she had understood *exactly* what he wanted. It was reflected in those mesmerizing eyes, which left little to the imagination.

After dinner the women had retired to the drawing room while the men had remained to enjoy their port and cigars. Lily had been restless, until *he* had appeared in the doorway half an hour later. Relief had flooded through her as he walked toward her, holding her with his eyes, not caring what anyone thought. Neither had she, much to her amazement. Lily had been somewhat surprised that she had remained excited and anxious to have him closer to her.

Once he had come to a stop, he had said, "I need to speak to you alone, Mrs. Overton."

She had simply nodded, and he had put his hand under her arm and ushered her to a distant corner near a potted palm.

"I must see you again, and as soon as possible," he had muttered once they were by themselves, his eyes riveted on hers. "And I do believe *you* would like that, too." As he had spoken, he had inched closer and increased the pressure of his hand on her arm, and there was such naked desire written across his face that she had found her mouth turning dry.

For a moment she had simply gazed up at him, totally under his spell.

"Please," he had begged.

Bright color had flooded her face, and she had felt flushed.

"Tomorrow," he had murmured hoarsely. "Better still, tonight. *Later tonight.* Oh, please say yes."

Finally finding her voice, she had whispered, "Tomorrow. In the afternoon. At four."

"Shall I come to your home? Or do you want to—"

"My home," she had cut in, dreading the thought of a meeting at a hotel. A public rendezvous would be improper, and she had quickly told him where she lived.

The following day, Lily had asked herself why she had become so quickly entranced by this young man, one who was obviously so much younger than she. And she had known the answer immediately. *Overwhelming sexual desire.* On both their parts. And so she had seen her housekeeper off at two o'clock; fifteen minutes later she had sent the maid home as well.

Alone, she had bathed and perfumed herself, brushed and dressed her golden hair in a loose, girlish style, put on pretty white undergarments, and selected a pale green chiffon-and-lace afternoon tea gown. The style was simple, loose and floating, tied around the waist with a broad, pale green ribbon belt. Even though it was a cold day, she had wanted to wear something young and pretty which also gave him easy access to her. She had known what to expect; he would attempt to seduce within the first half hour.

She had been ready an hour before he was due and had paced the floor, prowled around the house, checking on everything, hardly able to contain herself. She was acting like a young girl without experience. These feelings had truly taken her by surprise, since she *was* very experienced indeed.

Edward had arrived at five minutes to four, for afternoon tea. She had served him herself, and his gaze had never left her. Lily had been fully aware that the absence of staff and her flushed face signaled that her aim and intentions were indeed the same as his. But then he had known that before he had come. It had been telegraphed to him the evening before.

He had taken a sip of tea, and so had she; he had talked to her for a short while about Oxford, his close friendship with Will, and how much he liked Vicky Forth, *her* friend. Lily had listened attentively, loving the timbre of his voice, which was deeply masculine, mellifluous and cultivated.

And then Edward had stopped abruptly, risen and walked to her chair. Bending over her, he had said softly, "Won't you come and sit with me on the sofa? You seem so far away."

Before she could even answer, he had taken her hand, brought her to her feet, and led her to the sofa positioned near the fireplace.

"You're trembling, Mrs. Overton," he had said, sounding surprised as he pressed her down, seated himself next to her. "Are you all right?"

"Perfectly" had been all she could manage to say.

"I'm afraid I'm not," he had murmured and immediately drawn closer. "I've been extremely agitated since last night. You see, I haven't been able to stop thinking about you." When she did not respond, he had asked, "Dare I hope that you've given a little thought to me?"

She had nodded.

He had leaned into her then, put his arm around her shoulders, and brought his mouth to her cheek. She had remained quite still as he kissed her cheek again and found her mouth with his. She had kissed him back. Why pretend, she had thought, why pretend to be overly virtuous when he knows how much I want him? Within the space of a few seconds his hand had been on her breast; he had pulled her closer to him, holding her tightly in his arms, and with one dexterous hand he had unbuttoned the front of the gown and slipped his hand inside, lightly touching her nipple. When she had not shown any resistance to these advances, he had grown bolder, slid his hand down her leg, lifted the loose skirt of her dress, slipping his fingers along her inner thigh and between her legs. It was at this moment that she had exclaimed softly, "Please, we must stop. This is most unseemly."

He had pulled away from her gently, staring into her face, an amused look on his, and laughed. "Oh, Mrs. Overton, *really*." He had laughed again, and so had she, and then he had shaken his head and asked, "Could we perhaps go upstairs, Mrs. Overton? I do believe it has become quite pressing for us to find a bed."

"Only if you stop calling me Mrs. Overton and call me Lily instead, Edward," she had answered with a light laugh.

"And you must call *me* Ned."

Together they had climbed the stairs, and she had not been at all self-conscious; she had led him into her bedroom, then had suddenly turned her head and given him a most cryptic look.

His response had been to take her immediately in his arms, press her close to his body, his hand sliding down onto her buttocks. She had felt so small, feminine, and defenseless, because he was so tall, broad, and masculine, the most masculine man she had ever met.

When he had pressed her even closer, molding her to him, she had felt his erection against her body, and she had begun to tremble.

As if he understood her trepidation, he had not made another move, had simply stood perfectly still, looking down at her, his expression suddenly loving. Very slowly, he had begun to remove her clothes, untying the ribbon belt around her waist, letting it drop to the floor, unfastening the rest of the buttons on the front of her dress. Slipping it over her shoulders, he had let it fall to the floor, a pool of pale green lace at her feet. A moment after he had started to loosen her undergarments, he had stopped and led her over to the bed. Without a word, he had taken off everything else, until she was completely naked.

It was only then that he had spoken, saying in an awed voice, "Oh, Lily, Lily, you are very, very beautiful."

She had remained silent, simply staring up at him through eyes filled with longing, desire written all over her face.

Everything had gone very swiftly after that. He had risen, shed his own clothes, stretched out next to her on the bed. Pushing himself up on one elbow, he had leaned over her, kissed her deeply, passionately, his tongue sliding into her mouth for a moment of true intimacy. All of his movements were slow, gentle, tender, and soon one hand had roamed over her, stroking and caressing every part of her until she cried out in pleasure.

Soon after this he had taken her hand and placed it on his groin, and she had been startled by the size of him. But when he had entered her, he had done so with immense gentleness, and she had found herself opening up to him, thrilled by his virility, knowledge, and experience. Their coupling had been rapturous, ecstatic, as they had both known it would be from their first moment of meeting.

She had made supper for him, and he had stayed on and on, in the end not taking his leave of her until the early hours of the morning. He had been insatiable, and so had she, and she had realized that night that he was the best lover she had known.

And so had begun the most extraordinary relationship Lily had had with any man, one that had given her unusual happiness.

Ned saw her whenever he came up to London, and occasionally, giving in to his pleading, she visited him in Oxford. With the passing of time, she had grown to love him while understanding that the gap in their ages was too enormous to bridge. Nonetheless, she resolved to remain his mistress for as long as he wanted and needed her.

There was very little she did not know about him; she understood him completely. He was a sensual and extremely romantic man; she found him mature for his age; he had a brilliant analytical mind that would sometimes stun her. These attributes aside, his looks were heart-stopping, yet there was no vanity in him about his appearance, and he was kind, compassionate. Perhaps the most remarkable thing about Ned was his charisma. He possessed a special kind of natural charm that was so captivating it ensnared everyone. This characteristic, plus his amiability, immediately put people at ease. All gravitated to him, wanted to be part of his circle.

Yet Lily was very much aware that, behind that charming, polished facade, there was a wholly different kind of man, one of dogged determination, who harbored great ambition, was full of resourcefulness, and had a will of iron. Very quickly she had come to accept that he could be absolutely ruthless when he deemed it necessary.

Few people recognized any of these characteristics, because they took Edward at face value, and also because he did not permit them to know him intimately. Inevitably they underestimated him, much to her amusement and frequent irritation. They tended to characterize him as lazy, indolent, and a man of no consequence. How wrong they were.

Lily rose from the chair when she heard the front door bang, and her ponderings were pushed to one side. He was on the staircase, coming back to her, and her look was questioning as he entered the small sitting room. "Was the cabbie willing to wait?"

"For as long as I wish," he answered, giving her a faint smile. He seated himself on the sofa and stretched out his long legs.

"Do you want me to give you a shoulder massage?" she began, and instantly stopped as she saw him shaking his head.

"I just wish to sit here with you, Lily, for a while, and relax, if I can. I'm so filled with grief I feel that anything I do which would give me an ounce of pleasure tonight would be completely wrong."

Looking across at him, Lily merely inclined her head. A silence fell between them, but it was a compatible silence, and for a while the only sounds were the ticking of the grandfather clock in the corner and the crackling of the logs on the fire.

Eventually, Lily ventured, "I felt the same way as you do now when my first husband died . . . that I shouldn't enjoy anything, that it was somehow disrespectful. But that's not the case, you know. And having a woman love you, and loving a woman in return, is actually a wonderful affirmation of life." When he made no response, Lily pushed herself to her feet and went to sit next to him on the sofa.

Resting one hand on his leg, she said with great care, "Do you think that making love to me when you are in mourning would be unseemly? Or something like that, Ned?"

"I suppose so . . ." He left his sentence unfinished, leaned back against the sofa and stared at her, his expression both worried and perplexed.

"I fully understand, and as I said, I have been *there*, where you are at this moment in time, so full of sorrow," Lily murmured. "It's sorrow mixed with anger, and a sense of helplessness. It's only natural to feel like that, and perhaps worse for you, because you have lost not only your closest and dearest family but several other relatives as well."

He took her hand in his, held it tightly. "Yes," he murmured, "you're correct."

"I learned long ago that it is important to put death to one side and get on with *everyday* things. Life *is* for the living, Ned, and understanding that does help to ease the sadness."

He ran his hand through his red-gold hair and sighed heavily. "You're wise, Lily, and I agree with you on an *intellectual* level, but it's very difficult to accept that emotionally." He sighed again and offered her a rueful smile. "Anyway, I don't think I would be able to make love tonight, I really don't."

But he was. And he did. With Lily's loving help. Life *was* for the living. And tomorrow was for revenge.

eight

I don't think there is anything untoward about my coming with you to Deravenels this morning, Ned," Neville said, walking across to the fireplace as he spoke, standing with his back to it. "I consider it quite normal that I accompany you. After all, my father and brother were killed along with yours in Carrara."

"Oh, I totally agree with you," Edward was swift to answer, staring at his cousin, perplexed, and then continuing, "And it was *you* whom Aubrey Masters decided to telephone once he had received the tragic news. However, why do you bring it up?" Ned frowned. "Do you envision some sort of problem about *us* arriving together?"

"Not at all. I was just running everything through my mind. Some persnickety member of the staff might wonder out loud about a cousin who has nothing to do with the company arriving on their doorstep with you, that's all. It was always my understanding that several of Henry Grant's employees were a trifle touchy about your father's relatives."

Edward chuckled. "Correct, they were, and most especially the French whore, as Father used to call her. She was the most vociferous."

Neville raised a brow, giving Edward a swift look. "The French whore," he repeated and began to laugh. "I remember now, your father did occasionally mutter something about the true paternity of her son, Edouard. I do believe he wondered aloud about the ability of Henry to perform; well, that was the way he put it."

"My father was convinced that Henry was impotent, and possibly sterile as well, and he made no bones about it at home. He was convinced that their son was fathered by one of Grant's cohorts."

"Making Edouard a bastard, of course, and therefore not of his blood, and therefore not entitled to take over De-ravenels one day."

Edward nodded. "Anyway, I have not been in touch with Aubrey Masters. Have you?"

"No. I purposefully chose not to announce our arrival. I thought it would be more interesting to walk in out of the blue, so to speak."

Neville's carriage took the two men around Berkeley Square, into Piccadilly, and through Trafalgar Square, continuing in the direction of the Strand. The splendid, horse-drawn carriage finally came to a standstill outside the imposing office building of the great global trading company.

Eyes turned as the two men alighted. Both were elegantly dressed in dark suits and black overcoats, the fabric, cut, style, and tailoring proclaiming the garments to be undoubtedly from Savile Row and made to measure.

Passersby paused to stare at the tall, distinguished men as they strode confidently toward the front doors of the De-ravenel Company. Gentlemen with a bit of a dash and dazzle, toffs from the upper class, that was how they were perceived, and mostly without any resentment. England in 1904 was a world of class distinction, and everyone knew it and accepted it. Nothing had changed much over the centuries.

The two men went through the ancient portals and stood for a moment in the marble-clad lobby, the ceiling of which

soared like that of a great cathedral. The veined marble was
in tones of black and a deep terra-cotta, and it covered the
walls, many high-flung circular pillars, and the vast floor. It
reeked of money and success.

A uniformed doorman, positioned inside at a small desk
in the winter weather, hurried over to them. Immediately he
recognized Edward Deravenel, and his famous cousin, the
tycoon Neville Watkins. He had always liked Master Edward, such a tall, good-looking young man with burnished
red-gold hair and brilliant blue eyes. The son of the late
Richard Deravenel, and wasn't *he* one of the finest gentlemen in the world? the doorman thought, and then said politely, "Good morning, Mr. Edward, Mr. Watkins. Please go
right up to the first floor."

"Thank you, Johnson," Edward answered, giving the
commissionaire a warm smile. "And how is your son doing?
The last time we spoke he was joining the Indian Army."

Flattered that Edward had recalled their last conversation,
Johnson nodded, smiling with real pleasure. "Very well, sir,
thank you. Good of you to remember my Jack, sir."

Edward inclined his head slightly, and he and Neville
headed toward the wide double staircase of carved mahogany that floated up to a wide landing. The two men
climbed the stairs to the first floor, where the executive offices were located, aligned along a wide corridor which
ended at the giant double doors leading into the company's
boardroom. Edward thought of that room now; as a small
boy he had often wished he would dominate it when he grew
up. He felt a sudden sinking feeling as he saw his father's office in his mind's eye. He was not certain that he could face
going in there today, although perhaps he should. Putting it
off was ridiculous, wasn't it? Nonetheless, he balked at the
idea. It smacked of more pain.

Halfway up the red-carpeted stairs, Neville paused, his
hand resting on the banister. "Once the greetings are over, I

think it would be wise to move right in with your questions, Ned. Let us avoid procrastination. You know how Aubrey can be."

"Long-winded, to put it mildly," Edward answered. "And you don't have cause for concern. I'm as impatient as you are to get to the bottom of this situation. Let us hope he can give us satisfactory answers."

Neville nodded, and the two continued up the stairs. They were both filled with apprehension; they dreaded what they would soon learn about the terrible deaths of their loved ones. Although they had not discussed it, both men realized that the fire must have been a brutal and terrifying way to die.

The wide landing was more like a room. Placed in its center was a large desk, and behind it sat an attractive young woman in a black, long-skirted suit and white blouse.

She glanced up as Edward and Neville approached; her eyes automatically swung to Edward, whom she recognized at once. "Oh, Mr. Edward, good morning," she murmured, offering him a small half smile. She wanted to say something about his father's death but knew it would be improper. It was not her place to make any kind of personal remark to him.

"Good morning, Mathilda. This is Mr. Watkins, and we're here to see Mr. Masters."

She inclined her head in Neville's direction, then stood up. "I'll let Mr. Masters know you're here, sir." She hurried off down the corridor.

Edward and Neville took off their overcoats and hung them in the coat cupboard, and a moment later Mathilda was back, drawing to a standstill next to them. "Mr. Masters will see you immediately," she said and led them down the corridor, ushered them into an office, and closed the door behind them.

Aubrey Masters came around the desk to greet Edward

and Neville. He was a fussy, small, somewhat rotund man in his late forties, dark-haired with a florid complexion and brown eyes set close together.

Grasping Edward's hand, he exclaimed, "Mr. Edward, my boy, come in, come in, and sit down!" Turning to Neville, he shook his hand also and indicated the other chair in front of the desk. "Welcome to Deravenels, Mr. Watkins, it's some time since you've been here. Over a year, if I recall correctly."

"That's true," Neville responded and lowered himself into the chair. His gaze remained focused on Masters, who had gone to sit down behind the desk.

"Please accept my condolences, Mr. Edward, for this awful loss you have suffered, and you, too, Mr. Watkins. My deepest condolences to you both," Masters began. "This tragedy has been a blight on the company since we received the dreadful news. Everyone has been plunged into sorrow and gloom—"

"Thank you," Edward said, cutting Masters off sharply. "My cousin and I are most appreciative of your kind thoughts and sympathy, and we certainly thank you for sparing our mothers undue and additional heartache. To have received the news by telephone would have been perfectly ghastly for them both."

"Yes, it seemed to me at the time that contacting your cousin was the right and proper way to handle the matter," Masters answered, leaning forward over the desk, his hands clasped together.

"Most sensitive indeed," Neville interjected as he studied Masters, weighing him up.

"Mr. Watkins and I are very anxious to know exactly what happened to our fathers and brothers in Carrara. We hope you will supply more of the details."

Clearing his throat several times, Masters nodded. "I'm sorry to say I do not have a great deal of information, Mr. Edward. All I know is that a fire started in the hotel last Sunday night. I was informed on Monday, by telegram from Carrara."

"And who sent the telegram?" Edward asked, keeping a tight rein on his emotions. He was rediscovering his inherent antipathy toward Masters, who had never been a favorite of his father's either. There was something shifty about him, and Edward was convinced that his loyalty was for sale and always had been. He now wondered about the man's integrity.

Masters, staring at Edward in return, said in the most matter-of-fact voice he could summon, "I was informed of the tragedy by Alfredo Oliveri."

"Isn't he the manager of our business affairs in Carrara?"

"Yes, he is. He works with the superintendent of the mines."

"I see. And there's another manager in Florence, isn't there?" Edward remarked. "Fabrizio Dellarosa."

Masters nodded. "Dellarosa runs our overall business in Italy, and he was the one who worked most closely with Mr. Richard, er, your father."

"Has he been in touch with you?"

"Yes, he has." Aubrey sat up a little straighter, detecting hostility. A rush of panic hit him. Had he forgotten something? Did they know more than he did? If there *was* more to know. Clearing his throat, he announced in a clear, firm voice, "Look, I *have* told you everything I *know,* Mr. Edward."

"Were they badly burned in the fire?" Neville asked, not permitting his heartache to surface.

"I'm sorry, I'm afraid I don't know. Oliveri told me by telegram that they were found in the hotel and that their bodies had been taken to the hospital in Florence. That they were being held there until the arrival of the family members. That is yourselves, of course."

"And that's all you know?" Edward said, incredulity echoing in his voice.

Masters appeared to be mystified by this question.

"There's not much else to know," he murmured, looking confused and worried.

"Were they all together? Were they in a lounge or the foyer? Or in their bedrooms? How long did the fire burn? Why were they not rescued before it was too late? What did the police report say?" Edward stared hard at Aubrey Masters, his eyes narrowed. "There's a great deal more *I* want to know about this matter, and so does Neville."

"Oh, dear, maybe I've made an error."

"What do you mean?" Edward asked quickly, fixing his bright blue gaze on Masters.

"Perhaps I should have gone to Italy at once, to look into the situation, instead of leaving it to the Italian managers."

"Perhaps you should," Edward shot back coldly, glaring at him.

The silence in the room was deafening.

Edward sat perfectly still, filled with frustration. Was Aubrey Masters really a nincompoop, or was he a clever dissembler? Edward wasn't sure, and suddenly he made up his mind to leave this office at once. There was nothing he and Neville could learn here, that was patently obvious. Once they arrived in Italy, they would gather the facts themselves.

Out in the street, Neville spoke to the driver of his carriage. He and Edward then walked across the Strand and entered the Savoy Court, the forecourt to the Savoy Hotel and the adjoining Savoy Theatre. Neville broke his stride as they approached the theater, and turning to Edward, he said, "It's thanks to the Gilbert and Sullivan operettas that Richard D'Oyly Carte was able to build this theater and the hotel a few years ago, you know. With all those profits from them, he made a veritable fortune."

Edward nodded. "My father loved the operettas, especially *The Mikado* and *H.M.S. Pinafore.*"

"Not to my taste. I much prefer Mozart."

Edward made no comment, and they continued on at their

fast pace, entering the Savoy Hotel, crossing the entrance foyer, heading for the men's cloakroom. After depositing their overcoats and freshening up, they went into the Savoy Grill for lunch.

Once they were seated at their table, Neville ordered a bottle of dry white wine and sat back, regarding his cousin intently. "You don't like Aubrey Masters, do you, Ned?" he said at last.

"It's not a question of liking or disliking him. . . . I'm not sure that I trust him. He never was a favorite of Father's, and when we were at the offices I began to wonder if he was stupid or a clever dissembler."

"If he's given to dissimulation, then he's a mighty fine actor. Personally, I think he's a trifle dim-witted. Which brings me to a leading question. Why *is* he in that position? Who made him head of the Mining Division?"

"Henry Grant, of course. Aubrey Masters is a relative, a cousin twice removed, I do believe."

"Nepotism again, eh?" Neville shook his head. "Weren't you surprised not to hear from Henry Grant, not to receive his condolences?"

"Not really. You see, before Father left for Italy, he told me that Henry was out of sorts, that he had gone into a religious retreat in Cumbria for two months. So presumably he's still there, and perhaps no one's bothered to inform him of our tragedy."

"If that is so, I find it quite preposterous he's been kept in the dark."

"So do I. But never mind that. We have better fish to fry, you and I, Neville. It is imperative that we set off for Italy as soon as possible. Will and I are both prepared to leave immediately. You just have to say the word."

"We depart on Saturday, Ned. All the arrangements are being made by the Thomas Cook agency. I merely have to confirm the hotel to them later today."

"The Ritz in Paris is fine, as I told you."

Neville nodded and picked up a menu. "I've hardly eaten for days, and I know it's been the same for you. However, I do think we should order a decent meal, if only to keep our strength up."

"You're right. The problem is I've lost my appetite."

Edward studied his menu for a moment, then put it down and remarked, "You know, the pious Henry Grant might be purging his soul and reveling in his religion, but his wife is here in London. Condolence letters *could* easily have been sent to us and our families, don't you think?"

"Look to the source, Edward. That she-wolf doesn't know any better. Now, let's order something to eat and relax. This afternoon we must go over our plans. We really do have to know whether there was foul play, and then act accordingly."

"I'm hoping the two managers in Italy will have more information for us, especially Alfredo Oliveri, since he resides in Carrara. My father always liked him and often spoke about him. With some affection, I might add."

"Then he's our man, and no doubt he'll have the police report. Or at least access to it. That will be a start."

"I thought Masters was most cavalier in his attitude, and it infuriated me," Edward confided.

"I know it did. I can read your eyes even when you keep a poker face, Ned. Anyway, I do feel there is a way to get the better of the Lancashire Deravenels," Neville said. "I predict I will have you sitting in Henry Grant's chair in less than six months."

Edward was silent for a moment, and then he protested. "I'm so young, Neville. Let's not forget I am not yet nineteen."

"Let's not forget that William Pitt the Younger was only twenty-four when he became Prime Minister of England."

"But—"

"No buts, Ned. You *will* run Deravenels."

"But only if you are by my side," Edward exclaimed.

"And I will be, have no fear of that, Cousin," Neville promised.

nine

FLORENCE

They had come here to take the bodies back home to England. But they were also in Florence to find out what had happened to their kin. And now that they were finally in Italy, the thing Edward dreaded the most was viewing the bodies. He was only too well aware that to gaze upon the lifeless faces of his father, brother, uncle, and cousin would have a devastating effect on him. Conversely, he did need to see them in order to be convinced they were *really* dead.

Edward was standing in the window of his hotel room, staring out at the river Arno and the hills of Florence beyond. There was no sun on this cold Wednesday morning, and the sky was bloated with gray clouds. A mist floated over the surface of the river, obscuring the dark waters, a mist that reminded him of London's winter fogs.

He had arrived here last night from Paris, accompanied by Neville and Will, and they had checked into the Hotel Bristol. This was a well-known hotel built in the second half of the nineteenth century, much frequented by the English aristocracy, and it had come highly recommended. It was near the Arno, and their rooms faced the river and the hills scattered on the outskirts of the city. Edward and Will occupied rooms next to each other, while Neville was in a large suite just a few doors down.

Turning away from the window, Edward strode over to the mirror and began to tie his fine black silk cravat. Once this was arranged to his satisfaction, he added a beautiful pearl stickpin in the center of the carefully draped and folded knot. The pin had been a gift from his father for his eighteenth birthday, and he treasured it more than ever now.

Walking over to the wardrobe, he took out his waistcoat and slipped it on, returned to the cheval mirror, stared at himself, thinking how pale he looked, even haggard. With a small sigh he headed back to the wardrobe to retrieve his jacket.

And it seemed to Edward, as he walked back and forth, that the awful dread he had just experienced trailed along with him, surrounding him as if it were the mist off the river. He shivered involuntarily, paused next to a chair, rested his hand on it. He closed his eyes, and his gaze turned inward.

I must be absolutely in control of myself today, and I must reveal nothing. My face must be unreadable at all times. I share Neville's opinion that the fire was no accident. How we will find out the truth I do not know, but we must try. Will is of same mind. I'm glad he came along. He gets on well with Neville, and we have both enjoyed his company.

Somehow I must get through the ordeal of viewing the bodies this morning. And then we will go to Carrara, no matter what. I am set on that course. I must see the hotel where they met their untimely deaths. Then, I hope, this Italian nightmare will come to an end. Later this week we will take their bodies home, to Yorkshire, where we will bury them in that benign earth, and they will rest in peace—

Insistent knocking on the door interrupted Edward's thoughts, and he strode to open it. Will was standing there, appropriately dressed in a black suit and carrying a black overcoat on his arm. "I'm not too early, am I?" he asked, a brow lifting.

Edward shook his head. "Come in, Will." He opened the

door wider and moved into the room, his friend following closely.

"Have you had breakfast?" Edward asked as he took his overcoat out of the wardrobe.

"Yes, thanks, and so have you, I see," Will responded, glancing over at the tray which stood on a small side table. He frowned. "Coffee and a roll. Is that all you've eaten?"

"I'm not very hungry." Edward glanced at the clock on the wall and continued, "It's only ten past nine; we're a trifle early, I think. Fabrizio Dellarosa is not due here until ten-thirty."

"I know, but I was certain you would be up, and I thought we could take a breath of fresh air before his arrival. By the way, is Alfredo Oliveri also joining us?"

"Dellarosa didn't mention him in the letter I received last night. But I'm presuming he is. After all, he's the one who lives in Carrara, and will therefore have the most information. At least in my opinion he will."

Will nodded in agreement, sat down on a chair, and folded his overcoat across his knees. "Have you ever met him? Or is *he* a stranger, too?"

"He is a stranger, just as Dellarosa is, but my father always spoke so highly of Oliveri. He obviously liked the man, and I think the feeling was mutual." Edward buttoned his three-quarter-length jacket, put on his overcoat, and said, "Shall we go, Will?"

"Perhaps we ought to let Neville know we're going out," Will ventured as they left the room.

"It's not necessary. The arrangement was for us to meet in the main lounge at the given hour. Let's leave it at that, shall we?" Edward's voice was clipped.

"That presents no problem to me," Will answered, stealing a glance at his friend. He knew Edward was filled with apprehension about what lay ahead. As strapping as he was, and so very masculine, Will knew that Ned was a sensitive

man inside. Just contemplating the manner of his families'
deaths must be an agony for him. Ned was devoted to his
family. They came first with him, and he had been particularly close to his brother Edmund, and his father and he had
been tightly bonded.

The two men were silent as they went down the wide
staircase which led to the grand entrance foyer and several
opulent lounges. Marble abounded, and ceramic tubs holding potted palms were placed here and there; on the walls
hung a number of lovely paintings of Florence in heavy
gilded frames, and pieces of sculpture on plinths were
placed along each side of the foyer.

Within a few seconds they found themselves standing
outside the Bristol on the Via dei Pescioni, near the Santa
Maria Novella and directly opposite the Palazzo Strozzi.
This was one of the most elegant districts in the city, where
other important hotels as well as fine shops, art galleries,
and museums were located.

"Here we are, in the greatest Renaissance city in the
world, Ned," Will said, taking hold of his arm. "Let's stroll
along and enjoy the sights for a short while."

Edward nodded. "I'm sorry, Will. I know I'm being
gloomy . . ." He did not finish, merely shook his head, his
expression suddenly sorrowful.

"Think about this," Will remarked, ignoring Ned's comment. "Here we are in the city of Dante, Petrarch, and Boccaccio. Just *think,* Boccaccio wrote the *Decameron* here, and
that book became the model for prose the world over, a
model that's been popular for hundreds and hundreds of
years. And still is."

Ned glanced at his friend. "Niccolò Machiavelli lived
here and wrote *The Prince* in Florence, let us not forget
about *him.* We can all learn quite a lot from Machiavelli,
you know."

A silence fell between them, and as they walked Will
wondered how to bring a little cheer to Ned. Instantly he re-

alized nothing could make his friend feel better at this moment in time. First he had to deal with the dead, and only then would Edward be able to see his way to the future. He needs to close this ghastly affair, Will thought, in order to pick up the pieces and create a life of his own making. A new life.

ten

Neville was a striking man. Tall, though not quite as tall as Ned, he was of slender build, without an ounce of extra fat, very athletic. His face was sharply chiseled; he had an aquiline nose and a smooth, rather high brow. His wide-set eyes, under curved black brows, were a curious light blue, almost turquoise. Clear and transparent, they were alive with immense intelligence. His coloring was dark, and he had black hair, like most of the Watkins clan; on occasion he had a strong look of his father's sister, Cecily Watkins Deravenel.

This morning he sat at an antique writing table in the sitting room of his suite in the Hotel Bristol, endeavoring to put some of his thoughts on paper for the upcoming meeting with Fabrizio Dellarosa.

After a few moments he put his pencil down, satisfied he had covered the relevant points. He sat back in the chair, staring out into the room, his eyes narrowed.

Neville's motto, borrowed from his father, was this: Think with the head, not the heart. This he always did in business, and often in his private life as well. Long ago his father had cautioned him to be ice-cold at all times in business. Without emotion, inscrutable. "Never display weakness, never show face. That is what your grandfather taught me," his father had explained when Neville entered the world of commerce. They were words Neville had never forgotten, and he had always lived by them.

I must train Ned to be like me, Neville now thought. Certainly his father taught him many things, but I'm not sure Richard knew how to teach Ned to be truly coldhearted. After all, Neville's uncle had been a warm and loving man. Grumbling about inequities and his rights, and what should have been his, and was in fact *his,* had accomplished nothing and made many enemies within Deravenels. Deadly enemies, if the truth be known.

Neville's mind remained focused on Ned. His cousin had a superior intelligence, and he was not afraid of anything or anyone. He had enormous self-confidence and a charisma the likes of which Neville had rarely seen. And he could be utterly ruthless if he needed to be. Furthermore, Ned had always had a good head for business, most especially finance.

Convinced that Ned could easily run the Deravenel Company with the right guidance, Neville was ready, willing, and able to ensure his success. Together they would rule that empire one day, there was no question in Neville's mind. With his own knowledge and experience, and Ned's natural abilities and charismatic presence, they could accomplish almost anything. With a little luck, of course. Luck always had to be factored into the equation.

Folding the piece of paper on which he had made his notes, Neville slipped it in the pocket of his jacket and rose. Walking across the room in long strides, he stood in front of the window, gazing out at the leaden sky. The sun was beginning to filter through the oppressive grayness, and he decided it might turn out to be a better day after all. He loathed dismal weather, used to it though he was, and craved the sunlight, warmer climes. Just as Cousin Ned did, hence their sojourns in the South of France over the years.

Thoughts of Ned lingered. Neville held him dear, admired him. There was only one problem with Ned as far as he could see, and that was his addiction to women. Older women. And widows at that. Blond widows. As long as he remained single, there was no problem with his penchant for romantic and sexual dalliances, but when Ned married, which he would one day, he would have to curb his lustful behavior, or at least be much more discreet. Although Ned was not aware of it, Neville knew all about his current alliance with Lily Overton. There were some who thought it a trifle inappropriate.

Ah well, he's just a man after all, like all of us, poor creatures that we are, Neville thought with a small, wry smile.

The three men were dressed almost exactly alike. Each wore a black suit with the three-quarter-length jacket that was so fashionable. Their white shirts were impeccable, as were their black silk cravats. Basically they were in mourning clothes, and they cut quite a swathe as they strode across the lobby of the hotel. Some of the other guests eyed them with curiosity, and several of the women with open admiration. All three men were tall, good-looking, obviously English, and aristocrats, an appealing combination anywhere, anytime.

As they entered the lounge, a waiter came forward, smiling and showing them to a large, round table which Neville had reserved a short while before.

Once seated, they ordered coffee, and when the waiter departed, Neville turned to Edward and said, "As I did when we went to Deravenels, I am going to let you take the lead, Ned. After all, Dellarosa is an employee of the company, and at this moment answerable to you."

"Your father was killed in the fire as well," Edward murmured, frowning slightly. "You can say anything you want to him, ask him anything, as far as I'm concerned. We're in this together."

"Yes, indeed we are," Neville shot back. "But do take the lead, Ned, please. It will give me a chance to weigh him up, and you, Will, can give your attention to Alfredo Oliveri if you would. I think we should attempt to decide whether these men will be allies or adversaries. After all, Deravenels have a lot of business interests in Italy, aside from the marble quarries."

"I understand," Will answered at once, nodding. "I have a feeling Oliveri will be a friend, not a foe, from what Ned has said about him so far. Correct, Ned?"

"Oh, yes, Father had enormous respect for him. But the strange thing is he wasn't mentioned in Dellarosa's letter to me, so I have a feeling he won't be here this morning."

"Why do you make *that* assumption?" Neville asked, eyeing his cousin in alarm.

"I have a . . . *gut instinct* about it, to use a phrase of yours."

At this moment the waiter returned with the tray of coffee cups and tall glasses of water, and served them. Again smiling and nodding, he backed away. Neville took a sip of the water. He approved of this Continental custom of serving a glass of water with other beverages. It was most civilized.

"Could this be Dellarosa?" Ned muttered a moment or two later, staring at the arched doorway of the lounge, where a well-dressed man stood glancing around. He was of medium height, slim, and blond, like many Northern Italians. Ned hurried on, "He's heading this way, so it is him, I'm certain."

Edward rose, moved toward the Italian, extending his hand. "Signor Dellarosa, I presume," he said with a faint smile. "I'm Edward Deravenel."

"Good morning, Signor Deravenel," Dellarosa responded. "Welcome to Firenze. I wish this occasion was not such a sad one. I am sorry for the loss of your family."

"It is sorrowful, yes," Edward replied. "But please, come and meet my cousin Neville Watkins, and our good friend Will Hasling."

Neville and Will were already on their feet, and after shaking hands and exchanging greetings, the four men sat down together at the table.

Dellarosa turned to Neville and murmured, "I am so sorry, signore, for your loss also."

"Thank you." Neville inclined his head, his expression quite unreadable.

"Would you care for some kind of refreshment? Coffee, tea?" Edward asked.

"*Sì, grazie,* Signor Edward. I will partake of the coffee."

Edward motioned to the hovering waiter, ordered the coffee, and then focused all of his attention on Fabrizio Dellarosa. "What time are we going to view the bodies?" he asked.

Clearing his throat, Dellarosa said, "In about half an hour. They are at a hospital. Santa Maria Novella. It is nearby. We can walk."

"I understand. My cousin and I have been wondering why the bodies were brought to Florence."

Again, Dellarosa cleared his throat. "Because it was necessary to have them embalmed."

"I see, and what you are saying is that there are no facilities to do this procedure in Carrara?"

"Yes, Signor Edward, that is so."

"What did they die of?" Ned asked.

"Excuse me?" Dellarosa's brow furrowed, and he gave Edward a long stare.

"Our fathers and brothers were in a fire in the hotel." Edward's look was intent, focused. "So were they badly burned? Did they die of their burns? Or was it smoke inhalation that killed them? We have been told nothing about their deaths."

"Smoke inhalation, I believe, was the cause of death."

"And they were not burned at all?" Edward asked, sounding puzzled.

"No. There are no burns on their faces."

"But perhaps on their bodies? Is that what you're implying?"

"I'm not implying," Dellarosa shot back swiftly, raising a blond brow. "I was told they died of smoke inhalation."

"What information do you have about the fire? How did it start?"

"I do not know, Signor Edward. I was not there."

"Does anyone else know? Perhaps Alfredo Oliveri?" Ned probed.

"He knows no more than I do."

"I see. Tell me, Signor Dellarosa . . ." Edward paused, leaned forward, giving the Italian another penetrating stare. "Why is Oliveri not here today? I thought he had been informed we were coming. By Aubrey Masters."

The Italian nodded, looking suddenly worried, and his voice faltered slightly when he replied. "I told Alfredo it wasn't necessary for him to come. I am here, and I run the Deravenel business interests in Italy. He knows nothing. Nothing more than I do."

"So you are saying that the cause of the fire is a genuine mystery. And also that our family members were not even burned in this fire. Very interesting. Very interesting indeed, Dellarosa."

The Italian was silent, staring back at Edward and asking himself why he suddenly felt threatened by this young man, who had the coldest blue eyes he had ever seen. Steel, Dellarosa thought. *This* Deravenel is made of cold steel. And he was unexpectedly afraid. Edward Deravenel was not like his father, and he would be trouble. Dellarosa could not wait to escape, to return to his office and communicate with London.

Edward announced, "Well, it seems you have nothing more to say, Signor Dellarosa. So please take us to the hospital so that we can finally view the bodies. Oh, and what arrangements have you made for the bodies to be taken back to England?"

Dellarosa coughed behind his hand and then said quickly, "They will go by ship. I have booked passages for you and

Signor Watkins." He paused, glanced at Will, and added, "I will book passage for you, Mr. Hasling. If you wish to accompany your friends."

"I do," Will answered at once.

Neville exclaimed, "I don't think so, Signor Dellarosa! What I mean is, I don't think we shall be traveling by ship. Nor will the bodies of our fathers and brothers."

Dellarosa gaped at him. "I am not understanding—"

"Then let me explain," Neville cut in. "It is January. A journey by sea could prove quite dangerous at this time of year. There are far too many storms." He shook his head and gave Dellarosa an odd look. "I shall make the arrangements myself. We will take the bodies back to England by train. So much safer in the long run, wouldn't you say?"

It was the registrar of the hospital, Roberto Del Renzio, who greeted them at the reception desk and led them down a long corridor to the morgue. A tall, heavyset man, he was dressed in a starched white shirt with a stiff wing collar, black tie, black jacket, and pin-striped trousers. He had a somber voice, but his expression was bland, and it seemed to Edward that the man was lighthearted in spirit, the kind of person who was ready to laugh if the joke was a good one. But he did not laugh or joke or even say very much as he accompanied them now to the north wing.

The registrar paused when he came to a waiting room, and turning to Dellarosa, he said, in stilted English, "Perhaps you would please to be waiting in here." He swung his eyes to Edward and asked, "Just the two of you will enter the morgue?"

"I'm not sure," Edward answered and looked over at Will. "Would you like to come in with us?"

"If that's all right with you, yes, I would, Ned. I wish to pay my last respects to them all. Do *you* mind, Neville?"

"So be it," Neville murmured and followed the silent Ned and the registrar, with Will immediately behind him.

Much to Edward's surprise, the four men's bodies were already in their closed coffins. He had expected them to be in the long metal drawers banked around the room.

A moment later, a white-coated doctor joined them, and after being introduced, he proceeded to open the coffins.

Together Edward and Neville stared down at the waxen faces of their fathers and brothers. It was true, they had not been burned. There wasn't a mark on them. At least, not on their faces.

Although they did not know it, both men were thinking the same thing: that these were no longer their loved ones, not now that their souls had left them. All that remained were these frozen carcasses.

Edward touched his father's shoulder and closed his eyes. *Good-bye,* he thought, *good-bye.* Then he moved on to look at his dearest brother. But the Edmund he had known and loved was not here either. He touched his shoulder, said good-bye to the boy inside his head, and moved on sadly.

Neville followed suit, silently saying his farewells knowing that what had made these four men so special were their spirits; they were merely empty shells now, dead flesh. And Will, slowly moving behind them, felt utterly bereft. For he, too, understood death now, its total finality.

Within minutes it was all over.

They collected the relevant papers from the registrar and took their leave of Dellarosa. They left the hospital, hurrying across the piazza Santa Maria Novella to the hotel.

The letter arrived in the late afternoon. It was pushed under the door of Edward's room. But when he opened the door, no one was there. He looked up and down the corridor, only to discover it was empty.

Opening the envelope, he took the letter out. It was short, only a note.

As he scanned the words, he felt his stomach lurch, his

mind race. There was no salutation. Only a few lines, brief and to the point:

> *Nothing is the way it seems.*
> *Come to the place your father visited last.*
> *Tomorrow. Go to the building with a familiar name.*
> *I will be waiting.*

Edward knew immediately that the note was from Alfredo Oliveri. The place his father had visited last was Carrara. And the building with the familiar name was Deravenels. Of course.

Folding the letter in half, Edward put it in his pocket and walked to Neville's suite. He knew deep within himself that tomorrow they would find out the truth.

eleven

CARRARA

From the moment Edward had arrived in Carrara with Neville and Will earlier that morning, he had wanted to turn around and leave. There was something about this town in Tuscany which truly depressed him.

He knew that, in part, this feeling sprang from the fact that his father and brother, uncle and cousin had died here, and in tragic circumstances. Yet he genuinely disliked certain aspects of the place; he found it cold, unwelcoming, and reeking of danger, and he felt oppressed by the mountains that encircled Carrara on three sides and seemed to close it in like a prison.

Marble dominated here. Great slabs of it gleamed whitely high on the mountainsides of the Apuan Alps; its gray-white dust floated on the air, settled on the buildings and the ground, on the people as well; it penetrated their clothing and hair. There was the constant sound of marble being chipped at in studios, workshops, and apartments along the streets, where artists and artisans were working on sculptures, frescoes, urns, and many other artifacts. Carrara was busy in the town as well as up on the mountain ranges.

Edward understood that he must get himself through this meeting and then get away as fast as he could. In his mind, Carrara would be forever associated with death and grief, and he never wanted to return here as long as he lived.

He was sitting in the offices of the Deravenel Company, studying Alfredo Oliveri, who was speaking to Neville, suggesting they stay the night and adding that he would be happy to have them as guests in his home. "Far better than a hotel," he was murmuring.

They had arrived about twenty minutes ago, having traveled for some hours by hired carriage from Florence, an arrangement made by the head concierge of the Hotel Bristol.

Edward already knew that he trusted this man. He now realized why his father had liked Oliveri so much, had had such confidence in him. There was something about him, his face, his manner, his way of expressing himself that spoke to Edward of integrity, honesty, and loyalty.

Alfredo Oliveri was not at all what he had expected. To begin with, he had the brightest of auburn hair, that intense red color usually referred to as "carrot-top" in England. And second, he was very English. After they had introduced themselves and entered the manager's private office, Neville had commented on Alfredo's perfect command of English. It was then the other man had explained that he was born of an English mother and an Italian father, that he had spent every summer in London with his maternal grandparents during his childhood. Later he had attended an English boarding school for four years, returning to Italy for the summers.

"No wonder you sound like an Englishman," Neville had remarked. "In fact, you are one, of course," he added, hoping he hadn't sounded patronizing when he had meant to compliment.

"Half and half," Alfredo had murmured and smiled faintly, obviously gratified. "My Englishness usually takes visitors from the London office by surprise. Although it never surprised Mr. Richard." He looked pointedly at Edward when he added, "Such a good man, your father was. *Too* good, if the truth be known."

"You're the one who knows everything about things here,

Mr. Oliveri," Edward ventured. "And the fact that we came at once after I received your note must tell you something—"

"That you are suspicious," Alfredo cut in swiftly, his eyes riveted on Edward.

"Yes, we are. What did you mean when you wrote 'Nothing is the way it seems'?"

"Exactly that." Alfredo gave Edward a knowing look. "So many things appear to be quite straightforward. But when you look beneath the surface, well, that's a different matter altogether. There's very often something else at play. At least, that's the way I've frequently found it."

"So we are right to be suspicious about their deaths?" Neville asked quietly.

"Indeed," Alfredo answered. "I would like to tell you about the night of the fire, tell you everything I personally know and what I found out later." He raised a brow quizzically.

"Yes, please do," Edward encouraged, leaning forward, every part of him alert, expectant and also somewhat afraid.

"It was Sunday night, just over a week ago. I had dined with your father and uncle, and the two young men, Mr. Edmund and Mr. Thomas. I left them at the small hotel, the *pensione,* at about eleven o'clock and went home. As I learned later, the fire apparently broke out in the early hours of Monday morning, around one o'clock. It seemingly started in the right wing, spread to the foyer, and then to the left wing, where your family were staying. It was a sudden fire, and because of the wind that night, it kept spreading; in fact, it became a real conflagration at one point. And—"

"But they weren't burned," Neville interrupted. "We've seen the bodies, and their faces were not scarred. If it was an inferno, as you suggest, how can that be?"

"The wind suddenly dropped, and it also began to rain. Very heavily. Anyway, almost immediately the alarm was raised, and many of the townsfolk came out with buckets of water, helping to douse the fire."

"So you're saying that the fire was put out quickly, but that our family members died of smoke inhalation at the beginning, when the fire was at its height?" Edward asked.

"That's exactly what the death certificates say," Neville pointed out. "Death from smoke inhalation."

"There was no smoke inhalation," Alfredo began and cleared his throat several times. "They did not die as a result of the fire. They died from their injuries of earlier."

"Injuries?" Edward sat up straighter, once again fixing his vivid blue eyes on Alfredo. Neville and Will were also on the edges of their chairs, staring intently at the manager, aghast at what they were hearing.

Alfredo steadied himself and said in a low tone, "Your father, uncle, and cousin sustained head injuries, Mr. Edward." And then he looked across at Neville and continued. "All three men died instantly. Dr. Buttafiglio told me—"

"Someone attacked them? Killed them? Are we understanding you correctly?" Edward cut in, his voice rising.

"You are. . . . I'm so sorry to give you this dreadful news, and you, too, Mr. Watkins. Very, very sorry."

"And so the fire was started to conceal the crime? Is that what you're suggesting?" Neville asked, his expression grim, his voice hard.

"Yes, I am. That is the doctor's theory, and I concur. The men of your family were killed, and the fire was set in order to burn their bodies to a crisp, so nobody would know that murder had been committed. But whoever did this had not bargained for the rain. It was a *deluge.* It stopped the fire."

"You mentioned my father, uncle, and cousin, but not my brother," Edward exclaimed, staring at the Carrara manager. "What of Edmund?"

Alfredo had been dreading this question, and for a split second he could not speak. But he knew that he would have to tell Mr. Edward, so he took a deep, steadying breath and said, "It appears that after I left Mr. Richard and the others at the hotel, Mr. Edmund went out again. No one knows where he went, and by that I mean the police, who made inquiries later to no avail. They found out nothing. Anyway, as he was returning to the hotel, probably just before the fire was started, Mr. Edmund was waylaid in one of the side streets and attacked. He—"

"*By whom?* Who would attack my young brother?" Edward demanded, his face growing flushed.

"I don't know. No one knows; no one here understands it at all. Everyone is baffled, believe me."

"And no one saw it happening?" Neville asked in that same sharp voice, like a whiplash.

"Not the actual attack, no. But Benito Magnanni, the owner of the Coliseum Restaurant, was on his way home after closing up, and he saw two men bending over a body. It just so happens there was a streetlight on in the alley where they were standing, and he began to run down the alley, shouting at them. They immediately fled. They were English, though."

"How do you know that?" Will asked quickly, staring hard at Alfredo. He was aware Edward and Neville were too distressed to speak, so he took charge.

"Because Benito told the police that they looked English, and that he heard one of the men say something about London, and the man made a remark like 'let's ski diddle.' This phrase didn't make sense to either Benito or the police. But it did to me. I believe what the man actually said was 'Let's skedaddle back to London,' something like that. We all know the word *skedaddle;* it means 'run off in haste,' now doesn't it, Mr. Hasling?"

"Yes, you're right." Will nodded. "It's slang, of course, but we all use it."

"How did they kill him?" Edward asked in a voice so low they could barely hear him.

Alfredo hesitated, wondering if he should lie to save Edward Deravenel's feelings. But he knew he could not; he must speak the truth. He owed it to Edward and to his father. "He died very quickly," Alfredo replied at last. "Dr. Buttafiglio told me it must have been an instant death."

"But *how*?" Edward pressed.

"They cut his throat," Alfredo answered in a shaky voice, as quiet as Edward's had been.

Stunned shock filled the air, was nearly palpable.

Then, rigid in the chair, his face draining of all color, Edward cried out, "No! Not my lovely Edmund. To die like *that*. Such a brutal way. No, it can't *be*. Who would commit such a foul crime? He was only seventeen, for God's sake, an innocent *boy*—"

Edward broke off, tears glistening in those bright blue eyes. He brought his hands to his face, and he grieved a second time for his beloved brother.

At once Neville was on his feet. He bent over his cousin, encircled him with his arms. After a moment, Edward struggled to his feet, turned to Neville, and clung to him as though his life depended on it. For a while the cousins stood together in tight embrace. They were united more than ever in their mutual grief.

Eventually the two men broke their embrace and went back to their chairs. It was Neville who spoke first. Looking across at Alfredo, he said, "Let me ask you something. . . . Do you personally believe that Mr. Edmund was killed because he was a Deravenel? That it was not just an odd coincidence that he was attacked that night?"

"I don't think the attack on Mr. Edmund was a coincidence. Not at all. He was killed because he was a Deravenel and Mr. Richard's son. They did not find him at the hotel when they killed the others, so they went looking for him, in my opinion." Alfredo shook his head vehemently. "Nothing will convince me otherwise."

"Do you think Mr. Edward is in danger?"

"Yes, I do. Perhaps not here in Carrara, not now. The murderers have fled back to London. But I do think he's in danger. Because he's Mr. Richard's son. In my opinion, Mr. Watkins, your Uncle Richard was killed because he was the true heir to Deravenels. Everyone knows it in the company. . . . Deravenels was stolen sixty years ago by the Lancashire Deravenels. Some of the directors are happy with the status quo, but not everyone. There are those who have always believed Mr. Richard should have been sitting in the chairman's seat. Quite a few of us, actually.

"Henry Grant is ineffectual, always has been in my opinion. He's been riding on the coattails of the two Grants who went before him: his grandfather, who usurped the company, and his father, who made it greater. But it's slipping. Things are not good. He's an absentee landlord, just as Mr. Richard always said. He has no head for business or finance, and he's dominated by his French wife and her followers. Margot Grant has quite a few supporters, you know, who do her bidding."

"I did know. My uncle confided in my father." A deep sigh rippled through Neville, and he shook his head, sorrow shadowing his light turquoise eyes. "My father and brother died because they were in the wrong place at the wrong time . . ." His saddened voice filtered away, and he pursed his lips. "God rest their souls in Heaven."

"And so Deravenels, the company started by my ancestor Guy de Ravenel is actually being run by a young woman who is not even a Deravenel by birth. That has to make you shudder, Neville," Edward remarked in a voice dripping ice.

"Actually, it makes me laugh, if a little hollowly," Neville retorted. "That woman is a joke; she doesn't know what she's doing. But of course she's being used by James Cliff and John Summers. It is they who have the power there. Still, I do think she is dangerous; she has no conscience whatsoever, and it's more than likely she's behind the murders. Don't you fret, Ned. We *will* have our revenge, as I said we would at Ravenscar. I will not permit a young and incompetent woman to get the better of you, be assured of that."

twelve

KENT

"Why aren't you pursuing the matter with the police?" Lily cried, her face growing flushed, her eyes filling with indignation. "I don't understand, I really don't, Ned."

"You should. I've already explained it several times!" Edward shot back, striving to keep his temper in check. "But I'll attempt to do so once again. This is *not* a matter for Scotland Yard. The crime was *not* committed under their jurisdiction. It occurred in Italy, in Carrara, to be precise, and the—"

"I know that, Ned," she interrupted. "I was referring to the police in Carrara. Why aren't they continuing their investigation? *That* is what I meant."

Clenching his fists, taking a deep breath, Edward answered in as controlled a voice as he could manage. "They've done their best for over a month now. And incidentally, Neville and I, and Will, spent hours with the local police chief attempting to get to the bottom of things. He was very cooperative. Certainly he had done a very detailed investigation before we got there, and come up with nothing. All the police had, in fact, was the information given to them by a local restaurant owner, who told them he had seen two men attacking someone in an alley late at night. He ran to the rescue, shouting at the attackers, who instantly fled. He was too late, of course; my brother was dead when he got to him. Benito Magnanni, the restaurant owner, also reported hearing the two men, the attackers, shouting at each other in English. And that is it . . . there is nothing *more*."

Lily did not respond. She merely sat back on the sofa, staring across at him, shaking her head, a nonplussed expression crossing her face.

Staring back at her, Edward realized she looked as if she were about to burst into tears; it was for this reason he tried his best to let go of his irritation. He unclenched his hands, relaxed his rigid body, adopted a more casual stance in front of the fire roaring up the chimney. He knew she was not a stupid woman, quite the contrary, but she could be maddeningly dense about certain things, and this drove him to distraction.

Taking another deep breath, he adopted a lighter tone. "Alberto Oliveri truly went out of his way to probe every aspect of the murders with the police and, of course, the cause of the fire, everything to do with it. But there's not much anyone can do when there are no murderers loitering on street corners, no arsonists hanging around, for that matter. The whole affair is clouded in mystery . . ." He paused, sighed, added, "Without credible evidence, the Carrara police are totally stalled." He shifted on his feet, and another small sigh escaped him as he finished. "This is not the first case which will go unsolved, Lily, I can assure you of that."

"And so can I," Will said from the doorway, walking into the study of his sister's house in Kent, where the three of them were spending the weekend with Vicky. He went on, "It's also extremely frustrating, since we more or less know who is at the root of this ghastly crime, yet there's nothing we can do—"

"Why not?" Lily cut in, sitting up straighter, looking from Will to Ned, who remained standing in front of the fire.

"Because we cannot retaliate in kind," Edward snapped after a moment, his annoyance rising to the surface. "We can't go around killing people off just because we think they are behind the deaths of my father and brother,

Neville's father and brother. Certainly Scotland Yard would be involved *then* . . . they'd be on *our backs*."

Lily reached into her pocket for a handkerchief, blew her nose, patted her eyes. "It's such an . . . agony," she muttered, crumpling her handkerchief between her long, supple fingers, playing with it nervously. "I don't know how you can stand it, Ned."

The room became still.

The fire spurted; fabric rustled like a faint whisper as Lily moved on the sofa; light rain began to patter against the windowpanes. Otherwise there was total silence. Neither man spoke. Lily herself swallowed the sentence on the tip of her tongue, afraid to utter a word, accepting she had just said the wrong thing.

Slowly, almost cautiously, Will walked across to the fireplace where his best friend stood. He put a hand on Ned's arm as if to steady him, then took a position next to him.

For his part, Edward looked exceedingly perturbed; a veil dropped over his face, obscuring his true feelings. He breathed deeply.

After a moment or two, Edward focused his entire attention on Lily. He said, in a cold, clipped voice, "How can I stand it? you ask. If the truth be known, I can't. But I have to. I have no choice. Now, let us bring this discussion to a close, shall we? There is no real point to it. We are helpless as far as prosecuting those whom we believe are responsible. A week ago Neville and I buried our loved ones . . . they are at peace now. There is nothing more to say—" He broke off, leaned forward, staring at her most intently, his face resembling a mask of stone. "The matter is now at an end."

No, it's not, it's just starting, Will thought. It won't end until Ned and Neville have destroyed the Grants. Each and every one of them. That is irrevocable. And as these dire thoughts swirled in his head, Will felt the hackles rise on the back of his neck, and a cold chill swept over him.

• • •

Vicky's second husband, Stephen Forth, a banker of some standing, had gone to New York on business, and she had talked her brother into spending a weekend in the country with her. Will, in turn, had coaxed Ned into joining him. Because Vicky and Lily were close friends, Lily had been invited to come as well. Edward had been delighted to accompany Will, whom he always enjoyed being with, and the fact that Lily was so obviously welcome was an added bonus.

Stonehurst Farm, not far from Aldington in Kent, was close to the Romney Marsh, and long ago it had ceased to be a working farm. Dating back to the 1600s, it had undergone a bold transformation in recent years. Now it resembled a manor house, was, in fact, a gentleman's farm, a country residence.

Edward had stayed here before, and he had always been given the same room, one which he particularly liked because it looked out toward the marsh and the sea beyond. He closed his eyes, leaning his head against the back of the chair, let himself slide down into his innermost thoughts.

I promised my mother after the funeral at Ravenscar that I would protect and look after her and my siblings, see to their welfare and their comfort, and to the future. It will be done.

Of course my mother is safe, because she has her inheritance, which Neville will now manage, but I must take from the company all that is my due. I must find out why my father was always so impoverished and rectify that situation as soon as I can. And I must find myself a proper place to live. My mother owns the house in Charles Street, and although she offered it to me, I cannot take it from her. That would be most unfair, since it is hers by inheritance from her father.

Before I left Ravenscar I told my mother about the black notebook, which Alfredo Oliveri mentioned to me in Carrara. A notebook constantly used by my father, who made

*daily jottings in it. I couldn't find it at Charles Street. She
will look for it at Ravenscar.*

*Oliveri will be most useful to us, and he has promised to
help in any way he can. He is an undoubted ally. I am lucky
to have him on my side. He says we can win. I believe him.*

Will had been coming to Stonehurst ever since his
sister had bought the place, twelve years ago. She
had purchased the property not long after the death
of her first husband, Miles Tomlinson, wishing to leave the
hustle and bustle of London for the tranquillity of the Kent-
ish countryside. She had also turned the restoration and dec-
oration of the old farmhouse into a project to help keep grief
at bay.

To some extent she had succeeded in this effort, and Will
had been her willing helper. He had grown to care for Stonehurst as much as she did, in winter as well as summer. The
old farmhouse was surrounded by 150 acres of wonderful
land—there were fields and pastures as well as a pond and a
bluebell wood, and beyond the vast flower gardens was the
Romney Marsh.

To Will, the marsh was mysterious, a magical place with
its wild, blowing grasses and winding paths, its mists, which
rose at dusk and floated over the landscape, obscuring everything. And at this twilight hour, the salty smell of the sea was
carried in on the light breeze, reminding everyone how close
the English Channel was.

In olden days the locals had latched their windows at this
time of day, believing that the mists caused the ague; others
had fastened their shutters tight because they were certain
ghosts were at large on the marsh. Vicky generally laughed
at these old wives' tales, which were still told to whomever
would listen, and when it came to the mention of ghosts, she
usually muttered under her breath to Will, "More like the local smugglers winding their way inland from the sea, haul-
ing their tobacco, their wines and brandy from France." He

agreed with her, fully believed the smugglers still plied their dubious trade here.

This afternoon, as he strode along the flagged path which led from the back terrace to the gardens, he could not help thinking how beautiful the landscape was, even on this cold February Saturday. It was almost dusk already, and the gray sky of early afternoon had darkened and was filled with rafts of fiery red and purple along the horizon. Or was that the sea? Some of the low-lying marsh was well below sea level, and frequently it seemed to him that the sea in the distance was high in the sky. A most curious illusion.

"Will, Will! Wait for me!"

Will swung around at the sound of Ned's voice and stood waiting as his friend hurried down the path.

"Why didn't you ask me to come for a walk with you?" Ned demanded, peering at Will. "Or did you feel like being alone? Am I intruding?"

Putting his arm around Ned's shoulder, Will shook his head, drew closer to his friend as they walked on together. "I thought I'd better leave you to your own devices after lunch. You seemed so upset this morning and were rather silent at lunchtime."

"I was, and with good reason, don't you think?"

"Yes, I do. Anyway, I knew you were in your room alone, since Lily and Vicky took the horse and trap into the village after you disappeared. I just saw them coming back, so I ducked out here."

"For a man who protests so much about country living, you certainly seem attached to Stonehurst," Ned remarked, sneaking a surreptitious glance at his friend.

"I *have* grown attached to it, actually, perhaps because I helped Vicky bludgeon it into shape when I was a youngster and because we shared a unique relationship during that time just after Miles died. We worked well together and bonded. She has always reminded me that I helped her to combat her grief. I like to visit Vicky because we're so close. And I'm fascinated by the marsh. But to be honest, Ned, I wouldn't want to live in the country permanently."

Ned laughed. "Ah yes, I do understand. It appeals to the young, adventurous lad who still exists inside you . . . stories of smugglers, and baccy and brandy running, and God knows what else. But I understand what you mean, and I also appreciate that the Romney Marsh has a genuine history to it." Peering ahead as they came to the edge of the lawns, Ned added, "And there's romance there, too . . . a fair wind for France tonight and all that, eh?"

Will had the good grace to smile, knowing full well that Ned was teasing him. "Well, perhaps you're right, perhaps that's so, the romance of it," he agreed. Then, in a concerned voice, he said, "You are all right now, Ned, aren't you?"

"I suppose I am. However, I must admit I thought Lily was being as thick as a plank earlier today. And like you, Will, I have always considered her to be, well, rather a clever woman."

"I concur, I mean about her being somewhat dense this morning. On the other hand, I believe she's intelligent. She's also thirty-two and an experienced woman of the world. But you know, I remember now that Vicky once told me Lily thinks she's an expert on the law, because she was married to a solicitor for a number of years. Obviously she believes that she's got one up on all of us."

Ned said, in a soft but emphatic voice, "I've really endeavored to put my grief in its own place. It is *there,* and it always will be, but it's buried now, deep in my heart. I have had to do this in order to go on, Will. I must concentrate on the present and the future. My past and those tragic deaths will always be with me. However, I cannot allow grief to dominate me. I must move forward, and I know *you* understand this."

"I do, and yes, I think that Lily did probe a lot, somewhat unduly. But she wasn't trying to hurt you *intentionally,* she was just being . . . assertive, and she probably thought she was showing concern." He lifted his shoulders in a shrug. "After all, she's a woman, and who on earth can understand those adorable but tantalizing creatures, what they do and say? Not I."

The two men walked on silently, content to be in each other's company. They were like brothers, and their bond was true and strong. It would last a lifetime, though neither of them knew that at this moment.

When they had left the lawns behind and were standing close to the sea front, Will suddenly murmured, "Fair wind for France indeed, Ned. Just look over there. The lights of the French coastline are shining very brightly; they are so *visible*. What a marvelously clear night it is."

"With no mist off the marsh," Ned responded. "And soon there'll be a full moon, mark my words. Not a good night for our smugglers."

"You're right. But listen, did you know that the Romney Marsh is as famous for its smugglers as the Cornish coast?"

"I did." Now turning slightly to the right, Ned continued, "Let's go and sit on that wall for a moment. I need to talk to you about something."

Will nodded. Bundling their scarves and coats around themselves, the two men sat down, staring out toward the encroaching sea. It had grown truly dark; the stars glittered, and far off the Dungeness lighthouse flashed, its wide beams bouncing on the land and back onto the water.

Knowing that Edward would speak only when he was ready, Will waited, wondering what this was about.

At last Ned said, "What of Oxford, Will? You haven't gone back there to continue your studies. You're long overdue."

"Oh, but I'm not going back."

"Not ever?" Ned's surprise was evident in his tone.

"That's correct. I went up to Oxford, saw everyone, bade my farewells after I had explained my reasons for not finishing my education."

"And your father? Isn't he angry?" Ned probed.

"He was, but only momentarily. You know, the old man gave up on *me* a long time ago, and I suppose he knew it was futile to argue with me."

"Did you go to Leicestershire to see him?"

Will shook his head. "It just so happened my father was in town on business last week, and we dined at his club. At first it was a bit of a sticky wicket for me, but in the end he came around to my way of thinking. He agreed I could lead my life as I wanted, and he actually wished me well. He was a brick really, Ned, since he hasn't withdrawn my monthly allowance."

"That *was* generous of him," Ned murmured. Frowning, he then asked, "But, Will, what are your plans? Do you still wish to join a firm in the City?"

"No, I don't . . ." Will's voice trailed off, and he sat quietly for a moment, then continued. "I would like to work alongside you, Ned, if that would be at all possible."

Startled, Edward turned to stare at his friend. "At *Deravenels*? Is that what you mean?"

Will nodded.

"I don't have a job myself, not yet at any rate. So I can't very well give you one, old chap."

"The day will come when you can. I'm prepared to wait," Will responded. "If I know you and Neville Watkins as well as I think I do, I won't have to wait very long."

"You sound positive about our success," Ned muttered.

"I don't doubt it for one moment."

Ned said, "I have to present myself there next week, and very frankly, I quite dread it. I know the top brass will simply greet me, give me an office, and let me rot, twiddling my thumbs. That's their modus operandi. But I have other ideas; for one thing, I'm not going to let them stick me in a poky little room in the back. I'm going to demand my father's office."

"That's the spirit!" Will exclaimed. "You *must* have your

father's old office. Start the way you mean to go on, that's my advice."

"I most certainly will do that."

"Is it agreed then?" Will asked. "About me working with you?"

"If you wish to work at Deravenels, it would certainly please me, but I can't tell you exactly when that would be."

"As I said, I'll wait."

"Why?" Ned asked a short while later, as they started walking back up to the farmhouse. "Why are you so keen on Deravenels?"

"Because I believe I can be of use to you, and because I want to be with you, Ned. Now, to change the subject, what are you going to *do* about Lily?"

"Why nothing," Ned answered swiftly, turning to stare at his friend in the moonlight. "I'm going to walk back into the farmhouse and be as cordial as I can be. After all, there's no point in flogging a dead horse. Anyway, Vicky probably put Lily straight, wouldn't you say?"

"I would indeed," Will answered, pleased that Ned had decided to be his old charming self. His charm had disappeared of late. But things would keep normalizing . . . so he hoped. He felt a ripple of worry then, wondering why he would think things were going to be *normal*. They weren't. Not at all. Their world was about to go mad.

thirteen

LONDON

Neville was about to meet three men, each one of them very different. As he walked back and forth along the back portico of his Chelsea house, he focused on them. He was well aware that each would bring something unique to the meeting; what they said, and what was ultimately agreed upon, would change many lives, some for the worse, others for the better.

As Neville turned once more and headed back along the paving stones, a door flew open and a child stepped out. It was his small daughter Anne, and as soon as she saw him, she ran toward him. She was waving and crying out, "Papa! Papa! Here I am!"

Laughing, he hurried forward, caught her in his arms, swung her up, held her close to his chest. "Hello, my little sweetheart," he said against her glossy light brown hair. "And you should be wearing a coat, my pet. You'll catch a chill in this cold weather."

"But the sun is shining, Papa," she answered, staring into his eyes.

"It's still February, Anne."

"The flowers are coming out," she countered, pointing to the snowdrops and purple and yellow crocuses peeping up out of the dark earth of the borders set around the lawn. "Spring flowers, Mama says."

"They are indeed. However, we must go inside, where it's warmer. And you and I, well, we shall see each other later."

"Mama says Ned is coming. Will he bring Richard with him?"

"I don't think so, sweetheart, not this morning. We are having a business meeting."

"Today is Saturday, Papa," she said, sounding reproachful.

He grinned at her. "I know," he answered and suddenly recognized the disappointment in her eyes. Her face had become sad, he thought.

"You like your cousin, don't you?"

She nodded.

By this time Neville had reached the door, and putting her down, he ushered his daughter into the house, then stepped inside after her. Before they had even moved across the central gallery, he heard his wife's footsteps on the polished wood floor. He always recognized them; only she in the household walked with such determination. Slap, slap, slap, her feet went, and a moment later she was entering the gallery. "Ah, there you are my little one," Nan Watkins exclaimed when she spotted her namesake. "I've been looking all over for you."

"She came out in search of me," Neville remarked, walking across to his wife, putting his hand on her shoulder affectionately. "She was really looking for young Dick, though, I do believe." He smiled at her, his eyes full of love. "You know how attached she is to him, Nan; she's his shadow whenever he's staying at Thorpe Manor with us."

Anne Watkins, known as Nan all of her life, nodded and took hold of her daughter's hand. "She's been attached to him since she took her first steps and stumbled into his arms . . . arms that were certainly on the ready to catch her."

Neville was silent for a moment, looking intently at his wife. "A good thing it is Richard she has taken into her heart and not the other one. I never quite know about *him* . . . the middle one, that is."

"What do you mean?" Nan asked, a pale brow lifting eloquently.

"The breeding is there, but not the stamina."

"You sound as if you're talking about horseflesh."

Neville threw back his head and laughed, highly amused. But then his wife frequently amused him with her remarks. Shaking his head, he said at last, "Touché, my dear."

Nan glanced at him sideways, smiling, flirting with him, and then, looking down at her younger daughter, she murmured, "Come along, Anne, it's back to the nursery for you. Miss Deidre is waiting to give you and Isabel a painting lesson."

"I am here," a small voice said, and another pretty child came dancing into the gallery, her fair hair gleaming in the sunlight filtering in through the many leaded windows. She moved toward her father, pirouetting to show off her skills as a budding dancer. "Good morning, Papa," she said as she came to a standstill.

Bending down, Neville kissed her cheek, hugged her to him; then holding her away, he gave her a warm smile and said, "Aren't you the graceful one, Isabel? I am very impressed with your talents."

She smiled, bobbed her head prettily, and asked, "Is Georgie coming with Ned, Papa? Mama told me Ned would be here for lunch today."

"That's true, darling, Ned *is* coming to have lunch with me. However, it is about business. And no, Georgie isn't going to be here, and neither is Dick. You'll have to see your little gentlemen friends another day."

"Oh." She pouted a little and shook her curls. "I thought we could play together . . ." She let her voice trail off as she caught the warning look in her mother's eye, saw the stern expression settling on Nan's face.

Nan said, "I will talk to Aunt Cecily later, and perhaps we can arrange something, perhaps—"

"Cecily's still in Yorkshire," Neville interrupted, shaking

his head, pursing his lips. "She decided to stay at Ravenscar for a little longer before coming up to London." He gave a light shrug. "I do believe she's trying to settle herself down, come to grips with . . . things."

"As is your mother. I understand, Neville; it's only to be expected."

"Go along, my sweetlings," Neville told his girls. "Up to the nursery for your painting lesson. I need to spend a few moments with your mother."

"Yes, Papa," they said dutifully and ran out together.

Taking hold of her arm, Neville led his wife into the nearby library and closed the door behind them. Turning her to face him, he said in a low voice, his eyes full of concern, "I'm afraid Cecily and my mother aren't doing too well at the moment. They are still in shock, in my opinion. After all, the deaths were so sudden. There has to be a period of adjustment and of grieving."

Nan nodded vigorously. "Of course, of course, Neville, and I don't know why the girls are so focused on the two youngest Deravenels at the moment. I really have no clue."

"Well, Anne has always been like a little puppy trailing after Richard; as for Isabel, she's seemed to gravitate to George. Although *that* doesn't particularly please me. Still, there's nothing strange, darling; they've known those boys all their lives, grown up together, and after the week we just spent in Yorkshire, and being with them so much at Ravenscar, I think they're missing their little playmates. That's quite understandable, isn't it?"

"Yes, I suppose so." Standing on tiptoe, Nan kissed his cheek and led him out of the library. "I must go and spend a few minutes with them, my dear, show my interest in their painting lesson."

"I know, I know." He watched her walking off down the long gallery, thinking how beautiful she was in her refined and delicate way. She was the only woman he had ever loved; there had been others, but they had been merely sexual liaisons. His sweet Nan was the love of his life. They were extremely happy together, he and she, and the only thing that caused him the odd moment of regret was the lack of an heir. He longed for a son; Nan had had several miscarriages, and she had not yet conceived again. The terrible yearning for a boy child surfaced in Neville for a split second, and then he pushed it away. He was a lucky man, and he counted his blessings. And Nan and he were still young enough to have many more children . . .

Once Nan had disappeared up the staircase, Neville turned and went outside again. He began to walk up and down along the portico, his thoughts now focusing on the impending arrival of his three guests.

The first he expected was his cousin Edward. Neville was very anxious to see Ned, to listen to what he had to report. Ned had been working at the Deravenel offices in the Strand for the past week. They had spoken briefly, and Neville had received several enigmatic notes from Edward, but nothing of real importance had been conveyed. This had been puzzling. But Neville trusted Ned in all things and especially trusted his judgment, and it was patently obvious that Edward was being discreet. Far better to talk in the privacy of his house than on the telephone, and he was well aware how easily notes could get lost, fall into the wrong hands, or be stolen.

Alfredo Oliveri would be the second to come. He was in London, ostensibly on Deravenel business, but he had really come to see Ned and Neville. Oliveri had made his loyalty and devotion to the Yorkshire Deravenels known when they were in Carrara, and to have him on their side was an immense bonus. He was well trusted in the company and part of the old guard, having worked for them for over twenty years. Although he might not exactly be a member of the inner circle, he certainly knew a lot.

Neville had made a plan, and the secret to its success was

information. The more Oliveri was able to tell him about everyone and everything in the company the more *he* was likely to succeed.

His last guest for lunch was Amos Finnister. *Amos.* He turned the name over in his mind; he had known Amos for twelve years and employed him for ten. Amos was a private investigator, and the best in that line of business as far as Neville was concerned. He ran his own firm, which had only one client—Neville Watkins. It was Neville who actually owned the detective agency through several straw men. This arrangement worked well for both of them.

Neville smiled as he continued to think about Amos. Taking the man under his wing had been a brilliant piece of strategy. Amos was diligent, logical, and persistent, like a dog with a bone when it was necessary. Calm and cool whatever the circumstances, he was loyal, discreet, and on call night or day. And he had a knack for picking men to work for him who had similar characteristics. Among the things Neville considered of unquestionable value were the contacts Amos had, in all walks of life. They were key to being a successful private investigator.

Before he had left for Italy with Edward and Will, Neville had given Amos a list of names, for the most part names of people who worked at Deravenels and were known adherents of Henry Grant and, therefore, more than likely to be enemies of Edward.

Since returning to London, he was more convinced than ever that his cousin needed protection; he had been made aware of that by Alfredo Oliveri. But from whom *exactly*? Who were the real wielders of power at Deravenels? Margot Grant, obviously, and John Summers. But Harry Grant himself? Maybe. Maybe not. He was a weak man, lazy, ready to pass on the burdens of business to his wife, who was keen to grab those so-called burdens as fast as she could. And naturally there were others who were against Edward, simply because he was the son of Richard Deravenel, the true heir to the company.

Amos would find out, if he hadn't already; Neville could not wait to see him.

I have to triumph, Neville told himself as he struck out toward the end of the garden. When he came to the ancient stone wall that fronted onto the river Thames, he leaned against it, staring into the distance. It was a slow-moving river today, black like ink, and the sky above had suddenly changed. The pale blue had curdled, become a mix of gray and a strange bluish green.

It's going to rain after all, Neville decided, lifting his eyes. And this thought had hardly surfaced when he felt the first drops of cold rain on his upturned face.

Swinging about, he hurried up through the garden and into the house, crossed the central gallery, deposited his overcoat in the hall closet. He made his way back to the library, a large and elegantly appointed room, his favorite in the lovely house, which dated back to the Regency period. He had always thought of the library as his haven, which closed him off from the ugliness of the world outside.

A fire blazed in the hearth, and the softly shaded lamps had all been turned on during his absence, giving the room a welcoming, roseate glow. He realized he had grown slightly chilled outside, and he went and stood with his back to the fire.

His mind was alive with ideas and plans. He *was* going to put Ned in the seat of power, however long it took him. And he himself would be the one to wield the power.

fourteen

RAVENSCAR

The North Sea glittered like highly polished chain mail, rippling under the light breeze. Above, the sky was a cloudless arc of brilliant azure filled with golden sunlight. Sunlight without warmth on this cold morning. Nonetheless, Cecily Deravenel had been lured outside by it, and wrapping herself warmly in heavy woolens and a fur-lined cape, she had braved the cold.

She stood inside the old ruined stronghold on the promontory, somewhat protected by its high walls, staring out across the sea. Her thoughts were with Edward in London; a week ago he had presented himself at Deravenels, and his professional life had begun. She shivered, but not from the cold. How would they continue to treat him? And how would he fare in the long run? She was well aware that her son had dreaded going there. In the past week he had told her little, his two phone calls kept extremely brief. Yet Neville had reassured her, as best he could, that it would be all right. At least for the moment. No one would make a move against Ned. Too soon, he had explained. Also, Alfredo Oliveri was there; ostensibly, he was on a business trip to the London headquarters. But he was really there to keep an eye on Ned. *Keep an eye on him.* What a silly euphemism that was. Protection was what her oldest son would ultimately need. Ned was sitting in a nest of vipers.

Cecily shivered again and hunched into her warm clothes; her gloved hands fumbled with the ends of the scarf around her head. As she tightened it, her mind raced.

Neville had been honest with her the other day; he had admitted that all of her sons were in danger. Still, he had also managed to convince her that her two youngest were quite safe here at Ravenscar. She trusted her nephew implicitly, knew how clever he was, and brilliant. He was also loyal to family, just as Ned was, and as her father and brother had been. Rick, her only sibling, was gone forever, and Thomas, his youngest, was dead and buried with him. Now she must rely on Neville, and his brother John, both older than Ned. Dear Johnny. Her face softened at the thought of him. Less flamboyant, less ambitious than his brother, a loving young man and wholly devoted to Ned.

We are a strong family unit, the Watkins and Deravenel clans. We will stand together in this battle to come. We will prevail. These thoughts made her lift her head higher, and with great pride as she remembered who she was, her lineage, and whom she had married: *Richard Deravenel,* rightful heir to the Deravenel business empire. His widow now. She must do his memory justice. Her eyes blazed with a new determination.

She came to a sudden decision. She would not permit herself to be frightened by the likes of Henry Grant and his avaricious French wife, or by their cohorts. Never. She would stand up to them, stand tall, just as her father had taught her to do. As for her grief, she would bury it deep. It was not for public consumption. Nor for sharing with anyone, not even her children.

Her children. She must focus her attention on them now, protect them at all costs, ensure their safety. "Of course nobody's going to come and murder them in their beds," Neville had reassured her with a laugh. "All I'm saying is . . . Well, just keep an eye on them." And that she would certainly do; she would protect them with her very life.

Chilled from the wind coming off the sea, Cecily turned around, climbed the steps intersecting the tiered gardens and entered the house through the French doors on the terrace.

She was shedding her cape and heavy jacket in the Long Hall when she heard a yell, almost a war cry, and there was George nearly hurtling down the stairs, blond hair rumpled, clothes askew, face flushed with anger. Margaret was fast on his heels, looking equally distressed. Only Richard, following them slowly, seemed sedate and perfectly in control.

"Good Heavens! *Children!* What on earth is going on here?" Cecily demanded as she pulled off her gloves and scarf, threw them on top of her outer garments on the chair.

"It's not my fault! Not mine, Mama. I didn't smash the wall in," George yelled as he scurried toward her and, as usual, flung himself against her body. "It's not my fault, Mama," he repeated in a whining voice. "I'm not to blame, she pushed me."

Automatically, Cecily's arms went around the eleven-year-old boy in that protective way she had with him, but she looked over his head to his sister Meg, who was straightening her jacket, then smoothing her blond hair back into the black silk bow at the nape of her neck. She also looked as if she had been in a tussle, obviously with George.

Hesitantly, Meg took a few steps toward her mother and said in a trembling voice, "It *was* George's fault. He started it all."

"No, I didn't!" he shouted back.

"Be quiet!" Cecily exclaimed, staring down at George. Instinctively, she believed Meg, who was usually so loyal to George. Why would she turn on him unless he deserved it? Looking across at her daughter, Cecily continued, "Please explain the situation to me, Meg, since you at least seem to be in control of yourself."

"I'm the one in control," Richard volunteered.

"I see that," his mother answered. "Come now, Meg, what *is* this fuss about?"

"We were in the old nursery playroom. Richard was reading, I was working on my stamp collection. George was idling his time away, and growing bored. Suddenly, he swooped down on me and took my album. Actually, Mother, he grabbed it very rudely. Then he pranced around the room, waving it in the air. I thought he would damage some of my best stamps, which Papa had given me over the years, so I jumped up, to try to get it. But George kept dodging away from me, taunting me, and he made me angry. I lurched toward him, and naturally he endeavored to avoid me, and he tripped over a footstool and fell against the wall next to the fireplace. It caved in, just like that. George fell inside the wall, but it was very strange, because there's actually a room there."

Cecily froze. *The priest hole.* Closed permanently by Richard when Anne, their first child, was born. He was fearful that a small child might lock herself inside and suffocate before she could be rescued. And so he had made it safe. And no one had ever known about the priest hole except them, and the Deravenel ancestors of the past, of course.

Cecily opened her mouth to speak, then closed it as the youngest in the family slowly approached her. His face was solemn, his eyes grave, as they frequently were. And he was totally in control of himself, just as he had said he was.

What had silenced Cecily was the black leather notebook Richard clutched in his hands. Surely it was her husband's missing black notebook. The one she had searched for, and Ned, too, in his father's rooms here and in London.

"I climbed into the wall," the boy was saying to her. "To help Georgie, Mama. He was flat on his back on the floor. Between the walls. That's what I thought at first, but when I went to him, I found I was in a *little room.* There's a chest in there, and after I helped Georgie to get up, I opened the drawers; well, not all of them because one was locked. Anyway, Mother, I found this." Moving closer to Cecily, he thrust the book at her.

Cecily disentangled herself from George's embrace and accepted the book from her youngest child. "Thank you very much, Dickie," she murmured.

Holding it, she experienced a flare of hope. Her husband had jotted notes in it almost every day. She opened the book eagerly and saw lines and lines of numbers, but few words. There were odd sentences here and there but none of them made any sense. Disappointment swept through her, and her heart sank. For a brief moment she had thought the book would reveal something important—*important to Ned*. However, the notes were an enigma. Unless there was someone who could decipher them. Was this a code of some kind? Perhaps.

Oliveri. Instantly, Cecily thought of the Italian, who had apparently been a close colleague of her husband's and was so willing to help them. Would he know what the numbers meant?

Meg interrupted her thoughts when she said, "Mother, George *did* take my album, whatever he says. He grabbed it and ran around the room with it."

"I did not," George cried.

"George, tell me the truth. Did you do what Meg says?" Cecily asked, her tone icy.

"No, I didn't," he began, and then his voice faltered under his mother's sharp scrutiny.

"I'm asking you for the final time," Cecily informed him.

"I only . . . wanted to . . . have a look at the stamps," he muttered, sounding guilty, looking shamefaced, and he blushed as his mother held him away from her by his shoulders, stared into his eyes.

"I will not tolerate lying, George. Now apologize to your sister."

"I'm sorry," he mumbled without looking around at Meg.

"Please, Meg, come forward. That's right, stand next to George. Now George, turn to your sister and say you are sorry and shake her hand. And Meg, you must apologize, too."

The two of them did as she asked without further argument.

Cecily said, "Well, George, you're not hurt, apparently, so do stop whining. *Please.*"

The old nursery playroom at Ravenscar was entirely paneled in dark wood. Except for the gaping hole made when George had fallen, it looked perfectly in order. But Cecily understood that part of the paneling might be fragile. After all, it *was* centuries old.

Ravenscar had been built in the Elizabethan period, almost four hundred years ago, which was when a priest hole had been created behind a wall which adjoined the fireplace. During the early part of Elizabeth Tudor's reign there had been a certain amount of religious persecution after the Catholic risings in the north, and many renowned Catholic families like the Deravenels had built priest holes in which to hide priests in the event of sudden surprise, such as the unexpected arrival of soldiers.

Bending down, Cecily felt the wood around the hole which George had made, and a few pieces instantly crumbled in her hand. Stepping away from the damaged wall, she tried to recall where, all those years ago, her husband had hammered in the nails, and she was gratified when she had no trouble remembering. Six feet up from the baseboard, at the top of the second panel, a couple of feet away from the fireplace: that was exactly where he had nailed the small door shut.

Taking a chair from around the circular table in the middle of the room, Cecily pulled it over to the fireplace wall. Tall and athletic, she was very agile. Lifting her long black skirt, she climbed onto the chair and, reaching up, felt around for the nails. They weren't there anymore, just as she had suspected. She could actually feel the little holes where the nails had been; they had been darkened over with varnish or dark boot polish, and quite recently. There was no question in her mind that Richard had pulled them out, just as he had hammered them in place not very long after Anne came into the world.

Stepping cautiously off the chair, Cecily hurried to the fireplace and picked up the poker. Leaning forward, squinting in the firelight blazing up the chimney, she finally spotted the tiny metal lever set in the lower part of the brick fireback. It was covered in soot and difficult to find even when someone knew exactly where to look for it, as she did.

Lifting the poker, she struck the tiny lever, and instantly the panel swung open.

After replacing the poker, Cecily went to the hole and maneuvered herself inside. She was startled to find the space relatively clean. Obviously Richard had swept out the dust whenever he opened the priest hole.

Her main target was the chest; it took only a moment to locate the locked drawer, which she pried open with a pair of scissors. The drawer slid out easily, and she experienced satisfaction and a rush of hope. She had known full well that there would be something inside the locked drawer, something put there for safety by her husband, and indeed there was. It was a second black leather notebook. This one was slightly larger than the one her youngest son had discovered; it had her husband's initials embossed in gold in the bottom corner, and her hand trembled as she left the priest hole, opened it, and began to read. Her excitement grew as she stood there in front of the nursery fire, scanning the pages.

She did not read for long; she had perused enough to know how important it was for Edward to have this. She went immediately downstairs to the small sitting room which adjoined her bedroom and seated herself at the desk.

Placing her hands across the top of the private diary, for that was what it was, she stared off into the distance, thinking. She did not want to post the book to Edward; it might get lost. She could send Jessup up to town with it; a sealed package was safe from prying eyes. Or perhaps she should take it herself? But she didn't want to leave the children here alone. She could take them with her, of course. What to do . . . what to do?

part two

golden boy

edward and lily

Very tall of personage, exceeding the stature almost of all others, comely of visage, pleasant and broad breasted.

POLYDORE VERGIL

He had courage, determination and resourcefulness, which he used to his own advantage, and was pragmatic, generous, witty and ruthless when the occasion demanded it.

ALISON WEIR

She walks in beauty, like the night
Of cloudless climes and starry skies;
And all that's best of dark and bright
Meet in her aspect and her eyes;
Thus mellow'd to that tender light
Which heaven to gaudy day denies.

LORD BYRON

fifteen

KENT

"What to do? What to do?" Lily murmured, staring at Vicky. "Please tell me what to do, because I really don't know."

Vicky put down her coffee cup and sat back in the chair, contemplating her friend for a second or two, and then, shaking her head, she answered softly, "I don't think there *is* anything you can do at the moment, my dear. You must let the matter rest, and just wait."

"That's the hardest part, you know, waiting. Waiting for him to send a note by messenger, or put a letter in the post, or just arrive on my doorstep, as he so often does. This total silence all week is rather unusual, I must admit. I have to think he is still angry with me. Perhaps he even wants to break it off." A blond brow lifted.

"I doubt that. He's much too much enamored of you, Lily. I know he was a trifle put out with you last weekend; on the other hand, he seemed to calm down later. Also, Edward doesn't bear a grudge, he never has. Very simply, he's just not made that way, it's not part of his nature."

"If you say so, then I must believe you, Vicky, and it cheers me up a little. This whole week without a word from him has been nerve-racking; it's seemed like an eternity."

"And it would, since that's all you've focused on, waiting

for a word from Ned. I know for a fact he's been busy. It was his first week at Deravenels, remember."

"Will told you he's been busy with work? Is that what you're saying?"

"Absolutely. Will hasn't seen him either. Seemingly, Ned has kept to himself. He dropped Will a note saying that he was trying to work out the way the company runs, and that Will shouldn't expect to see him until next week, that is the coming week."

A smile flitted across Lily's face, and her eyes suddenly sparkled. "Thank you for telling me this; it makes it easier, knowing I'm not the only one Ned's ignoring. His best friend is going through the same thing."

Vicky began to laugh, stood up, walked across the small morning room at Stonehurst Farm, where the two women were having morning coffee on this windy Saturday. "If I'm picking up the correct vibrations from my darling brother, I think he has better fish to fry," she remarked as she brought the coffeepot over to the table. "Would you care for another cup?"

Lily shook her head. "No, thanks anyway."

After filling her own cup, Vicky placed the silver pot on the table and sat down, looking thoughtful. Stirring her coffee and taking a sip, she went on, "I do believe Will has a new lady in his life."

Lily stared at her, taken by surprise. "Really! How odd that Ned hasn't mentioned it to me; after all they are so close, those two, inordinately so. He must know."

"I doubt that Ned would say anything to anyone . . . he'd consider it Will's business. He's not the kind of person to gossip."

"Edward's an odd duck, though, in some ways, don't you think?"

Vicky frowned, not quite understanding what Lily meant. She gave her friend a questioning look.

As if reading her mind, Lily exclaimed, "What I mean is he seems much older than his actual age. Also, he certainly has a penchant for older women. I know for a fact that he had a flirtation with his mother's secretary, a widow."

"He does have a weakness for older women, and most especially *widows,* but don't complain, Lily. *You're* his favorite, so do be happy."

"I am happy, although a little worried at the moment."

"Oh, darling, don't be concerned. You haven't heard from him this week because he's only just stepped into his father's shoes and gone into the family business."

"It's not his absence or his silence that's really worrying me," Lily murmured, leaning closer across the table, "but something else altogether." Dropping her voice, she confided, "I'm afraid I might be pregnant with his baby."

This was the last thing Vicky had expected to hear. For a moment she was speechless, and then, sitting up straighter in her chair, she asked in a quiet tone, "Are you *sure*?"

Shaking her elegant blond head, Lily answered swiftly, "No, not yet. But I have . . . missed . . . a month. Last month. I have to wait and see what happens. . . . I'm due in ten days." Taking a deep breath and blowing out air, Lily added, "Before you say it, I know he won't marry me if I *am* expecting. And I wouldn't want him to, I'm much too old for him. Anyway, I think it goes without saying that Ned is not really marriage material. He's too much of a Lothario at the moment. And Edward Deravenel is undoubtedly expected to make a brilliant marriage when the time is right."

Vicky nodded. "What you say is true, but what on earth are you going to do if you are carrying his child? There are doctors who . . . well, you know, terminate unwanted pregnancies. But I think that might be a dangerous course to take."

"Oh, I agree with you! And I would *never* go that route! Believe me."

"So what *will* you do?" Vicky pressed, filled with concern.

"I would have the baby. There's nothing else to *do*, if you think about it."

Vicky was silent for a moment, biting her lip. "You would have the baby and bring it up yourself, is that what you're saying?"

"Yes." Lily nodded. "I would have it *and* keep it."

"But Lily, darling, think of the scandal. What will you tell people? And who will you name as the father?"

"Well, I hadn't actually thought of all that. No, I definitely haven't puzzled that out yet. But I don't suppose I would name Edward. Why would I want to cause trouble for him? After all, I do love him, Vicky, very much. And I understand that he can never marry me, for a variety of reasons, not only our age difference. But I think . . . Well, you know, I do think I would like to have his baby, and I know I'd enjoy bringing up his child."

"What lovely sentiments, Lily," Vicky murmured, smiling at her friend. "And I'm perfectly certain Ned would help you financially."

"Oh, but I don't want *money* from him, Vicky! How could you think such a thing? My goodness, I have plenty of money from my late husbands . . . money to burn, in fact. Why would I burden Ned with something like that? Especially since he never has any money of his own. Well, hardly any. He did tell me once that his father had been as poor as a church mouse. The money in the family comes from his late grandfather Philip Watkins."

"Yes, I'm aware of that." Vicky sat quite still, ruminating for a few seconds, and then she nodded to herself and gave Lily a smile of affection and warmth. "I must say, you're a most unusual woman, Lily Overton, quite remarkable, in fact."

"Thank you." Lily rose, walked over to the window, stood looking out toward the Romney Marsh yet seeing only Ned in her mind's eye. She did love him to distraction, but there was no future for them, not in the long run. She would remain his mistress for as long as he wanted her, she had always known that. She was utterly devoted to him. He was a great gift to her, one she had never expected. He had brought her to the height of fulfillment, introduced passion and sexual excitement to her life. And she knew that, in his own way, he truly cared about her. And that was enough.

Her two marriages had been affectionate, and of course, she had fulfilled her marital duties. However, lovemaking with her late husbands had been lackluster. But they had provided comfort and protection, and ultimately, they had made her a wealthy woman, giving her independence.

Swinging around, she said slowly, "I can well afford to raise a child, Vicky, and that's what I *am* going to do. Bring up Ned's child. In the country. That would be the most comfortable place to be. Perhaps here in Kent. Somewhere near here, near you. What do you think?"

"I agree with you, of course I do. Far better to be down here than up in town, where everyone tittle-tattles and pries. And you know I am here for you, my dear. I'll do anything I can to help."

Lily walked over to Vicky, gave her a quick embrace, and sat down at the table. "Thank you, Vicky, I'm lucky to have you as a friend. But I might not be pregnant at all, you know."

Vicky merely smiled and thought: I'm certain you are. There's a wonderful bloom on you. And Edward Deravenel, almost nineteen, is as virile as any man could ever be.

When Vicky went into the kitchen later, she saw that Cook had everything rolling along in her usual efficient way. Florry, the young woman who came up from the village to help, was beating eggs in a bowl, and she glanced up, smiled cheerily at the sight of her mistress.

Vicky smiled back, nodding, and then said, "I see all is

very much in order in here, as usual, Mrs. Bloom, so I'll just leave you to it."

"That's right, mum, I'm on my schedule, right on time, that I am. The cheese soufflé will be ready at one-thirty, as you requested, and there's no problem with the roast chicken; fortunately, the bird won't spoil."

"I'll make sure we sit down at one twenty-five, Mrs. Bloom, never fear. Your soufflé won't drop if I've anything to do with it."

Mrs. Bloom glanced over her shoulder at Vicky and began to chuckle.

Vicky hurried out and walked across the hall into the dining room. It was cozy and welcoming with the fire burning brightly in the grate, and there was the smell of beeswax and pinecones intermingled with the hint of smoke in the air. It was a mixture of those unique and lovely country smells that never failed to remind Vicky of Compton Hall, the Hasling family seat where she and Will had grown up. That lovely old manor house had always been redolent with the perfume of burning wood, mellow fruit, baking bread, and homemade honey. She thought with a rush of affection of their late mother, who had turned that ancient pile of stones into a welcoming home where children were loved and cosseted.

Slowly Vicky began to set the table, selecting a linen cloth with embroidered edges, crystal water tumblers, knives and forks and linen napkins; and as she moved around she thought of her dear friend Lily Overton.

Lily had been very brave when she had explained what she would do if she was pregnant. She did have only three choices. Lily could endeavor to get a termination, a risky business in more ways than one; she could have the child and give it up for adoption immediately, a miserable, heartbreaking prospect; or she could keep it and bring it up herself.

Lily had elected to do the last, and Vicky couldn't blame her. She would manage very well, in Vicky's opinion, because she was practical by nature, a good organizer, and she had her own money. *That was the key, the money. It protected her and the child.*

Having a child out of wedlock was like committing suicide for most women. An enormous stigma was attached to illegitimacy, and unless a woman was protected by the man involved, she was doomed. Even in this new Edwardian era, which was more relaxed than Queen Victoria's time, the stigma remained. Despite the antics of the aristocracy and the licentiousness which was so prevalent today, there remained prudery, snobbery, discrimination, class distinction, and—

"I shocked you earlier, didn't I?"

Swinging around, Vicky exclaimed, "Goodness, Lily! You did give me a start. I didn't hear you coming down the hall."

"I'm sorry," Lily apologized. "But I *did* shock you, didn't I?"

"No, you didn't, actually. *Surprised* me, yes."

"I've made up my mind not to think about it, for the moment at least. . . . It *could* be a false alarm, you know."

Vicky nodded. "That's a wise decision." She fell silent as Lily glided into the room and came to stand next to the fireplace. Vicky couldn't help thinking what a beautiful woman she was, with her perfect pink-and-white complexion, green eyes, and blond hair. Her features were very even and smooth, and she looked much younger than her years. No wonder Edward Deravenel was so smitten with her. What man wouldn't be?

Margot Grant came in from the garden, took off her coat, hung it in the armoire, and went into the dining room. She stopped dead in her tracks, staring at the room in horror. *Mon Dieu!* What had happened here? The mahogany dining table had been pushed up against one of the end walls, the twelve antique dining chairs arranged in four rows of three, like the pews in a church, and the table itself had been transformed into some strange homemade altar. Above the table, hanging on the wall, was the crucifix. How had Henry managed to nail it up there? she asked herself.

Dismay swept over her, and she did not move for a moment, her mind churning. Henry was off on one of his mad jaunts again, filled with religious fervor, reveling in the belief that he was a monk, and that he had his own church, where he preached to a congregation. That there wasn't one present never seemed to bother him at all.

But he wasn't here preaching to the empty chairs now. So where was he? Terrified that he might have wandered out of the garden of their Ascot home and gone onto the main road, she rushed out to the garden. Shading her eyes from the sunlight, she looked around frantically, calling, "Henry! Henry! Where are you?"

He did not respond to her calls, and she began to search for him. Within a few minutes she saw him flitting through the trees in a small copse at the end of the lawn. Her heart sank. He was wearing the dark brown monk's robe again and carrying a wooden cross. As she drew closer, she heard him singing, off-key as usual.

Margot felt nauseated. Her husband was stark raving mad, there was no question about that. What if someone found out how truly crazy he was? And that he had been in asylums? She might have to put him in one again. *Mon Dieu! Mon Dieu!*

"Henry, Henry, *cheri!*" she exclaimed as she moved into the copse. "Come along, let us go inside. It is cool today."

He turned around, gaping at her, his eyes vacant. "Daughter in Christ," he mumbled. "Daughter in Christ, good morrow to you."

Pushing her spiraling anger to one side, Margot took hold of his arm, and murmuring cajoling words, she led him across the lawn and into the house. Once she had maneuvered him into his bedroom, she swung on her heels, left the room, and locked the door behind her. What a mentally disturbed old fool he was. And one thing was imperative. She had to keep him hidden from the world until he became himself again.

Margot shook her head as she went downstairs. It was better when he went into catatonic shock. At least then he sat in a chair all day not moving, not speaking.

sixteen

LONDON

Edward came striding into the library of Neville's Chelsea house, bringing with him a rush of energy, vitality, and exuberance. *Ned's feeling better,* Neville thought, putting the grief behind him. *He's ready and able to move forward.* He was pleased for his young cousin, and relieved at the change in his demeanor.

There was a smile on Edward's face, an apology on his lips as he drew to a standstill in the middle of the room. "Sorry to be late. I'm afraid I had trouble finding a hansom cab this morning."

"There's no problem, Edward," Neville murmured, coming forward to greet his cousin. After they had quickly embraced, Neville stepped away, seated himself near the fireplace. Edward chose to stand, propped himself against the mantelpiece, and asked, "What time are the others due to arrive?"

"Alfredo Oliveri will be here in about ten minutes, Amos Finnister fifteen minutes after that."

"You haven't really explained who Amos Finnister is," Edward remarked, looking across at Neville, an eager and rather curious expression settling on his face. "All you said is that he has worked for you for some years, that you trust him implicitly, and that he will be invaluable to me."

"He will indeed, I've no doubt. But you'll soon understand about Finnister. Before they arrive, please tell me about the past week. Your notes were rather enigmatic, and you were not at all forthcoming when you telephoned."

Edward nodded and explained. "There wasn't a lot to tell you, and quite frankly it was a god-awful week. I loathe Aubrey Masters. I'm putting Oliveri in his place, making him head of the Mining Division, if we win."

"*When* we win, but do continue."

"Masters is bumptious, argumentative, and full of his own importance. And basically he's as thick as a plank. I'm more certain than ever that he's there purely because of Grant family connections. Anyway, he was going to give me the worst office in the building until I put up a fight. I insisted on my father's office, which is the tradition, and he wouldn't hear of it. I went at him hammer and tongs, but he was absolutely bloody-minded about it. Obdurate. Finally he brought John Summers in to mediate, and much to Masters's surprise, Summers agreed with me. Masters was furious, but Summers is his superior. I won. I got my father's old office."

"So John Summers was on your side, was he?"

"I wouldn't exactly say *that*!" Edward shot back, throwing his cousin a pointed look. "However, he did insist that I was to be given Father's old office, just brushed aside Masters's objections. After that he disappeared. I never saw him again last week. He went to Wales, so I was told."

"Did Aubrey Masters give you anything to do?"

"Not a damn thing. I was left to twiddle my thumbs. I went to the office every morning and was greeted fairly cordially by almost everyone, except Masters, of course, who was grumpy, almost to the point of rudeness. The other men treated me with the utmost civility, and that was that. Then they just ignored my presence."

"I see. Well, I'm not surprised. They're accepting you because they have no alternative; you have every right to be there. That's the company rule: the son steps into the father's shoes, gets his office, becomes a junior director although not on the board, and then works his way up through the ranks. However, they've rendered you ineffectual by not passing on work for you to do. Clever in a sense; on the other hand, it's rather ridiculous of them in the long run. It's as transparent as glass."

"I agree. However, dull and boring though it was, I did learn a few things."

Neville leaned forward, looked at his cousin intently. "About what?"

Edward answered, "For one thing, about the morale. It happens to be very low, and quite a few employees believe the company is not only in the doldrums but more than likely in the red. I also managed to ascertain that there are a couple of people who are in our camp, so to speak. And finally, I have begun to understand a little bit about the workings of the company. Also, I now recognize how truly enormous it is. I have always known, obviously, that it is one of the biggest trading companies in existence today. But Neville, until one is actually faced with it on a day-to-day basis, one doesn't really understand what *global* means. Deravenels is just that . . . the whole bloody world."

"First things first," Neville responded. "Who told you about the morale? *And* the red ink?"

"I picked up on the low morale almost immediately, just through chatting to people. Oliveri had steered me toward those employees he thought might be friendly, those who think Henry Grant should be removed. And they were the same ones who muttered about the company being in the red and not being what it once was," Edward told him. "As far as the vastness is concerned, Father had always drilled *that* into me. But it was only when I stood in front of that huge map in his office and counted the little red flags he had placed there that I *really* understood. Deravenels covers the *world.* We seem to be in every country."

"Almost, yes." Neville leaned back in his chair and brought his long fingers together in an arc, thinking for a moment. Then he said quietly, "What you've told me is very good news. A company with low morale, because of bad management I presume, and which is also in the red is very, *very* vulnerable, Ned. It can be picked off and taken over. *By us*. Of that I am absolutely sure. This is the most heartening information, and it corroborates everything Oliveri has muttered about lately."

Harrison, the butler, knocked and opened the door. "Excuse me, sir, Mr. Oliveri has arrived."

Neville nodded, rose, and went to greet Alfredo Oliveri.

After shaking hands, the two men walked over to Edward, who hurried to greet Alfredo. In the past week in London their friendship, begun in Carrara, had been carefully cemented.

Neville said, "Would either of you care for a drink?"

Both men shook their heads, and Edward murmured, "Perhaps a glass of wine at lunch, but nothing now, thank you."

Alfredo indicated his agreement, then unexpectedly plunged in rather abruptly. "In my considered opinion, you may have more supporters and friends than enemies at Deravenels, Mr. Edward. That may surprise you, but I feel sure that I am right."

Both Edward and Neville appeared taken aback, and then Edward said, "I did note that several of the men you introduced me to were exceptionally cordial, but I just assumed I had mostly *enemies* there—"

"Oh, you do have *some*," Alfredo cut in, "those who are cronies of Henry Grant, whose fathers have been on his side, usually because of *their* fathers and old loyalties. Let's not forget, that particular faction of the Deravenel family has been in control for sixty years now."

"Far too long," Neville murmured, giving Edward a knowing look.

Edward asked, "Who *are* my friends? I'd like to know their names."

Oliveri pulled a piece of paper out of the inside pocket of

his jacket, opened it, and began to read: "Rob Aspen, David Halton, Christopher Green, Frank Lane. Those men are well disposed to you for sure, Ned. They've made that perfectly clear to me this week, and of their own volition, I might add. I also believe that Joshua Kennett would be in your corner. Certainly he has long been dissatisfied with current management, has begun to grumble more loudly about the company being mismanaged."

"I know that John Summers is my enemy, and also Aubrey Masters," Edward began and fixed his eyes on Alfredo. "So who else has me in their sights?"

"James Cliff, who's exceptionally close to Summers and also very chummy with Margot Grant, as is Summers. Then I would add Andrew Trotter, Percy North, Philip Dever, and Jack Beaufield. Several of those men are on the board, because of their fathers' connections to the Grants over many years. But, of course, your friends Rob Aspen, David Halton, and Frank Lane are board members as well."

"It looks as if it's fairly evenly balanced," Neville interjected, sounding pleased. "The thing is, we must try to win more of the men over, don't you think, Oliveri?"

"Absolutely, and don't forget, *I* am on your side as well, even though I'm in Italy part of the time. But you can always count on me. And if I'm back in Carrara, I'll come at once if you need me to be in London."

"That reminds me of something," Edward said, smiling at Alfredo. "When we win this war, I shall get rid of Aubrey Masters immediately. And I am offering you his job now. It would please me if you'd take it."

Alfredo chuckled. "Talk of self-confidence, you certainly have it, and in spades. And I agree with you, we *will* win, and of course I'll take the job. Thank you. I've wanted to move to London for several years now. I even discussed it with your father at one point, and he agreed that I should really be here. But naturally nothing ever happened."

"What about your wife? Would she mind moving?" Neville asked.

"No, not at all. She's English, as you know, and whilst she loves Italy as much as I do, I know she would welcome a change." Alfredo smiled at them. "It's a done deal as far as I'm concerned."

"The news you've brought us today is a real boost," Neville remarked, nodding in affirmation of his words. "We must *all* gather as much information as we can in order to mount a case against Henry Grant. Information will prove to be our greatest weapon, you'll see, and when Amos Finnister arrives, we'll hear what he has discovered. Ah, here he is now," Neville exclaimed, jumping up to greet Amos, who hovered in the doorway with the butler.

After the two men shook hands, Neville said, "Edward, come and meet my good friend Amos Finnister. . . . This is my cousin Edward Deravenel, and my other guest is Alfredo Oliveri, whom I've mentioned to you."

Amos greeted them pleasantly, and the four men sat down in a grouping of chairs near the fireplace. Neville took charge and explained, "Before we went to Italy, I talked to Mr. Finnister and asked him to start digging in Henry Grant's backyard, and in anyone else's backyard if he thought it was appropriate to do so. I want to know everything there is to know about our enemies within Deravenels, and Finnister is the best private investigator there is in London, if not in the whole of England."

Amos smiled faintly, his gaze at Neville steady. "I don't know if I would go as far as that, Mr. Watkins."

"But I would. Now, what have you dug up? Lots of dirt, I hope."

"Not so much dirt as facts, sir, which are more important in the long run, wouldn't you say? First off, I'd like to say this. . . . In my opinion, Henry Grant is not simply pious, scholarly, and religious, as everyone claims. I believe him to be so seriously unstable it's more than likely he's actually *insane*. I discovered that he has been in two different mental institutions in the last few years. And no, they were not *retreats,* as was claimed at the time. They *were* insane asylums."

There was a moment of silence, and then Edward said in a low tone, "Oddly enough, my father once said to me that he thought Henry was extremely unbalanced, but he never said anything else. Not to me."

"Good God!" Neville looked at Edward and then at Amos. "Surely that's enough of a reason to have him removed from the chairmanship of Deravenels." He stared hard at Ned, his eyes full of questions. A brow went up, eloquently.

"Listen," Alfredo cut in, "I've heard it said he was off his rocker, a doddering fool, loopy, nutty . . . words like that. But yes, if he *was* in an asylum, it suggests much worse, doesn't it?"

"It does," Ned finally said. "And I think you're right, Neville, insanity would justify removal from the board and from the company. And not just at Deravenels, at any company. It's common sense, pure and simple."

"If I might suggest something," Amos murmured. "Perhaps no one ever really believed he was seriously mentally disturbed, perhaps everyone thought he was just an . . . ineffectual sort of chap and let him be."

"Maybe," Neville agreed. "Otherwise he would have been removed promptly by Summers and his gang."

Alfredo stood up and paced in front of the fire for a few seconds. Then turning to Neville, he said, "I must tell you, this news is most lethal. And it's a huge weapon for us." Turning to Amos, he asked, "Do you have *proof*? Hearsay and innuendo won't be enough to convince the Deravenel board. We must have absolute proof that he was in *two asylums,* at different times, presumably. Otherwise, they'll laugh in our faces."

"Proof *does* exist, Mr. Oliveri, but I don't actually have it in my hands, I'm afraid," Amos replied.

"But could you get it?" Neville asked, his eyes narrowing.

"Oh, yes, course I could, Mr. Watkins. But you do understand I'd have to have it . . . *stolen.* I would have to get . . . one of my *contacts,* so to speak, a *specialist* in that area, if you get my drift, to break into the two asylums and pinch their records."

"Then have it done. At once," ordered Neville without hesitation.

"Would anyone guess *we* had stolen those records? I can't help wondering that." Edward looked pointedly at Amos.

Amos answered swiftly, "No, no, they *wouldn't,* because his incarcerations have been secret, or more accurately, it's been passed around that he was in religious retreats. Correct?"

Edward nodded. "True."

"So nobody's going to point a finger at you," Amos continued. "Anyway, someone might have *brought* those documents to you . . . as a good deed, let's say. Someone who wanted the record set straight for the good of the company."

"How soon can you get them? Because I do agree with my cousin that you should go after them," Ned said, staring at Amos.

"Not sure. It'll take a bit of working out, getting the proper crew together. Can't afford mistakes."

Alfredo went back to his chair. Turning to Edward, he said, "We can't have any scruples at this moment in time. Very simply, we can't *afford* scruples. There's a great deal at stake here; not only justice for you, Mr. Edward, and you, too, Mr. Watkins, because of the deaths of your kin, but there's also a huge company at stake. A company that employs thousands of people all over the world. We must think about them, too."

It was Neville who spoke first. "Yes, you're correct, Oliveri. It would be criminal to let Deravenels go down the drain after eight hundred years of trading. Besides, it belongs to Mr. Edward; at least the top job belongs to him. It's his inheritance, and I aim to make sure that he gets his inheritance and that Deravenels not only survives the thieving Grants but goes on to become bigger and better than ever under our management."

Edward pondered for a moment, then addressed Neville. "Stealing the records to prove Henry Grant is insane is only one step. Surely we need much more to wrest Deravenels from their hands. They could easily put Margot Grant in to run the company until their son, Edouard, came of age."

"They wouldn't dare," Alfredo exclaimed, shaking his head vehemently. "Trust me on that. Yes, she manages to insinuate herself these days, but she does not have a role, a position, or a title."

"I have it on good authority that she is extremely unpopular," Amos told them. "Only Summers, Cliff, and North are her true adherents. Oh, and by the way, people are saying that her son is the half brother of John Summers, that it was his father, not pious old Henry, who impregnated Margot."

"Old? He's only thirty-nine," Edward muttered.

Neville glanced at him and said, "Too old to beat you." Then turning to Amos, he continued, "So, that old story has sprung up again, has it?" He began to laugh uproariously, and then, clearing his throat, he said, with another glance at Amos, "It might be a good idea to get those chaps of yours on it, the ones who are so good at spreading damaging gossip. Have them circulate the old story that Margot's brat is a bastard. Everything helps, you know. Let's get some really damaging propaganda out on the street, not only inside the company. Blacken the name of the Grants, that's all par for the course. Anything scurrilous they can think up they can use, tell them, as long as it doesn't stretch the imagination too far."

Harrison hovered in the doorway. "Lunch is served, sir," he announced.

◆ ◆ ◆

Nan Watkins sat alone in the conservatory, sipping a tall glass of mint tea and nibbling on a smoked salmon tea sandwich. She was happy to take her lunch alone in this sunny glass room filled with potted palms, exotic rubber plants, and her prized white orchids. It was a tranquil, peaceful spot in their busy household.

The girls were having lunch on the nursery floor with Nanny, and Neville was entertaining his guests in the dining room. She herself had planned the menu with Cook, and she hoped they were enjoying her choices.

She had selected Neville's favorites, as usual wanting to please him. The first course was a light vegetable soup, something similar to minestrone, which she knew Alfredo Oliveri also enjoyed; the second was grilled plaice, served with parsley sauce, croquette potatoes, and peas. For dessert she had asked Cook to make her famous bread pudding, with extra creamy custard and raisins, which was everyone's favorite. She had left the wine selection to her husband as she usually did.

Her husband. Neville Watkins. A man she had fallen in love with at first sight when he had come to her family home in Gloucestershire. He had had business with her father and ended up marrying her. She had never quite recovered from the shock. That this most handsome and extraordinary man had even deigned to look at her never ceased to amaze her.

In this Nan did herself an injustice, and she knew it. But she still always thought of herself as thin and pale, not at all enticing. In reality she was very pretty, with shining, golden brown hair and huge, soulful gray eyes that were beguiling to most men. She had perfect white skin, shapely breasts, and lovely long legs. But it was her femininity and fragility that appealed to the opposite sex. Instantly they wanted to protect her, as indeed did Neville Watkins. He not only considered her beautiful but had soon discovered she was a very sexual woman as well, a partner who craved him and showed it in ways no other woman ever had.

Nan knew this because he had confided in her; he had also told her how sexually exciting she was to him. She smiled to herself now as she thought about their lovemaking that morning. After her complaint the night before that he had taken Saturday, a day which belonged to them, away from her, he had awakened her very early with intimate kisses and a clamoring sexual desire. Their passion had been enormous, their longing slaked several times, and he had eventually whispered against her neck that perhaps they had made a child together this very day. And this she prayed for, prayed for a son so that he would have an heir. A baby conceived at this moment would help to assuage the pain and grief he felt at the loss of his father and his brother Thomas.

Nan stared into the room absently, thinking of young Tom. How Neville had grieved in the last few weeks. But she had helped him as best she could, and so had his brother John. Johnny they all called him, such a kind and gentle young man.

She would never dare say a wrong word about Johnny to Neville, but she knew deep in her heart that it was Ned who held his loyalty and love. She also knew that Edward Deravenel knew this, and sometimes it disturbed her.

Instinct, she thought. I have instinctive feelings about such things, instincts I cannot and must not fault. I'm right more often than I am wrong, aren't I?

It was the same with young Richard. There were times when Neville treated him like the son he hoped one day to have; Richard was the stand-in perhaps; yes, in a sense it *was* that. But Richard's absolute loyalty was to his brother Edward first.

Then there was George, the middle Deravenel brother. He had no loyalty to anyone but himself, of that she was certain. One day it will all go up in smoke, Nan said to herself, and then wondered why she had had such an irrational thought.

The clans of Watkins and Deravenel were intertwined forever. An unbreakable bond. That was what they all said. She just hoped it was true . . .

seventeen

The four men at the table in Neville's handsomely furnished dining room were quite different in style and personality, as disparate as any men could be.

Seated at the head of the table was the host, Neville, an aristocrat. At the other end of the table sat his cousin Edward, who dominated the scene because of his height and physique. Facing each other across the table were Alfredo Oliveri and Amos Finnister. They appeared to be at ease with each other, as well as with the patrician cousins and their luxurious surroundings. As usual, Alfredo appeared very English in his plain, dark gray suit. His pleasant demeanor attracted people to him and gave them confidence in him.

Amos Finnister was in his mid-forties, tall and thin with a slight stoop. His jet-black hair was touched with strands of gray, but his pencil-thin mustache was as black as his coal-dark eyes. He, too, was from the lower middle class. Street smart and intelligent, he was a man with strong instincts about people; it was this psychological insight which made him such an excellent private investigator.

Amos had started his professional life as a policeman on the beat. His years with the force had served him well, and he had nurtured most of his contacts long after he had left the force. Contacts who were as diverse as Scotland Yard de-

tectives and coroners, thugs, thieves, and underworld characters with information to deal or to sell.

Conservatively dressed in a black suit this afternoon, he
was always unremarkable in his appearance; Amos could
move through the diverse worlds he traveled without causing
a ripple or drawing attention to himself. He liked to boast
that he was invisible, and this was true.

Despite their differences, the four men were, conversely,
very similar. They all had integrity, a deeply ingrained sense
of duty and of what was right and wrong. They also shared
the same motive, which was to put Edward Deravenel in the
seat of power at Deravenels. They were convinced that, as
Richard Deravenel's son, he was the rightful heir to the company, knew without a trace of doubt that they were righting a
wrong committed over sixty years ago. Each of them had
vowed to stop at nothing in order to achieve their goal. And
because they were so certain they were fighting a deadly enemy, there were no holds barred.

For the last hour they had touched on many subjects which
interested them but had not mentioned their business at hand.
Neville had made it clear as they walked across the hall to the
dining room that it would be wiser to wait until they were
alone again before discussing their imminent plans.

Now, as they sipped their coffee and nursed their balloons
of Calvados, Neville said quietly, "So, let us review things."
Turning to Amos, he went on. "You have given us the best
ammunition so far, the knowledge that Grant is most probably insane. And you *will* get us the medical records as soon
as you can?"

Amos nodded. "Consider it done. And my people will
take any other records pertaining to Grant. We'll make a
good job of it, have no fear, sir."

"Excellent, and I think now would be a good time to fill
us in about John Summers and his crew. You did say you had
information."

Amos shifted slightly in the chair and cleared his throat.

"That's right, Mr. Watkins, I do. About Summers himself, there's nothing, nothing at all. He's as clean as a whistle. And so is Margot Grant, by the way, except for the resurfacing of that old rumor about her son's legitimacy. But some of the others, well, they're tarnished, sir, and in my opinion that plays in our favor."

His three companions leaned forward.

Amos smiled thinly as he explained. "They are so tarnished, in fact, they have left themselves wide open to blackmail."

"Have they now?" Neville exclaimed, his eyes narrowing. But he was not at all surprised. "Please do fill us in, Amos."

"James Cliff has rather foolishly antagonized both his wife and his mistress. He's caught in a vise between the two of them, who are both coldhearted females. Each is demanding more of his time. There's a strong rumor that his mistress is pregnant, which would really throw a spanner in the works, since his wife is the one with the money." Amos began to chuckle.

Everyone laughed with him, and Neville said disparagingly, "Yet another fool about to take a fall."

Amos continued, "Then there's Philip Dever, a secret homosexual with a hot young buck for a lover. No one knows this, of course, including his wife. And Jack Beaufield, I have discovered, has extremely sticky fingers. Financial problems and complications in his last position at another company. Not too careful, our Jack, when it comes to other people's money. That's all I have at the moment, but there'll be more. My operatives are still digging."

"Well done, very well done indeed," Neville said and took a long swallow of the brandy.

"I'm wondering about Aubrey Masters," Edward began, and his eyes met Alfredo's. They shared a knowing look, and Ned went on. "Finnister, did you manage to get anything on the head of the Mining Division?"

"Not a lot, Mr. Edward," Amos replied. "Masters is con-

sidered a little weird by the other employees. He's a vegetarian, and there's nothing amiss in that, except that he follows
a strange diet, consuming roots, seeds, pods, flowers, grains,
and all manner of unusual things, and he's attempted to get
others to join him. With no success, I might add. He has a
wife but no children, as you no doubt know. The wife stays
in the background, a bit of a recluse seemingly. He's considered an indifferent manager, dismissed by many as ineffectual and boring, and he's definitely not popular. He doesn't
seem to like to travel, which irritates his staff because he *is*
the head of the Mining Division."

"That's absolutely true about the traveling," Alfredo said.
"And that was one of the complaints Mr. Richard had about
him. Masters has long ignored our mining interests abroad,
has never gone to India, South Africa, or South America, and
he's only once been to Carrara. Somehow, Masters has always managed to shove those field trips onto his underlings.
I've long doubted his ability, and most people are at odds
with him. As for the peculiar diet, I don't know anything
about that, and I don't think it really matters." Shaking his
head, Alfredo finished. "Everyone believes as I do, that he's
in that job because he's the cousin of Henry Grant."

"My father said the same," Edward murmured and
glanced at Neville, laughed hollowly. "It's a pity Aubrey
Masters is in such good health."

"Isn't it just?" Neville responded with a cold smile. "But
please, don't anyone bring up that famous old question Who
will rid me of this turbulent priest? Or whatever it was. We
don't need murder in the cathedral at this moment."

"Too true, Cousin. Let us not turn Masters into a martyr
like Thomas à Becket."

Although he knew what the cousins were alluding to, Alfredo changed the subject. "Earlier you asked me how long I
would be in London, Mr. Edward. I have another week at the
head office, but I can stretch it to two if you wish. I have a

great deal to do on the situation in Carrara, and there are decisions to be made, so it could take longer."

"Do you think Masters will agree to your suggestion of purchasing new quarries?"

"It's a decision for the board. However, I believe they will listen to me. The old quarries are almost depleted; we must buy new ones to stay in business. That's what I think—"

Neville interrupted. "I think you must try to stay here as long as you can, Oliveri. We need you to gather as much information as possible since you're our only inside man with access to everyone. You're invaluable, you know, having been so long at Deravenels, and because you are so well trusted. And there is another reason. I can breathe easier knowing you are with Edward on a constant basis."

Nodding, Alfredo answered, "I will do my best to extend my visit. I'm as anxious as you to know what they're planning, and I agree, it's good for me to be able to keep an eye on Mr. Edward."

Focusing on Neville, Amos said in a firm voice, "Mr. Watkins, I know you worry about your cousin, but in my opinion Mr. Deravenel is perfectly safe, sir. I doubt that John Summers will do anything to hurt him or have him hurt by others. There's been excessive gossip about the fire in Italy and the family losses. After all, your father and Mr. Richard Deravenel were well-known figures in the business world. Summers is far too canny to do anything rash; he wouldn't want to attract attention to himself or to the Grants. Not after the fire in Carrara. Nor would he want to stir up old animosities. . . . The Grants are not particularly popular in the City. Some old hands haven't forgotten about Henry Grant's marauding grandfather."

Something struck Edward, and he murmured, "That's another thing, why not get some propaganda going about *that* old story? It won't do us any harm to paint the Grants black, you know. Actually, it would gain us even more sympathy if we remind people about those events, don't you think, Finnister?"

"I do indeed, sir, and I'll get my chaps on it at once."

For the next hour the four men remained seated at the dining table, avidly plotting and finally reaching decisions. As the afternoon drew on, they became even more confident of their ultimate triumph over their enemies.

eighteen

I'm so sorry I wasn't able to attend the lunch yesterday," Will said, his gaze fixed on Edward, who was sitting opposite him in the hansom cab. "I had to be in Leicestershire to meet with the family solicitors about the legacy my aunt left me."

"So you said," Edward replied, then added, "I hope it was a decent inheritance."

Will laughed. "Very decent indeed, Ned. Really generous. I was her only nephew, and she never married, so there were no children. I was her sole heir. Anyway, I couldn't get back to London until last night. How was the lunch with Neville and Oliveri?"

"It went very well," Edward responded. "I was very impressed with this man Amos Finnister. He's the private investigator Neville is using. I think he's going to prove invaluable to us. He's already dug up a lot of dirt, and most important, he discovered that Henry Grant has been incarcerated in *two insane asylums*. Finnister's convinced Grant is actually insane."

"Good God!" Will exclaimed, sitting up straighter, his amazement written across his face. "That *is* interesting news, and certainly it works in our favor."

"Yes, it does. Finnister has to get the medical records, because as Oliveri pointed out, the board of Deravenels will want proof in order to believe."

"If then," Will muttered. "You know the place is riddled with his cohorts. They'll defend him any way they can, do whatever it takes to keep him in power."

"Maybe they won't be able to do that," Edward answered, and in a low, rapid voice he began to tell Will everything that had been said, and ultimately agreed upon, at the lunch.

When Ned had finished, Will sat back, looking thoughtful for a few moments, and then he shook his head. "Certainly this Amos Finnister chap has handed you a number of lethal weapons . . . the possibility to blackmail, circulate bad propaganda, those kinds of things, but stealing the records might not be quite so easy."

"Neville assured me that if anyone can do it, it's Finnister. Or rather, some of the men he employs. I get the impression they're professional thieves."

"Well, I certainly trust Neville's judgment. By the way, have you told him I would like to work at Deravenels, once you've taken over?"

Edward began to laugh. "Another confident soul, I see, not even questioning the outcome. And yes, I have told him, and he was delighted. He even wondered aloud if you would consider working for him, until you could join me, and I said I would ask you."

"Neville wants me to work for him? Good God! But look here, Ned, what would I do?" Will's expression was one of total puzzlement.

"Chiefly, you would be . . . my boon companion," Edward explained. "Except you wouldn't be able to accompany me to Deravenels. However, he does want you to be with me at all other times. He's got a bee in his bonnet about my safety, even though Amos Finnister assured him they wouldn't dare make a move against me, *physically* that is, at the moment. Finnister says the deaths in Carrara have brought attention to the Grants. There's a lot of gossip going around about the tragedy, and about the Grants, too. Look, Will, Neville feels I shouldn't be wandering around town alone, and he thinks you're the best person to be at my side."

"But he doesn't have to employ me to do that, Ned! Surely he understands about our deep and abiding friendship."

"Of course he does. I suppose he wanted to put you on his payroll because he thinks you have to earn a living—"

"That's no longer necessary, because of the money my aunt has left me. It's not a great fortune, Ned, but it's enough to keep me quite comfortably, and my father still gives me a small allowance."

Edward nodded and said swiftly, "I hope you're not offended by his offer of money."

"Don't be silly, and the answer, by the way, is yes. I will certainly be your boon companion; that's not work, it's total pleasure."

Both young men laughed, and then Will's face became solemn and he said in a serious voice, "Rest assured that I *will* protect you. With my life. And always. Because like Neville, I believe the Grants will eventually try to get you in some way. And I don't want my best friend dead . . . I want him alive."

Edward nodded and gave Will a somewhat wry smile. "And your friend wants to stay alive, I can assure *you* of *that*." There was a moment's pause before he continued. "I'm certainly glad my mother decided to come to London. I've worried about them, especially the children. I'll be much happier having them at Charles Street with me. I know it is perfectly safe at Ravenscar, a house well protected by its location and the locals who are so devoted to us. Still, I have been concerned about them being there without me."

"That I understand, Ned, and you never know in life." Will sighed. "You just never know what might happen." He looked out of the window for a second, and then, bringing his steady gaze back to Edward, he asked, "Do you think your mother was afraid there? Is that why she's coming back to town today? Do you think she considered herself vulnerable at Ravenscar?"

"No, I don't, in all honesty. I know she's always felt safe there, but from what she said on the telephone last night, she became lonely without my father. Also, she had previously engaged John Pennington to tutor the boys and Perdita Willis to act as Meg's governess here for the next few months. Mind you, Will, she did say they have *all* missed me."

"She's done the right thing, coming back, and I feel better myself, having you all in *one* place," Will confided and then exclaimed, "Well, here we are, Ned, King's Cross Station!"

A moment later the two men were alighting from the hansom cab. Swinton, Edward's butler, was getting out of a second hansom just behind them, and he came to join Edward and Will. "I shall go and round up some porters, sir," Swinton announced. "Mrs. Deravenel told me there would be a quantity of luggage."

Edward nodded. "Mr. Hasling and I will go to the usual barrier and wait there, Swinton."

"Righto, sir."

Edward and Will hurried to the platform where the morning train from York would be pulling in within the next few minutes.

It was a cold Sunday afternoon, and the two men were bundled up in thick winter overcoats and woolen scarves. Tall, handsome, and well dressed, they stood out in the crowd, and it suddenly occurred to Will that Edward Deravenel would always stand out, because of his height and looks and that head of burnished red-gold hair. How to make him invisible? he asked himself. He had no answer. Yet he did know one thing, and it had troubled him for some time.

He was well aware that, as soon as the battle between the cousins began in earnest, Ned would be a moving target. How strange to think of murder—they lived in a civilized country, in a civilized age—yet he knew that dark powers were at work. Even Cecily Deravenel had said *that* to Edward.

Of all the Deravenels, Edward was the most vulnerable because he could take over the company, whereas his two brothers were just little boys. He is the true threat to the Grants, Will told himself, and on the back of his neck his hackles rose.

God help us all when it starts, Will thought, and his mind began to race as he wondered again how he would be able to keep his best friend safe. There was no obvious way, except to surround him with a phalanx of bodyguards. Which Ned wouldn't tolerate. But Neville would, and Neville would pay.

Will's thoughts were suddenly interrupted by Edward, who leaned closer to him. "I went to Belsize Park last night hoping to see Lily," he confided. "The housekeeper told me she had gone to the country for the weekend. Is she with Vicky in Kent, Will?"

"Yes, she is. They were planning to return tomorrow."

"I hope she's not angry with me. I didn't get a chance to see her last week, I was so preoccupied with Deravenels."

"Did you leave her a note yesterday?"

"I did."

"Then she'll be fine, Ned." Will looked at his friend and told him in a lowered voice, "She really loves you."

"And I love her."

"It can't go anywhere, though, now can it?"

"Nowhere at all, Will. But I do want to continue seeing her for the moment. She's a great comfort to me."

"We all need a little comfort at times," Will agreed.

At this moment a train whistle began to blow, and the York train came rumbling toward the barrier at Platform Five where the two men were standing.

Edward noticed Swinton, followed by two porters with luggage wagons, and within minutes, through the billowing clouds of steam and smoke, he spotted his mother. She was elegantly dressed in black, surrounded by his siblings. He saw her greet the butler and watched as she indicated the suitcases and trunks being unloaded onto the platform.

A moment later, his two brothers became aware he was waiting, and they raced toward him like greyhounds. The boys were suddenly flinging themselves at Edward and at Will, and the two young men were unexpectedly entangled in a mass of boyish arms and legs. And then there was Meg, looking so beautiful and sedate, followed by his mother, who was smiling at him.

Edward knocked on the door of the parlor and waited, entered the room only when his mother called, "Come in, Edward." She was seated at her small, kidney-shaped desk in the bay window and glanced up as he closed the door behind him.

"Peace reigns at last!" she exclaimed, shaking her head and sighing. "I thought that George would never stop chattering. And that Will would never leave."

Edward sat down in the chair facing the desk and exclaimed, "Yes, George was unusually garrulous, and as for Will outstaying his welcome, that was all my fault, Mother. I did invite him to have tea with us, and it somehow got out of hand. I'm so sorry." He studied her for a moment, then asked quietly, "Are you not feeling well?"

Cecily Deravenel gave him a long, puzzled look. "I'm perfectly fine, Ned, thank you. And please don't misunderstand, I like Will—No, let me correct myself, I love him, and you know very well he's been like a member of this family for years. The only reason I became so impatient was that I needed to be alone with you, and you seemed so embroiled with the children and Will."

He laughed. "Yes, my brothers most especially were all over me like chicken pox."

She smiled, her love for her eldest son written all over her face. Cecily leaned forward and fixed her soft blue-gray eyes, so like Richard's, on him intently. "The reason I came to London *today,* instead of in a few weeks' time, was to see you, Ned, and bring you this." She patted a small package wrapped in red silk which was on the desk.

"What is it?" he asked, eyeing the odd-looking bundle.

"The famous missing notebook," she replied a little triumphantly.

"I can't believe it! I thought *that* was lost forever! Where was it?" His excitement was apparent, his blue eyes sparkling.

"In the priest hole."

"*The priest hole.* There's a priest hole at Ravenscar?"

"Yes, there is," she answered and proceeded to tell him what had happened the day before, and explained the history of the old hiding place. When she had finished, she removed the red silk scarf, handed him the notebooks, and added, "There is a second book, Ned, full of jottings by your father. Most illuminating, *I* think, and it will be more useful to you than the actual notebook."

As he took the two black leather books from his mother, Edward asked, "But why would that be? I mean, Oliveri said my father always had his nose in the *notebook*."

"Maybe he did, but only your father understood what he was writing in it. I don't. It's full of numbers which seem quite meaningless. However, perhaps Oliveri will understand, or perhaps you yourself will. Your father spent a lot of time talking to you about Deravenels over the years."

"Yes, he did, but he never spoke to me about *numbers,* Mother." Ned opened the smaller notebook, scanned several pages, and then shook his head. "I see what you mean. I'm baffled, too. There *are* sentences here and there, as you no doubt saw, but I don't have a clue as to their meaning. Oh, here's a line that makes some sense. He wrote this. 'Necessary to talk to my compadre about two and eleven.' " Edward glanced up and shrugged his shoulders. "What on earth can that mean?"

"I have absolutely no idea, Ned. I wondered when I read

the sentence yesterday if it might be Oliveri he was referring
to as his *compadre.*"

"Perhaps. But it could be anybody, you know. However, do I
have your permission to show the notebook to Oliveri?"

"Of course. And as I said, I think you will find the second
book much more fascinating. It *is* going to help you achieve
your goals."

Edward jumped up, obviously anxious to delve into the
pages. At the door, he swung around. "Thank you for bringing the books to London, Mother, and so promptly."

"It seemed the safest way to get them to you."

Edward took the stairs two at a time. Once inside his room,
he locked the door, not wishing to have any intrusions
from his younger brothers. They had been so excited to
see him, he half anticipated a visit from one or both. He was
glad they were here in London, but at this moment he wanted
total privacy to read the notebook and the slightly larger
book, which looked like a diary. From the way his mother had
spoken, he believed the diary contained information about
Deravenels, Henry Grant, and his cronies. And Margot Grant.
He knew how much his mother hated the Lancashire faction,
the usurpers, as she referred to them with great bitterness.

Settling himself in front of the fire, Edward put the diary
on the floor and looked at the notebook first. Lines and lines
of numbers, page after page; an occasional written comment
that was meaningless, although he did realize, rather quickly,
that the comment usually referred to a number. The numbers
two, eleven, thirty-one, and thirty-nine recurred a lot. Not understanding what they referred to, Edward impatiently put the
notebook on a side table and bent down to retrieve the diary.

After scanning the many pages swiftly, he sat back and
turned to the beginning of his father's jottings. There was no
date at the top of the page, so he had no idea when his father
had started to write this, except that the ink was black, un-
faded, the white page crisp, new looking.

Edward's eyes were glued to the page; he began to read, filled with eagerness and not a little trepidation.

I am at my wit's end. I do not know what to do about Margot Grant. She is worse than ever, and I worry about Harry. My cousin is not a bad man, nor is he evil, like his wife. Actually, Henry is just a poor soul, out of his depth. We were such good friends when we were younger, spent much time together, and I was not only loyal to him but a devoted cousin, his close friend, just as he was mine.

The trouble with Henry is that he has always been the most pious of men, entangled with priests, full of devotion, wanting only to mingle with the clergy. And he made them his companions, listened to them, took their advice. And he loved to go to church, studying the Bible. His thoughts were always on God, not business, and it is still that way. Deravenels never really meant anything to him. Nor does it now. Oh yes, he was, and is, proud to be the chairman, sitting in the seat once occupied by his magnificent father, and his grandfather before that. But he did not want to run the company, cannot run it, and he knows that now. This is the reason I call him the absentee landlord.

He is a vague, distracted, lazy man; contemplating God is his favorite pastime, so he lets the French-woman do his job, at least he permits her to give orders to John Summers and James Cliff. They are devoted to her, but they do not follow her guidelines. They dismiss her orders, believing they are far too clever to be instructed by her. Especially Summers. He takes after his late father; like him he is a handsome man, personable, intelligent. And ambitious. He means to take more and more power, I know that.

I worry about Harry because he's no match for Margot, or for them. He's daft in the head, I believe. It has come back, the dementia which so incapacitated him seven years ago. For one year he was like a zombie; he was wandering around as if in catatonic shock, or in a trance. Until they put him in an asylum for treatment. But they lied to all of us in the company, said he was in a religious retreat.

Long before his marriage to the Frenchwoman, he made me his heir because he knew full well I was the true heir, and the board asked me to take charge when he was put away. Put in a padded cell. And I did. I executed my duties well. Then, suddenly, he was back. He had made a remarkable recovery. And I stepped aside, which was only right.

Within days Margot gave birth to her son, Edouard. Her heir. But was he Harry's heir? Was he really Harry's son? I doubt it; many doubt it. Harry Grant has always lived like a monk. In every way. And the dates were doubtful. Everyone said so.

I was never her enemy in the beginning. But she has always treated me as one, and over the years she has been vicious to me and mine. And she has succeeded in turning me into her enemy. What a fool she is.

And I fear for Henry, fear for his welfare. His wife has such ambitions. For her son. For herself. For John Summers.

I have no proof, but I do believe he warms her bed, as his late father did. And surely her son is Summers's half brother. So Edouard does not have a drop of Deravenel blood in him.

Edward sat back, holding the book on his knee, staring into the flames, his thoughts racing.

First of all, his father had confirmed Amos Finnister's story that Henry Grant had been in and out of insane asylums. Well, at least *once*, according to this diary. But wasn't his father also saying that his cousin had always been as mad as a hatter . . . "daft in the head," those were his father's damning words.

Turning the page, Edward began to read once more, and then he realized that his father was now writing only about Ravenscar and his great love for his ancestral home. Edward scanned the pages swiftly, genuinely wanting to know what his father had to say yet impatient to move on to more important entries.

Suddenly there it was, a new entry on a new page, and the date was written very clearly: September 1, 1902. Almost a year and a half ago.

Holding the book tightly, Edward read his father's words rapidly; from the very first line he felt a tingle of anticipation.

> *I have made my mind up. I shall no longer procrastinate. I shall gather all of my notes together, notes made over the years, and I shall prepare my case. And I do have a case to present to the board of directors. Long, long ago, my ancestors made a rule—that any director of Deravenels, whether a board member or a junior director, could present a case to them if he had a serious grievance against the company. I do. I have a complaint against Henry Grant. He is allowing Deravenels, one of the greatest trading companies in the world, to be run into the ground. By himself, a man who is daft in the head. I have the proof. I shall use it. I will take what is mine to take. They cannot refuse to hear me. It is my right as a director, and as a Deravenel, which is even more important. I am going to fight them. I hope I shall win. I think I shall win. The board must remain neutral, and they know this; I believe there is enough neutrality among them to permit justice and fair play to prevail. I must find my copy of the company rules; all of those old documents are important for backup. The board won't deny my petition to speak, but it is always a good idea to be prepared.*

Now there was not a doubt in Edward's mind that his father had given him powerful weapons to fight the Grants; first, he had confirmed that Henry Grant was mentally deficient and unable to run the company. Edward knew enough about the company rules to know that Deravenels could not under any circumstances be run by "stand-ins," as his mother usually called Grant's cronies. Now there was the old company rule that gave a director the right to present a case to the board. Obviously, his father had never done what he'd vowed to do. But *he* would. By God, he would.

Edward continued to read for another hour, finding a lot more useful information. But as far as he was concerned, he had already found the most important.

L ater that evening, Edward and his mother discussed his father's diary. They were both in agreement that he had some potent weapons in his hands now.

She promised to find the old documents among which were the company rules; he told her all about Amos Finnister and his discoveries.

They made their plans.

nineteen

Edward Deravenel knew he would always remember how he felt this morning as he mounted one side of the great double staircase that rose up from the central lobby of Deravenels.

He felt like a new man. He was filled with pride; he was happy; his self-assurance was at its height. As he glanced around, he felt reassured by this gargantuan building, which in a sense was his and where he now knew he would spend the rest of his life. He was secure in the knowledge that he would win, and not only a battle or two. He would win the war. He would rule Deravenels. It was his destiny.

His parents had raised him to understand fully who he was, what he was about, and where he came from. Naturally he had grown up to be self-confident. He was proud of his heritage, but there was not one ounce of snobbery in him; he was at ease with himself and with everyone else, from whatever walk of life. In part, this ease would prove to be the secret of his success, but he did not know this now.

When he had started working here last week, he had felt slightly inhibited, and certainly he had been on guard. Everyone was suspect as far as he was concerned; and he was still wary of the men who were employed here, especially Henry Grant's cronies. But he had a better understanding of the various echelons now, thanks to Alfredo Oliveri.

He truly understood about his right to be head of this ancient company. *He was the rightful heir.* Because of that he would never permit the progeny of usurpers to mismanage it, and he would oust the "stand-ins" along with Grant himself. Only a Deravenel by birth could be managing director or chairman, and other than Grant, he was the sole one available.

As Edward strode along the corridor to his father's office, which was now his, he thought of the diary. It had hardly been out of his mind since last night, when his mother had passed it on to him. There was so much in it, so many guidelines from his father. It was going to be his Bible. Every word was meaningful, and possession of it had made him feel *entitled*.

He had just taken off his overcoat and hung it up when Alfredo came barreling into the office, his arms full of books and papers. "Good morning, Mr. Edward." The manager gave him a cheery grin from behind the books.

"Good morning, Oliveri, and here, let me help you with all this stuff. What is it, anyway?"

"Homework, sort of. Yours, to be exact."

"Mine?" Edward gave him a questioning look as he lifted some of the books and papers off the top of the pile. "Are you serious?"

"Indeed I am." Alfredo deposited everything he was carrying on the desk, as did Edward, glancing at the titles as he did so. "Aha! Books on mining I see! And *wine.* And the making of Egyptian *cotton.* You want me to study these books so I know something about the various divisions, what we trade in. Am I right?"

"Yes. You said you have a photographic memory. Is that true?"

"Absolutely. But why do you ask?"

"Because you can't merely read, you've got to memorize some of this material, and there's lots of it. Once you're chairman of the company, you must be able to hold your own with the heads of the various divisions, who are obviously knowledgeable. You're going to be boss, you'll be *it*. I must make sure you're fully prepared."

Edward knew that Alfredo meant every word he was saying, and he was touched that the man had gone to all this trouble for him. "Thank you for doing this. Really, Oliveri, this is very decent of you, and I appreciate it."

Edward sat down behind the desk, and Alfredo pulled a chair closer to the desk. "Now shall we begin? I'd like to start with the Mining Division, because I am involved with it, and you told me the other day you're interested in diamonds, in the mining of them and—"

"Listen to me for a moment," Edward cut in. "I have something quite extraordinary to tell you. My mother found the notebook."

Alfredo was startled, and for a moment he was speechless.

"Here it is," Edward said, taking the notebook out of his pocket and handing it to him. "See if you can make head or tail of it."

Alone in his own office, Alfredo started at the beginning of the notebook, concentrating on every page, trying to decipher the numbers. But they meant nothing to him. He could not fathom what Richard Deravenel had been getting at, nor could he hazard a guess about the person Richard referred to as *compadre*. Certainly Mr. Richard had never called *him* that, nor had he ever discussed *numbers* with him.

Alfredo thought back to the last time they had seen each other . . . in Carrara, just before Mr. Richard had been killed. The older man had complained bitterly about Grant in a most confiding way, and he had said he was alarmed by the spiraling problems in the company, Grant's colleagues, and the problems with the Carrara marble quarries. But that was it. Alfredo had told Mr. Edward everything he knew, although Edward Deravenel had seemed to expect *more*. There was nothing more.

After an hour of studying the notebook, Alfredo got up, put it in his pocket, and went back to Edward's office down the corridor.

Knocking and then walking in, Alfredo exclaimed, "I'm sorry, I'm as baffled as you. Bloody annoying it is. The notebook is gibberish."

Edward was standing in front of the enormous map of the world which hung on the wall behind the huge Georgian partners desk. He swung around at the sound of Alfredo's voice. There was a peculiar look on his face as he said slowly, in a low voice, "Come here, look at this."

Staring at Edward, Alfredo asked, "But what is it? What's wrong? You have a strange look on your face."

"Just come over here. Please."

Alfredo did as he was asked, stood next to Edward in front of the map.

Edward put his middle finger on his tongue, dampened it, and touched a small number on the map. The ink bled out. "See how the ink runs? That's because the number's been written on this map, not printed. And written by my father, of that I am sure. It's the number *two,* and it sits up there at the top of India, just between Delhi and the Punjab. See it?"

"Oh yes, indeed I do."

"Now look over here, at South Africa, and you'll see the number eleven. Let your eyes sweep over to South America; the number thirty-nine is written there." Stepping back slightly, looking closely at Alfredo, Edward asked, "So you tell me. What do those three numbers have in common?"

It was obvious that Alfredo was excited. "The numbers are written on the countries where Deravenels have mines: diamond mines in India, gold mines in South Africa, and emerald mines in South America."

"Correct!" Edward grinned at him.

"My God, how did you discover the numbers?" Glancing at the map again, Alfredo added, "You almost need a magnifying glass to find them."

Pointing to the books open on his desk, Edward explained swiftly, "I was reading about diamond mines in India, especially the famous Golconda mines. I knew ours were somewhere nearby, so I got up to look at the map. I noticed the number there all of a sudden, almost by accident, just below the Punjab, and I realized it hadn't been printed on but *written* by hand. My eyes roved over the entire map, I was so intrigued, and I kept finding numbers—" He broke off, shook his head. "It hit me then! The country numbers were those which were repeated so often in my father's notebook."

Alfredo was nodding his head slowly, enlightenment spreading across his pale face. "Listen, your father gave each country a number, and then used the number in the notebook instead of a name. It was a coding system. I think he didn't want anyone to know which countries he was targeting for some reason. Anyone picking the notebook up would be baffled."

"But why didn't he want anyone to know which countries he was referring to?"

"I think he'd stumbled onto something. In Carrara he told me he was worried not only about the quarries there, which were dwindling, but about lots of the other mines as well. I asked him if they, too, were dwindling, and he said no, there were other difficulties. But he didn't go any further than that."

Alfredo took the notebook out of his pocket and passed it to Ned, then went and sat down in the chair. "You'd better have that. I'd hate to lose it."

Sitting down himself, Edward confided, "I think I know who he meant by *compadre*. My uncle Rick Watkins."

Alfredo frowned. "Why Rick?"

"Because they *were* the best of friends, true *compadres,* and had been close for donkey's years. Rick was my mother's brother, and therefore family, and obviously someone he trusted absolutely. Then there's yet another thing. Rick Watkins was probably the greatest magnate in this country; there was no other tycoon like him. Therefore, my father could rely on his judgment. It just suddenly made sense to me as I was staring at the map. Rick came into my mind, and I knew I was right."

"I agree. Who better than Rick Watkins to advise your father? Unless it was his son."

"True. However, I'm sure my father was much closer to Neville's father."

Sitting back in his chair, staring into space for a moment or two, Edward seemed to drift into another world, a world only he could envision. Then he sat up abruptly and looked at Alfredo intently. Lowering his voice, he said, "That's why Rick and Thomas were killed. They were murdered on purpose. Not because they just happened to be there in Carrara. The Grant faction was afraid of Rick Watkins, his power, his wealth, his brilliance as a businessman. They knew if push came to shove, Rick would throw everything he had at them to support my father and his claim for the top job at Deravenels. My brother was murdered *because* he was a Deravenel, a contender for the top job if anything happened to me."

Pale as he was, Alfredo appeared to grow paler. He did not speak for a moment. Finally he murmured, "I can't argue with you, Mr. Edward, I really can't. I think you are right. And—"

The door of the office burst open, swinging back on its hinges. "So here you are," a woman's shrill voice exclaimed, and as she strode into the room Edward knew at once that this was Margot Grant.

He had met her several times, but when he was much younger, and he had forgotten how very beautiful she was. Her skin was white and flawless, her hair raven black and luxuriant, glossy, upswept into the latest style. Large, luminous black eyes stared out from under perfectly arched black brows. Her incomparable and dramatic beauty was matched

by her willowy figure and her clothes, which were the height
of fashion.

Coming fully into the room, she closed the door behind
her and gave Edward a cursory look, then turned her attention on Alfredo furiously. "I've been looking all over for
you!" she cried in perfect English only slightly accented.
"How dare you hold these meetings about the Carrara quarries without my presence!"

Alfredo took a deep breath, obviously striving to control
his temper. "The matter is urgent, and you were not here last
week, Mrs. Grant. Because of the urgency, I held my meetings with Aubrey Masters and other executives involved in
the Mining Division. But you know all this. And there is nothing wrong with my doing that, you know."

"I represent my husband at this time. I run this company,
and I will not tolerate insubordination."

"There wasn't any," Alfredo shot back. "And I won't have
you suggesting that there was."

"You must not speak to me in that tone—"

"Hey, hold on a minute," Edward cut in. "Let me just
point out one thing to you, *madam.* You do not run this
company!"

"Oh, but I do," she exclaimed. "And why are *you* here?
You have no right to occupy this office. Pack your posses-
sions and get out."

"Oh, but I have the right. You had better go and look at
the company rules, Mrs. Grant. You will quickly discover
that I have every right to be here at Deravenels, to occupy
my father's office, to be a director of this company, and to
work here. For one very simple and undeniable reason. *I am
a Deravenel.* You are not a Deravenel by birth, and therefore
you cannot run this company; you shouldn't even be here.
Because in those company rules you will find a clause which
says only a woman who is a *born Deravenel* can work in the
company and hold a directorship. Other women may work

here as secretaries and receptionists but not hold a position as an executive."

"Ah, ce n'est pas possible!" she cried, reverting to her native French.

"Oh, but it is possible!" Edward responded, a knowing smile playing upon his mouth. He moved forward and was suddenly standing in front of her.

Staring up at him, Margot Grant saw the handsomeness of this man, became aware of the raw sex appeal oozing out of him, and she stepped back, glaring. But she was silent for once, taken aback by his charismatic presence. He overwhelmed her.

Edward continued. "I will not get out, and don't you ever dare suggest that to me again. You are the one who is a trespasser here, not I, *madam.*"

Feeling unexpectedly humiliated, Margot swung around and left Edward's office without another word.

Once the door had closed behind her, Alfredo grinned at Edward and said, "That was telling *her* where to get *off.*"

"She's one of the most beautiful women I've ever seen," Edward said almost wonderingly.

"But she's also a bitch, and evil," Alfredo pointed out in an almost inaudible voice. "Don't ever forget that."

Neville met Edward and Alfredo for lunch at Rules that day. The wonderful old restaurant just off the Strand was a favorite of his, and after Edward's urgent telephone call, he had made a reservation for one o'clock and been accommodated immediately.

The three men sat at the best table in the house, studying their menus as they waited for Amos Finnister to arrive. They had just selected their food and were relaxing with aperitifs when Amos hurried in.

"So sorry to be late," he apologized, "but I got caught up with . . . some of my operatives." As he took a seat opposite

Neville, he added, with a small, satisfied smile, "I have set things in motion, sir. Regarding those . . . er . . . records."

Neville smiled warmly. "I have no qualms about you," he replied. "I know how dedicated and efficient you are. Now, have a look at the menu and let's order lunch. In the meantime, would you like to join us in a glass of sherry?"

"Thank you kindly, Mr. Watkins, but I won't, if you don't mind. I've got my hands full today. And I'd better be sober."

Laughing, Neville nodded. "As you wish, Amos, although I don't think one drink would do any harm."

Again Amos declined, picked up the menu, and studied it. Within a few minutes the four men had ordered, and with their heads together, Neville said, "Now that we're all here, let's have it, Ned, my boy. What is your important news? Other than finding the notebooks and your father's diary, which you informed me about already."

Keeping his voice low, Edward told Neville and Amos about the discovery of the numbers on the map, and what he believed they meant. He also confided that he thought Neville's father had been the person Richard referred to as *compadre*.

"To tell you the truth, my boy, that had occurred to me, too. Who else would your father trust so implicitly? Now, to the discovery of the numbers on the map. Let me ask you something. Why did your father keep listing those particular mines in the notebook? Not just because they were *mines*, surely. There's another reason."

"I think there is something wrong with the mines," Alfredo volunteered. "What this is I can't hazard a guess. But something's amiss, I feel positive. Mr. Richard was troubled when he was in Carrara, and as I've told you before, the reason *he* came to Italy instead of Aubrey Masters was that he wanted to get to the bottom of the problem there. Which is the dwindling of the marble in the quarries we own. As for the mines in those other countries, maybe they have the same problem."

"I doubt it," Neville answered. "I think my uncle would have told my father, and certainly my father would have mentioned it to me. It's something else."

"But what?" Edward asked worriedly. "What *could* it be?"

"I don't know." Neville shook his head. "You and Oliveri here have to keep your eyes and ears open. You mustn't miss . . . a trick."

"I understand," Edward replied and then laughed. "I had quite a run-in with Margot Grant this morning."

"He was superb, really told her off," Alfredo said proudly.

"Did you?" Neville raised a brow, his pale blue eyes twinkling.

"I told her that she had better go and read the company rules. That she would soon discover she wasn't even allowed at Deravenels. Well, that's an exaggeration. But she left without another word."

"I'm afraid we haven't heard the last from her," Neville muttered. "Not by a long shot."

At the end of the afternoon, Edward went to see Lily. He had missed her, and he knew he must make amends for having neglected her the previous week.

It was Mrs. Dane, the housekeeper, who opened the door, and immediately her face lit up. "Why, Mr. Deravenel, good afternoon, sir. How nice to see you."

"Good afternoon, Mrs. Dane," he answered and smiled at her warmly.

Her immediate response to his undeniable charm was to open the door wider. "Please come in, Mr. Deravenel. I'll tell Mrs. Overton you're here." Closing the door and turning the key, Mrs. Dane continued, "She hasn't been too well today. Please, do come into the drawing room."

"I hope it's nothing serious," Edward said, sounding concerned as he entered the drawing room, which faced the frosty-looking garden.

"Oh no, sir, I think she's just a bit under the weather."

Mrs. Dane offered him a small smile as she hurried away, adding, "Please excuse me for a moment, sir."

Edward wandered around the room, feeling slightly on edge, wondering what could be wrong with his darling Lily. As he thought of her, of her femininity, her blond beauty, her loveliness and warmth, her kindness to him over the year they'd been together, he suddenly realized something vital about her. Lily's beauty was soft, genuine, angelic; Margot Grant's beauty was dramatic but cold, hard. She was a hard-boiled woman, a woman filled with ambition, a woman on the make . . .

"Mrs. Overton would like you to join her in the upstairs parlor," Mrs. Dane was saying from the doorway.

"Thank you," he answered and hurried out. At the bottom of the staircase he turned to the housekeeper. "I'll find my own way up, thank you so much, Mrs. Dane."

She nodded and disappeared in the direction of the kitchen. Realizing that he still wore his overcoat, that the flustered housekeeper had forgotten to take it from him, he slipped it off and laid it on a nearby chair.

He was halfway up the staircase when a vision in floating white chiffon and lace appeared at the top. *"Edward. Darling!"* Lily exclaimed. "It's lovely to see you here."

He took her in his arms and brought her close, kissed her cheek, her neck, her hair. "I've missed you so much, my darling," he said softly, then held her away and looked deeply into her face. "What's wrong? Mrs. Dane said you're not feeling well."

Lily touched his cheek lovingly. "It's nothing. I felt tired today, Ned, a little weary." She laughed lightly. "I suppose I'm getting old."

"Old. You? Never." Putting his arm around her, he walked her into the parlor. It was as cozy as ever, with a fire burning in the grate; the gas lamps had been lighted, creating a roseate glow, and vases of fresh flowers gave the room a feeling of spring.

"I must apologize, Lily," he said, sitting on the sofa as he usually did. "I ought to have been in touch last week, but I was swimming in deep waters, so to speak."

"It's all right," she murmured. "I wondered what had happened to you, and then this weekend Vicky told me how busy you had been with your work." She gave him a pretty, dimpled smile, and finished. "So you're forgiven."

"I hope to God I am. Because I couldn't do without you, Lil, I really couldn't. You make me feel happier and more relaxed." He paused and looked her up and down. "Amongst the many other *things* you make me feel, you temptress," he added, his brilliant sapphire eyes growing most seductive.

Lily was silent for a moment. She pulled her white peignoir around her body and smoothed a hand over her hair. "I'm sorry I'm not properly dressed. You see, I was in bed when you arrived."

"Why don't we go back there, my love? What better place for us to be"? As he spoke he rose, strode across the room, bent over her. Tilting her face to his, he kissed her lightly on the lips. "Come back to bed, Lily. This time with me. Let me love you, sweetheart, let me pleasure you, we won't do anything too . . . hectic since you're not feeling well. Actually, you don't have to do anything at all. *I* will make love to *you*."

"Oh, Ned, there's no one like you," she breathed softly, smiling up at him, all of her anxiety about him instantly blown away.

"I hope not . . . at least, not in *your* heart. Come on, my pet." He pulled her gently to her feet and led her across the landing and into her bedroom. Within moments he had her resting on the bed, and he was kissing her tenderly. He stopped abruptly, went back to the door and locked it, then took off his coat and waistcoat, threw them on a chair, unknotted his tie, walked back to the bed. He began to unbutton his shirt as he stood looking down at her, smiling knowingly. Once it was unbuttoned, he brought Lily to her feet, held her close. "You'll never know how much I missed you last week," he murmured and untied the white silk ribbon at her throat. Slipping the peignoir off to reveal her smooth, creamy shoulders, he went on, "And I know that you missed me, didn't you?"

Their eyes met. Deep green impaled brilliant blue and locked. Neither looked away. At last he bent down to her, kissed her, let his tongue slide into her mouth . . . so warm, so soft. The taste of her thrilled him. He gave the nightgown a slight pull, and it fell to her feet; he took off his shirt and brought her to him, closed his arms around her. "Remember what I said, nothing hectic," he whispered against her tumbling gold hair.

"But I want it to be wonderfully hectic," she whispered back and began to unbutton his trousers, fumbling as she did so.

"I'll do it," he muttered, and she went back to the bed and lay down on her side, watching him finish undressing. As he walked toward her, she was momentarily startled. How had he become so aroused so quickly? She shivered slightly. He seemed so potent, so virile, more than ever at this moment.

One of the things Lily loved about Ned was that he did not rush at her, handle her roughly. He was always gentle, loving, giving her pleasure before he took his own. And this afternoon was no different; he stroked her, touched her, kissed her breasts, brought her nipples to tender points. His hands trailed over her lightly, touched her neck, her hair, her stomach, slid between her thighs, encountered her most feminine part, brought her sighing to pleasure until she was calling his name. Entering her, he pressed his hands under her back and lifted her toward him, and their movements together were rhythmic: as always they were in tune with each other, as one. And they soared together, carried by their joy in each other, and their ecstasy. And when he was spent, when he rested against her, sighing and stroking her face, he said quietly, in a low, very serious voice, "Only you, Lily, only you."

• • •

It was almost nine o'clock when Amos Finnister arrived in Whitechapel. As he stepped out of the hansom cab, he said to the driver, "Wait for me here. I'll be about an hour, no longer."

The driver touched his cap. "I'll be right 'ere, guv."

Amos walked away, thinking what a lovely night it was. Sky like black velvet, splattered with an array of silver stars. Dazzling. Cold, but not too cold. No wind. Yes, a nice night. He stood for a moment looking out toward the Thames. He had always loved this long, flowing river; when he had been a small boy, his father had brought him down here to the East End, brought him to the docks, told him wonderful, magical stories . . . stories of the tall ships which sailed in from all over the world, carrying chests of tea from Ceylon, gold from Africa, diamonds from India, sapphires from Burma, spices from the West Indies, silk from China . . . exotic goods transported and traded. . . . How adventurous it had sounded to him then. It still did, if the truth be known.

Whitechapel. A mixture of humanity—folk from all over the world. He knew this place so very well, not only from those childhood visits to see the big ships and eat whelks and winkles out of a bag with his father. But from his days on the beat, when he had patrolled this place every night. Friend and foe alike down here near the docks. Still, it was colorful, and cheerful, despite the poverty that prevailed, the degradation and the vice, the crime. He had many friends down here. Some of them were the costermongers, who sold their goods from barrows and carts, and their pearly kings and queens who ruled the roost, talked rhyming slang and boasted of being born within the sound of Bow bells. Good people.

Not a bad place, Whitechapel. Worse places in this heathen world.

Amos sniffed. What a fragrant smell that was, floating to him on the night air. He sniffed again, transported to his past for a split second. Thoughts of his father returning. His Da, such a good man. Killed too soon, in the line of duty. A copper like he had been, and perhaps that was why he had become a bobby. To honor his father's memory.

Amos stopped. Sniffed again. And decided to buy a meat pie. His mouth was watering so much he simply couldn't resist.

Within seconds he spotted the man with the cart and increased his pace. As he drew to a standstill, the vendor touched his cap respectfully. "Evenin', guv. Want a Cornish or a meaty?"

"A meat pie. With plenty of gravy, please."

"Best in Whitechapel, me wife is, best cook is wot I means, a'course." The vendor took a pair of tongs, clamped them on a pie, and showed it to Amos. "See its crusty top? Bootiful brown, guv." As he spoke, the man placed the pie in a small white paper bag, picked up a ladle of gravy, and dribbled it over the pie.

"How much is it?" Amos asked, anxious to take a bite.

"Tuppence, guv."

Amos paid, took the bag with the pie, bade the man good night, and walked off; he was smelling the pie with pleasure, waiting for it to cool. A moment or two later he sat on a wall under a streetlamp and slowly munched on the meat pie, enjoying himself better than he had in a long time.

The pie was his supper, and such a treat. Much tastier than the slice of bread and cheese Lydia perpetually offered him, or her other mainstay, cold lamb on a bread bun. He sighed to himself, hating his sudden critical thoughts of his wife. She wasn't well, really. It was her migraines which bothered her the most. And sometimes rheumatism. Poor Lydia. Full of aches and pains. Always miserable. Never a happy thought these days. Poor Lydia. Indeed.

Amos had demolished the pie in short order, and now, as he wended his way down toward Limehouse, he decided he needed a drink. Perhaps a pint to wash down the pie, he decided. Why not?

The Black Swan was hereabouts; the Mucky Duck the locals called it. As it hove into sight, Amos hurried his steps, was swinging in through the double doors within seconds.

At the bar he asked for a pint of bitter and swigged some of it down immediately, frothy, delicious. He might even have another one.

The bartender came back, peered at him in the murky gaslight. "Used ter be a copper round 'ere, din't yer?"

"That's right." Amos smiled at him. "Retired now. Finnister's the name."

The bartender chuckled. "I remembers now. Sinister Finnister we used ter call yer."

Amos laughed with the man, drank up his beer, put his money on the counter, said good night, and promptly left. He set out again for Chinatown in Limehouse, an area filled with small shops where all manner of goods were sold, from silks, clothes, and jewelry to medicines and herbs; Chinese laundries, Chinese shops, restaurants, and even opium dens also dotted the streets. Amos loved the food the Chinese made, and he had forgotten about it until this moment. He had fallen hard for the fragrant wafts of the pies of his youth. Too late now to partake of the Chinese food. Another night.

It was not long before Amos reached his destination. Mr. Fu Yung Yen had a small shop set back from the street; the light was burning in the window as Amos hurried toward the door. After he rapped several times and proclaimed, "It's Amos Finnister," the door was finally opened.

Fu Yung Yen was dressed in a long black cotton gown with a small stand-up collar; he had a long pigtail, and a round porkpie hat was perched on top of his graying hair. He smiled when he saw Amos and said in his whispery voice, "Come inside. Cold night."

The shop was dimly lit, and there was a strong smell of spices, herbs, and roots in the air. Mixed in was the whiff of camphor and perfumed oils. It was not an unpleasant smell, and Amos never minded coming to the shop.

"How is wife?" the Chinaman asked, smiling.

"Bad migraines again, Mr. Yung Yen. I need her usual headache powders, please."

The Chinese herbalist nodded and went behind the counter, began taking portions of white powders out of various pots. Finally, after pounding them together, he poured the mixture into a small paper packet, sealed it, and handed it to Amos.

"I need the ointment for her aches and pains . . . pains in the limbs."

"Ah yes. Understand. My balm." This too was quickly produced, already in its own small glass pot.

Leaning over the counter, looking at Mr. Yung Yen intently, Amos handed him a small piece of paper. "Do you happen to have this in stock?"

The herbalist read it and nodded. "How much you need?"

"Whatever you think."

"For one good long sleep, yes?"

Amos nodded.

"Wait minute." The Chinaman disappeared through a door, and it was a while before he returned. He put a small package wrapped in purple paper on the counter.

"Thank you," Amos said. "How much do I owe you?"

Smiling, Fu Yung Yen made out a bill.

Amos read it, read it again, took out his money, and paid without protest.

After putting the various packets away in his overcoat pockets, he nodded. "Good night, Mr. Yung Yen. And thank you."

"Come back."

"I will," Amos answered, but as he left the shop he wondered if he ever would. Well, he did have what he had *really* come for, didn't he? The contents of the packet made of purple paper. That was what mattered, not how much it had cost. He patted his pocket: Yes, it was safe there, safe until it had to be used.

twenty

It was late when Edward left Lily's house, much later than he had intended. And now, as he crossed Belsize Park Gardens and headed toward the main road, he realized hansom cabs were scarce in this area. There was not one in sight. Glancing around again, noting that the road was almost devoid of traffic, he set out to walk, telling himself he would come across a hansom in no time at all.

As he headed for Primrose Hill, leading toward the center of London, his mind automatically went to the numbers in his father's notebook and the conclusion he and Alfredo had come to that there was some kind of trouble with the mines producing gold and precious gems. The number for Burma had not been written in the notebook, so they both presumed the production of sapphires was continuing without problems, as it had for some years.

The man who approached him had sprung up from nowhere, or so it seemed to Edward.

"Egscuse me, guv," he said in a guttural Cockney voice. "Can yer tells me 'ow to get ter 'ampstead? I be lost."

Edward shook his head. "I'm so sorry, I'm afraid I can't," he replied, as polite as always. "However, if you keep heading north, I think you'll be going in the right direction."

The blow came from behind, the heavy truncheon striking him on the shoulder and then on the back. The brute force of the blows brought him to his knees, and he cried out, clutching at the air as he fell, almost as if he were reaching out for the stranger who had just spoken to him. The man was not there, Edward realized; he had disappeared.

Another blow came down, this time on the crown of his head. Edward fell forward instantly, his face hitting the ground. He was knocked unconscious.

There were three men altogether, the pedestrian who had distracted the target and the two giant bruisers who were armed with truncheons. The three men conferred for several seconds; then one of the assailants bent over Edward, peered at him, and straightened.

"Don't t'ink e's breeving, mebbe 'e's dead," the assailant whispered and straightened. "Best we get goin' afore the bleedin' coppers get 'ere."

The men ran off down the road. It was so deserted the sound of their boots was like thunder. Drizzling rain and the wind, which had now blown up, were keeping everyone at home tonight.

Edward lay on the pavement where he had fallen. The road remained empty for a long time.

Neville sat with Amos in the waiting room of Guy's Hospital, silently praying that Ned would be all right, that he would regain consciousness soon. He had been badly beaten, but it was the blows to the head which were causing the problems.

The two men remained silent. Neville, ashen-faced, his expression bleak, was so worried he did not want to talk; Amos did not dare. He was afraid to intrude on his distracted employer's thoughts.

The door opened suddenly, and Neville's wife, Nan, stood there with Cecily Deravenel. The two women hurried in, and Neville instantly went to greet them. Placing his arm around his aunt, he led her over to a chair and introduced her to Amos.

Nan had already met Amos, since he was a frequent visitor to the house. It was she who now turned to him and said, "Thank you, Mr. Finnister, for everything you've done for Mr. Deravenel. If it hadn't been for you, I don't know what would have happened to him."

"It was lucky I happened to have my man on duty, keeping an eye on Mr. Edward," Amos murmured. "I know the young gentleman will be better in a few days. I feel it in my bones."

Looking intently at Amos, Cecily said in a warm voice, "I want to thank you, Mr. Finnister, for all you've done for my son. But I'm still not sure what exactly happened last night." She glanced from Amos to Neville. "Who was it that attacked Ned?"

"We don't know, Aunt Cecily. The police think it was a random attack, more than likely a robbery. Edward had only loose change on him, no banknotes when he was found. They must have been in a hurry, because his gold pocket watch was not taken." Neville shook his head. "The problem is the police have no leads."

"Why do you say *they,* as in 'They must have been in a hurry'?" Cecily asked, staring at her nephew.

"For obvious reasons, Aunt. Edward is taller than most men, and very strong. It would take several men to overpower him, in my opinion."

"Yes, of course, I see what you mean." Taking a deep breath, she went on softly in a saddened voice, "You would have told me if there was any news, so I'm making the assumption there isn't any."

"I'm afraid not." Neville touched her arm consolingly.

Cecily bit her lip, tears suddenly brimming, and she instantly stood up, walked across to the window and remained there looking out until she had recovered her equilibrium.

Returning to the chair, she said to Amos, "Would you be kind enough to tell me the whole story, Mr. Finnister? I'm afraid I'm a little confused, perhaps because I'm so upset."

"It's not surprising, Mrs. Deravenel, under the circumstances. I'd be happy to fill you in, so to speak. It's like this. . . . From time to time, Mr. Watkins and I have discussed the possibility that Mr. Edward might be . . . well, in danger, because of the situation with the Grants. For most of his spare time, he's with Mr. Will Hasling, but we decided, Mr. Watkins and myself, that when he was alone he ought to have, well . . . a bodyguard. My man, Harry Forbes, is on duty every day, but he's not always needed. Late yesterday afternoon when Mr. Edward left the office, he was alone. There was no sign of Mr. Hasling. My man immediately followed Mr. Edward, who went to Belsize Park, and—"

"To see Mrs. Overton?" Cecily interrupted.

Surprised though he was to hear this, Amos nodded and went on. "My man hung around in the vicinity. Mr. Edward was at the house for about three hours, and he left soon after nine. It was very dark last night, and apparently the area was lonely, no one around and no hansom cabs. My man realized that immediately. He was some short distance behind when Mr. Edward was attacked by two very big men and—"

"The bodyguard was outnumbered," Cecily said quietly.

"That's right, Mrs. Deravenel. Once the men, three altogether, had fled the scene, my employee ran to Mr. Edward and was relieved to find him alive. He then went in search of a policeman. Luckily he found one at the top of Primrose Hill. More help was fetched, and Mr. Edward was brought here."

Cecily nodded. "Thank you, Mr. Finnister, now I understand." Glancing at her nephew, resting her hand on his arm, she murmured, "Could we go outside for a moment? I'd like to talk to you, Neville."

"Of course." He helped his aunt up out of the chair, and the two of them walked into the corridor.

Once they were alone, Cecily leaned closer to Neville, staring into his face. "It's the Grants, isn't it?"

"I'm afraid so," he confirmed, grimacing. "The whole thing was handled very clumsily, so it's most transparent.

His watch was left in his suit pocket, and so was the notebook. Only banknotes were taken. To make it look like a robbery."

"But he never has very much money on him," Cecily pointed out. "As often as not, Swinton has to pay the hansom cab out of the household petty cash when Ned comes home."

"It's the Grants, there's no question in my mind about that. Who else could it be?"

"What are we going to do about them, Neville? They're a menace."

"Reprisals. There will have to be reprisals, I think. To put them on notice that they have met their match in Ned and myself. However, I want to think things out carefully, not act in haste. We must be subtle, and we can't do anything that would involve us with the police. Don't you agree?"

"I do indeed, and I will leave it to you, Neville. You are the smartest man I know . . . you take after my brother, your father."

Michael Robertson," the doctor announced as he came into the waiting room, just before noon. He was smiling as he approached Neville, who had risen and was walking toward him.

"Neville Watkins, Dr. Robertson. I'm Mr. Deravenel's cousin. From your expression, I'm encouraged to believe he has regained consciousness."

"Yes, indeed he has. However, he is sleeping at the moment, and we feel he must not be disturbed for a while."

"I understand." Neville introduced Cecily to the doctor. "This is Mr. Deravenel's mother, Dr. Robertson, Mrs. Cecily Deravenel."

After shaking the doctor's hand, Cecily asked, "Was my son in a coma?"

"Not a coma, no. But he was unconscious, and he still has a concussion. I can assure you, though, he will recover from this, Mrs. Deravenel. He really will."

twenty-one

As he blinked in the dim light and slowly awakened, Edward was momentarily disoriented. Blinking again and trying to push himself up in the bed, he realized that every bone in his body ached.

Looking around the room, so white, sparsely furnished, he understood at once that he was in a hospital. Sinking back against the pillows, he endeavored to focus his mind, and as he did he began to remember the events of the night before. Leaving Lily's later than he had intended, walking up from Belsize Park Gardens, looking for a hansom cab. The stranger stopping him, asking for directions, and then the unexpected attack from behind.

Lifting his arm, he gingerly touched his head, felt the bandages, then slowly let his fingers roam over his face. He knew it must be bruised, even a little battered, because it hurt when he touched it. His shoulders and back ached; now he remembered those heavy blows, the way he had gone down onto his knees so quickly, had lurched forward as additional blows had landed on his head.

Who had attacked him? Thieves, wanting to rob him? Or had the attack been arranged by the opposition at Deravenels? He had no idea. Neither did he know who had found him, or how he had been brought to this hospital.

After a few moments, Edward managed to sit up; throw-

ing back the bedclothes, he swung his long legs to the floor.
For a moment he thought he could not stand, but eventually
he did, although he felt weak and slightly dizzy. He sat down
again heavily on the bed, wondering how to summon a
nurse. He needed to know more.

Dizziness overwhelmed him, and he flopped back against
the pillows, but he did not have enough strength to lift his
legs back onto the bed. He was not certain how long he lay
sprawled like this, half in and half out of the bed. Perhaps
twenty minutes. Then he felt a waft of cool air as the door
opened, and he was filled with relief. The nurse at last.

"Good heavens, Mr. Deravenel! What on earth are you doing?" a voice exclaimed, and a split second later, the owner of
the voice was bending over him, looking concerned. "Are you
all right?" the man asked in a kindly tone.

"Yes. Just felt a trifle dizzy . . . when I tried to get out
of bed."

"I'm not surprised. Come along, let me lift your legs into
the bed for you." As he spoke, the man got him settled properly. Once this was accomplished, he explained, "I'm
Michael Robertson, by the way. Your doctor, Mr. Deravenel."

"So I've gathered," Edward answered, attempting to
smile. He guessed the doctor was forty or thereabouts, dark-
haired, pleasant-looking, and wearing a white coat over his
dark suit. A stethoscope dangled around his neck. He had an
air of competence.

"Am I badly hurt?" Edward asked at last, a brow lifting.

Noting the anxiousness in his patient's voice, Dr. Robertson was quick to reassure him. "I believe you are out of danger. You were brought in here unconscious last night. You
had a concussion. But you appear to be much better. How
does your head feel? Any pain? Headache?"

"No, not a headache, but my head does feel . . . well, sort
of *top-heavy*. And my face is sore."

"Were you hit in the face, Mr. Deravenel?"

"No. But the blows to my back and shoulders were very

hard, and I fell forward. My face grazed the pavement. I remember being hit on the head. I obviously passed out. However, I don't think I have any other injuries. Or do I?"

"No, you don't. Not as far as we can tell."

"So I can go home today?"

"I don't think so, Mr. Deravenel. I need to keep you here for a few days. Under observation. Just to be on the safe side. I want to be absolutely certain we haven't missed anything."

Edward was silent for a moment, and then he asked, "Has my mother been informed that I am here?"

"She has indeed. She was here at the hospital, in fact, but I understand from Mr. Watkins that your mother and Mrs. Watkins have gone to your home to have food prepared for you. They will return with a hamper shortly. In the meantime, your cousin is very anxious to talk to you. Are you able to see him now? Or would you prefer to wait a little longer?"

"No, no, I'm really all right, Dr. Robertson. I would like to see him. And let me thank you for looking after me so well."

The doctor nodded and stepped closer. Bending over him, Michael Robertson put the stethoscope in his ears and listened to Edward's heartbeat. Then he shone a small flashlight in his eyes and finally placed a cool hand on Edward's forehead. He appeared well satisfied. He nodded, gave Edward a brief smile, and hurried out.

W hat I don't understand is how I got here," Edward murmured, giving Neville a close look and frowning slightly. "And how did *you* find out? Was my wallet still on me? My name and address are in it, you know. But thieves would have taken the wallet, surely?"

"Indeed they did," Neville replied swiftly, pulling the chair closer to the bed, and he lowered his voice when he added, "But thieves they weren't, I'm convinced of it. However, more about all that in a moment, Ned. Since you patronize an excellent Savile Row tailor, a small piece of tape with your name on it is always stitched on the reverse side of the pocket which is on the inside of your jacket. That was how you were identified by the police, who brought you to the hospital. But actually there's another story. . . . I mean about the way *I* was informed that you had been injured and were here."

Staring up at Neville, his eyes startlingly blue in his bruised face, Edward appeared puzzled. "Do tell me, I'm filled with curiosity."

A faint, rueful smile flitted across Neville's mouth. "With my permission, Finnister has had one of his operatives keeping an eye on you. You were attacked by *two* heavily built men last night. Finnister's man was outnumbered, and there was nothing he could do to help you . . . except run off looking for the police. Once he had ascertained you were still alive, of course."

"He saw the attack, did he?"

"From a distance. He also noticed a stranger stop you, and later he saw the same man conferring with the two bruisers . . . before they all made a dash for it." Neville shook his head. "Odd, don't you think, that *your* father and *mine,* and my brother, died from fatal blows to the head?"

Edward closed his eyes for a moment, and when he opened them they were stark. He pushed himself up on the pillows, staring into Neville's face. "Same modus operandi, is that what you're saying?" he muttered bleakly.

"Yes. There is no doubt in my mind that you were attacked by men working for the Grant faction. They're obviously having you followed, just as Finnister was. It was a good thing he took that precaution, because his man reported in to him quickly, and Finnister telephoned me as soon as he knew. I, in turn, informed your mother."

Edward remained silent, turning everything over in his mind, and at last he said softly, "I know you're going to suggest that I have a proper bodyguard, *several* men, presumably, to look after me, and you will not receive any argument from me, Cousin. Will can now go on your staff until he works with me at Deravenels, and you and Amos can seek out the other men."

"Thank you, Ned, for being so sensible. I know what a nuisance it's going to be, but unfortunately it is necessary. I cannot permit anything to happen to you." Neville reached out, grasped his cousin's hand in his, and held on to it tightly. "We are in this together. I promise you I will be your rock."

"And I will be yours, Neville, there for you should *you* ever need *me*." Edward laughed and then instantly grimaced. "When I move my face, it hurts like hell. But I was going to say, Not that you will ever need me."

"Ah, don't say that, do not tempt Providence. We never know when life is going to come and hit us in the face. *Catastrophe* is ever present, a specter that lurks behind every corner. For someone."

Edward felt an involuntary shiver run down his spine on hearing these words, but he remained silent.

Neville released his cousin's hand and sat straighter in the chair. "I have a good thought, Ned. It occurred to me earlier that my brother could come to London. Johnny and Will and you have often made a good threesome."

"Indeed we have, and Johnny has been special to me all my life. But can you spare him?"

"Yes, I think so. The managers of the northern offices have all been well trained. By us both. Anyway, my brother needs a change. It will do him good to be here in London . . . and I am sure we can find a place for him later. At Deravenels."

"Again, if you can spare him," Edward responded, laughter suddenly sparkling in his bright blue eyes. John Watkins was close to his heart.

"We will have to retaliate, you know," Neville announced.

Edward stared at his older cousin. *"How?"*

"I don't know. Yet. Don't you worry about it. Something will come to me. There's no hurry."

There was a sharp knock on the door, then it opened with

a burst. And before Edward could catch his breath, his mother and Nan, his brothers and sister were rushing into the room, followed by Will Hasling.

Neville jumped up and led Cecily forward to the bed, while his wife shushed George, just as Margaret was doing. "Do calm down," Meg told her younger brother, hanging on to his hand. Richard, of course, was silent and worried. His genuine concern shadowed those blue-gray eyes. He could not bear that his adored Ned was hurt.

Cecily clutched her eldest son's hand. "Ned, oh, Ned, your *head*. Your poor face. You took such a beating." She, who was usually so controlled, discovered her eyes were filling with tears.

"Not too much damage done, Mother. The doctor says I'm perfectly fine. Please try not to worry. I'll be up and out of here very quickly," Ned told her and then looked over at Richard, beckoned for him to come forward. "I'm alive and well, Little Fish. I do promise you."

For the first time that day Richard smiled and ran to the bedside, took hold of Ned's other hand. "Mama told us you were set upon by thieves, Ned."

"Were you frightened?" George asked. He had wriggled free from Meg's grasp and was now standing next to Richard by the bed.

"No, he wasn't! Of course he wasn't!" Richard exclaimed, glancing over his shoulder at his brother. "Ned is *never* afraid, are you, Ned?"

"I didn't have time to be, as it happens," Ned responded, his voice full of affection for his younger siblings.

Meg joined her brothers, and gazing down at Ned, she asked, "Is there anything you need, other than the food Mama and Aunt Nan have brought?"

"To come home to your loving care, Meg darling. But Dr. Robertson has suggested I stay here. Overnight. Just to be sure that . . . my old noggin is in working condition."

"Is there some problem with your head injuries?" his mother asked, alarm flaring on her face.

"No, Mother. It's just a precaution. You know very well how hospitals are." As Edward turned his head, his eyes met Will's, and he said, "Thanks for coming, old chap. And what's that you're carrying?"

"A picnic, Ned. Swinton's put together quite a lavish spread, at least so I'm told. I asked the ward nurse if she could find a small table so I can unpack it. Oh, here she is now."

After they had had their merry picnic, everyone left except Neville and Will. They wanted to stay because there were important matters to discuss, and also because the police were coming. Neville felt they should be with him during the police interview.

He had just finished explaining everything in detail to Will and asked him to join his staff when Dr. Robertson entered the room, accompanied by a uniformed policeman and a detective.

Once they had all been introduced, Inspector Laidlaw, the plainclothes detective, stepped forward and asked, "Would you mind telling us exactly what happened to you, Mr. Deravenel, please? We do have a report from the constable on the beat in Belsize Park, but that's about it. Nothing much at all, sir."

"Of course, Inspector Laidlaw, I'm glad to do so," Ned answered. "I'd been visiting a friend in Belsize Park Gardens in the late afternoon. I did stay for supper, and I was therefore longer than I'd planned. I left about nine o'clock and walked up to the main road, seeking transportation. The problem was there were no hansom cabs around. I was surprised. However, there was nothing I could do about it, and I decided to walk. I was heading for Primrose Hill, where I thought I would probably find a hansom. I was stopped by a pedestrian who asked me directions to Hampstead. It was when I was speaking with him that I was struck from behind. First across the shoulders and then on my head. I fell forward. And passed out. That's all I know, Inspector. Until I woke up here today."

Inspector Laidlaw compressed his lips. "Not much to go on, sir, I'm afraid, but it's the truth, nevertheless. The pedestrian who asked directions, can you describe him?"

"Medium height, light eyes, ordinary face. Wearing a cloth cap, a muffler, oh, and a worn looking overcoat. Nondescript sort of chap, actually. I thought at the time that he looked . . . a bit down on his luck."

"What about his accent? Can you pinpoint it?"

"Oh yes, certainly. A Cockney. Born and bred. And within the sound of Bow bells, Inspector."

Nodding, the inspector put away his notebook. "I understand your wallet was taken, Mr. Deravenel, but nothing else. Not even your gold pocket watch or your gold cuff links. So my question to you, sir, is this. Was it really a robbery? Or was the attack on you . . . well, let's say, a *personal attack*?"

"Good Lord, Inspector, how on earth would I know!" Ned exclaimed, looking properly askance.

"Any enemies, Mr. Deravenel?"

"None as far as I know."

"I understand, sir. Well, it looks as if we've hit a brick wall, so to speak. If you do recall anything, anything at all, please get in touch with me, sir."

"I certainly will, Inspector."

twenty-two

John Summers, usually a patient and self-contained man, was agitated. He paced the floor of his office, filled with a mixture of frustration and anger. Unable to sleep the night before, he had risen at dawn and come here earlier than usual. None of his colleagues had yet arrived; therefore he could not question them or confront them.

Last evening, just after dinner, he had been informed that Edward Deravenel had been physically attacked and was in hospital, badly injured. His anger sprang from this unwelcome news. He did not need problems at this moment, and an injured Deravenel was indeed a problem. If any of his people were involved, they would pay heavily for it.

Finally, he stopped pacing and walked across to the windows, looked down into the Strand. Even though it was not yet nine o'clock, the traffic was heavy horse-drawn carriages, horse-drawn omnibuses, hansom cabs, a few hand-carts, and lots of pedestrians, all jostling together, a mass of humanity on the move on this sunny morning.

Turning away absently, Summers went over to his desk and sat down. Steepling his fingers, he gazed around the large and handsomely furnished room, thinking about the consequences of the attack on Deravenel. The prospect of retaliation alarmed him.

At twenty-eight, John Summers was an attractive man

with a pleasant, clean-cut face. Very English in looks, he had a fair complexion, brown hair, and light gray eyes. Slender, almost wiry, and athletic, he was just above average height. He dressed well but in a most conservative manner, which reflected his outlook on life.

He was Henry Grant's man, always had been, as was his father before him. In fact, the Summers family had been allied to the Deravenel Grants of Lancashire for over two hundred years. And at this moment in time, Summers ran Deravenels. There was no one else to take on the burdens of this vast global company. Henry Grant was a bewildered, absentminded man, pious and harmless, yet far too involved with monks and priests for his own good. Certainly he understood nothing about business these days, even though he had in the past.

Henry's French wife, Margot, liked to think she was in charge, but this was a figment of her imagination. She was not shy in coming forward with advice and ideas. Summers allowed her to rant on, but he paid very little attention to her ravings and edicts, yet was clever enough not to let her know this.

Margot Grant. Beautiful, even beguiling to most men, and dangerous. He sat up straighter in the chair. Could *she* be behind the attack on Edward Deravenel? He sincerely hoped not.

Summers did not like Deravenel. He was far too glamorous, oozing charisma and bonhomie. But he was not stupid or soft. Unlike most other people at Deravenels, who thought of Edward as lazy and a playboy, Summers knew instinctively that the young man had steel in his bones. Ned liked women, the good life. But he was driven, ambitious, and strong, a man who was determined to win, no matter what.

That was why Summers was afraid of him. And even more afraid of Deravenel's cousin. *Neville Watkins.* A great magnate, a man of unimaginable wealth. Cold and ruthless when it came to business. They made a matchless team, in

Summers's opinion, and he loathed the idea that these two were ranged against him. Warriors, and hell-bent on winning. He had to stop them in their tracks, and very soon.

Restlessly, Summers rose and went out of his office, heading for the reception room at the far end of the corridor. When he went in a few seconds later, he switched on the crystal chandeliers and glanced around. Hanging on the walls were a collection of portraits of the men who had steered this company over the centuries. Mostly they were Deravenels from Yorkshire; only two Grants—Henry's father and grandfather—hung there. Until sixty years ago, the Deravenels of Ravenscar had dominated this company. And that was what Edward Deravenel wanted again. As did Neville Watkins.

Leaving the reception room, Summers flung open the door of the elegant dining room, his eyes scanning the handsome antiques and the priceless paintings which hung on the red-brocade-covered walls. So many magnificent luncheons and dinners had been given here for important clients, politicians, and foreign guests. But not lately. It was not possible to put Henry Grant on parade. And, ostensibly at least, it *was* Henry who was head of the company.

Retracing his steps down the long corridor, Summers considered going to the first floor, where many of the heads of divisions had their offices. Perhaps Aubrey Masters was already here; he could question Masters, find out what *he* knew. A reliable ally.

Instantly Summers changed his mind. Taking out his pocket watch, he glanced at it, nodded. In a short while his secretary would arrive, along with the telephonists and typists, the clerks and other members of the general staff. And certainly by ten o'clock the key executives would be behind their desks.

Although he had managed to calm himself, Summers felt a sudden flare of apprehension. He did not need this Edward Deravenel matter; there were too many problems as it was.

Trouble loomed. And yet he had to investigate the attack, get to the bottom of it. He must put a stop to this sudden . . . *violence.*

W hat in God's name is wrong with you?" Summers demanded, looking from James Cliff to Jack Beaufield, and then more pointedly at Andrew Trotter. "You're all laughing about the attack on Edward Deravenel, enjoying this . . . *catastrophe*! For that is indeed what it is! When what you *should* be doing is steeling yourselves for a powerful retaliation. Are you such fools that you don't understand what's going to happen?"

"Nothing, nothing at all," Trotter answered, a grin still lingering on his long, saturnine face. "That arrogant young pup got a whipping, and so what! Hopefully it will teach the little bugger a few manners."

At this moment there was a knock on the door, and Aubrey Masters hurried in, looking both harried and apologetic. "So sorry I'm late. The Strand is jammed with traffic, worse than ever."

"That's perfectly all right, Masters, do come in and sit down."

Masters took a seat, then glanced around at his colleagues. Instantly he detected the tension in the room. "What's wrong, gentlemen?" he asked, frowning.

Summers told him about the Deravenel incident and then finished. "I want to know *who* amongst you is behind the attack. And I will find out, whatever it takes." Now his eyes settled on James Cliff. "You're not saying anything this morning. So unlike you. Please tell me what you know."

"Oddly enough, I don't know a damned thing," Cliff answered in a mild voice. "I truly don't."

"Really," Summers answered swiftly, giving him a cold look. "Usually you're not squeamish . . . about *anything*, just so long as it serves your purpose."

"For this company, not my *own* purpose," Cliff shot back

and smiled a trifle smugly. "You know very well I am devoted to Deravenels and work for its success. And there's no reason to drip acid on me today. I'm not involved in this bit of . . . *violence*." Swinging his head, Cliff looked at Jack Beaufield. "Come on, do confess. You and the lady have been rather cozy lately, wouldn't you say?"

Beaufield's face tightened at this act of treachery, and a small vein started throbbing on the side of his temple. He said, in an icy voice, "I had nothing to do with the attack on Ned Deravenel. In fact, no one in this room did. However, Cliff is right that I have been . . . sequestered, shall we say, with the lady of the house, this house, and more than usual. She *is* behind it, Summers. She asked me to hire someone to teach Deravenel a lesson. But I refused. It is my belief she managed it all on her own. It's not so difficult to hire thugs."

Summers sat back in his chair and let his eyes roam over the men sitting across the desk from him. Finally his glance settled on Masters. He said slowly, "Now, Masters, you know everything that goes on here, because everyone confides in you. Can you throw any light on the matter?"

"Actually, no, I can't. But I do believe Margot Grant has it in for Deravenel. They had some sort of . . . *run-in,* I suppose one could call it. I think she was determined to clip his ears. Well, that was the expression I heard around the office."

"Since several fingers have been pointed in that particular direction, I shall have to have a word with the lady when she comes in today, if she does come in, that is," Summers said.

"She's already here," Masters announced. "I just saw her going into her office. Well, into Henry's office."

Summers jumped up. "Let us adjourn, gentlemen. Please excuse me." Without waiting to hear another thing, he hurried out of his office.

When he came to the chairman's office, he went in without knocking and immediately stopped short. Margot Grant was sitting behind the giant-size Georgian partners desk while her husband lay stretched out on a sofa near the window.

Taken by surprise at the sight of Henry Grant, looking somewhat disheveled and certainly quite unwell, Summers nonetheless recovered himself at once. Always the gentleman, he said pleasantly, "Good morning, Margot." Then, hurrying over to the sofa, he went on, "And good morning to you, sir. How're you feeling?"

"Not too badly off, John," Henry answered in a somewhat feeble voice. "How're you? And how is your father?"

"I am well, sir, thank you," Summers answered and ignored the question about his late father.

Margot stood up, walked around the desk, and came toward Summers with a wide smile playing on her face. "Have you heard the news about Deravenel?" she asked and began to chortle, her merriment reflected in her eyes.

Summers chose not to respond. Instead he turned to Henry and murmured, "Would you excuse me, sir? I need to take Margot back to my office. I wish to go over several business matters with her, rather urgently."

A faint smile glanced across Henry's vacant face, and he waved his hand in a dismissive gesture. "Go along, my boy, go along."

Opening the door and standing back, Summers looked at Margot and said in a low voice, "After you, please."

He was silent as he walked with her down the corridor, and it was only when they were inside his office and he had closed the door that he turned on her, his anger rising. "I know you are responsible for the attack on Deravenel, so don't deny it. I think you hired thugs to beat him up."

She looked at him intently, her dark eyes still full of laughter, holding his, and then, leaning closer, she said softly, "Why are you so angry, my dear? Apparently he got a whipping. Someone taught him a lesson, and that makes me happy. That's the end of it. The end of Ned Deravenel. He will not be a problem anymore. Someone did us a favor." She was jubilant.

Grasping her arm tightly and leaning into her, his face

filled with fury, Summers said in a harsh but controlled voice, "You foolish, foolish woman. This is not the end of anything. It is the beginning of a war. You have just unleashed a terrible force."

"Oh, John, do not be so . . . *melodramatic*—"

"There's going to be a catastrophe," he hissed, glaring at her with sudden animosity. "They will retaliate. I have no doubt about that."

Margot looked genuinely puzzled. "I do not understand—"

"No, you don't," he snapped. "And there is another matter we must clarify. Please do not bring Henry to the office until he is in better health. And if that *should* happen, and you do choose to bring him, make sure he is properly dressed."

"John, please, let us not quarrel, not you and I. You know I do not wish to upset you. I am your friend, your ally—"

Suddenly remembering his manners, he nodded and said in a less angry tone, "I know you mean well, Margot. Now, if you will excuse me, I have work to do."

She stared at him, still nonplussed by his earlier anger. Without another word she turned on her heels and left.

Once he was alone, Summers gazed at the door and then snapped his eyes shut for a moment. When he opened them, he shook his head as he went to his desk.

Why in God's name had he ever succumbed to that woman's charms? But he had, and he had no one to blame but himself. Thank God, he had never been intimate with her. Their relationship was still only a flirtation, which must now end.

Aubrey Masters left Deravenels early that day. Once a week he went to see his supplier, and today seemed like a good day to stop by the small shop to purchase his roots and grains. It was a sunny afternoon, quite mild for March, and as he walked up the Strand at a brisk pace, he endeavored to shed his anxieties about business.

John Summers was in a fury about Margot Grant, that was obvious, and Masters couldn't say he blamed him. She was always interfering in things, and this did not sit right with Summers or some of the other executives at Deravenels. Masters himself found her irritating, and besides, there was no room for women in the company. It was not their place to be involved in business. Her being the wife of Henry Grant was no reason to permit Margot Grant's presence in the man's world of commerce.

Masters's thoughts veered away from Margot Grant and settled on Alfredo Oliveri. Now there was an enigma. He had never liked the man, had always found him ambitious, competitive, and absorbed by his sense of entitlement. Oliveri had worked for the company all of his adult life and believed this gave him untold privileges.

Years ago Masters had wondered if Oliveri wanted his job, and this idea had lately surfaced yet again. Oliveri was hanging around London far too long. Now Masters couldn't help wondering why this was; Oliveri ought to be back in Italy, overseeing things there. Could it be that he was a traitor? This unexpected thought jolted Masters. Was Oliveri now in Edward Deravenel's camp? Had he changed sides? The more Masters thought about it, the more he believed it to be true. Why else would Oliveri be hanging around headquarters? Also, he had just learned that Oliveri was helping Deravenel understand the many divisions in the company, from mining to winemaking.

Once again, it struck Masters that Oliveri really did want his job; that was undoubtedly why he had allied himself with Ned Deravenel. Perhaps they had become close in Carrara. I must find a way to discredit Alfredo Oliveri, he thought, get him out of the company. This is my priority.

So busy was Masters with his planning and plotting that he had not noticed a well-dressed couple were following him up the Strand at a distance.

Continuing on his regular route, he crossed Trafalgar Square, wending his way through the jostling crowds. Once more he had no idea that another person was now following him as well. This was a young woman, nicely dressed but not quite as fashionably as the man and woman. After a brief word with them, the young woman fell in behind them, again keeping her distance. However, she made certain they were always in her sights, as they had instructed her to do.

Although it was a fairly long walk from the Strand to Piccadilly, Masters was enjoying it this afternoon. Striding along the wide thoroughfare, he glanced to his left and immediately noticed how verdant Green Park was looking, living up to its name. Spring was not too far away.

Turning down Half Moon Street, he was on Curzon Street within seconds. He thought of going into his favorite barbershop to purchase a bottle of his aftershave lotion, then changed his mind. He was far too anxious to reach Shepherd's Market.

It was at this moment that the young woman who had been following him turned the corner of Half Moon Street herself. And she hurried to catch up with Aubrey Masters. She was a little out of breath when she tapped him on his arm and said, "Sir, please excuse me."

Startled, Masters swung around, sharp words springing to his tongue. But when he found himself staring at one of the prettiest girls he had ever seen, the words remained unsaid. Her loveliness unhinged him slightly, and he found himself asking in a warm voice, "How can I be of assistance to you, young lady?"

"I'm sorry to trouble you," she apologized, smiling at him and showing lovely white teeth, "but I'm not from these parts, and I find myself lost. I'm looking for Shepherd's Market, but I can't find it."

Struck by the sweetness of her smile and her soft voice, Masters beamed at her and exclaimed, "I will be happy to help you. It just so happens I am going to Shepherd's Market myself. Come along, let us walk there together. It's not far, just up the street."

The girl smiled again. "What a relief. And how kind of you, sir, to take me there." Falling into step with him, she went on, "Is it a big place, Shepherd's Market? Do they sell many different things?"

"Oh yes, indeed, but it's quite a small area, compact, actually." Looking down at her, he was struck by her beauty again. "And I suppose you are looking for some pretty things for yourself?" he murmured in a voice that was wholly unfamiliar to him.

The young woman shook her head. "Oh no, sir, I am hoping to find the shop that sells grains and pods, and other vegetarian things. For my mother. Her stomach's been acting up, and a friend advised her to forgo foods such as meat and fowl, to eat much more lightly. She now wants to partake of vegetables and the like."

"How curious!" Masters answered, his eyes sparkling. "I myself am a vegetarian, and it just so happens I am going to the very shop you're looking for."

"How lucky I am," she said and stopped walking. Thrusting out her hand, she added, "May I introduce myself, sir? I am Phyllida Blue."

Shaking her hand, full of smiles, Masters said, "And my name is Aubrey Masters. So pleased to meet you, Miss Blue."

"Please call me Phyllida. Everyone does."

As they walked up Curzon Street together, Masters told the young woman about the items he purchased from the shop, extolled the virtues of vegetables and grains, and the importance of vegetarianism. Within a few minutes they were entering the cobbled yards which made up Shepherd's Market, where in the center of the shops, small restaurants, and coffeehouses stood the favorite shop of Aubrey Masters.

"Here it is, Phyllida," he announced, opening the door and ushering her inside.

"'Ello, Mr. Masters," the man behind the counter said. "I was expectin' you today." He eyed the young woman, and just like Masters, he couldn't help smiling at her. What a pretty one *she* was, with her golden curls, large blue eyes, and pert mouth. A tasty bit if ever he'd seen one.

Noticing the man's reaction, Masters muttered somewhat possessively, "This is Miss Blue, Phineas. She is looking for certain items for her mother. But I shall show her around first."

"Please be my guest," Phineas answered, and as Masters turned his back, he smiled at the young woman and winked.

She smiled in return and followed Masters, saying, "I was told to get dried mushrooms, lentils, sago, and various nuts and pods. And certain dried flowers and roots as well."

"Yes, yes, I will help you, my dear," he responded, finding himself so attracted to the young woman he was amazed. She looked as if she was in her early twenties, half his age, and she was so lovely she stirred something inside him which had long been dormant. He wondered how he could arrange to see her again. For see her again he must.

H e's hooked," Phyllida Blue said three hours later when she joined the fashionably dressed couple in the tap-room of a pub in Maiden Lane, up behind the Strand.

"So tell us all about it," the man said, grinning at her.

"Easy as eatin' pie," Phyllida replied and smiled at the man and his companion. "He fell for me hook, line, and sinker. Took me for coffee afterwards, and he wants me to meet him next week. Same time, same place, Charlie."

"Good girl."

The woman eyed her fob watch. "We'd best be going. We've all got to be at the theater soon."

"We're all right for a minute or two, Sadie," Charlie answered. "We don't have far to go."

Looking across at Phyllida, he said with a throaty chuckle, "You're a good little actress, Maisie. I trained you well."

"You did, and thanks for watching out for me today," she replied.

John Summers was so unsettled that evening he found it difficult to eat the excellent dinner his cook had so carefully prepared for him. Finally throwing the white linen napkin down on the table, he left the dining room and swiftly retreated to the library.

A moment later Fellowes, his butler, knocked on the door and came in. "Is everything all right, sir?"

"Everything's fine, thank you," Summers responded in a quiet tone.

"Cook is worried, sir. Did everything suit?"

"Yes, it did. My compliments to Cook, Fellowes, and please pour me a Cognac, would you?"

When he was finally alone, Summers settled back in the leather wing chair in front of the blazing fire, nursing the balloon of brandy.

Uppermost in his thoughts were the events of the day. In many ways his eyes had been opened. Now he knew exactly where he stood with his executives, understood much more about them, knew their weaknesses. Finally. And certainly he had been startled by the knowledge that Margot Grant had a truly ruthless streak. He also realized that she was something of a liability. On the other hand, Henry Grant relied on her, and loved her . . . if love was an emotion that could be felt by such a lost and demented man.

Summers sighed and looked across at the small painting of Georgina which stood on the table next to the fireplace. If only his fiancée had not been killed in that bizarre accident several years ago, his life would be very different now. He would have a wife and a family, and they would have eased his loneliness. As it was, his life was unbearable at times, because he missed Georgina so much, and because he had no confidant, no close friend whom he could trust. He was utterly alone. Except for his brothers, living in Somerset, and they were not all that close these days.

He took a long gulp of the brandy and then put the glass down on a nearby table, closed his eyes, and sat as his mind filled with myriad thoughts. One thing was suddenly paramount: Thank God he had had the wisdom not to fall into the sexual trap that was Margot Grant. A narrow escape, he thought. And he pitied Jack Beaufield, who was apparently her new victim.

Summers knew he had his work cut out for him in the next few months. The problems at the company would not go away. He was damned if he was going to let the House of Deravenels fall. Somehow he would find clever solutions. With the help of a few good men, he would bring the company back up on top. He must.

twenty-three

At times Cecily wished she had been born a man. There were many things she could do better and faster than some of the men she knew; but because she had been a child of Victoria's reign and was now a woman of the Edwardian era, so much had been, and still was, forbidden to her. Over the years she had suffered her frustration and impatience in silence, as had so many other women she knew. Many men, in public and private, complained about Mrs. Pankhurst and her fight for the rights of women, but Cecily could not help but admire her and her efforts on behalf of the female sex.

At this moment, Cecily wished she had been standing in her late husband's shoes over the last few years. *She* would definitely have challenged Henry Grant about his mismanagement of Deravenels and his right to run it. Curiously, Richard had never really done so, perhaps out of sentiment and a lingering affection for Harry, whom he had known throughout his life, since Henry's childhood, in fact.

It was all here, all the documents which would have brought the situation to a head if Richard had so wished. Earlier that morning she had gone to the vault in the basement of the Charles Street house and opened it with Swinton's help. Once she was alone, Cecily had removed a large pile of documents, which Richard had secured in a white linen pillow-case, and taken them up to the dining room.

Now these were spread out in front of her, and she studied them carefully. The papers were actually copies of documents so fragile they were stored in the vaults at the Deravenels offices in the Strand.

Long ago Richard had told her that every five years or so, before the copies themselves yellowed and aged, they were copied afresh. He had gone on to explain that those originals in the office vaults dated as far back as the founding father of the dynasty, Guy de Ravenel, and were extremely valuable and of great historical interest.

As she read, turned the pages, and read on, Cecily quickly came to understand that everything Richard had written in his diary was correct. She was struck most forcibly by the fact that he himself could so easily have presented a case to the board, yet for some reason he had not. He had only written about doing it.

Once more, she wondered why. Sentiment aside, Richard was not a fearful man; certainly he was capable of standing up to anyone. He had never been cowardly, just the opposite, in fact. Yet in this instance he had backed away from the fight, had merely continued to grumble about the sixty-year-old usurpation and his inalienable rights, and had angered people in the process. She could not comprehend why he had not acted, and now she would never know. He had taken that reason to the grave with him.

Two hours later, fully informed about the rules and regulations of Deravenels and understanding everything, Cecily collected the papers and carried them up to her bedroom in the pillowcase. Placing them on her bed for a moment, she opened a drawer in the chest which stood in the corner and placed the documents inside.

She would show them to Edward when he returned from lunch with Neville and Will. Even though her husband had never seen fit to take advantage of her many talents and insights, when it came to business, she knew her son would. And this pleased her. Ned had always paid attention to what she had to say, knowing he would benefit from her wisdom.

I can't believe it's you, Johnny!" Edward exclaimed, rushing across the library of Neville's Chelsea house. "No one told me you would be here today!"

Hurrying forward to greet his favorite cousin, Johnny Watkins explained, with a wide grin, "That's because no one knew I would be arriving last night."

Meeting in the middle of the floor, the two men shook hands, then stood apart; both wore appraising expressions as they eyed each other with great affection. Suddenly they both laughed, remembering so much. They were not only first cousins but the best of friends, having bonded when they were growing up in Yorkshire, Johnny at Witton Castle, Rick's splendid home in the Dales, Edward at Ravenscar. They were regular visitors to each other's homes, and also often stayed with Neville and Nan at Thorpe Manor near Ripon.

Although Johnny was a few years older than Ned, they had always seen eye to eye, shared the same values: honor, integrity, loyalty to family, and devotion to friends. These were their sincere and genuine beliefs and the two men had remained steadfast in their love for each other.

Standing away from Edward, Johnny swept his gray eyes over his cousin's face and said, with a faint smile, "You don't look like the wounded warrior to me."

"I'm *not*. Not anymore, Johnny. It's two weeks since the incident, so the bruises are almost gone. I'm no longer black and blue, and the shoulder pains have also fled."

Johnny touched Ned's arm lightly, his expression suddenly serious. "Thank God you're all right. You could've been killed, you know, Ned. And then where would I have been? Where would all of us have been? After losing my brother Thomas and your Edmund, and our fathers, well, I don't think I could have survived the loss of you."

There was a moment's silence.

Ned's brilliantly blue eyes turned dark with pain before he said slowly, "I know, it's still a raw wound, and for all of us. But we do have our families, and each other, Johnny."

"For life," Johnny answered.

Ned nodded, smiled at his friend and cousin. And at this moment he had no way of knowing that it would not be so. Not in the end. Other loyalties would tear them asunder and almost break Edward's heart.

"How is Isabella? And your boy?" Ned asked.

"Wonderful, and if my sojourn here becomes a more permanent situation, she will come with our son to London. Neville is well satisfied that things are under control in Yorkshire. The woolen mills in Bradford are turning out the best cloth, a lot of it for export, our heavy-machinery manufacturing plants in Leeds are booming. The coal mines are operating better than ever; in fact, all of our industrial interests are at full throttle. My father had everything running smoothly when he was killed—" Johnny broke off, looked away for a second before adding, "And Neville has always had his business interests on an even keel. That's why he decided I should come here and keep you company, so to speak. Until we take over Deravenels."

"And that we will certainly be doing in the not too distant future!" Neville announced self-confidently from the doorway and came striding into the library accompanied by Alfredo Oliveri and Amos Finnister.

Once he had greeted Ned affectionately, he introduced the other two men to his brother.

Although Neville and Johnny bore a marked family resemblance, they were quite different. Neville, the eldest, was always elegance personified, dressed in the best. Johnny was not at all flamboyant, and he dressed rather simply in good, understated clothes. Johnny was as good-looking as all of the Watkins clan, and like his older brother, he bore a strong resemblance to his aunt Cecily Watkins Deravenel.

As for his character, he was hardworking and disciplined but not quite the slave to business his brother was. He frequently teased Neville that he lived in his business attire as he traveled the length and breadth of England. Johnny liked the quiet country life, was something of a homebody, unlike Neville and Ned, who thrived amidst luxury, glamour, and splendor, and loved the gilded life of society.

Neville indicated the men should sit down near the fireplace. "It's still rather cold," he pointed out and seated himself near the hearth.

A moment later Will Hasling came striding in, greeting everyone in his usual cheerful manner, and then he hurried over to Johnny; they shook hands. They were old friends and trusted each other implicitly.

Neville said, "Oliveri has a few things to tell us, so I suggest he speak first."

Alfredo nodded, and sitting slightly forward in the chair, he said, "The first thing I want to report is the general attitude at Deravenels after Mr. Edward was so brutally attacked two weeks ago. I noticed the tense atmosphere myself, but most of my information came from Robert Aspen and Christopher Green, who have finally fully revealed themselves to me. They are on our side. Anyway, they told me, *separately,* by the way, that John Summers was really furious, that he hauled his executives over the coals regarding the attack and demanded to know who was responsible."

"I'll wager they all denied having anything to do with it," Ned exclaimed pithily, glancing across at Neville.

Alfredo nodded vehemently. "Naturally they did. And then James Cliff did something quite treacherous; he said, rather pointedly, that Jack Beaufield ought to know who was behind it since he was rather cozy with Margot Grant quite a lot these days."

"Really," Neville remarked, then laughed heartily at the thought. "Well, we sort of knew that already, didn't we, Finnister?"

The private investigator smiled knowingly but remained silent.

"Beaufield admitted that he was friendly with her," Alfredo explained, "but insisted he had refused to help her do harm to Ned. He suggested she hire thugs to do her dirty work."

"It's more than likely she did," Amos now interjected, "but we'll never be able to prove it."

"John Summers has cooled on Margot Grant, angrily turned away from his queen bee, but not for long. Green says they are once more just as friendly as ever, whilst Jack Beaufield has been relegated to a back bench." Alfredo sat back, his eyes on Neville.

"None of this is really surprising," Neville began and then stopped abruptly, considered things for a moment. "However, come to think of it, it's not such a bad idea, having them all at each other's throats."

"They won't be for long," Ned interrupted. "They are all smitten by that woman, solidly behind her."

Alfredo said, "I would like to speak to you all about Aubrey Masters now. Aside from the fact that he's been acting somewhat strangely, he's apparently got it in for me. I hear he is trying to have me thrown out of the company. And out of the country. He's blackening my name, I'm afraid, and I don't like the look of things."

"He must be stopped. Immediately," Neville said in a cold, hard voice, staring at Amos. "He should be induced to retire."

"He has become a bit of a . . . nuisance," Amos murmured, struggling to find the right word to describe Aubrey Masters. He looked as if he was about to say something else, but he stopped himself.

"Who will rid me of this turbulent priest?" Will said, a quirky smile playing around his mouth.

Neville glanced at him, then said softly, "I knew we would hear that famous question before long." Turning to Amos, he added, "Perhaps we can find a way to persuade Aubrey Masters to cease and desist. He must be made to understand he can't speak ill of people, most especially Oliveri here."

"I will certainly try, sir." Amos looked doubtful as he said this.

"To my last and perhaps most important discovery," Alfredo announced, looking from Neville to Ned. He began in a low, confiding voices. "I think I've found out what's wrong with the mines . . . what your father discovered, too, Mr. Edward."

The room went quiet. No one moved. Everyone was waiting for Alfredo's words.

"Somebody is stealing the product, skimming diamonds, emeralds, and gold. Or money off the top."

"But who?" Ned asked, incredulity echoing in his voice.

"In my opinion it could be the local managers," Alfredo answered.

"They wouldn't dare!" Neville exclaimed. "Or would they?" His eyes narrowed slightly, and he threw Alfredo a pointed look. "Unless they had approval from the head office. A partner in Deravenels?"

"That was my guess." Alfredo nodded. "And Rob Aspen agrees with me. I'd been working late last week, and so had he; that was when he drew my attention to discrepancies he was finding. I knew at once what this meant. I gathered he did, too. Anyway, I asked him not to reveal this to Masters, or to anyone else. At least for the moment."

"Why?" Ned asked, then swiftly added, "I understand; don't bother to answer my stupid question. If the other side finds out we know about the discrepancies, they'll try to cover them up. Somebody in London *is* running this scheme."

"Precisely." Alfredo gave Ned a knowing smile.

"So we're not going to deal with it until we're running Deravenels ourselves, later in the summer," Neville announced. "Let's leave this matter in abeyance and move on. Finnister informed me several days ago that he now has in his hands all of the records from the two insane asylums where Henry Grant was sequestered. Let's hear about it, Finnister."

"Mr. Watkins told you the most important part of my story," Amos began. "We are indeed in possession of the records. They are very detailed and extremely useful. I have hired a well-known doctor to study the records and give a written report on what they mean. In other words, how will Henry Grant behave over the next few years? Is he on the brink of going totally mad? Is he already suffering from dementia? What are his chances of survival? And finally, is he capable of running a company such as Deravenels?"

"I think the doctor will have no problem giving you the best written opinion there is, and likely it will be the kind of opinion which will serve us best," Neville said, and threw Amos a questioning look.

"You are right, sir. The doctor I engaged, Mr. Rupert Haversley-Long, is a psychiatrist who has been a colleague of the famous Dr. Sigmund Freud."

"I have no fears he will do the job perfectly," Neville murmured. Rising, he continued, "Let us all go into the dining room. We will be able to discuss everything further over an aperitif before we partake of lunch."

The others followed Neville out of the library.

Ned said to Alfredo, "Don't worry, old chap, we'll neutralize Aubrey Masters in some way or other. We can't lose *you;* we especially need you here in London these days. *Permanently.*"

"I agree. When are you returning to the office?"

"On Monday morning. The hospital gave me several examinations this past week, and everything is apparently quite normal. In my opinion, they've been overly cautious, but my mother insisted on these extra tests, and I don't think even Dr. Robertson had the nerve to contradict Cecily Deravenel."

Alfredo smiled. "I know what you mean. There's no one quite like your formidable mother. Anyway, she was right. Head wounds can be dicey, very dicey indeed."

twenty-four

Lily stood in the center of the drawing room in Vicky's Kensington house, taking everything in, a delighted smile on her face. "It's absolutely beautiful, Vicky," she said at last. "But then you've always been so clever in the way you decorate your homes."

Vicky's eye lit up, and she exclaimed, "Oh, I'm so glad you like it. To tell you the truth, I've been a little worried, wondering if it was all too—*pale.*"

Walking over to Vicky, who was still standing in the doorway, Lily said emphatically, "Not too pale at all. . . . The room is perfect; in fact, I love the way you've mixed all these creams and whites together, and the touches of green and lilac are charming."

"It's not too feminine?"

"Of course it isn't. Anyway, the antiques are dark and help to give the room exactly the right balance."

"I just pray that Stephen's going to like it."

"I know he will," Lily reassured her best friend and then asked, "And when is he getting back from New York?"

"In a week. He had to go to San Francisco unexpectedly, and that delayed him, but his business has gone well, and he'll be sailing from New York in a few days. I can't wait to see him, it's been ages."

"I know what you mean," Lily murmured and walked

slowly across the room, went and sat down on a plump, curving love seat upholstered in pale apple green damask. As she settled back against the lilac and apple green silk cushions, she said, with another glance around, "The flowers are lovely, Vic. You've managed to create a feeling of spring here today."

"Thank you, darling." Vicky took a seat in a chair next to Lily, and looking at her intently, she asked, "Have you told Ned?"

Lily shook her head. "No, not yet. I saw him only once last week, after he came out of the hospital, and I felt it wasn't the right time. But I am going to tell him, please don't worry."

"Good. I'm glad. Now, you'll be interested to hear that I've found a house quite near us in Kent. I think it's lovely and not too big, and I was hoping you could come down to see it with me on Monday or Tuesday, before Stephen arrives in London."

"Oh, Vicky, darling, how wonderful! I'd love to," Lily cried, beaming at her friend. "To tell you the truth, I've also been thinking about moving from Belsize Park Gardens. To a house I saw in South Audley Street, in Mayfair."

"I see. I hope you're not taking on too much—in your condition, I mean."

Lily laughed. "I really feel wonderful. Very fit and healthy, and it's only the morning sickness getting me down at the moment. Also, the house in Mayfair is compact really, yet very adequate for me, the child, and a small staff. I just hate the idea of Ned being stranded the way he was in Belsize Park when he was attacked. I need to be in the West End."

"I understand." Vicky fell silent for a few seconds, and then, leaning toward Lily, she asked in a quiet voice, "You do still plan to keep the baby, don't you?"

"Oh yes, I could never give it up! Why it's part of me and Ned. I might tell him today, Vicky, then I might not. But please be assured that when I do, I will explain that I want to be quite independent. I don't want anything from him, as you know."

"That's brave of you, Lily. *I* have something to tell *you*, by the way. It's rather important. At least, I think so."

Lily looked at her alertly. "What is it? You seem very excited."

"I am. I've made a decision about something I've thought about for a while. I'm definitely going to do voluntary social work with my friend Fenella Fayne—"

"The widow of Lord Jeremy Fayne?"

"Exactly. She's been a friend for years, and as I think I once told you, she runs a women's . . . *shelter* in the East End. I've always admired her work, and I want to do something useful with my life. There's so much poverty and misery in London, greatest capital in the world though it might be. I simply can't bear the discrepancy between the lives of the rich and the desperate, miserable existence of the poor."

"I'm very happy you finally decided to make a move. You've been hankering after doing work like this for as long as I can remember." Lily gave her friend a loving smile and took hold of her hand. "And I think you'll be wonderful at it. Fenella Fayne must be thrilled to have you."

Vicky began to laugh, looking embarrassed. "I haven't actually told her yet, but she knows how interested I've been in her work for a long time. I plan to visit her next week and volunteer my services."

"Stephen won't mind, will he?"

"I don't think so. He understands that I'm . . . well, that I feel women should be able to make contributions if they wish to do so. He thinks I'm rather emancipated really, and he's one of the few men I know who believes Mrs. Pankhurst has the right idea . . . about women's rights. Frankly, Lily, he's proud that *I* am emancipated."

Lily nodded. "And you're so very right about the poverty in London. There are some terrible slums, such as Providence Place, and those ghastly tenements . . . they're called rookeries, aren't they?"

"Yes. And the women who live there are beaten down and desperate, poor, *and* frequently in ill health, and often abused by their beer-swilling husbands. It makes my blood boil when I think about the wealth in England and the self-ishness of so many people who could help to make a few lives easier—"

Vicky stopped and jumped up, went to the window, saw the carriage coming to a stop.

"Oh, Lily darling, I think it's my brother, with Ned, and, oh my heavens, *Johnny Watkins*. They're earlier than I expected."

Amos settled himself at a corner table for four in the Mandarin Garden, the little Chinese restaurant which was his favorite in Limehouse. Six o'clock was early for him to eat his Sunday dinner, but Charlie had requested this time, so he had acquiesced.

His thoughts settled on yesterday's lunch with Neville Watkins and the other men. When he considered the infor-mation that had passed amongst them, the decisions made, he filled with a rush of pleasure and satisfaction. Every-thing was coming together much faster and better than he had anticipated.

The medical records were in hand, the renowned doctor was studying them; Alfredo had produced valuable informa-tion about the Mining Division as well as the names of their allies within the company; and now, thanks to Charlie, he had two men whom he could use to tackle James Cliff, Jack Beaufield, and Philip Dever. *Tackle* was a strange choice of words, he decided, smiling to himself. The two actors were going to pose as aristocrats and reveal that they had lethal information about the private lives of these three men. Blackmail, in other words.

Right on time as always, Charlie came hurrying into the restaurant. Amos glanced up, raised his hand in a wave. A moment later Charlie was sitting opposite him, a grin spreading across his handsome face.

"Evening, Mr. Finnister."

"Good evening, Charlie. Would you like a pot of this jasmine tea I'm having? It's most refreshing."

"Indeed I would, sir. And thank you very much." Charlie sat back in the chair and glanced around the restaurant, which was still relatively empty. "It appears we are the sole diners," he added.

"Playing the toff this evening are we, Charlie?" Amos asked with a wide smile. He was extremely fond of the young actor, and they had worked together on many *projects,* as Charlie was wont to call them. For ten years, at least.

"I am the toff tonight, sir. Don't forget I'm stuck with a posh part at the moment, so I try to keep my voice in character with the character, if you get what I mean. Makes my life easier."

"It's quite extraordinary the way you assume such different voices, can flip from one accent to another," Amos remarked, giving him a thoughtful look. "You're the best mimic I know, except for Maisie."

"Thanks, guv."

The waiter came hurrying to the table, and at once Amos ordered jasmine tea and asked to see the menus. Then he continued, "I think it's a genuine gift, Charlie, your voice."

"Mebbe it is, mebbe it ain't." Charlie grinned at Amos cheekily as he dropped with the greatest of ease into his native Cockney. "Fings ain't wot they used ter be around 'ere, Mr. F, so I'm off to America wiv me sister."

Startled by this announcement, Amos sat up straighter, an expression of disbelief on his face. "Well, I'll be blowed! So you made your mind up to do it at last. She must be thrilled."

"She don't know nuffin yet. Yer see, I ain't told 'er nuffin. It's a serprise, guv."

"Very good, very good indeed, Charlie. I'm delighted that you're going to remove yourself from these shores. I shall miss you, of course, but I think perhaps it's . . . well, a *wise move,* shall we say?"

"Wiv me sister by me side, I think we can mek it big in America, Mr. F, an' we do 'ave a double act, yer knows."

"So you've told me, and I—" Amos broke off when the waiter came scurrying back with the pot of tea and a cup on a tray, along with the menus. He gave these to Amos, poured the tea for Charlie, and bowed low, then disappeared again.

Once they were alone, Amos leaned across the table and said in a much lower voice, "Is everything set for tomorrow?"

Answering in his cultivated voice, Charlie murmured softly, "It is, Mr. Finnister. Maisie has arranged to meet Aubrey Masters at the coffee shop in Shepherd's Market. She will explain she's going to be away for a week visiting her grandmother, and she'll give him the going away present."

Amos simply nodded and reached into his pocket. A second later he placed a small packet on the table between them.

Charlie eyed it, then picked it up and looked at it. "*Purple paper.* Very fancy." He slipped it into his pocket without further comment.

"Maisie knows what to do with it?" Amos gave him a penetrating stare.

Charlie nodded. "She's to mix it in with the grains and pods she's giving him in the brown paper bag."

"Correct."

"What is it, by the way? What is it going to do to him?"

"It'll give him loose bowels for a few days, keep him at home. Away from the office, which is the purpose of this exercise. And for your information, it's a mixture of dried herbs and seeds, that's all."

"That's awright then, innit? " Charlie muttered, having again reverted to his natural Cockney. Now he pulled a piece of paper out of his jacket pocket. "Wiv these 'ere two lads yer won't go wrong, guv."

Amos glanced at the paper. "Real names?"

"Naw, ain't a good idea ter give real names, yer knows

that. Aliases, like my Maisie called 'erself Phyllida Blue. Cor blimey, don't arsk me where she got that from."

"Has she used that name with anyone else?" Amos asked, suddenly sounding worried.

"Naw, course not, Mr. F. I mean, I'm not bleedin' daft, yer knows. Invented it she did an' all, on spur of the moment, so she told me."

"And your two fellow thespians will meet us here in an hour?"

"That's right."

"So we should order dinner? Or should we wait for them?"

"Naw, naw, they won't be eatin' wiv us. They 'ad Sunday lunch wiv their mums down Whitechapel way."

"Very good. I shall have duck with orange sauce, and would you like to have your usual, Charlie?"

"I will, thanks. Sweet and sour, and steamed rice, please."

After Amos had ordered from the waiter, he looked across at Charlie, his brows furrowing. "Maisie *is* leaving tomorrow as planned?"

"She is, an' as I told yer, I'm going wiv 'er. To Liverpool. On the evening train. Board the ship the next day, that we do. And off we goes, sailin' away ter America, where the streets are paved wiv gold."

Amos nodded and felt a surge of relief that Charlie was leaving London. It would be better in the long run. Too many people knew they were associated, and, in view of future events, it was much smarter to terminate their business relationship.

"I shall miss you, my friend," Amos murmured again, sadness creeping into his eyes. Charlie had always brought laughter and loyalty into his life, and he had been reliable, devoted.

"Same fing for me, Mr. F. Yer've been a good 'un, 'elped me out when I've needed it. But now I'm gonna be a good bruvver to Maisie. She deserves it."

"She does. And by the way, just make sure she *never* uses

the name Phyllida Blue again. And tell her to dispose of the blond wig."

"I got yer, Mr. F. I understands."

Reaching into his inside breast pocket, Amos removed a thick packet and handed it to Charlie. "Put that money safely away, my lad. Tomorrow there'll be another one like that when I meet you at the railway station. And by the way, don't forget to stay in touch with me when you arrive in New York."

Charlie's cheeky grin spread across his face once more, and he reached out and grasped Amos's hand resting on top of the table. "Friends for life, Mr. F."

And, as it turned out, they were.

Margot Grant stared at herself in the Venetian mirror. Satisfied that she was looking her very best tonight, she went and sat down on the big, plump sofa in front of the fire. Leaning back against the many soft cushions, she willed herself to relax at last.

After a moment, her eyes roamed around her small private sitting room in the grand house on Upper Grosvenor Street where she lived with Henry Grant—when he was not away at a retreat.

The room this evening was just as perfect as she herself was. She had set out to create an enticing roseate glow in this most intimate place in the house, and she suddenly realized, yet again, how well she had succeeded.

The walls were covered in a pale pink watered silk, while a deeper rose-colored ribbed silk upholstered the big over-stuffed sofa, several chairs, and a small love seat set against the back wall. The tied-back draperies at two tall windows were the same color as the sofa and chairs but were made of light, floating taffeta. Beautiful landscapes by several French masters hung on the walls, and a number of priceless French objets d'art were scattered around.

The lighting was soft. The pink silk shades on the pink alabaster lamps added to the rosy feeling, as did the blazing fire. Margot sighed. It was a room designed for seduction, and she hoped it would work wonders tonight.

She smiled inwardly. Jack Beaufield, her latest flirtation, had called it the honeypot, and what a fitting name that was. He had added that it was feminine, sexual, and with her at the center, even more exciting. But she had made it clear to him that she was unavailable.

There was a faint smell of roses in the air, and she wore the same attar of roses perfume. John Summers's favorite. *He* was her favorite. She must win him back, she needed him by her side. How foolish she had been to antagonize him. He had always been her champion; she thought of him as her knight in shining armor, and of herself as his queen.

Despite his genuine adoration of her, she had never claimed John in her bed, made him hers as she had his father years ago, when she had been only a young girl. But she must do it. Tonight. She could not wait for him any longer. Her whole body raged for him. It was imperative that she own him sexually, not only to satisfy her rampant desires but to bind *him* to *her* forever.

Margot closed her eyes, thinking of him. He was a man she had wanted for a long time now, the perfect man for her, and she knew he would be a passionate lover, knew it in her bones. She needed a man she could trust, who would meet her voracious sexual appetite with a raging yearning of his own. *How she had yearned for him. For so long.*

She had never believed she would end up married to a man like Henry Grant. They were total opposites. She prided herself on her vivid intelligence, her education, her many talents—she played the piano like a true artist, could paint and embroider, and had knowledge of gourmet food and the great wines of France. Her grandmother had trained her in etiquette and manners; she had taught her how to run great houses and manage country estates. Her father and grand-mother had made sure she was a great lady, as befit the daughter of a French industrialist.

The marriage to Henry Grant was one of convenience. Henry had bestowed on her a famous name; she had brought him a grand dowry. And her father's business holdings and land in Anjou would be his one day, through her.

Proud, spirited, and undeniably the most beautiful of women, she had come to England full of expectations. She had come to marry the head of Deravenels, the most famous trading company in the world, and she was excited about this arranged union. At fifteen she had expected a dashing En-glishman. He was twenty-four, and she had imagined a vig-orous and experienced lover, a man of charm and elegance. She discovered instead that she was marrying . . . a *monk*. More or less. And a monk who was daft in the head.

She had been married to Henry for fifteen years, and now, at thirty, she was in full bloom. Frustrated in every way. What she longed for was a man in her life and in her bed. But not just any man. A particular man, one who was already deep in her heart, John Summers. Her female longings aside, he was the man who was actually running Deravenels, and she wanted to be by his side, learning from him for her son's sake.

Looking at the antique ormolu clock on the mantelpiece, Margot suddenly rose and went to the window, hoping he would come soon. She did not have long to wait. Within a few minutes the carriage arrived; he alighted, and she sped across the room and out into the black marble entrance foyer. Before he could lift the knocker, she had opened the door.

He appeared startled to see her on the front steps.

"*Cheri*," she murmured in her low, breathy way. "Come in, come in."

"Good evening," he said in his cultured voice and smiled at her.

Smiling in return, she took his overcoat and placed it on the wooden hall bench, and ushered him into the sitting room.

He glanced around, then turned and kissed her lightly on the cheek. "It's nice to see you, Margot," he murmured, his eyes taking in the décolletage of the pink silk gown, which showed off to advantage her perfect breasts, tiny waist, and curvaceous hips. "Thank you for your unexpected invitation," he added, dragging his eyes away from her.

"Sit down, please, here on the sofa in front of the fire. I shall bring you champagne. Yes?"

"That's a good idea," he said as he sat down and leaned forward, reached his hands toward the fire. "It's turned into a cool evening." He sat back and watched her intently as she floated over to a console table and poured champagne into two crystal flutes. A moment later she was handing one to him.

"Ah, my favorite. Pink champagne."

She laughed as she seated herself next to him. "It matches the room." She clinked her glass next to his. *"Santé."*

"Your health, my dear. And how is Henry?"

"The same . . . always the same. Resting at this moment."

"Will he not join us then?"

"Ah, non, non, ce n'est pas possible ce soir."

"I am sorry he can't come down. So . . . it's just the two of us then?"

She gave him a careful, guarded look. *"Oui, les deux."*

He sat back, keeping his thoughts to himself.

John Summers was nobody's fool, and he had suspected that Margot had invited him here to seduce him. But suddenly, it didn't seem to matter one iota. He was tired and lonely, and frustrated in a variety of ways; he carried the endless and heavy burdens of Deravenels on his shoulders and never had a moment's joy. So let her try, he thought, let her try to inveigle me into her bed. And let us see what happens.

Mistaking his silence for lingering anger after their recent quarrel at the office, she said softly, "I am sorry I annoyed you the other day. Please say you forgive me. I want so much to have your forgiveness, and your respect."

"You have both," he responded swiftly in a neutral voice.

"Oh, thank you! You have made me so happy. *Merci, Jean*," she cried, pronouncing his name the French way.

Impulsively, she took hold of his hand. "I have been so worried you would no longer be my friend. And I am alone, and lonely."

His mouth twitched with hidden laughter. He finally remarked, "But I've been so friendly toward you this past week; we even had lunch together. Didn't you realize I was . . . back in the fold?"

"Are you?"

"Yes."

She leaned closer, revealing a portion of her beautiful breasts,. and kissed him on the cheek. Then she looked at him pointedly, raising a brow.

He stared at her, mesmerized. God, she was beautiful. The most beautiful woman he had ever seen. He took in the perfect white skin, the flawless complexion, the arched black brows, the dark eyes full of hidden depths, the cloud of black hair, unbound tonight and loose around her heart-shaped face. Her mouth was a brilliant red from lip rouge, and it was luscious. *She* was luscious. Ripe for the picking. Such a temptress, tempting him. He felt a stirring between his legs as they held each other's eyes.

He said, after a few seconds, "You have a questioning look on your face." His voice sounded hoarse to him. "Ask me, whatever it is."

Margot put down the champagne glass, drew closer to him. He could smell the perfume of roses on her neck and breasts, and he felt himself growing hot. At last she whispered, "Will you be mine?"

Before he could stop himself, he asked bluntly, "In the

way my father was? Is that what you mean? All of me? Not just my loyalty to your cause? Is that what you want?"

He had startled her. "Yes," she answered finally.

"I have a question, too," he announced after a moment's consideration.

"Ask me."

"What of Jack Beaufield? . . . What is there between the two of you?"

"There is nothing between us. There was only a mild flirtation, of no consequence. There has never been anything between me and anyone else. That is, other than your father." She focused on him intently. "Truly. I promise. I am not a liar, whatever else I am."

"I believe you, don't protest so."

She smiled, and then she began to giggle like a girl.

John gaped at her. "What is it?" He frowned, staring at her in bafflement.

"Jack Beaufield said this room was like a honeypot."

"Did he now?"

There was a long moment of total silence between them, and then, quite unexpectedly, John took hold of her and pulled her almost roughly into his arms. He kissed her on the mouth; it was a deep and passionate kiss, and she returned it fully, sliding her tongue into his mouth, wanting to devour him.

John still held her tightly and kept on kissing her; then abruptly he moved his face and said against her ear, "But he was wrong. *You* are the honeypot."

"*Your* honeypot?" she whispered.

"Ah yes. *Mine.*" After a moment, he said, "What of Henry? Is he sleeping?"

"I gave him a sedative," she admitted.

"The staff?"

"It's Sunday. They have the night off."

"So, we are alone. Nevertheless, I must lock the door and draw the curtains."

"Yes, do," she murmured, leaning back against the cushions, fiddling with the buttons of the peignoir.

He was gone only a moment. When he came back to the fireplace, he switched off two of the lamps, saying, "It's just a little too bright."

As he turned around to face her, he saw that she had opened the top buttons of the pink gown, then realized it was a robe, not a gown at all. Even more of her beautiful breasts were revealed, and she was gazing up at him, a yearning expression on her face.

He took her in his arms and held her close, whispering her name over and over, then began to kiss the voluptuous mouth. Within seconds they were both aflame.

Reaching for his hand, she placed it on her leg. He glanced down, saw that her legs were bare . . . soft, smooth, and firm beneath his hand. He knew it was an invitation to explore. And he did so, running his hand along her inner thigh and across her stomach.

He heard her catch her breath, and he looked down at her intently.

"I am yours. Do what you want with me." As she spoke, she tugged at the front of the peignoir, and it came open fully.

Now she truly was revealed to him, and as he gazed at her slender white body, he caught his breath. "Oh, God, you're beautiful, Margot!" And he leaned over her, buried his face against her breasts.

"Take me, take me," she moaned against his hair.

It took him a moment to get undressed, but when he was finally free from his jacket and trousers, he flung off his shirt and cravat, and lay down with her on the huge sofa, which enveloped them like a bed.

Their kissing and touching became more frantic, her arms and legs went around him, and he was poised over her, looking down into eyes the color of jet.

"Please, please," she begged, "take me to you."

And very slowly and carefully he did so, making himself

part of her. They began a long ritual of rhythmic moving and kissing, and he found himself drowning in her. And then, in a moment of sudden and absolute clarity, he wondered why he had ever fought her off, fled from her sexual desire for him. She was sheer bliss.

twenty-five

Every morning when he arrived at Deravenels, Edward spent several hours studying the books, brochures, and pamphlets which Alfredo Oliveri had given him. As Alfredo had intended, Edward was gaining a greater understanding of all the divisions of his family's huge company.

Almost immediately, Edward had found himself gravitating to the Mining Division, discovered he was particularly interested in diamonds and precious stones. In only a few weeks he had become extremely knowledgeable, especially about the diamond.

He had always had a prodigious memory, and when they were at Oxford together, Will had announced that it was photographic. It was true that, after reading something twice, Edward knew it by heart. "You would have made a good actor," Will had once told him, and Edward had laughed and agreed.

This morning he was immersed in a book about Jean-Baptiste Tavernier, the merchant and traveler who had journeyed from Paris to India in the seventeenth century, usually heading for the famous Golconda mines, now extinct. Tavernier was the first person to bring diamonds back to Europe from the subcontinent of India. Louis XIV had bought diamonds from Tavernier, as had other members of his court who were able to afford them.

As he went on reading eagerly, Edward made notes. He had recently become intrigued by those very special diamonds which were both big and perfect, and because of this were given names. Each one became famous, much coveted. He had just discovered that one of the first of these was called the Grand Mazarin, named after Cardinal Mazarin, who had owned it. On his death, the cardinal had bequeathed it to Louis XIV.

The door of Edward's office burst open, and as he glanced up, Alfredo came rushing in, looking troubled.

Always pale-skinned, Alfredo was now so white that his freckles seemed to stand out most prominently across the bridge of his nose and his cheekbones. Edward knew at once that something was seriously wrong, and his stomach lurched. He couldn't help wondering if Alfredo had been pushed out of the company, or at least instructed to return to Carrara.

Drawing to a standstill in front of the desk, Alfredo stood staring at Edward. He seemed to have lost his voice.

"Whatever's the matter?" Edward asked.

"Aubrey Masters is dead."

Dumbstruck, Edward simply gaped at the other man. He **felt a chill run** through him.

Alfredo sat down heavily in the chair.

Edward leaned across the desk. "When did he die?"

"Tuesday . . . last night, that is."

"Who gave you this news?"

"Rob Aspen. He came into my office a few minutes ago and said, 'Masters is no longer with us, he passed away.' I was just as shocked as you are now. I had a meeting with him on Monday afternoon, but he told me he'd have to cut it short because he had an unexpected appointment. He was more cordial than usual, though, which seemed a bit odd to me. Anyway, he left in a hurry. Yesterday I ran into him in the corridor, and although he was somewhat preoccupied, he looked in good health."

"Did Aspen tell you what Masters died of?"

"He didn't know." Alfredo lifted his hands in a helpless gesture and added, "It must have been a heart attack or a stroke, something like that."

"Whatever it was, it was certainly *sudden*," Ned remarked, frowning. "And how did Aspen get the news? From whom?"

"The horse's mouth, of course. *John Summers.* Summers is related to Masters, they're cousins three times removed or some such thing. And as you know, they are both related to Henry Grant. Hence their dedication to the Grant cause, and the reason they both work here. Or rather did, as far as Masters is concerned."

"I'm not going to play the hypocrite and say I'm sorry he's dead," Edward said. "He was, after all, my father's enemy, and my enemy as well. And very frankly, I've wondered for the last few days whether he was involved with the problems in the Mining Division—" Ned broke off, drew even closer to Alfredo. "You know what I mean, the skimming, or whatever is going on in India, South America, and South Africa."

Alfredo nodded. "I had the same thoughts."

There was a knock on the door, and John Summers opened it before Edward could say another word.

Summers hovered in the doorway for a moment, then said, "Good morning, gentlemen."

They responded in unison, and Edward said, "Do come in."

As Summers walked across the office, his eyes on Edward, he said, "I suppose you must have heard the terrible news . . . about Aubrey Masters."

It was Alfredo who answered quietly, "Yes. Rob Aspen came to my office a short while ago and told me, and I have just informed Mr. Edward."

Edward asked, "What did Aubrey Masters die of actually?"

"We don't know as of this moment. His wife telephoned me this morning to inform me of his death. Apparently he came home on Tuesday night and seemed perfectly fit and well. He prepared his own vegetarian dinner, as usual, and he ate it alone as always, in his study. About an hour later, he staggered out of the study complaining of chest pains. Later he became violently ill. Apparently he was having what Mrs. Masters described as convulsions. She had their housekeeper telephone for the doctor whilst she endeavored to help her husband. But to no avail, I'm afraid. The doctor arrived fairly swiftly, only to find that Masters had just passed away."

"Perhaps it was a stroke," Edward suggested.

"It's impossible to know anything now," Summers responded. "The doctor arranged for the body to be taken to the hospital, where they are probably doing an autopsy at this very moment."

"So we should have some news later today," Alfredo said.

"I hope so. In the meantime, I am going to go to their house in Hyde Park Gate to be with Cousin Mildred. I think I'm about the only family she has other than her sister. I shall come back to the office as soon as her sister arrives from Gloucestershire."

All of these last comments had been directed at Alfredo, and he now said, "Yes, of course, and would you like me to have Rob Aspen cover for Aubrey—" He cut himself off, then said, "Deal with anything Masters was working on?"

"Yes, that will be all right, a good idea actually, Oliveri," Summers replied. "Under your supervision, of course. And by the way, perhaps you should postpone your return to Italy. For the moment."

Later that day, Edward had a short meeting with Neville at his cousin's office in the Haymarket. Will and Johnny accompanied Edward, and the four men sat together in the vast boardroom to discuss the death of Aubrey Masters.

"A sudden death such as his can be caused by any of a number of things," Johnny pointed out. "The obvious things are natural causes, such as a heart attack, a massive stroke, a brain hemorrhage, or the ingestion of something poisonous."

"Talking of poison, he does eat a number of very weird things," Edward said, throwing his cousin a pointed look. "He could have eaten some sort of poisonous mushrooms, for example. Don't you remember when we were children, one of the stable boys at Ravenscar ate a toadstool and was violently ill? Luckily for him he ate only one, that's why he recovered."

"His name was Sammy Belter, I remember him well," Johnny replied and grimaced. "The poor lad was horribly sick."

"Didn't Amos say Masters ate pods and seeds, all sorts of strange roots and such?" Edward now asked Neville.

His cousin nodded. "He did indeed, and perhaps Aubrey Masters ate something that killed him. On the other hand, he could have had a stroke or a heart attack. Look, we're just speculating right now. A waste of time, usually. We'll know soon enough what he died from. What else did Summers have to say?" he asked, changing the subject swiftly.

"That he was going to be with Mildred Masters until her sister arrived from Gloucestershire, that the body had been taken for an autopsy. He also agreed with Oliveri that Aspen should work on Masters's various tasks under Oliveri's supervision." Edward leaned back in the leather chair and said with a wide smile, "And he made a point of telling Oliveri that he should remain in London for the time being."

"That's good to know!" Will exclaimed.

"Isn't it just," Johnny cut in with a laugh.

"How long does it take to get the results of an autopsy, Neville?" Edward now asked quietly, raising a blond brow.

"Do you know, I've absolutely no idea," Neville answered. "A couple of days, perhaps? Unless one knows the pathologist involved. And in this instance we don't."

"So what you're saying is we'll just have to wait," Will interjected.

"That's right," Neville replied, "and how he died doesn't really matter to us, does it? In the meantime, I just want to say that I for one will not be sending any condolences to the grieving widow, if indeed she is grieving. Finnister led me to believe there was an estrangement in that marriage."

"And I won't be offering any sympathetic words either," Edward announced in a sharp voice. "In view of the fact that we never received any condolences when our fathers and brothers were murdered in Carrara."

"Now, gentlemen, shall we repair to my club for a few drinks before dinner?" Neville suggested. "I think it might be rather nice to raise a glass to one another under the circumstances." He shook his head, then remarked, "It's a pity Oliveri's not here."

"It is, I agree," Edward murmured. "But his mother is in hospital, and he wanted to go and visit her. However, we can toast him, can't we? After all, it looks as if he might inherit Masters's job."

"Indeed he might," Will agreed. "Let's face it, this sudden death might very well play in our favor."

At seven o'clock that evening, Edward arrived at Lily's house. As he alighted from Neville's carriage, he said to Will and Johnny, "Enjoy your dinner, and come back around ten o'clock, please."

Johnny grinned at his cousin and saluted. "Yours to command, sire."

Edward laughed as he went up the steps to the front door. It was Lily, not the housekeeper, who answered his knock, and she opened the door wider, her smile radiant. "I'm so glad you were able to come tonight, Ned. I must admit, I've missed you."

As the door closed behind them, he took off his overcoat, chuckled, and shot back, "I saw you on Saturday afternoon for tea, at Vicky's for goodness' sake!"

"But we weren't alone," she reminded him in a low voice; slipping her arm through his, she led him into the drawing room. "Would you like to have a whiskey?"

Ned shook his head. "No, thanks anyway. I had several at Neville's club earlier."

As usual he went and stood in front of the fire with his back to it, looking across at her. She had seated herself on the sofa, and he couldn't help thinking how lovely she looked in the pale blue silk gown with pearls on her neck and ears. He suddenly wished he had money so that he could buy her a gift.

"You're looking rather pensive, darling. Is something wrong?"

"No, Lily, nothing's wrong now that I'm here with you. I was just thinking how beautiful you are, and wishing I had some money so that I could buy you diamonds and emeralds, cover you in jewels."

Shaking her head, giving him an indulgent look, Lily laughed. "Don't be so silly, you don't have to buy me anything! I have everything I could possibly want." She patted the sofa and said, "Come and sit down, tell me about your day."

He did as she asked, gazing at her intently. "You look like a rose in full bloom, Lily. Your skin is perfect, your eyes are sparkling . . . simply ravishing, that you are. But a little different somehow." Leaning forward, he kissed her on the cheek and sat back. "Well, you asked about my day, and I can only say that it's been a bit hectic. Aubrey Masters died last night, very suddenly."

"Oh my goodness!" Lily's eyes narrowed, and she went on swiftly, "Wasn't he the head of the Mining Division? The one you had the huge argument with about your father's office?"

"He was indeed."

"Was he ill?"

"Oh no, well, as far as we know he wasn't. John Summers told us that Masters had chest pains last night, and that by the time the doctor arrived he was gone."

"Masters wasn't very nice to you . . ." Lily slowly shook

her head. "My mother always said God doesn't pay his debts in money," she added pithily.

Before Edward could respond, there was a light knock on the door, and Mrs. Dane poked her head around it. "Dinner's ready, madam," the housekeeper said and added, "Good evening, sir."

"Evening, Mrs. Dane," Edward responded, smiling, and stood up, offered his hand to Lily, brought her to her feet.

As they went across the hall to the dining room, Lily murmured, "I asked Mrs. Dane to make some of your favorite things, roast leg of lamb and roast potatoes, and I had Fortnum and Mason deliver their best Scotch salmon and Russian caviar, Beluga actually, I—"

"Lily, I'm afraid you're spoiling me!" he cut in. Then he put his arm around her shoulders as they walked into the room together.

After supper they retreated to the drawing room, and for a few minutes Lily fussed with pouring Edward a cup of coffee and then a balloon of Napoleon brandy. As she was doing so she said in an almost offhand way, "I'm thinking of buying a house in Kent; it's not far from Stonehurst Farm and is rather charming. Fortunately, it's in good condition, not a wreck like Vicky's farm was when she bought it."

Edward looked at her, his eyebrows drawing together in a jagged line. "That's always a blessing, not having to engage in remodeling and such. But Lily, why on earth do you want a house in Kent? I never realized you had a partiality to the country."

Lily realized that he was genuinely puzzled, and she replied quickly, "Oh, I do enjoy being out of town for part of the time, Ned, as long as there are friends nearby. However, I have another reason for buying the house." She cleared her throat, sat down on the small sofa, and continued, "There's something I want to tell you. But please, I don't want you to be upset. I'll take care of everything, you won't have to do a thing, I promise you."

Frowning again, Edward asked in a puzzled voice, "Lily, what *are* you talking about?"

"I'm pregnant, Ned," she announced in a strong, steady voice. "I'm expecting your baby—our baby."

He gaped at her in astonishment and instantly experienced a rush of happiness. "Lily, darling!" he cried. "We're having a baby! And that's what is different about you." He grinned from ear to ear. "You've put on weight, not a lot, but you are definitely a little plumper. Not that I mind, it's rather charming."

Rising, he went to sit next to her, encircled her in his arms, and kissed her on the cheek in the most loving manner. "*A baby.* Well, fancy that, we're having a baby."

"You're not angry with me, are you?" A look of worry crossed her eyes.

"How could I possibly be angry with you of all people? And anyway, let's not forget what Will always says. It takes two to waltz." Drawing away, gazing deeply into her face, he murmured, "I'm just as responsible as you are for making this child, and I will always feel and *be* responsible for him, or her."

"You don't have to be, I mean in a financial way," Lily assured him. "And I do understand you can't possibly marry me. I'm much too old for you. You will have to make an important marriage one day, you know. But of course, it would make me happy if you could see our child, spend time with us, visit us." A gentle smile flitted across her face. "You must understand, I'll never make any demands on you, Ned. Never ever."

There was an odd expression on his face, and he took her hand, brought it to his lips, kissed it, and held it between his own. "You're the most extraordinary woman I've ever met, and you are very special to me, my darling Lily."

twenty-six

I'm certainly glad you've recovered from that nasty little attack upon your person, Mr. Deravenel," Inspector Laidlaw said in his hearty voice, shaking Edward's hand with a firm grip. "I'm afraid we came to a dead end on that, sir. No suspects, as you know. Mind you, we've not closed the case. It remains open."

"I'm perfectly certain you'll never be able to pin it on anyone, Inspector," Edward replied and chuckled. "Those boys were long gone that very night, wouldn't you say?"

"I would indeed."

"Now, Inspector Laidlaw, I would like you to meet my colleagues Alfredo Oliveri and Robert Aspen. They both worked rather closely with Aubrey Masters for a number of years. They'll be happy to answer any questions you have, as will I."

"Pleased to meet you, gentlemen," the inspector said, shaking Alfredo's hand and then Rob's. "I do have a few things I would like to discuss with you both, and Mr. Deravenel."

The four men were standing in the middle of Edward's office, and he now said, "I think we might be more comfortable over there near the window, where we can all sit down." As he spoke he walked across the room and seated himself on the sofa; the other three men followed, and each took an armchair close to the leather sofa.

"By the way, Inspector, do you have the results of the autopsy yet?"

"Yes, I do, Mr. Deravenel. Two nights ago Mr. Masters died from the ingestion of digitalis."

"Isn't that a heart medicine?" Rob asked in surprise. "I didn't think one could die from it. My mother has a heart problem, and the doctor prescribed digitalis last year."

In his late thirties, Rob Aspen was a pleasant-looking man who appeared much younger than his years and wore his clothes with a bit of dash. Women found him attractive, wanted to mother him, but so far he had eluded all of them and was still single.

"It is indeed a heart medicine, Mr. Aspen," the inspector answered. "And that was one of the things I wanted to talk to you all about. Did Mr. Masters suffer from a heart condition, do you know?"

"I don't think so," Alfredo answered, "but then Rob would know better than I, because he works here in London all the time. I go back and forth to Italy, to Carrara, to be exact."

Rob exclaimed, "I'm pretty certain he was in the best of health. On the other hand, how can I be sure? We were business colleagues, not close friends, and he did not confide in me. Surely Mrs. Masters would know about his health?"

The inspector nodded and leaned back in the armchair, a reflective look on his face. After a moment's thought, he continued slowly. "Mrs. Masters insists that her husband did *not* have a heart condition, and therefore was not taking digitalis. I've also spoken to his physician, Dr. Fortescue. In fact, we had a long chat. The doctor cannot explain why Mr. Masters took digitalis. Certainly he did not prescribe it."

"Could there be another doctor involved?" Edward asked, giving the policeman a hard stare. "Perhaps Aubrey Masters wanted a *second* opinion, and certainly he wouldn't have wanted to offend Dr. Fortescue. Or perhaps he didn't want his wife to know he had developed a heart condition and *secretly* went to see another physician or specialist."

"Or any kind of condition," Rob suddenly volunteered.

"What are you suggesting, Mr. Aspen?" the inspector asked, pinning his eyes on the other man.

"It's something I've just remembered—" Rob left his sentence unfinished, shaking his head. "No, no, I'm sure there's nothing to it."

"To what?" the inspector asked.

"A remark Masters made to me about six months ago. I thought it was an odd comment, not at all like him. Out of the blue one day he muttered that life was so much easier for women, that all they had to do was lie down, whereas men had to stand to attention." Rob shook his head. "I was being something of a dunce that afternoon, I suppose, because I didn't get the innuendo at first, not until he chuckled and winked at me. Frankly, I was astonished. I suddenly realized he was making a reference to his . . . sexuality, or perhaps I should say lack of it. About a week later I took some papers to his office, but he was out. I placed the files on his desk, and it was then I noticed a writing pad on which he had drawn a number of hearts in red pencil, doodles really, and just below the hearts was the name Dr. Alvin Springer. I thought nothing about it at the time. It just came back to me now."

"I will have that name checked out, Mr. Aspen, and thank you very much indeed," Inspector Laidlaw said. "There's a possibility that Dr. Springer *is* a heart specialist, in view of those scribbles."

"It might be a clue, yes," Rob responded. "On the other hand, the doctor could be one who specializes in sex therapy. There are a few now practicing in London, I hear from a friend of mine, who suffers from . . . well, er, shall we say a certain inadequacy. He has also been going to a psychiatrist. Springer might well be a doctor who treats head problems."

Edward, who had been swallowing laughter, now glanced at Inspector Laidlaw. Immediately he saw the laughter in the policeman's eyes, although his expression was one of total solemnity.

Rising, Edward walked over to his desk, endeavoring to turn his spluttering laughter into coughing. A moment later, fully in control, he said, "Do excuse me, I'm so sorry."

The inspector, obviously suppressing *his* laughter, said, "Do you need a glass of water, sir?"

Edward walked back to the sofa, shaking his head. "No, no, thank you, I'm fine."

Laidlaw now said, "Mr. Aspen, you've been very helpful, and I will personally speak to Dr. Springer." Clearing his throat several times, he then went on. "I don't suppose any of you would know if there was—well, another woman in Masters's life?"

Edward again thought he would burst into laughter at the preposterousness of this idea, but he managed to control himself, as did Alfredo and Rob. They simply shook their heads, as did Edward, and kept their faces straight.

After a moment, Edward turned to the inspector. "If Aubrey Masters *did* have a heart condition, and had been prescribed digitalis, which is a *heart* medicine, then why on earth did he die because he took it?"

"It was an overdose, Mr. Deravenel. I'm sorry if I didn't make that clear at the outset. Accidental or on purpose, we don't know yet. And this leads me to another point, Mr. Masters's demeanor. How was he in the last few weeks? Despondent about anything? Did he appear worried? Or did he perhaps behave differently in some way?" He looked at Alfredo in particular.

"He was totally normal, Inspector," Alfredo announced in a firm voice. "Actually, he was in an especially good mood on Monday, although in a bit of a hurry to get away from the meeting we were having. He explained he didn't want to be late for an appointment out of the office. The following day, Tuesday, we bumped into each other in the corridor here, and he was very cordial. But I must admit, he did appear to be preoccupied. That's all I can tell you."

"He was *very* preoccupied, Inspector," Rob volunteered.

"And I concur with Alfredo. I myself thought he was in a good humor on Monday, and certainly normal in everything he did."

Inspector Laidlaw nodded. "It's probably all very simple really. No doubt he did have a heart condition he was hiding from his wife and everyone here. He must have gone to Dr. Springer, who put him on digitalis, for that reason. The other night, he more than likely misjudged the dose."

"Is there going to be an inquest?" Edward asked.

"Oh yes, of course, sir. It will be held next week according to the coroner." Standing up, Inspector Laidlaw thanked them for their cooperation. "I'll be in touch with you, gentlemen, as soon as I have more information."

Edward escorted the inspector down the corridor. As they walked along, Edward said in a low voice, "There is the possibility he committed suicide, isn't there?"

"Yes, indeed, Mr. Deravenel."

"I didn't know Aubrey Masters well, but he didn't strike me as the kind of man who would misjudge the amount of medication he should take. He was rather precise," Edward confided in the same quiet voice. "And yet he did take an overdose, didn't he?"

The policeman nodded and murmured in an equally low tone, "If you have any more thoughts or information to pass on, you can reach me at Scotland Yard, Mr. Deravenel."

When Edward walked back into his office a few minutes later, Alfredo and Rob were laughing uproariously.

"What's the joke?" he asked, and then began to laugh himself. When he finally sobered, Edward said, "Honestly, Aspen, I thought I was going to explode. There you were, mincing your words, being ever so discreet. You could have just come out with it and said Masters couldn't get an erection. The inspector was striving to suppress his own laughter. I saw that immediately."

Alfredo pulled out his handkerchief and wiped his eyes. "You sounded like your own maiden aunt, Aspen."

"I know," Rob admitted, looking suddenly chagrined. "It was rather foolish of me, but I was simply trying to say what I had to say without being—bloody vulgar."

"Inspector Laidlaw's one of the boys, a good sport, I can tell you that," Edward remarked, grinning again. "I think he would have appreciated a good laugh, in fact."

Alfredo walked over to the window and looked down into the Strand, then swung his head and said to Edward, "I think Masters might have committed suicide because of the *skimming*. You and I both think he might have been involved in that, and so does Rob, by the way."

Rob, who was leaning against the desk somewhat nonchalantly, nodded his head. "It's bound to come to light in the next few months—unless there's a real cover-up. It'll be miraculous if they make it go away."

"You're correct in that," Ned answered and sat down behind his desk. "I told Inspector Laidlaw that I'll be in touch if anything comes to mind, so put your thinking caps on, my lads, and think hard. I'd like to help Laidlaw if I can. He's a nice chap."

Alfredo said, "I couldn't believe it when the inspector asked if Masters had another woman. Can you imagine that, Aubrey Masters and a lady of the night?"

"Please don't," Ned muttered, grimacing. "It's certainly not something I want to envision. Masters was rather a strange duck in my opinion, quite ghastly, actually."

Rob chuckled. "You're right, and it's certainly hard to envision him as a ladies' man, even when the lady isn't a lady. Think of that."

"God forbid!" Ned exclaimed.

twenty-seven

He paused, his hand on the knob of the library door, listening acutely, wondering if he had been mistaken. No, he had not. He *could* hear someone sobbing, but he hesitated for a moment before entering. He was not sure who was in there, but whomever it was sounded extremely upset.

Quietly, Edward opened the door and looked into the long, elegant room. In the dim light, the library looked dark. Nevertheless, he saw his sister at once. Meg was bent over the mahogany reading table, her head on her arms, weeping as if her heart would break. He experienced a swift rush of love and concern for the girl and went into the room, closing the door softly behind him.

Although he was tall and well built, Edward moved lightly and with enormous grace; he was halfway across the floor on silent feet before his sister lifted her head and saw him.

Instantly, she jumped up and flew across the room, threw herself against his body. His arms went around her, and he held her tightly.

In a low, loving voice, he attempted to soothe her, stroked her hair. Like many large men, Edward Deravenel was gentle, tender, especially with women and his younger siblings.

Within a few minutes, her heaving slowed to a few gasps, and bending over her, he lifted her chin and looked into her eyes. "Too many tears for such a beautiful girl as you, Meg.

Now, what's this all about, my love? Why were you crying so hard?"

"I don't know," she began, her voice faltering, and shook her head. "I'm worried, I suppose—" She broke off, compressed her lips, and the tears welled again.

"And a little frightened, I suspect," he said gently. Leaning in to her, Edward wiped the tears from her face with his fingertips, kissed her forehead. Then he pulled a handkerchief out of his jacket pocket, and offering it to her, he said, "Come along, blow your nose, and let's go sit over there and have a little chat."

She nodded, took his handkerchief, and walked back to the circular reading table. Edward followed her, glancing around the room, thinking how peaceful and quiet it was on this sunny Saturday morning.

The walls were covered in a dark green damask fabric, offset by the white-painted woodwork, ceiling moldings, the door, the white marble fireplace, and the line of white-painted bookcases. These were filled with hundreds of volumes collected by his forebears. With its dark green silk draperies, red leather chairs, Oriental rugs, and a Chesterfield sofa covered with paisley fabric, it was a masculine room, yet not oppressively so.

Edward pulled out a chair next to Meg and sat down. "Tell me what's troubling you, sweetheart. Perhaps I can help."

"I suppose you were right when you said I was also frightened, Ned. Such terrible things have happened lately . . . too many for one family to bear. Papa and Edmund murdered, Uncle Rick and Thomas as well, then the attack on you. You could have been killed, all those blows to your head." A deep sigh rippled through her before she added, "It's as if the Grants are trying to kill off all the men in our line, render us helpless by turning us into a family of women."

Edward's blood ran cold as she said this, but he smiled at her and teased, "You and Mother are my *Amazons*, my warrior queens. Neither of you is helpless, Meg. Just the opposite." When he noticed her frown, he continued, "I'm not trying to make light of what you're saying. A lot *has* happened, but remember, bad things do happen to everyone at different times. Life is very hard, you know, and often comes back to hit one in the face. The most important thing is learning how to survive, to fight back, to hold one's own. That's what we must all do."

"I know, I must be brave," she murmured. "I'll try." She stared at her brother intently. "I worry about George and Richard, and you, too, Ned, about your safety."

"Listen to me, Meg darling. None of the Grants are going to destroy *me*. I'm going to get *them* first, don't you know?" He grinned at her, his bright blue eyes full of sparkle. "As for George and Richard, the Grants wouldn't go after children." As these words left his mouth, he knew, with a sinking feeling, that they would if they had to.

But wanting to calm his sister, he insisted, "You're quite safe, Meg, you and the boys, here in this house with Mother and the staff. And *me*. Don't forget, *I* live here, too."

"You go to work with them, and they could hurt you again."

"Yes, I do work at Deravenels during the day, and I go out at night, but now I have two bodyguards, Will and Johnny. Anyway, I seriously doubt that the Grants will attempt anything in the near future. They would be very foolish if they did."

"I hope they won't. I love you, Ned, and so do George and Richard." She suddenly smiled. "He adores you, your Little Fish."

"Yes, I know, and I feel the same about him, about all of you, and really, you mustn't worry about the Grants."

"When will they stop hurting us?"

"Soon."

"How do you know?"

"We'll make them stop, Neville and I."

"Why have they been doing bad things to us?"

"It's a long story. Basically, for money and power. They stole those things from our line of the family sixty years ago, and they are desperately trying to hang on to that power. But they *are* going to lose it, and lose it to us. We are going to reclaim what is ours by right."

Meg looked at him, her eyes shining. "Do you promise me, Ned?"

"I do indeed promise you, Margaret, and I want you to put these worries about the Grants out of your head. *You* must promise *me* that."

"I do promise." Leaning back in the chair, she murmured in a quavering voice, "I miss Papa and Edmund."

"So do I, and I truly understand your grief, Meg. I want to tell you something." Ned leaned closer and said sotto voce, "I carry them in my heart. Always. And you must do that, too. It helps to hold on to them and the memories of being with them, of having them in our lives."

Slowly she nodded her head. "I will do that. And I know I'll never forget them." She took his hand in hers, clung to it.

"*I* promise I will always protect *you,* be there for you," Ned reassured her.

"And I will be there for you," she responded. And some years later she was to prove her loyalty, a loyalty that never wavered, for all of his life and afterward.

"That's good for me to know. And we're going to be fine, the entire family is going to be all right. Trust me, the Grants will fall into oblivion."

"*When?*"

"I told you, *soon.* However, I see you want me to be more specific. Neville thinks we'll oust them in a few months. By the summer, he says, I'll be running Deravenels. Now, Meg, tell me about your days here. Are you enjoying being in London?"

"I prefer Ravenscar. I wish we were there now."

"Well, we're going there, how about that, my girl?"

"Did Mama tell you this?"

"No, she didn't. I just decided it now. So it's *our* secret, for the time being. Now, tell me about Perdita Willis. Do you like her as much as you did last year?"

"Yes, I do. More, really. She loves botany as much as I do, and she's teaching me such a lot of new, interesting things. I was studying a special book before I became sad and started to cry. I want you to look at it, you'll see how lovely the illustrations are." She pulled the large book toward her and confided, "I found this in the library at Ravenscar, and I was fascinated by it. So is Richard. He keeps saying that it belongs to him."

"Why is that?" Edward asked, looking somewhat amused at the idea of his Little Fish asserting himself.

"Because it does have his name on it." Opening the book, Meg showed Ned the name inscribed on the faded bookplate on one of the front endpapers. In beautiful copperplate it announced: "Richard Deravenel: His Book."

Looking down at the page his sister was showing him, Edward realized at once how old the book was. Very early Victorian, he thought. It was undoubtedly a gem. He suddenly remembered the story of the boy who died, and he exclaimed, "There *was* another Richard Deravenel, other than Father, many, many years ago. And that is his name on the bookplate, I feel sure. He died when he was about your age, Meg, of typhoid fever, I think. His full name was Richard Marmaduke Deravenel. This *did* belong to him, there's no doubt in my mind."

Edward turned the page and looked at the front. "What an odd title," he exclaimed. "*Fatal Flowers*." He glanced at his sister a little quizzically.

"It's about flowers that are so poisonous they can kill, and there are lots of them, Ned, growing in everybody's gardens. But do look at the pictures, they're so lovely."

"More than lovely, Meg," Ned remarked as he turned the leaves of the book. "These watercolors are simply superb."

Suddenly Edward stared at the two pages open in front of him. There was a painting of the tall and elegant foxglove on the left, and on the right the name of the flower in bold letters:

THE FOXGLOVE (DIGITALIS)

He read the heading again, hardly able to believe his eyes. *Digitalis,* he read once more, then dropped his gaze to the details written below. His eyes widened as he read:

> *The common foxglove grows in almost every Victorian garden. It is a flower beloved by all. Tall and graceful, it has many other names, such as fairy thimbles, fairy gloves, fairy bells, and dead man's thimbles, because its flowers do resemble the fingers of "fairy gloves." The curious names originated here in the British Isles, where our ancient people believed that the small spots on the bell of the flower were the fingerprints of fairies, hence the name "folks gloves," meaning the gloves of the little folks. The elegant and colorful foxglove is often referred to as "dead man's thimbles" because of its shape and the poison it contains. The Latin genus Digitalis refers to finger or thimble. This beautiful natural ornament for the Victorian garden, so graceful, so tall, is fatal if eaten.*

Oh, my God, Edward thought. He sat frozen, continuing to stare down at the page. He knew that Meg wanted to talk about the book with him. Whereas he wanted to think. Was that how Aubrey Masters had died? Had he eaten foxgloves? Had they been ingested with his vegetarian dinner? An accident? Suicide? Murder?

His fertile brain raced. If Masters had been murdered, who had done it? And how had the perpetrator managed to put foxgloves in his food?

"Ned, Ned," Meg exclaimed. "What is it? Why are you so interested in the foxglove in particular?"

Finally he lifted his head and forced a smile. "Because it's so strange, that a thing of such beauty is so deadly. Now I understand the title of the book."

Will was waiting for Edward in the library of White's, the gentlemen's private club in Whitehall where he and his father were members. Arguably the most famous club in London, it was believed by many to have been the first to open its doors; it had begun as a chocolate house in 1693, and Pope and Swift were among its regulars. Certainly it was a male bastion where members could go to eat, drink, smoke, gamble, play billiards, and read. Women were barred. None of them really wanted to go anyway, preferring the men in their lives to have places where they could be left to their own devices.

While waiting for his friend, Will had been perusing *The Times,* but he had now read enough and took it back to the table where the newspapers were always placed after use. As he swung around to return to his chair, Edward came rushing into the room but slowed his steps when he noticed a couple of older members present. Usually the club was deserted on weekends, with everyone in the country.

"So sorry I'm late," he said, clasping Will's arm.

"No problem, but shall we go for lunch? I'm positively ravenous."

"Let's do that."

The two young men left the library, crossed the grand entrance foyer, with its marble floor and dark mahogany furniture, and went into the dining room.

After they were seated and had each ordered a glass of champagne, Will looked at Edward and said, "This is a nice surprise. I didn't expect to see you today, especially since we're invited to have lunch with Neville and Nan tomorrow."

"I know, but aside from us and Johnny, there'll be Nan

and their girls, my mother and my siblings. It's going to be a family Sunday lunch with all the trimmings, and I don't think we'll have a chance to speak privately."

"So what's on your mind, Ned? Is something troubling you?"

"I wouldn't say troubling, more like tantalizing."

"I'm not sure what you mean by that."

"Did your mother have foxgloves in her garden when you were a child?"

"Yes, she did, and there are still foxgloves growing at Compton Hall." Will appeared puzzled when he asked, "But what are you getting at?"

"She was growing *digitalis,* and it is still growing in flower gardens."

Nonplussed, Will shook his head. "Come on, Ned, you're not talking sense."

Swiftly and with precision, Ned told him about the book from Ravenscar and what he had discovered that morning about the common foxglove. "Foxglove leaves and seeds are very poisonous, and I think that somehow they got into Aubrey Masters's food. Because nobody really believes he has a heart condition, do they?"

"No, they don't," Will answered and paused as the waiter arrived with their flutes of champagne. Once they were alone again, touching his glass to Edward's, Will murmured, "Cheers."

Edward responded in kind and went on quickly. "I telephoned Neville this morning to discuss the matter with him, but he had gone to the country for the day with Nan. So I'll mention it tomorrow before lunch if that's possible."

There was a moment of silence, and the two men exchanged knowing looks.

At last Will asked, "Do you think that our side has something to do with that digitalis in Masters's food? If indeed there was some there."

"I don't know. Anyway, how could they have?"

"God knows," Will muttered, shaking his head.

Late that afternoon, when he arrived home at the Charles Street house, Edward went in search of his mother. He found her in his father's den, and she glanced up as he opened the door.

"Oh, hello, darling," she said, smiling at her eldest son. "Nice lunch with Will?"

"Yes, very pleasant, thanks. Is this an inconvenient time to drop in on you, Mother? You do seem to be rather busy with your accounts."

"No, they can wait, and I was hoping to have a chat with you anyway, Ned."

"About something special?" he asked as he walked over and sat down in a chair near the desk.

"No, just things in general. And what about you?"

For a moment his eyes rested on the pile of bills on the desk; after a moment, he said, "Why did Father never have any money? After all, he was in a good position at Deravenels—assistant managing director. He must have had a decent salary."

"Not really. Naturally he had a salary, Ned, but it was not very much, of that I can assure you."

"And what about his father and grandfather? Didn't they leave him any money?"

"They, too, were on low salaries, and the Grants cheated them of their bonuses most of the time, just as they cheated your father. There *was* a small annuity from his father, and now that comes to me. Somehow your father always managed to pay for the upkeep and repairs at Ravenscar, but not the staff, I'm afraid."

"You pay their wages, Mother, and you maintain this house. I understand all that." Edward shook his head. "So unfair, isn't it? The Grants have stolen from us for donkey's years. Stolen our money, but fortunately not our spirit and our pride."

"True. And it's over sixty years now to be precise," she replied in a pithy tone.

"I aim to rectify that," he exclaimed. "I vow to you."

"I hope you will, not out of any avarice on my part but because Deravenels *does* belong to the Yorkshire branch of the family. I think it's about time there was a little justice and fair play."

"Neville and I will bring it about, Mother, never fear."

Cecily leaned back in the large desk chair and looked at her son speculatively for a moment. Then she said, "I've been thinking about money myself. I want to buy a house for you in London, close to here, and I was wondering how to do it. Actually, I was going to discuss it with Neville."

"But, Mother—"

"No buts, Edward. You're a grown man, you have your own private life now, and I think it's about time you had your own household. Don't you agree?"

"Well, yes, I do in a way. Will has mentioned it several times, and today at lunch he told me that a 'set' has come up at Albany. He wondered if I would be interested."

Cecily shook her head. "Those sets of rooms at Albany wouldn't be correct for you, not big enough. No, I think a house in Mayfair is much more appropriate under the circumstances."

"But that would be costly. I wouldn't want you to dip into your inheritance—"

"Sssh!" She held up her hand. "I had an idea about how to finance the house the other day." Rising, she walked around the desk and continued, "Come with me, Ned. I want to show you something."

It was gloomy in the cellar, especially at the far end near the wine racks. Ned suddenly realized his mother was heading in the direction of the vault, and he called out, "This electric light isn't very bright. Shall I go and ask Swinton for a few candles?"

"It's not necessary, there are some here, near the vault, and a box of Swan Vestas matches."

When he caught up with her, his mother was already lighting the candles, explaining, "I want you to open the vault, Ned; the handle is a little stiff for me. Now, let me tell you the numbers."

Within seconds the heavy door of the large vault swung open, and Cecily stepped closer to Edward and pointed to two dark green leather boxes, and another large one made of dark blue leather. Along with these there was a smaller fourth box, a faded red.

"Let's carry these upstairs, where the light is better. I'll take the red and blue boxes, they're lighter, Ned."

"Heavens, the green are heavier than I thought!" Ned followed his mother, saying, "If these are what I think they are, they must be purgatory to wear."

Cecily laughed but made no comment and climbed up the stairs to the entrance hall. "I think we should go into the drawing room, the light is exceptional there." She led the way. Placing the two leather boxes on a chair, she indicated the sofa to Ned. "Put those boxes over there. Now, darling, open them, please."

He did as she asked and gasped when he took out the first tiara. "Good Lord, Mother, this is extraordinary!" he cried, turning the tiara slowly, watching the light strike the diamonds, hundreds of them, catching the rainbow colors. "This is—*something special.*"

"Unique," she murmured. "It belonged to my mother."

Ned put it back in the box and took out the second tiara. Again, he exclaimed about its beauty. "And whose was this?"

"Mine," she answered. "My father bought it for me after my marriage, and this third tiara was left to me by Mother's best friend, Clarissa Mayes. She had no children and bequeathed it to me, along with this diamond necklace." As she spoke, Cecily showed him the tiara and necklace, and he seemed a little stunned.

"Mother," he said at last, "there's a small fortune here!"

"I know. I've been hoarding all of these for a rainy day, and now I shall sell them and buy you a house. What money's left over will pay for your staff."

"Oh, Mother, it's such a shame to sell these things. Why, they're family heirlooms. And what of Meg? She will need a tiara one day, after her marriage."

"*You* shall buy her a tiara, Ned, when the time comes. These are going to be sold so you can have your own establishment." Her voice brooked no argument.

twenty-eight

Edward stood on the threshold of the conservatory in Neville's Chelsea house, watching his brothers socializing with their cousins, Isabel and Anne.

The two little girls looked charming in their deep blue woolen dresses, each with a large white satin bow on top of her head. His brothers were equally smartly turned out, in their knee britches and jackets, black stockings, and highly polished black shoes.

With all the plants, and with sunshine pouring in through the many windows, it was an idyllic scene and brought a smile to Edward's face. George seemed to be holding forth about something; certainly he had captured Isabel's complete attention. Anne was talking earnestly to Richard, who was nodding his head and looking amused. Edward felt a little twist in his heart . . . they were so young, so vulnerable.

At the sound of footsteps in the hall, Edward swung around and smiled at Neville.

He joined Ned in the doorway, put his hand on his cousin's shoulder, and together they stood watching the children. After a moment, Neville said softly, "The future, Ned . . . they are the future of our two families, which are as one, and they must be protected at all cost."

"You're quite correct," Ned answered quietly. "We must guard them at all times. The Grants will stop at nothing."

"Unfortunately, you're right. I'm sorry I had to leave you to take the telephone call just as you were arriving." Neville glanced around. "I suppose Cecily and Meg have gone off somewhere with Nan."

Ned nodded. "They're in the drawing room."

"Right. Well, shall we meander along to the library and have a glass of champagne before lunch? Will and Johnny are already there, waiting for us."

"Why not?"

The two men walked down the entrance hall, but just before they reached the library, Edward paused and took hold of Neville's arm so that he, too, stood still. "Yes, Ned, what is it?" he asked.

"I need a word with you. Privately."

"Then tell me now, whilst we are alone here. Are you worried about something?"

"No, no, just curious. About the digitalis. We know Aubrey Masters died of an overdose, but I believe it was in the food . . . his vegetarian dinner, to be precise."

"Oh. *Really.*"

"Yes. Let me tell you about a book called *Fatal Flowers.*" Swiftly, Edward told his cousin of his discovery the day before, and the conclusion he had come to almost at once.

"I see what you mean," Neville replied, nodding. "But you said you were curious . . . about what exactly?"

"Did *we* have anything to do with Masters's ingestion of digitalis?"

Neville did not respond. He simply stood there, tall, elegant, and serene, his light blue eyes calm, his face without any expression.

Ned, leaning against a pillar, was equally steady. He waited.

After the longest moment, Neville answered. "I did promise you we would avenge the murders of our fathers and brothers. I never break a promise, Cousin."

Ned nodded his understanding, his own face wiped clean

of emotion, his eyes locked to his cousin's with intensity. And then he reached out, took hold of Neville's hand, and said in a low voice, *"Fidelity unto eternity,"* repeating his family's motto.

Cecily Deravenel was enjoying the luncheon party at her nephew's home. A lovely, flowing house overlooking the Thames, it was beautifully furnished in perfect taste. And because they were family, it was all the more pleasing to her. As for Will Hasling, she always thought of him as another son, and his devotion and loyalty to Edward had forever touched her heart. Yes, he *was* family, no question about that.

Her eyes roamed around the table, rested for a moment on her nephew Johnny. Dearest Johnny, a man of integrity and honor, Ned's champion. Then her glance settled on Neville. How alike the two brothers were in appearance, and they had the Watkins physical characteristics just as she did: dark hair, light eyes, the finest bone structure.

Neville was now the only senior male in the family, and it was on him that she must rely in many ways. Her brother, Rick, had managed her affairs, but now that he was dead it would be his son who would advise her on these matters. Only last week she had told him Ned needed an allowance. He had agreed. She trusted Neville; she had no reason not to do so. He was, after all, her nephew, and the richest magnate in England, a powerful man. That was the secret to him, of course, his power. Or rather, the secret was his *love* of power. Only the other day she had pointed this out to Ned, and he had smiled and retorted, "Do you think I don't know that?"

They had laughed together then, and the matter had been closed. She was well aware that her son had great judgment, and wisdom beyond his years. With Neville by his side, Ned would succeed in taking over Deravenels; it was just a question of time. From what Ned had said recently, perhaps it would be sooner than she had anticipated. There was nothing she could do except wait. She wanted to know that her children were safe, out of the reach of the treacherous Grants.

Cecily smiled inwardly as her eyes settled on Anne, Neville's younger daughter. She was an exquisite child, delicate in her beauty, intelligent, like quicksilver. How adoring Anne was of Richard; she trailed after him like a devoted puppy dog. And he did not seem to mind the little girl's attention, was responsive to her and very protective.

Anne was seated opposite Cecily, and as if she had read her aunt's thoughts, she announced in her light, clear voice, "Richard and I are going to be married, Aunt Cecily."

Everyone at the table looked at Anne in surprise. There was a trickle of warm laughter from the adults.

Richard said, "But not for a long time, Mama. Not until we're grown up."

"Of course, Dick, we do understand that," Cecily murmured, smiling at her youngest, her dearest child.

Ned said, "Well done, my boy. It's a good idea to stake your claim on a lady early. Just promise me one thing."

"What is that?" Richard asked solemnly, his gray-blue eyes so serious.

"Promise that I can be your best man."

Richard beamed at his hero and nodded enthusiastically.

Not to be left out, George now asserted, in a very grand voice, "And I am going to marry Isabel."

Isabel gazed at him, turned bright pink, said nothing. But she looked pleased, if somewhat startled.

"My goodness, all these sudden announcements," Cecily responded, staring at George, then smiling at Isabel.

Isabel smiled back, continued to gaze at George through loving eyes, euphoria flooding her face. She looked at her mother shyly.

Neville remarked in a light tone, "All these announcements indeed, Cecily! And yet no one has asked my permission."

Ned threw back his head and roared with laughter. "Nor my

mother's, nor mine," he spluttered, his laughter infecting the rest of the table. Hilarity reigned for a few moments.

Richard looked slightly embarrassed and threw an appealing glance at Edward.

His brother responded at once. "When you're grown up, Dickie, you can ask Uncle Neville for Anne's hand in marriage. As for me, I give you my permission now."

"What about *me*?" George demanded. "Do you give me your permission, Ned? After all, I'm older than Richard, and Isabel is older than Anne."

Yes, and she's the heiress to a vast fortune, Ned thought, if Nan doesn't give Neville a son. "Of course you have my permission," he responded at last, smiling. But he could not help thinking that his brother was showing some very dubious characteristics, avariciousness being one of them. He bears watching, Ned thought, he might spell trouble when he grows up. Years later Edward was to remember this day and marvel at his insight.

The music washed over him in waves, lulling his senses; slowly, he felt the tension easing out of his shoulders, and finally he relaxed in the seat. What a blessed relief this was . . . letting go, escaping into this world of thrilling sounds. The music was like an enchantment, taking him to another world.

Edward was with Lily at the Bechstein concert hall in Wigmore Street, attending the Sunday night concert. He loved music as much as she did, and tonight was special. The featured piece was Rachmaninoff's Piano Concerto No. 2 in C Minor, a concerto which was a favorite of theirs.

The second movement was coming to a close now, the crescendo engulfing him; he allowed himself to be engulfed. So many of the troubling thoughts running through his head fell away as he gave himself up to the music entirely.

Suddenly it was over. Everyone was on their feet, clapping and cheering. Lily leaned in to him and whispered, "Wasn't it thrilling, darling?"

"Stupendous," he answered. "Thank you for bringing me."

Smiling at him with adoration, she whispered, "Who else but you? Now tell me that." He just laughed. Protectively, he escorted her out of the hall and into the street, where the carriage she had hired for the evening was waiting for them.

In order to shake off Johnny and Will, wanting to be alone with Lily tonight, Ned had explained to his mother earlier in the day exactly where he was going, adding, "And my friend has hired a carriage. I'll be perfectly safe." After a moment's thought she had agreed with him, had excused herself and left the room. She had returned a moment later and handed him ten guineas. "But, Mother—" he had begun, and she had waved his words away, explaining that he must now have an allowance every week, that it had been arranged with Neville. "Take Mrs. Overton to dinner after the concert, and be the gentleman you are, Ned."

And so they were going to the Savoy Hotel for supper, and he was excited that for once he could take Lily somewhere elegant and pay for it himself.

Once they were settled in the carriage, he told her about lunch at Neville's that afternoon, and she laughed delightedly when he recounted the story of Anne's announcement that she and Richard were going to marry. In fact, they laughed all the way to the Savoy.

Heads turned as the two of them walked through the hotel lobby. They made a stunning couple, he so tall and handsome, she the most beautiful of women and elegantly dressed in a chic outfit of dark royal blue. After they had been seated in the dining room overlooking the Thames, Ned ordered a whiskey for himself and lemonade for Lily.

When they had settled down, he asked, "How are you feeling, darling Lily?"

"Healthy, Ned, thank you. Please don't worry so much

about the baby. It's the morning sickness which is the worst. Otherwise I'm fantastic. Really and truly."

He smiled at her, touching her cheek with a fingertip. "And that's how you look—absolutely fantastic."

As he savored his whiskey and soda, Edward told her about the tiaras his mother owned, and that she was going to send them to the jewelers to have them appraised and then sold. "She insists on doing this, Lily, in order to finance the purchase of a house for me. In Mayfair. I understand she's already seen one in Berkeley Square and thinks it's ideal for me. She wants me to have my own household."

Lily nodded, smiling, and was about to tell him she had been contemplating buying one for herself nearby, in South Audley Street. But she knew it would be inappropriate. The last thing she wanted was for him to think she was endeavoring to cling because of the baby she was expecting.

Ned said, "You looked as if you were about to tell me something, Lily, but changed your mind. What was it?"

"Nothing," she lied and went on. "Shall we look at the menu? I am a little hungry."

He nodded and signaled to the waiter, who was by their side in a split second. He gave them the menus, recommended various items, and departed.

Lily said, "I think I will have Dover sole, it's light."

"So will I. And what would you like first?"

"Nothing really. Well, perhaps a cup of bouillon. I find if I eat anything heavy at night I suffer from indigestion."

He smiled, leaned in to her, and whispered, "You poor thing. . . . I can't wait to see our child, hold her."

"Oh, you've decided on the sex, have you? A *girl,* eh?"

"Well, you know how much I love women," he answered before he could stop himself; he could have bitten off his tongue and shook his head, seemed somehow helpless.

Lily, being a wise woman, simply laughed.

Edward said, "What shall we call the baby? *Lily?*"

"I'd like to call her after *you,* so I prefer Edwina."

"Edwina Lily, how about that?"

"And Edward, if it's a boy. Is that all right with you, Ned?"

"Anything you want, my darling. I do adore you, you know."

The waiter returned and took their order, and they sat back, happy at being together in this elegant restaurant, sharing the evening, at ease in their relationship.

It was after their first course that Lily suddenly announced in a rather subdued voice, "Ned, I want to ask you something. It's really important for me to discuss it with you, and I must have an answer from you tonight."

Alarmed, he looked at her and exclaimed, "What is it, Lily? What on earth's the matter?"

"I'm not sure how to begin, because it's a morbid subject, but I have been troubled . . ." She took a deep breath. "Let me start again. As you know, I was an only child, and my parents are dead. I have no other family, only a few good friends, particularly Vicky. And because I'm alone in this world, I've worried about something quite a lot lately. Women do die in childbirth, you know. And I worry that I could die. Then what would happen to the baby? *Our baby.* So I want to know your thoughts on this, Ned. I couldn't bear it if the child were put up for adoption."

Startled by her words, Edward was also appalled at the thought of Lily dying and their child being lost to him forever. He didn't have to think twice before answering her. "You're not going to die, I promise you that. You're a healthy young woman, and you take good care of yourself. You'll both be fine. But if something ghastly did happen, you . . . died in childbirth and the baby lived, you know I wouldn't permit our child to be adopted. Never, Lily. I promise you I would take the child, bring it up."

"You'd do that alone? How would you handle it? What about other women? You'll get married one day. A wife might not be overjoyed at the thought of your illegitimate little girl or boy. Am I not right?"

"Yes, perhaps you are. But I believe my mother would happily raise the child with the help of a nanny. And of course I would see the child all the time. Does that satisfy you?"

"Yes, it does! It was the answer I was hoping you would give, Ned. You see, I know women, know how easily the child of another woman could get in the way in a relationship." Lily gave him a huge smile and squeezed his arm. "If anything goes wrong, then your mother can take over. . . . I'm so happy you suggested this."

He took her hand in his, squeezed it. "Lily, let's not talk about your dying . . . I can't stand that thought, I really can't. Let's be happy tonight, happy that we're together."

twenty-nine

Edward Deravenel was not easily rattled. In fact, he was almost always composed, and hard to read. On this Wednesday afternoon, as he walked at a measured pace down the corridor to John Summers's office, he was perfectly at ease with himself and with the world. And he had a good idea why he had been sent for. There was news.

When he arrived at the door of Summers's office, he knocked and walked straight in; he was not at all startled to see Inspector Laidlaw sitting there with Rob Aspen.

"Hello, Inspector," he said and looked across at the two other men. "Afternoon, Summers, Aspen."

They both responded, and John said, "Come and join us. "We're waiting for Oliveri so we can begin."

At this very moment Alfredo knocked and walked in, looking somewhat harassed. "Afternoon, everyone," he said in a rather casual way and took a chair next to Edward.

Inspector Laidlaw pushed his chair back a little so that the other four men were all in his line of vision. "Well, gentlemen, I'm here to tell you that I don't have very much news. We have done an intensive investigation into Aubrey Masters's death, and we've come up empty-handed."

"What exactly does that mean, Inspector?" Summers asked, steepling his fingers, a habit of his, and frowning.

"There are no suspects. We don't believe anyone gave

him digitalis, because there seems to be no reason anyone would want to kill him. He led a plain life, somewhat humdrum, in fact. It was a dull marriage, his wife is a bit reclusive, but there were no other women."

"But did he have a heart condition?" Rob asked, "and did you manage to trace Dr. Springer?"

"He did *not* have a heart condition, nor was he prescribed digitalis, because he didn't need it," the inspector explained. "We *did* find Dr. Springer, and he turned out to be a psychiatrist, a follower of Dr. Sigmund Freud. He could throw little light on Mr. Masters's life in general, although he did show us the medical files. He explained that Masters was concerned with his lack of sexual urge, worried that this problem was affecting his relationship with his wife. Apparently he believed she felt neglected."

The inspector paused, then added, "Dr. Springer was analyzing him."

"So *did* he die of an overdose of digitalis or not?" Alfredo now asked. He wanted this meeting to come to a conclusion so he could talk to Edward privately.

"Yes, he did," the inspector confirmed quietly.

"There was an inquest this morning, wasn't there?" Edward said, a brow lifting quizzically as he stared at the Scotland Yard man.

"Indeed there was, Mr. Deravenel, and the coroner brought in a verdict of accidental death." Laidlaw paused for a moment, then finished. "In my opinion there could be no other verdict. My sergeant and I believe that Masters accidentally poisoned himself with his vegetarian mix of seeds and pods, the stuff he ate and apparently had eaten for years. It could have built up, the toxicity; the medical examiner thinks that anyway."

"Didn't you examine the vegetarian mix at his home?" Edward gave the detective another probing stare.

"We did indeed, but there was nothing much there, and certainly there was no digitalis in the mixture we did find.

You see, the idea was to buy everything fresh several times a week, at least so Mrs. Masters told us."

"And where did he buy the mix?" Summers thought to ask.

"That's the problem, we don't know," Laidlaw answered and added, "His wife told us he brought the mixture home with him in a plain brown paper bag, so we have no idea what store he bought it at. As I told you, we've come up empty-handed, I'm afraid. Case closed, gentlemen."

"Thank you very much, Inspector Laidlaw," Edward said, immediately rising, walking over to the detective, and shaking his hand. "I, *we,* appreciate everything you've done to solve this, and I suppose it will always remain a mystery."

"That's right, sir, it will," Laidlaw answered and took his leave of them.

Edward walked the detective down the corridor, as he had in the past. When they reached the grand staircase, he turned to Laidlaw and said, "Inspector, if you ever need anything, whatever it is, please come to me. You've been most diligent, and very courteous. Deravenels and I appreciate everything you've done."

"Very little it seems to me, sir, and thank you for your kind offer. I'm sorry, too, Mr. Deravenel, that we haven't been able to solve the attack on you. It wasn't for the want of trying."

"Another mystery," Edward murmured, offering him a warm and genial smile.

A moment later, alone in his office, Edward reached for the phone on his desk. Then he instantly replaced the receiver. Why make a call to Neville now? The newspaper boys would soon be out on the streets, touting the latest afternoon editions. Best to let sleeping dogs lie, he decided, and waited for Alfredo Oliveri to come into his office.

He arrived within two minutes.

Seating himself in the chair, Alfredo gave Edward a long, questioning stare and said, "So, what do you think?"

"I think the inspector is a damned fine policeman who has found absolutely no evidence of murder."

"Do you think Aubrey Masters committed suicide?"

"I'm not sure, to be truthful. He might have killed himself, but let's take the coroner's verdict as the gospel truth, shall we?"

"But naturally, old chap," Alfredo said, poker-faced. "However, between you and me, I've found enough evidence to have had him hung, drawn, and quartered if he'd been alive. He was definitely skimming, and Jack Beaufield and James Cliff were in on it with him. And others on the job locally."

Edward grinned. "So we've got the two who are still alive by the short hairs, have we?"

"Oh yes, we surely do. It's taken a bit of digging, if you'll excuse the unintended pun, by Aspen and Green, but we now have even more evidence to get those two out. I can't wait to tell Neville Watkins."

Vicky had the hansom cab take her to Whitechapel; once they arrived at the High Street, she alighted, reminding the driver that he was to wait for her. Hurrying from the cab, she made her way through several bleak little streets until she arrived at the reclaimed old building now named Haddon House. She knocked on the door and waited, looking up at the darkening sky. A storm threatened, and it was beginning to drizzle on this cool Wednesday.

The door was opened within seconds, and the young woman standing on the threshold smiled when she saw Vicky. "Mrs. Forth, how nice to see you again, and so soon! Fenella is in her office, do please come in." She opened the door wider and ushered Vicky inside.

After hanging Vicky's topcoat in the hall cupboard, the young woman said, "Come along, I'll take you to her office."

"Thanks, Dora, but I do think I know the way by now," Vicky replied, laughing.

Fenella Fayne jumped up when she saw Vicky in the doorway and immediately came around the desk to greet her old friend.

"Let's sit over there by the fire," Fenella suggested. "It's turned chilly today, and it's damp as well."

"It's not very nice out," Vicky murmured, sitting down in one of the wooden chairs which Fenella had pulled toward the grate. Clearing her throat, she said, "I'd like to get straight to the point, Fenella. I've made up my mind, I do want to come and work with you here."

Fenella's face lit up, and she exclaimed, "Oh, Vicky! I'm thrilled. And I can truly make use of you."

"That suits me fine," Vicky answered and continued, "I know you're overworked. I can give you two full days every week. Would you like me Tuesday and Wednesday? Or Wednesday and Thursday?"

Without having to think twice, Fenella replied, "Tuesday and Wednesday is so much better, Tuesday being closer to the previous weekend. We get quite a few injured women coming in for help on Mondays and Tuesdays." She shook her head sadly. "You see, Vicky, their men have been in the public houses for most of the weekend, and the women get knocked about a little when the men come home from the pubs." Fenella grimaced and continued. "Not a pretty sight, I'm afraid. Black eyes, broken bones."

"I do have a few nursing skills," Vicky reminded her friend, "and you said the other day you needed someone who would make stews, soups, that kind of fare, and I'm quite a good cook actually." She smiled. "But I'll do anything you want, even scrub floors, I just feel I must help in some way. There's such poverty here in the East End."

"Vicky, there's so much you can do; even taking on some of my paperwork would be a godsend. Now, I would just like to mention, there are a few little rules. If I may explain them to you?"

"Yes, of course, please do."

"You won't be called Mrs. Forth once you start working with us, but Mrs. Vicky. It makes the women feel more at ease not using a surname, but they don't want to call you by your first name either. They also feel awkward about that, think it's too familiar. So I devised a compromise. The same thing goes for titles. I'm not Lady Fayne or Lady Fenella to them but Mrs. Fenella, and Dora is not Lady Dora but Miss Dora. Two other rules. Their husbands can visit them if the women are here for a few days. But they must be absolutely sober, and they must remain on the ground floor. Finally, we never press the ladies too hard if they don't want to discuss how they were injured. They are extremely protective of their men, you see. Oh, one other point. Sometimes they bring a small child with them, and we let the child stay until the mother is well again. And I think that's about it."

"I understand everything, and I'll certainly do the best I can. My heart will be in it, Fenella, I can assure you of that."

"I know that, my dear, and I can only say thank you from the bottom of my heart for volunteering in this way. You are a sight for sore eyes. How's Lily? I haven't seen her lately."

"She's very well, Fenella, and she did ask me to give you her love."

"Thank you, and mine to her. She's such a wonderful person. Only last week I received several bundles of clothes from her, all of them useful. They can be remade, simplified. I just sent her a note thanking her." Fenella suddenly stood up and continued, "When will you be able to start helping us, Vicky darling?"

"I'll be here next Tuesday morning, if that's all right."

"It is, and by the way, always remember to book yourself a hansom cab to pick you up in the late afternoon. They are very hard to find around here."

A few minutes later, as she walked back to the hansom cab waiting for her near the High Street, Vicky thought about her friend. Fenella was the widow of Sir Jeremy Fayne, who had been killed in a hunting accident several years before. She was now twenty-seven and had once told Vicky that helping the needy and downtrodden women in the East End had assuaged her grief to a certain extent, given her a purpose in life. Although she had worked at Haddon House, a charity founded by her aunt, Fenella had been somewhat reclusive in her widowhood until very recently. For the past nine months she had been socializing once more, living in two entirely different worlds. Vicky admired her fortitude, strength, and generosity of spirit, and she was going to do her best for Haddon House.

Edward sat in a comfortable chair in the Smoking Room at White's, waiting for Neville. Johnny, Will, and he had arrived twenty minutes earlier, but the other two had decided to "knock a few balls around the table," as Johnny put it, and had gone into the Billiards Room.

Nursing a whiskey and soda, Edward drifted with his thoughts, mostly thinking of Deravenels and the detailed plans for the takeover. Everything was coming together.

Occasionally he caught a wisp of conversation from other men in the room, and he smiled inwardly. Men could gossip just as easily as women.

The three men who sat at the table next to him, smoking cigars and relaxing after a day at business, were talking quite loudly. He cocked his ear for a moment.

"The king's going to Biarritz, dragging dray loads of servants with him, of course," one of the men said.

"And Mrs. Keppel, no doubt," said another.

There were a few titters, and then the third fellow exclaimed, "Heard what Churchill said recently? That Mrs. Keppel should be appointed First Lady of the Bedchamber."

All three men laughed uproariously, and even Edward

had to stifle a chuckle. The king and his long-standing mistress were often the butt of jokes.

Another voice piped up. "Northcliffe's *Daily Mail* is really backing Balfour and his government."

"Balfour won't last."

"The Tories *have* to stay in power."

"Couldn't agree more, old chap. By the way, I'm thinking of buying an electric car."

"Good Lord, that's brave of you."

"Oh, they're perfectly safe."

"Purchasing one of Mr. Ford's models, are you?"

"I'm not yet sure, old chap. Two English engineers, Mr. Rolls and Mr. Royce, are bringing out their own model. I might just wait for that."

"Stick with British made, that's my opinion, and that's what it's all about, you know. Got to keep the Empire flourishing. We're the greatest country in the world, don't you know?"

"I'll drink to that, Montague."

"Kipling has another book out. Amazing the way these chaps keep turning out masterpieces—Galsworthy, too, has a new hit. And George Bernard Shaw is putting on yet another play."

"Prolific, that's the only word for those writer chaps."

Edward cut off the chatter at the next table and fell down into his own thoughts, reminding himself that he had promised his Little Fish another book by Rudyard Kipling. He must order it tomorrow. And Lily's birthday was coming up. He wanted to buy her a beautiful piece of jewelry; he wasn't sure how to do this, unless he borrowed from his mother. *Money.* He needed it badly.

All conversation suddenly stopped. Edward glanced at the door and laughed to himself. Neville was standing there, looking for all the world like the reigning monarch of all he surveyed. Elegantly dressed as always, and supremely self-confident, he strode into the room with panache, nodding to the men who greeted him.

Edward rose and clasped his cousin's hand as Neville drew to a standstill at the table. "Where are the others?" he asked, sitting down.

Edward, also sitting, explained, "They went to have a game of billiards."

Neville nodded, motioned to the waiter, ordered the same as Edward, then settled back in the chair. "Would you care for a cigar?"

"No thanks," Edward replied and went on. "Inspector Laidlaw came to see us at Deravenels today." He gave Neville a penetrating look.

"I assumed he would. The coroner's verdict is in all of the afternoon papers," Neville answered. "Accidental death, so I read."

Their eyes locked, and there was a moment's silence.

Finally, it was Edward who murmured in a low voice, "Yes, that's what Inspector Laidlaw told us. He said no crime had been committed, also pointed out that there was no reason for Aubrey Masters to commit suicide, at least as far as he had been able to ascertain. The inspector characterized the man's life as humdrum, plain."

Neville nodded, pursed his lips, looked thoughtful. "The money he stole from Deravenels has to be somewhere, Ned. In his bank account, I presume, which is now his *wife's* bank account. Unless he had another woman in his life, or made other arrangements. It could well be *hidden*."

"Laidlaw made a point of saying there were no other women around. Well, to the best of his knowledge. But that doesn't mean Mildred Masters has it. He might have opened an account with another bank, which she has no inkling of," Edward suggested.

"Perhaps. In that case, the money is most probably lost, Ned, unless he left instructions with the bank, or in his will, regarding the disposal of his wealth. I doubt Deravenels will ever see a penny. If only we had some documentation about his personal finances—" Neville broke off, shaking his head. "Impossible."

"I agree, I don't suppose we'll ever get our hands on *that,*" Ned muttered, irritated at the thought.

"You may well be right," Neville agreed. *"C'est dommage."*

Neville picked up his whiskey and soda, which had arrived a moment or two before. "Good health, Ned."

Edward lifted his glass, brought it to touch his cousin's. "Good health," he repeated.

"Where would you like to dine tonight?" Neville asked, wanting to change the subject.

"Wherever you wish," Edward answered. "The Savoy? Rules?"

"Ah, here come Johnny and Will! Let's ask them."

M argot Grant stared at John Summers and cried, "Accidental death! This verdict is a travesty! Aubrey was murdered. I *know* he was . . . in my heart I know it. Oh, *mon Dieu,* it is a travesty."

"Margot, darling, please calm down. Inspector Laidlaw came to see me today and explained everything. Scotland Yard did a very thorough investigation, and they are certain no crime was committed."

"Nonsense! I know he was murdered. *They* did it! *They* killed him."

John leaned back on the sofa, his eyes focused on her intently. She sat behind the desk in the paneled library of her house in Upper Grosvenor Street and, as usual, looked impossibly beautiful, sexually inviting. And imperious. Also somewhat outraged. When she was angry, her voice grew shrill and her French accent became more pronounced, and he always wanted to flee for safety.

Taking a deep breath, John said, "There is no evidence that the Deravenels did anything. Laidlaw agrees with the coroner's verdict that this was an unfortunate accident. You know as well as I do that Aubrey had the weirdest eating habits. I am certain he ingested digitalis by accident."

"I do not believe this."

"If it was not an accident, then it must have been intentional, suicide," John suggested, his voice even, reflecting his unruffled demeanor.

"*Suicide.* Bah, he wouldn't do that! *Non, non, jamais.*"

John remained silent, thinking of the discrepancies he had recently discovered in the accounts which pertained to the Mining Division. As yet he couldn't quite fathom what Masters had been up to, and who else might be involved in the problem. If there *was* a problem. He decided not to mention this new development to Margot. He had no intention of inflaming her further tonight.

Suddenly the door opened and Henry Grant stood on the threshold, wearing an old blue velvet dressing gown and slippers and looking rumpled. There was a vacant expression on his face and in his eyes a lost look.

"Ah, Margot, there you are," he began and shuffled into the room, a man aged beyond his years.

At once Margot went across the floor and took hold of his arm. "Come, Henry, sit down. John is here, he came to visit you."

Henry turned. A gentle smile spread across his face when he saw his cousin. He shuffled forward, offering his hand.

Immediately, John was on his feet, shaking Henry's hand, smiling, affecting a look of pleasure. But inside he was dismayed. The head of Deravenels seemed more like a doddering old fool than a captain of industry. He had to be kept out of sight. That was imperative.

"Good evening, Henry," John said and led the other man over to the sofa. They sat down together, and John went on. "How're you feeling this evening? A little better, I hope."

"Oh yes. I was waiting for Father O'Donovan, but per-

haps he is late. Mmmmm. Ah well, never mind. And how is
your father? Haven't seen him lately."

Before John could respond, Margot interjected, "Now
John, Henry, shall we have a *coupe*? A little champagne
will be good, no? A healthy drink, my grandmother told
me." Without waiting for an answer, she rang the bell on
her desk.

"That will be nice," John responded at last.

Henry as usual said nothing. His eyes closed, he was
drifting with his pious dreams.

The butler appeared in the doorway. "Can I be of service,
madam?"

"*Oui,* Turnbull. Champagne please."

He inclined his head and left.

Margot moved toward her husband. "Henry, Henry, are you
tired? Are you sleeping?" She bent over him, solicitous.

Henry roused himself and sat up straighter. "Tired, yes. I
think I shall go back to my room."

"I will help you," she murmured in a kindly tone.

"No, no, John will accompany me." He turned to his
cousin in a helpless way and then smiled faintly. "Please."

"Of course, Henry," John replied at once and, taking hold
of the older man's arm, led him out of the library.

Margot stood in the middle of the floor, seething inside.
Men. They were impossible. Henry was a pious, ineffectual
idiot; John Summers was a fool. He believed this stupid policeman Laidlaw, believed the coroner's verdict. She was
right. She knew it. The Deravenels had murdered Aubrey
Masters, and they were getting away with it.

At this moment John came back into the room, followed
by Turnbull with the silver bucket of champagne on a silver
salver, and crystal flutes.

Within seconds they were toasting each other with the
sparkling wine and went to sit together on the sofa. Margot
made a tremendous effort to curb her anger. She said softly,

with a light smile, "And did Henry have secrets to confide in you, John darling?"

He shook his head and answered swiftly, frowning. "He wanted to talk about Edouard. He says he wants me to take him down to Eton to visit his son." John eyed her carefully, always curious when he mentioned the boy who might be *his* father's bastard, his half brother. "What do you think of that?"

"It's a splendid idea," she answered, not in the least put out. "He has not displayed much interest in Edouard lately. Will you do it?"

"Naturally. But you will accompany us, won't you?" Not waiting for an answer, he leaned in to her, kissed her full on the mouth. "It will be unbearable if you don't," he added.

"I shall come with you. And my *life* is unbearable without you. I need to see you alone, *cheri,* be with you." She dropped her voice. "I need to be with you in your bed, in your arms. Ah, John, my life is empty, miserable without you . . ."

Placing his glass of champagne on a side table, he then did the same with hers. Drawing closer, he pulled her into his arms, began to kiss her passionately. She responded with an ardor that more than matched his, then suddenly pulled away. Against his cheek, she whispered, "It is not safe here. Let's go out. *Now.* Take me to your house . . . please. *Please.*"

He longed for her just as much as she did for him. Within minutes they were in his carriage driving across town.

thirty

The streets of Whitechapel were dark by the time Amos Finnister arrived, and after paying off the hansom cab he went in search of his favorite pie man. All afternoon he had dreamed about one of those wonderful meat-filled pastry pies, oozing gravy, and he was now determined to have one if not, indeed, two.

Sometimes the vendor had his cart set up on Commercial Road, but tonight there was no sign of him. Amos knew he would be somewhere in the area and set off to find him. Ten minutes later he spotted the cart, and the most fragrant smells wafting toward him announced that it was the same chap he had patronized before.

The vendor greeted him with a cheery grin, said in his breezy Cockney way, "Evenin', guv, I knew yer'd be back 'ere again. Best pies, that I 'ave."

"You certainly do, and my compliments to your wife. I've never found any more delicious than hers. I'm even tempted to buy two tonight."

"Go on then, sir, 'ave a splurge."

Amos nodded. "I think I will."

The vendor lifted a pie out of the tray with the metal tongs, showed it to Amos, put it in a small white bag, dipped a ladle into a pot, and added thick beef gravy on the crust. He followed the same procedure with the second pie, then placed the two white bags into a larger one made of brown paper.

Reaching into his pocket, Amos brought out fourpence, handed the money over, and took the bag. "I'll be back next week, all being well."

"See yer, guv," the vendor said and saluted, grinning.

Amos walked through the streets until he found the cul-de-sac where he had eaten his pies in the past. It was a quiet spot, a bit off the beaten track; a gas lamp nearby added illumination. As he put the bag of pies on the wall and sat down, Amos glanced around. Immediately he noticed the old wooden cart, which hadn't been there before. Somebody had obviously dumped it; without wheels, it was dilapidated and of no use.

Taking a pie out of the bag, his mouth watering, Amos bit into it at once, savoring that first bite. Like this area, the pie reminded him of his father and the carefree time of his childhood. That was the reason he liked to come to Whitechapel these days. For the memories.

He had just taken a second bite when he heard a strange mewling sound, like a small animal in pain. He scanned the ground, but there was no stray dog or cat in sight. There it was again, the mewling. Amos glanced toward the cart and was taken aback at the sight of a small face peering over the edge. Light-colored eyes, enormous in the dirty face, were just visible under a flat cap. The mouth was distorted as if the boy was in some sort of pain.

Putting the pie down, Amos jumped up and walked to the cart; instantly, the boy scurried away from the edge, cowering.

"Now, now, what do we have here?" Amos asked in a soft voice, not wishing to frighten the child any further.

There was total silence.

He said again, "So, what do we have here then?"

"Nuffin'," the child answered, "nuffin'."

"Oh, but I think you're something."

"Ain't. I'm nuffin'."

"My name's Amos. What's yours?"

"Liddle Bugger."

"No, no, come along, lad, it can't be that. Tell me your name."

"That's wot 'e calls me."

"Who?"

"The man, 'im as kicked me out, kilt me muvver, 'e did."

Amos felt the hackles rising on the back of his neck, and an involuntary shiver ran through him. He asked in the same gentle voice, "Where do you live, lad?"

" 'ere."

"In this neighborhood?"

"Naw, 'ere."

"Do you mean you live in this cart?"

The boy nodded and sniffed, then sniffed again.

Amos suddenly understood that the child could smell the pie, and he cursed himself under his breath. Why hadn't he understood that before? The boy had looked out of the cart because of the pie. "Hungry, lad? Do you want something to eat?"

The boy nodded, suddenly came closer to the edge of the cart and looked at the wall where the pies were.

Amos said nothing more. He reached into the cart and lifted the boy out before he could protest. He was light as a feather, and as Amos put him down on the cobblestones, he wobbled slightly. The child wore an old, torn jacket, a pair of ragged pants, and broken boots. And he was filthy.

"Come along then, let's have some of that pie," Amos said cheerily.

Unexpectedly, the boy hung back, wary, his eyes darting around nervously.

Amos took hold of his hand in an easy way and said, "Let's tuck in together, shall we, laddie? Get to know each other."

The boy was silent but put up no struggle. Once they were

at the wall, Amos lifted him onto it, opened the brown bag, took out the other pie, handed it to him. "This is for you."

The boy hesitated for only a split second, then took it, gobbling ravenously.

Watching him, Amos was suddenly angry. What sort of country did he live in where little boys could roam the streets in dire need of food, clothing, and shelter? It made his blood boil. All the wealth in this lush Edwardian era and bairns starving on the streets of London. Appalling, it was.

The child suddenly stopped eating, and looking across at Amos, he offered him the pie. " 'Ere, 'ave a taste."

Shaking his head, Amos picked up his own pie and began to eat, and after a mouthful or two, he explained, "One each, you see, I must have known I was going to meet you."

" 'Ow yer know'd that then?"

"I've no idea, lad. I suppose I just did. Would you like a drink? Water, milk, something like that?"

The boy nodded, his eyes eager.

"We have to go and get it," Amos explained and took a bite out of his pie. "I'm full," he murmured, looking at the child. "Why don't you finish it for me?"

Shaking his head, the boy jumped off the wall and stepped backward, looking worried.

"Shame to waste it, really," Amos muttered and put the remainder of the pie on the wall.

After a moment the child started to reach for it, then paused, his big eyes resting on Amos. He wanted the pie but appeared afraid to touch it.

"It's all right, you can have it. I told you I'm full to bursting," Amos remarked.

Once the piece had been demolished by the child, Amos stood up, stretched out his hand, and said, "Come on, let's go and find that glass of milk, shall we?"

"Naw, can't go."

"Why not? It isn't very far."

"Can't leave me cart."

"It'll be quite safe, I'm sure of that," Amos assured him.

" 'Ow long?"

"You mean how long to get there? How far it is?"

The boy nodded.

"Ten, fifteen minutes, that's all."

Instantly the boy shrank back, shaking his head vehemently. "Naw, naw, stayin' 'ere. It's safe 'ere."

Crouching down to look into the child's scared face, Amos said in the warmest voice he could muster, "Tell you what. I know you're tired. How about I carry you there? We'll have a glass of milk, and then I'll bring you back to the cart. Or take you wherever you want to go. I promise."

The child stared back at him, his eyes appearing even larger, and he suddenly smiled. "Cross yer 'eart an' 'ope ter die?" he said.

"Cross my heart and hope to die."

Running to the cart, the boy scrambled inside and reappeared a moment later clutching a dirty cloth bag tied at the top with string. He clambered out of the cart and stood looking up at Amos.

"What's in the bag?" Amos asked, reaching for it.

The boy clutched it to his body, shaking his head harder than ever. "Naw, naw, it's me fings! Yer can't 'ave it."

"It's all right, laddie, I don't want it. I thought you might like me to carry it, that's all. Anyway, I'll carry you, and you can carry your bag, and that'll be fine."

There was only a moment's hesitation, and then the boy confided, "Me mam seys that . . . Cross me 'eart an' 'ope ter die."

"So she's not dead?"

"Yeah, she is . . . she's in Potter's Field."

Cursing himself once more for his thoughtlessness, Amos bent down and picked the boy up, carried him out of the cul-de-sac and up toward Commercial Road, singing, "Onward Christian soldiers, marching as to war, with the Cross of Jesus going on before!"

◆ ◆ ◆

As Amos walked along, singing his favorite hymn half to himself, he felt the little boy go limp in his arms almost immediately; his head rested on Amos's broad shoulder, one hand clutched his precious cloth bag, the other held tightly to the lapel of Amos's overcoat.

Poor little bairn, Amos thought, he's exhausted. Whatever will become of him? And where should I take him after we've had the milk at Haddon House?

It was while they were eating the pies in the cul-de-sac that Amos had had the idea to take the boy over to Haddon House, just off Whitechapel High Street. He was quite certain that Lady Fenella would be able to help. He had known her since she and her aunt Lady Philomena Howell had opened the safe haven for battered women three years ago, and he admired her, respected her for the extraordinary work she was doing.

After all, she was titled in her own right, being the daughter of the Earl of Tanfield, and, as the widow of Lord Jeremy Fayne, a wealthy woman. She was young, not yet twenty-eight, and considered something of a beauty in society—tall, elegant, with blond hair and gray eyes. As an aristocrat and socialite, she did not have to devote half her life to helping those in distress, yet she did, and with great efficiency, kindness, devotion, and love. All those who met her, from all walks of life, succumbed to her charms.

It was more than likely that she wouldn't be there at this hour of the evening but rather in her house in Mayfair. However, Amos knew that some of her helpers would be at Haddon House because Lady Fenella's policy was to keep the doors open twenty-four hours a day, seven days a week; no one was ever turned away. Perhaps the boy would be permitted to sleep there tonight, once he had been cleaned up a bit.

Amos loathed the thought of taking him back to the cul-de-sac and that decrepit old cart; in fact, he had no intention of doing so. It was so unhealthy and, furthermore, dangerous. It was inhuman to allow a child to exist in such a way. He decided he would make inquiries at the local Dr. Barnardo's Home tomorrow; perhaps the orphanage would be able to find a place for him.

All of a sudden, Amos thought of Charlie and Maisie, wished that they were here, that they still lived in Whitechapel. They would have taken the boy in without a second thought. That was the way they were.

As it was, the brother and sister were in New York, walking those streets they claimed were paved with gold, seeking work as actors. He missed them, especially Charlie, and looked forward to more cheerful letters from him. One had arrived already, and it seemed that their prospects were good.

Hoisting the boy, holding him close, Amos hurried now, wanting to get to Haddon House. One thing he was certain of was a warm welcome. All the women who worked there were pleasant and accommodating. He characterized them as the salt of the earth.

thirty-one

A ll the lights were blazing when Amos arrived at Haddon House, and they were a most welcome sight. Lifting the brass knocker, he banged it several times, and within a couple of seconds the door was opened.

To his utter surprise he stood staring at the familiar and lovely face of Will Hasling's sister, Mrs. Vicky Forth. She was looking equally surprised.

"Goodness gracious, it's you, Mr. Finnister!" she gasped, then immediately added, "Do please come in, won't you?"

"Evening, Mrs. Forth," he replied at once, stepping into the vestibule. "I didn't expect to see you here, ma'am, and especially in the evening."

"I'm helping Lady Fenella two days a week," Vicky explained, "and my presence here this evening *is* rather unusual, Mr. Finnister. There was an emergency, you see, and Lady Fenella asked me to come in to help her deal with it. But please, let us not stand here in the chilly foyer. Come into the great room, where there's a fire." Peering at the sleeping boy with immense curiosity, she then asked, "And who is this little fellow?"

"I found him out on the streets, Mrs. Forth," Amos answered as they walked into the large main room, where there were several big sofas, plenty of comfortable chairs, as well as a long trestle table covered with a white cloth. Amos quickly filled her in as they made their way to the fireplace.

The lamplight, the warmth, and the voices caused the boy to stir in Amos's arms, and he suddenly awakened and began to struggle. "Steady on, laddie," Amos murmured and placed the boy on the floor. Again he seemed a little unsteady on his feet, and then he looked up at Amos, appearing afraid. He was shivering excessively.

"Are you cold, lad?"

The boy nodded.

"Come on then, let's get you settled here by the fire for a little bit. And then I'll get you that nice glass of milk I promised you."

The boy clung to Amos's hand as they moved toward the roaring fire. "Sit here, laddie." The boy hesitated in front of the chair; Amos lifted him up and plopped him down in it.

"You'll soon feel much warmer," he murmured and hurried over to Vicky, who was waiting for him near the trestle table. "Could we get him something to drink, Mrs. Forth? Perhaps water, if you can't spare the milk. Although I did promise the little mite a glass of milk."

"Of course he can have some milk, but do you think he might like a cup of cocoa? Children love it, and certainly it would warm him up."

"Oh, what a grand idea, it is indeed! Thank you."

"I'll go and tell Mrs. Barnes to make a jug of cocoa for all of us. You look as if you could use a hot drink yourself. Back in a moment, Mr. Finnister."

Vicky was as good as her word; she returned at once and informed Amos that the cocoa would be made within minutes. "Now, please tell me more about the boy."

"I've told you most of what I know, Mrs. Forth. He said he'd been kicked out by the man who killed his mother, but of course, we don't know if that's true, the bit about the man killing her. However, I do have a strong feeling that his mother really is dead. He said something about her being in Potter's Field."

"Then I agree with you. She probably passed away, and the boy could easily have been unwanted after she was gone. Perhaps she was sent into the streets, if the man they were living with was not his father. You told me he said he had no name."

"That's right. Well, he did give me a name of sorts, but I couldn't possibly repeat it to a lady like you, Mrs. Forth."

Vicky smiled at him. "Oh, you can, Mr. Finnister. You'd be surprised what I've heard around here. Then again, you might not be. After all, you were once a policeman in these parts, so my brother told me."

"Indeed I was, ma'am, and I do know the area well. My father brought me here quite a lot when I was a boy." He sighed, and lowering his voice, he muttered, "He said his name was Liddle Bugger."

"How awful for the child." Vicky shook her head. "It staggers the imagination the way some people willfully hurt innocent children." She paused, looked toward the door. "Ah, here comes Mrs. Barnes with the cocoa."

Mrs. Barnes nodded and smiled when she saw Amos. Crossing to the long table, she placed the tray with the jug and cups on it and hurried off back to the kitchen. She, too, was a volunteer, and this was her night to look after the food.

"Thank you, Vanessa," Vicky called after her. At the table, she poured cocoa into the three cups. "Come along, here's a cup for you, Mr. Finnister," she said and carried a second cup over to the boy, who was curled up in the large armchair.

He raised his head when he saw her and instantly cowered. But then, as he focused on her, his eyes widened, and he sat up a little straighter, staring at her intently.

"Hello, little boy," Vicky said, offering him the cup. "Don't be afraid. Look, I've brought you a cup of warm cocoa. It's lovely, it tastes of chocolate. I know you'll enjoy it." As she spoke he listened most attentively, and his eyes did not leave her face.

Vicky leaned toward him, again offering the cup of cocoa. With a jerky movement, the boy reached out and touched her hair, then drew back swiftly.

Vicky simply smiled at him and handed him the cup. He let go of the cloth bag he was clutching and took the cup from her. His eyes were still wide, the look of surprise lingering on his small face.

She, too, was surprised; in fact, the child had startled her when he reached out. She had almost pulled back but managed, somehow, to remain still when he had touched her hair.

She noticed he was not drinking the cocoa; his eyes were fixed on her face: he appeared to be mesmerized by her.

Vicky said softly, "Have a sip of the cocoa. It's very good. I'm going to have a cup myself."

The boy finally nodded and did as she said.

Amos had been watching Vicky with the child, and now he came over to join her by the fireside, bringing the two cups with him. "Here you are, Mrs. Forth," he murmured, handing her a cup. "Ah, I see you're enjoying it, laddie. That's good."

The boy looked at Amos and nodded, then he said in a low mumble, "Mam . . . like Mam."

Frowning, Amos glanced at Vicky.

She said, "I think he's referring to his mother when he says *Mam,* it's a North Country word, from Yorkshire actually. I suppose he might be suggesting I look like her."

Amos raised a brow, then glanced at the boy, who was now drinking down the cocoa and no longer paying attention to them.

There was the sound of footsteps, and as Amos peered across the room, he saw Lady Fenella and, much to his surprise, Chief Inspector Mark Ledbetter of Scotland Yard. When Ledbetter spotted Amos, his face lit up. As he came to a stop, he stuck out his hand and exclaimed, "How nice to see you, Finnister."

"Evening, Chief," Amos replied, shaking his hand, and then he turned swiftly to Fenella Fayne. "Good evening, Lady Fenella."

"Amos, what a pleasant surprise! It's been a few weeks since you popped in. I've missed seeing you. Those clothes were most welcome, as I told you at the time. It was exceedingly generous of you and your wife, and I do hope you received my letter of thanks."

"We did indeed, Your Ladyship. We admire your work, try to help when we can."

Fenella nodded and then quickly glanced at the child. "And who is our young guest?" she asked.

Vicky said softly, "Mr. Finnister found him in the streets, Fenella. He seems to have been thrown out of wherever he was living. He had taken refuge in a cart."

"A cart!" Fenella cried, her eyes startled. "How horrendous!"

Vicky nodded and explained, "Perhaps it would be better if Mr. Finnister filled you in. Don't you agree with me, Mr. Finnister?"

"Happy to oblige, ma'am." Amos drew Lady Fenella and the chief inspector to one side of the room and rapidly told them everything that had happened that evening, from the moment he had gone into the cul-de-sac.

They both listened attentively, and Amos finally finished. "I didn't know what to do with him, Lady Fenella, and then I thought of you and Haddon House. He *can* stay here tonight, can't he? Poor little lad, he seems worn out, and he was starving. Very hungry and thirsty, and cold."

"Of course he can stay here tonight, Amos. Where else but here? However, I do think we have to take him into the scullery and give him a bath at once. Don't you agree?"

"Oh yes, indeed I do, Lady Fenella. He does need a bit of soap and water to make him . . . palatable."

At first the boy was reluctant to vacate the armchair, but eventually Vicky was able to coax him out of it. Even so, he did not want to leave Amos, who finally had to accompany the two women to the scullery. The boy held on to his hand tightly, looking frightened again.

Vanessa Barnes was standing at the big deal table in the kitchen, cutting up meat and vegetables, which she kept putting in the bubbling pot of beef soup on the stove. The boy's nose visibly twitched as they passed by the large black iron oven that also warmed the room. His steps faltered, as if he wanted to stop and eat. The adults noticed this, and glances were exchanged but nothing was said. Once they reached the scullery door, Amos got down on his haunches and said to the boy, "Now listen to me, laddie. I shall be right here in the kitchen with the lady who is making the soup. I won't go away. I'll wait for you, I promise. Cross my heart and hope to die."

The boy looked up at Amos and nodded. "Awright," he muttered and allowed himself to be led into the scullery by Vicky.

This was quite a large room with a stone floor and one window, tall cupboards for linen and supplies, and in one corner a large set pot where the washing was done. The fire underneath the set pot was always burning and kept the room warm as well as the water heated.

Fenella glanced across at the set pot and said, "I know that Vanessa filled it up with water earlier, so there will be plenty for his bath."

Vicky nodded and went to the end wall, where a small zinc bathtub hung on a metal hook. "I think this is the best size to use, don't you?"

"I do. I'll get soap and some of the disinfectants, Vicky. His hair especially will need attention—for the usual *problem*."

Within a few minutes the two women were taking jugfuls of hot water from the set pot and filling the bathtub on the floor in the middle of the room. "Come along," Vicky said to the boy. "You have to have a bath now."

The boy remained standing near the door, a fierce look on his face.

She went on, with a warm smile, "We must wash all the dirt away." She smiled again and beckoned to the child.

He remained stock-still, clutching his cloth bag next to his little body. He was totally mute.

Finally, Vicky said to Fenella, "I'd better start undressing him." Walking over to the boy, she knelt down in front of him. "We're not going to hurt you, child," she said in a gentle voice. "We only wish to make you clean."

Once again he seemed mesmerized by her, stared into her eyes, and taking advantage of his momentary distraction, she whipped the big, flat cap off his head before he had a chance to stop her.

The boy gasped, and so did Vicky and Fenella.

Masses of red curls covered his head. They were tied in bunches with bits of dirty string; obviously the idea was to conceal the curls under the cap.

The child began to tremble and hugged the bag tighter. Tears slid down his dirt-covered cheeks, making little channels.

Vicky and Fenella exchanged knowing glances, and Vicky asked quietly, "Are you a little girl?"

At first the child did not answer. Then there was a nod. "Yes," she whispered, her voice barely audible.

The two women were stunned momentarily, and Fenella came over and knelt down next to Vicky. "Do you have a name, little girl?" she asked, observing her acutely.

The girl shook her head.

"Will you help us? Will you let us undress you so we can wash your beautiful auburn hair, and also bathe you? We want to make you clean and pretty."

The child nodded, put the cloth bag on the floor, and stood on one end of it with both feet. Then she began to untie the filthy muffler around her neck. Vicky helped her to take off the torn jacket, the grubby shirt underneath, and, finally, the old boots were removed. The trousers came off next, but with some difficulty, since one foot had to remain on the bag at all times.

Once the little girl was stripped naked, Vicky led her over to the tin bath in the middle of the floor.

Fenella said to her softly, "I'm afraid I will have to take that bag from you, but only while you are having your bath. Otherwise it will get wet."

The child shook her head frantically and clung to the bag.

Pointing to the large hook where the bathtub had been hanging, Fenella said, "I shall put it over there on that hook, where you can see it. And you can have it back when you've been washed."

"Naw!" the girl cried. "It's me fings."

She was looking at Fenella, and once again Vicky acted swiftly. She snatched the bag away from the girl in one deft movement. The child instantly cried out.

Vicky placated her. "Don't cry. I'm not taking your things."

She hurried across the floor and put the bag on the hook. "There! You can see it all the time. Now, get into the bath, please."

Vicky's firm voice had the desired effect. The little girl stepped into the bath and sat down with a splash. Vicky rolled up the sleeves of her blouse, leaned over the girl, and began to untie the bits of dirty string. Within minutes, a cascade of auburn hair hung around the girl's face.

Taking a facecloth, Vicky dipped it in the water and began to wash the girl's face; then she tackled her body, asking the girl to stand up. As Vicky washed her, she noticed a few old bruises on the girl's body, but they might have been caused by sleeping rough in the streets. They did not look serious. The child was thin but not emaciated, and much smaller than she had appeared when dressed. Suddenly Vicky realized that the clothes had all been too big for her, and of course, they were a boy's clothes, not a girl's.

Once all the dirt had been washed away, Vicky told the child to sit down in the bath again, and she did as she was told. Vicky, peering at the girl's head, muttered, "I'm going to need the disinfectant, please, Fenella."

A moment later Fenella brought a bottle of disinfectant and a large jar of liquified soap, then went to get a comb and towels.

"Cover your face with your hands, please," Vicky said to the girl. She explained, "I'm about to wash your hair, and I don't want you to get soap in your eyes."

At the end of an hour, the most beautiful child stood before them, dressed in a white flannel nightgown. Her hair had been toweled hard and was almost dry as Vicky brushed it. It was a wonderful golden red and fell in curls around her lovely face. The other remarkable thing about her was the color of her eyes. They were deep blue, almost the shade of cornflowers.

Although Amos had been taken aback to see Mark Ledbetter at Haddon House, his surprise was mostly due to the hour. Usually Lady Fenella had gone home by this time, but Vicky Forth had said they were there tonight because of an emergency. And perhaps this was the reason Ledbetter was present as well. But not necessarily.

Amos was well aware that the chief inspector knew Lady Fenella and her spinster aunt, Lady Philomena Howell. Ledbetter's mother was a close friend of Lady Philomena's; the two women had come out together as debutantes years ago.

Amos had always liked Mark Ledbetter, had known him for over seventeen years, since the younger man had started at Scotland Yard. Mark had been a dashing aspiring detective when Amos was a copper on the beat. They had met in the East End on a strange murder case and had got on well since that time.

Mark, who had gone into Fenella's office, returned to the great room carrying two cups. He was a tall, slender, pleasant-looking man, with dark, wavy hair and warm brown eyes, and at thirty-nine, he was fit and athletic. With a brilliant analytical mind, superior intelligence, and dedication to work, he had quickly moved up the ladder at the Yard.

Amos studied him as he strode over to the fireplace, asking himself yet again why a man with Mark's looks, Cambridge education, aristocratic forebears, and wealthy mother would want to be a policeman. He had once asked Mark that question, and the younger man had answered that he wanted to help people in despair. Perhaps that explained his interest in Haddon House.

As he came to a standstill, Mark said to Amos with a grin, "I've just stolen some of Lady Fenella's brandy, but I'm perfectly certain she won't mind." As he handed the cup to Amos and sat down in the other leather armchair, he added, "She keeps a bottle in her office . . . for medicinal purposes or emergencies. I need this tonight, and I'm sure you do, too."

With a nod, Amos took the cup. "I do. Thank you, and good health, Chief." Amos took a swallow of the brandy, felt its warmth immediately.

"Cheers," Mark murmured and tasted the Cognac himself, then looked down into the cup, his expression thoughtful.

After a moment, Amos cleared his throat and asked quietly, "What was the emergency here tonight? If you don't mind me asking, Chief. Obviously something serious to bring you here."

Mark glanced at Amos and pressed his lips together. "I'm here by chance, actually. I was at a meeting with Lady Fenella and Hugh Codrill, the well-known barrister. We were discussing ways to improve Haddon House, raise additional funds. Codrill had come along at my request, just to help . . . well, kick a few ideas around, to be honest."

Mark paused, took a drink, went on. "We were still at her house on Curzon Street when she received a telephone call from Mrs. Barnes, who was here doing the cooking. A local woman had been brought in by two other women . . . neighbors. The woman was badly battered around the face, however, the troubling thing was she appeared to be almost unconscious. The nurse on duty was Clara Foggarty, and she was worried. She thought the woman might have a concussion and asked Mrs. Barnes to contact Lady Fenella. I came along because I was worried, too."

"And where is the poor woman now? Here? Or at the hospital?"

"Oh, at the hospital, of course. I immediately sent for an ambulance, and they took her away at once. I was pretty certain that there was a concussion. We were just about to go home when you arrived with the little chap." Mark shook his head, a sorrowful look sliding onto his face. "I wish there was more we could do for these destitute boys living on the streets. Despite all the wonderful work done by Dr. Barnardo's Homes and others, there are plenty of them out there still. Too numerous to count."

"I know that, sir. I used to think mud larks and urchins and all the little street thieves had disappeared finally, been rehabilitated. But I'm not so sure. I can't help thinking it's as bad now as it was when Charles Dickens was writing about them."

"That wasn't so long ago, you know——" Mark stopped abruptly, and his expression changed. He looked toward the kitchen door, bafflement flooding his face.

Amos followed the direction of his gaze, his eyes widening as he stared at Lady Fenella and Vicky. They were ushering a little girl into the room. A beautiful girl at that, with amazing golden red hair. *Oh, my God.* The girl was clutching the cloth bag. It couldn't be . . . She wasn't the boy, was she?

Almost as if she had read his mind, Vicky said, "Look what emerged from underneath all the dirt and grime, Mr. Finnister. This lovely girl who had been wearing a boy's clothes. From what she told me, her mother dressed her like that most of the time. To protect her, I should think."

Jumping up, smiling hugely, Amos came across the floor and stood in front of the two women and the child. He touched the girl's glorious red hair and murmured, "Will you tell me your name now, little one?"

"Mam . . . she call me her liddle rosebud," the girl answered, gazing up at him through her brilliant blue eyes. Her face was serious, her eyes suddenly sad.

"That's a pretty name indeed," Amos answered, smiling at her; then lifting his head, looking at Vicky, he raised a brow questioningly.

Vicky bent down to the child's level. "But that isn't your *real* name, is it?"

"Dunno . . ." The child's voice trailed off, and she looked bewildered.

Vicky noticed that the girl's hands had tightened on the bag, and she wondered what was inside. Possibly something which might explain who she was. But to get the bag away from her seemed an impossible task.

Fenella now knelt down in front of the girl and said slowly, "I am Fenella. And this"—she glanced up at Vicky—"is Vicky. And the gentleman who found you is Amos. Over there is Mark. And you are . . . *who?* Tell me your name so we can call you by it."

The little girl shook her head and then addressed Vicky, "Rosebud . . . Mam say."

Vicky smiled at her and knelt down next to Fenella, gazed at the child through eyes that were warm and tender. "All right then, *that* will be your name. We shall call you Rose. Do you like that?"

The child nodded. A faint smile flickered and was gone.

Vicky reached for the bag, saying as she did, "Let me lock this up for you, to keep it safe."

"Naw! Naw!" the girl cried and clutched it even tighter.

"That's all right, don't cry," Vicky murmured. "Come, let us go and have another cup of cocoa."

◆ ◆ ◆

An hour later, after the little girl had been put to bed, still clutching the cloth bag, Fenella and Vicky sat with Mark and Amos discussing the situation.

"We cannot put that little girl into an orphanage," Vicky announced, shaking her head. "I won't allow it. She's far too beautiful and vulnerable. Something bad will happen to her. I feel it in my bones."

There was a moment's silence, and then Fenella exclaimed, "She must stay *here*. There's no real reason why she can't, you know. Perhaps you can make some discreet inquiries in the area, Amos? Find out whether a little girl has gone missing."

"I will, Lady Fenella, but I doubt very much that anyone will claim her. I think she told the truth when she said that her mother was dead and that she had been tossed out onto the street. If only we had a name . . ." Amos's voice trailed off, and he shrugged helplessly.

"If only," Mark muttered, shaking his head. "I tend to agree with you, Amos, about her mother. And certainly with Mrs. Forth and Lady Fenella—she must stay at Haddon House until we decide what's best for her. Are we all agreed on this course?"

The three of them said they were.

Vicky found herself filling with relief. The little girl they now called Rose was safe. For the moment.

thirty-two

RAVENSCAR

Richard had pestered and then begged to go fishing all morning. Finally, after lunch, Edward had succumbed to his entreaties and taken him down to the beach.

Even though it was the middle of April and sunny, there was a high wind blowing across the North Sea, and it lashed at their cheeks and made their noses red.

"It's a good thing Meg wrapped you up well, Dickie boy," Edward said, staring at his brother, who was fumbling with his fishing rod. It was obvious that his woolen gloves were in the way, but somehow Richard was managing.

Edward smiled inwardly at the way Meg had protected the boy against the weather. She was always worrying about her beloved youngest brother, and today she had cocooned Richard in layers of clothing, adding, as a final touch, a red woolen scarf around his head and neck. Then she had placed a red knitted cap on top of the scarf, completely covering his head.

Meg would have cocooned *him* in the same way if Ned had allowed it, but of course, he had not let her get anywhere near him. However, he had seen the wisdom in wrapping a woolen scarf around his head, copying the way she had protected Richard's ears. But instead of a red woolen cap with a pom-pom on top, Ned wore a more sedate tweed cap over his gray scarf.

They crunched along together in their Wellington boots, making for a spot Ned preferred for fishing. The beach was a bed of shingle where old fossils were often found, along with pretty shells, all manner of odd sea specimens dredged in by the tides, and seaweed.

The two brothers did not talk much as they tramped ahead, both of them lost in their own thoughts. Edward was thinking of Lily, and Richard was overjoyed that he had managed to get Edward all to himself. George was always hanging around these days, trying to curry favor with their elder brother. But he didn't really succeed; Ned held back, and Richard was beginning to ask himself why.

Suddenly Richard cried, "Look, Ned! The Cormorant Rock!" Before Edward could restrain him, the boy had started to run along the beach. A worried frown struck Edward's face, and he held his breath, praying the boy wouldn't go sprawling.

Within minutes Richard had reached the Cormorant Rock and was clambering over the smaller rocks to get to it. Then in a flash, there he was, standing on top of it. Triumphant, grinning, waving to Ned, beckoning to him.

His elder brother waved back and trudged on, remembering how their father had brought him here with his brother Edmund all those years ago. It was from his father that he had learned some of the local fishermen's lore. Cormorant Rock was so called because the cormorants would emerge from the waves to stand on that one particular rock, with their wings outstretched, obviously drying them.

His father had always said he couldn't understand why a species of bird that spent such a great amount of time in the sea had not evolved efficient waterproofing, as so many other marine birds had. He constantly muttered that it was a mystery of nature, quite unfathomable.

Arriving at the cluster of rocks, Edward climbed up to join his brother, and when he was standing next to him high above the frothing, foaming sea, he said, "Just be careful, my Little Fish. I don't want to be . . . *fishing you out,* have you on the end of my line instead of a plump little cod."

Richard laughed, his blue-gray eyes dancing. "Yes, this is the place for cod! Papa told me that, and he also said that if you want to catch haddock, you must take a boat out a mile from the shore. That is where all the haddock are."

"That's right," Ned replied and pushed away the sudden thought of Edmund, at the age of ten, saying almost the same words. He snapped his eyes shut to obliterate the image of Edmund's innocent young face, then opened them almost at once.

"Let's put out our lines, Tiddler," Ned said to his youngest sibling and cast his line into the sea as he spoke.

Richard followed suit. They stayed there for over an hour, caught only a few fish. Freezing cold, their eyes watering, their faces bright red from the wind, they finally abandoned the rock to the cormorants and headed back along the beach. Their destination was the steps cut into the cliff face. These would lead them up to the lowest part of the moorland that flowed down to the North Sea.

A s they climbed slowly, Richard chattered away, interrupting his older brother's racing thoughts, which were mostly about Deravenels and those who currently ran it. The boy was forcing Ned to pull himself out of his rather reflective mood.

"Ask me questions about sea lore," Richard requested, tugging at Edward's arm.

Understanding that he would have to comply, Edward nodded and instantly remembered that this was a game they had played with their father only last summer. Stifling the rush of unexpected emotions, he said, "All right then, let's do just that, Little Fish, let's see how sharp your wits are today."

"Very sharp," Richard shot back.

"What is the one thing you must not do with a ship or a boat?"

"Change its name!"

"Correct. But why is that so, Little Fish?"

"Because it's *unlucky* to change the name of a sailing vessel."

"Very good indeed, Dick. Now here's another. . . . What were Admiral Nelson's last words?"

"Kiss me, Hardy."

"Clever lad, that you are. Now, which was Nelson's greatest battle?"

"Trafalgar."

"That's it, and Waterloo is another one. What else do sailors consider unlucky, especially when they're out at sea?" This was something of a tricky question, and Edward wondered if Richard had remembered that it was partially a joke among sailors.

"*Mermaids!* And I know I'm right. Edmund told me this . . . never take mermaids on board. Yes, he told me that last summer—" The boy's voice faded away, and he fell silent, his eyes grown the color of slate. He didn't say much for a while, and then he murmured, "I thought of Edmund, Ned, and that made me want to cry. I miss him. . . . Do you?"

"Very much," Ned answered and hoisted the fishing basket higher on his shoulder. It contained the cod, which were not heavy, but the leather strap kept slipping. "Let's keep going with the game, my lad," he went on. "When you go up the gangplank of a British battleship, what's the first thing you see as you step onto the deck?"

"A plaque that says, 'Fear God. Honor the King.'"

"You have an excellent memory, Dickie. I know Father taught you a great deal of this stuff, didn't he?"

"Yes, and he said he would have liked to have been a sailor in the Royal Navy. I think I would, too."

"Talking of the Navy, what do you do when you unexpectedly see a sailor?"

"Touch his collar for luck."

Edward began to laugh, and through his chuckles he murmured, "I think I'm actually running out of things to ask you about sea lore, do you know that?"

"It's all right, Ned, we're almost at the top of the steps. Are we going to give the fish to Cook? Perhaps she'll make it for supper."

"Perhaps, although I think the cod are going to end up as fish cakes; they *are* quite small, you know."

It was Will who greeted them when they got back to the stable yard. He was standing at the back door waiting for them, and he waved and exclaimed, "Do you two have a big catch then?" He was grinning from ear to ear and seemed anxious to talk to Edward.

"What's the matter?" Edward asked, looking intently at his friend as they went inside the house together. "You look *excited*."

"Not really excited, but well, sort of relieved, perhaps that's the best way to describe my feelings."

"Do tell me," Edward answered, putting the fishing basket down along with his rod, struggling out of the cap and scarf and layers of clothes, then helping Richard to do the same.

"Neville telephoned whilst you were out. Apparently Oliveri has had a telegram from his contact in Delhi. It looks as if his little team out there have come up with just the evidence we need. David Westmouth is going to send it all in a series of telegrams; seemingly that's the quickest way."

"Thank God we've heard from the fellow at last. I'd almost given up on him," Edward replied, and this good news brought a smile to his face. "Now, Tiddler," he remarked, turning to Richard, "here's the catch of the day. Take it along to the kitchen and tell Cook it's *our present* to her. If she wants to keep the cod for herself, she can. Will you tell her that?" Lifting the fishing basket, Edward placed the strap on Richard's shoulder. "Oh, and do me a favor, Little Fish.

Ask her to please send hot tea and crumpets to the library, will you?"

Richard nodded. "Course I will, Ned. I'd do anything for you." The boy hurried off down the corridor with the small haul of fish.

Will and Edward followed at a slower pace, a compatible silence between them. After they went into the library, Will said, "Once we have that information, everything can go ahead, according to Neville. There's nothing else we're waiting for, not really."

Going to stand in front of the roaring fire, still chilled from his sojourn on the beach, Edward nodded. "I'm anxious to get things moving, to be honest. The sooner the better. There's no real reason to wait once those telegrams are received. I don't want John Summers and that bloody woman to do any more damage."

He sighed and went to sit in a chair nearby, looked across at Will. "There's a lot of rebuilding to do, of that I am certain. Rob Aspen and Alfredo Oliveri, and Christopher Green as well, actually, will quickly pull the Mining Division into shape, but the vineyards in France are in need of an overhaul, and somebody will have to look after the northern offices. Things have grown slack, in my estimation."

"Perhaps Johnny will agree to do that," Will suggested. "After all, he has a fund of knowledge about the north, after working for Neville all these years, and he has a family home in Yorkshire."

"I expect he will have to take on that burden, if only for a short while. But I'll miss him, Will, he's invaluable." Edward smiled at his dearest friend and swiftly added, "I certainly can't let you work up here in the north. I need you in London with me."

"And that's where I want to be. By the way, Ned, I spoke to Vicky while you were off fishing. And—"

"Did she mention Lily?" Ned interrupted eagerly.

"She certainly did. Lily is fine, and she's expecting you next week. If you go up to town, I'll go with you, and Johnny will have to come, too. You know Neville's a stickler about protecting you."

"Of course, there's no question about that. Is that all she had to say about Lily?"

"She confided that your darling Lily was looking beautiful, that she was in good health, and that the baby was showing a little. That was about it."

Edward grinned. "Can you imagine that I'm going to become a father? It's hard to believe, isn't it?"

Will merely grinned and exclaimed, "And Vicky might well become a mother, Ned. She and Stephen are thinking about adopting that little girl Amos found in a cart. Don't you remember? He told us all about it at the last meeting we had. He seemed oddly touched by the child, and so is Vicky. More than that, actually, old chap. She's gone a bit potty about her, according to Stephen. However, he's all for the adoption because Vicky hasn't been able to become pregnant."

"I think that's wonderful, and such a kindness to the child," Edward replied. "From what Finnister told us, the girl is rather pretty."

"Yes. Still, they don't know anything about her. Vicky told me that when they took her in at Haddon House, she was sort of . . . well, permanently attached to a cloth bag, wouldn't be separated from it. Eventually they did get her to show them some of the things inside. But there was nothing to explain who she was. So they call her Rose."

"*Can* they adopt her?" Edward wondered out loud, giving Will a penetrating look. "I mean, *who* are they adopting her *from*? She was homeless. Can't they just . . . take her in and bring her up as theirs? It seems ludicrous to talk of adoption."

"Good Lord, I hadn't thought about that!" Will exclaimed. "Perhaps you're correct, maybe they don't have to do anything legal. Anyway, Fenella knows Hugh Codrill, the famous barrister, and he's apparently going to advise them."

"Then they're in good hands."

Before dinner that night, Edward went to his mother's upstairs sitting room. She was alone, reading a book in front of the fire; she looked up and put the book down when he came in.

"Yes, Ned, what is it?" she asked, smiling at him and beckoning him to enter.

"Can we talk for a few moments?"

"But of course we can. Is something troubling you?"

"Well, yes, as a matter of fact it is. I'm troubled about the tiaras, Mother. I don't want you to sell them so that you can buy me a house in order for me to create my own household."

"Ned, there's no other way to do it!"

"I think there will be, and really rather soon."

Cecily frowned. "You do? Please explain, darling."

"We have an enormous amount of evidence against the Grants and their adherents," Ned confided. "It's going to sink them once and for all. Actually, we could go ahead now, but Neville wants to wait until we have some telegrams which are coming soon from India. Oliveri has a good friend out there, a man called David Westmouth, and he's finally got the goods on Aubrey Masters and his dealings with the locals, those who are involved in the skimming I told you about. So we're mounting a case, and then we'll request permission to present it to the board."

"I understand. . . . When do you think you will do this?" she asked, her excitement reflected in her eyes and her eager expression.

"I hope it will be only a few weeks from now. In May."

Now Cecily could not keep the smile off her face. She beamed at her eldest son and asked, "Why are you still standing there? Come and sit with me for a moment and tell me more."

He did as she asked, lowered himself into a chair next to the fire, and explained, "There's not a lot to tell, Mother. You already know most of it."

"When are you going to London?"

"Next week. For a few days only, and then I'll be back for about a week. After that I'm going to be needed in town. You do understand, don't you?"

"Oh yes, I do, darling, I really do. I plan to remain here at Ravenscar for the summer. I know the London Season's not over, but that doesn't matter since we are a family in mourning and cannot participate. Therefore, in my opinion, we're better off here, and I think the children agree."

"I know Richard does . . . he loves Ravenscar."

"So does George, you know."

"Yes, that's true," Edward agreed and thought: He would love it for himself. He covets it in his own greedy way. But he can't have it. Ravenscar is mine.

"You will be running Deravenels, won't you, Ned?" Cecily suddenly asked, startling him.

"I will."

"And Neville?"

"Ah yes, Cousin Neville. Mmmmm. Let me think. . . . He will be advising me, helping me wherever he can, as will Johnny and Will."

There was a pause. Cecily was silent.

"What is it, Mother?" he asked when she remained mute.

"What does Neville hope to gain from all of this, Ned? He is the greatest magnate in England, and probably the richest. He already has everything. He doesn't need to help you run Deravenels . . ."

"I know that as well as you do, and I suppose he does, too. On the other hand, his father backed my father, the true heir to Deravenels. I believe he feels totally committed to do the same for me. There's his pride involved you know, and honor. And another thing. I would say he wants . . . *power.*"

"Oh, Ned, surely he has enough power."

"When is enough *enough* for an ambitious man?"

"So what you are saying is that Neville wants power through you. Is that it?"

"To a certain extent."

"Oh, Ned, be careful."

"I am not a toy on a string, he is not my puppet master. He doesn't control me. I am my own man."

"Ah, but does *he* know that?"

"I should think so . . . why Neville has known me all my life and has only my interests at heart."

"I say again, be careful, Ned. Be very careful."

thirty-three

LONDON

It's becoming very painful for me to leave the child at Haddon House," Vicky explained, looking from Fenella to her husband, Stephen. "And I worry about her so much when I'm not here. It's upsetting my life, my concentration, and almost everything I do."

"I know it is, my dear," Stephen said, touching her arm lovingly. "And I can't say I blame you. I realize you think there's a chance that someone might come and claim her, or that she might run out into the streets and disappear. However, I don't believe there is the remotest chance of either of those things happening."

"Neither do I!" Fenella exclaimed. "She has become very attached to you, Vicky, we understand that. She took to you the night Amos brought her, and she can't wait for the days when you come here."

Stephen sat back in his chair, a reflective expression shadowing his eyes. At forty-two he was a successful banker with a rising career; a man of independent means, through his mother's family inheritance; a Harrow boy and a Cambridge graduate, and something of an intellectual. He was also a practical man, who believed in all things English, in the King, and in God, in that order. He had an enormous sense of justice, of fairness, and he was known for his kindness and charity. His looks were typically English. He had light brown hair and a fair complexion, and his warm brown eyes could fill with compassion or twinkle with mischief, depending on the occasion. He was usually characterized as a nice man: nice-looking, nice by nature.

Fenella was thinking exactly that when she said, "So you are in agreement with Vicky, Stephen? About adopting Rose?"

"Oh yes, very much so. I think she is the most adorable child, and we can offer her so much." He glanced at his wife and added with a smile, "Vicky wants her, needs her in a sense, and so do I. Therefore, I will do anything I can to accomplish the adoption. Also, Fenella, Rose loves Vicky, we see that with our own eyes."

"Of course she does—" There was a knock, and Fenella broke off and then said, "Come in!"

Amos Finnister appeared on the threshold and smiled at them all as he entered. "Good afternoon, Lady Fenella, Mrs. Forth, Mr. Forth. I'm sorry I'm a bit late, but I was delayed on some other business."

They greeted him warmly, and Fenella said briskly, "Thank you for coming this afternoon, Amos, we really do appreciate it. Please, sit down."

Amos did so, and observing the expectant expression on Fenella's face, he shook his head and said, "I'm sorry, I haven't been able to find out a thing about little Rose. There are no children missing in the area. I've inquired everywhere. I've even gone farther afield. Let me put it this way, if a girl *is* missing, nobody's admitting it, or claiming her."

Stephen said, "And there was nothing in that old cloth bag, was there, Vicky? Nothing to give us a clue to her origins?"

Vicky bit her lip. "Absolutely not. Unfortunately. Yes, there were some interesting things. Obviously they mean a lot to the child; she still becomes frantic when we put the bag away for safekeeping. But they don't mean anything to *us*."

"Perhaps I could have a look at the things again," Amos murmured, "after we've had our meeting. Talk to her about them."

Vicky agreed. "I think that's a good idea."

Fenella now said, "Well, I do have some good news. I have spoken to Hugh Codrill, and he says he can find no legal reason why you and Stephen cannot adopt Rose, Vicky. Legalities aside, he made inquiries at one of the local Dr. Barnardo's Homes, and they have a good system when they take in children, whether they are off the streets or given up by parents who cannot keep them. Every child is registered at Barnardo's. Name, date of birth, other family details. When a couple come looking to adopt a child, they are given a copy of the registration certificate, and if they are approved, they receive adoption papers drawn up by Barnardo's."

Leaning forward over her desk, Fenella finished. "And he recommends that we follow their example."

Vicky beamed at her. "That's such a relief." She glanced at Amos. "As I told Lady Fenella, the other day Will asked me how we could adopt a child when we didn't know *who* we were adopting her from. And Mr. Codrill has given us the perfect solution."

"He has indeed," Fenella concurred. "He is currently drawing up a document for Haddon House to use in order to register Rose and the details of her arrival here. We can have it printed later, to use if any other children are brought here. However, I cannot encourage that, since we are not an orphanage but a safe house for destitute and battered women."

"I presume Mr. Codrill is also preparing documents for us to sign, Fenella?" Stephen asked. "In other words, proper *legal* adoption papers?"

"Exactly, and they will be as watertight as he can make them."

"And when will you have the documents, Fenella?" Vicky asked, her eagerness apparent.

"Within the week, but Hugh advised me that you may take Rose today if you wish."

When she heard this news, tears came into Vicky's eyes,

and she gave Fenella a faltering smile and said, "Thank you! Oh, thank you," her voice thick with emotion.

Her beaming husband put his arm around her shoulders. "You see, my darling, everything has worked out perfectly after all."

"I must say, it's a wonderful relief for me, too," Amos murmured, his face also ringed with smiles. "I've worried about the little bairn for weeks now." He focused on Fenella and said, "Thank you, Your Ladyship. Little Rose owes you a lot. Well, we all do, really."

It was Vanessa Barnes who took charge of the tea in the great room, with Vicky and Fenella helping. As the women set up cups and saucers and other accoutrements on the trestle table, Amos and Stephen sat and talked about the mysterious circumstances surrounding Rose.

"I just can't understand it," Stephen said. "How anyone could push a child like Rose out onto the streets staggers the imagination. It's frightening even to contemplate such a thing, never mind knowing it's actually being done."

"There are a lot of monsters passing for human beings out there, Mr. Forth," Amos said in a somber voice. "Take my word for it. Long before I became a private investigator, I was a copper on the beat, and right here in Whitechapel." He shook his head sadly. "I can't begin to tell you what I've seen in my day." He gave Stephen a long, knowing look, and continued. "How any person could throw Rose away like rubbish I'll never understand. She's such a beautiful child."

"Unique in her looks, I agree," Stephen was quick to say and then asked, "How old do you think she is, Mr. Finnister?"

"Please call me Amos, everyone does. I must admit, her age is hard to figure out. I don't think she can be any more than five, do you?"

"Isn't she a bit tall for five?" Stephen asked. "My wife thinks she's four, though. And I suppose we'll never know."

"I believe she's more than four; she's very bright and in- telligent, but not *more* than five, I'm certain of that. I tried to find out how long she had been on the streets, but she wasn't able to tell me. She doesn't have any sense of real time; few children do. But she was very dirty, and her clothes were filthy, so I can only think she was out there scavenging for herself for at least three or four weeks, possibly longer."

An involuntary shudder passed through Stephen, and he closed his eyes for a moment; when he opened them, there was a strange look in them, a mixture of sorrow and pain. He made no response to Amos's comment, just sat there looking sickened. After a few seconds, he said, "When we saw her earlier this afternoon, she was bubbling over with happiness that we were here. There's something quite lovely about her personality, when she's a little more relaxed."

"I know exactly what you mean, Mr. Forth," Amos replied. "She's full of life."

"That's a good way of describing her. Yes, Rose *is* full of joie de vivre, as the French say."

"Amos! Amos!" a child's voice rang out, and a moment later Rose was rushing across the floor to greet her friend.

As he watched her draw closer, Amos thought she had never looked bonnier. There was a big white ribbon tied on top of her auburn hair, and she wore black stockings, a navy wool dress, and a starched white pinafore. He knew they were clothes Vicky had bought for her.

As she drew to a stop, Amos grinned, picked her up, and swirled her around. And then he placed her on the floor, noticing at once how steady she was now, not wobbling the way she had when he found her.

"Hello, Rose," he said, giving her a broad smile. "You look beautiful in your new clothes."

"Fank yer," she said and bobbed. "Mrs. Vicky give 'em ter me. She's like me Mam."

Amos took hold of Rose's hand and led her across to the

sofa, where he sat down and brought her close to his knees, looked into her bright blue eyes. "Rose, will you do something for me, please?"

"Summfink 'ard, is it?" she asked, looking at him keenly, her head on one side.

"No, no, it's not hard. It's easy. I want you to go to Mrs. Vicky and ask her to unlock the special cupboard, so I can take a look at your things in your cloth bag."

"Wot yer wanna look at me fings for?" she demanded, suddenly suspicious.

"We want to try to find out how old you are. It's possible something in the bag will tell us."

Reaching inside the neck of her dress, Rose pulled out a piece of black ribbon on which hung the key. "Mrs. Vicky put key 'ere 'cos I cried for me fings wen she took 'em."

"Isn't she a nice lady? Well, come along, little one, let's go to the cupboard."

Smiling up at him and taking his hand in hers, Rose led him to a series of cupboards built along the wall facing the trestle table. She came to a standstill in front of one of them, pulled the ribbon over her head, and opened the cupboard. Then she reached inside for the cloth bag.

Rose was careful to lock the cupboard and put the ribbon around her neck before they went back to the sofa. When Vicky saw what they were doing, she hurried to join them. She and Amos sat down on the sofa, and a moment later Stephen walked over, carrying a cup of tea for his wife. After handing it to her, he said to Amos, "Would you like a cup?"

"Not at the moment, thanks, Mr. Forth. I want to concentrate on these items here." He indicated the cloth bag with his head.

Rose looked at Amos and asked, "Wot yer wanna see?"

"What about the photograph you showed me last time?"

Without a word Rose took the photograph out of the cloth bag and handed it to Amos. He stared at it for a moment, then stared at Rose and asked, "Is this Mam?"

She nodded several times rather vehemently. "Yeah."

"She always says that," Vicky volunteered.

Amos studied the photograph. It had been taken in a studio, no doubt in his mind about that, and it was by a good photographer. So it had cost money. Poor people did not have cash to spare to have their photographs taken.

Did this young woman in the picture come from money? She looked as if she did. Her hair was swept up on top of her head, with all the curls coming to the front in the style of Queen Alexandra.

The woman wore a dark dress, and the beautiful lace collar came across her shoulders and chest, and had the latest stylish high neck. Matching lace cuffs trimmed the long sleeves. As he peered at the photograph, Amos saw that the young woman was wearing a star-shaped brooch which looked as if it was set with diamonds. He had not noticed it before because he had been concentrating on the woman's features. He also noticed the earrings sparkling, and they looked real.

The face was lovely; her eyes were large, and she had a wide brow. The first word that came into his head was *class*. She had a great deal of it in Amos's opinion. So she obviously came from the Upper Classes. Suddenly, he knew that this was true. He glanced surreptitiously at Rose, who was talking to Stephen and Vicky, and caught a glimpse, fleeting though it was, of the young woman in the photograph. She *was* Rose's mother, he truly believed that.

Turning the picture over, Amos looked again to see if there was a photographer's name on it. No luck. If there had been a name, they would have noticed it when Rose first allowed them to open the bag.

"What can you show me next, Rose?" Amos asked, and she turned from Vicky and Stephen, looked in the bag, and brought out a key. She handed it to him.

It was a plain key, no name or markings on it. Amos shook his head. "I don't know what this is for. Do you, Rose?"

"Mam's key," she answered and looked at Vicky as if she could supply the answer.

Amos handed the key to the child. After putting it away, she brought out a piece of flannel, a scrap really. He knew what it held—the gold wedding ring. He took it out of the cloth, his eyes resting on it for a moment, and then he wrapped it carefully, and once more the little girl took it, placed it in the bag.

There were other small things, mostly a child's treasures. Several colored glass marbles, a flower pressed between two sheets of paper, a handkerchief, and a small prayer book. Inside he saw again the neat inscription: "To Grace from Mother." No date. Nothing else. Not a word.

A brick wall, he thought. We're facing a brick wall. Looking at Vicky and Stephen, his eyes full of disappointment, Amos murmured, "It's the same as last time, I'm afraid, I haven't found a clue amongst her things. I somehow thought that I might, that there would be something there that would be a lead, a clue, something I'd missed before. I'm afraid it's wishful thinking on my part."

"We understand," Vicky said. "And anyway, it will be like starting afresh, won't it, Amos? The three of us together . . . a new family."

Pushing herself to her feet, Vicky went over to Fenella, who was standing near the table. She slipped her arm through her friend's and said in a low voice, "Thank you for everything you've done, my dear, dear friend. I shall be forever grateful."

"Vicky, darling, I'm thrilled for you and Stephen, and for that simply gorgeous child. She's lucky, we're all lucky."

"If it hadn't been for Amos and Haddon House—" Vicky broke off and shook her head. "Imagine what might have happened to our little rosebud if Amos hadn't found her and you hadn't opened Haddon House?"

Fenella nodded and smiled. She seemed on the brink of tears, but she swallowed them back, took control of herself, and together the two women walked across to the big sofa near the fire. As usual, the child was clutching the cloth bag, and she appeared to be suddenly alarmed as the two women approached and came to a standstill in front of her.

Vicky said, "Don't look so frightened, Rose. I'm going home now—"

"Naw! Naw!" the child whimpered, and her face crumpled. Tears ran down her cheeks. "Please doan go."

"Ssssh," Vicky said softly and knelt down in front of her. "You're going to come, too, Rose, with me and Stephen, to our house. And you shall live there with us, and we shall look after you always, and we shall keep you safe."

thirty-four

The sunlight filtering in through the many glass windows in the conservatory cast a soft golden glow on everything on this sunny May Saturday.

Amos glanced around, admiring the room, which was airy and lighthearted yet extremely comfortable, with wicker chairs and sofas filled with plump cushions and matching occasional tables. It overflowed with white orchids and others of more brilliant hues. Nan Watkins's pride and joy, they were glorious, and Neville's wife had created an indoor garden that was a quiet haven.

Will, who was sitting with Amos, broke the silence. "I have finally met Rose, and she is the loveliest little girl. My sister and Mr. Forth are thrilled to have her, and Rose is lucky to have fallen into their laps, so to speak, thanks to you."

Amos looked across at Will, inclined his head. He had grown to like this young man, found him admirable in so many ways, not least in his devotion to Edward Deravenel. Will was also intelligent, well informed about business and politics, and a warmhearted, kind person.

"I wonder if you understand how *truly* lucky the child has been," Amos said in a low voice, throwing Will a penetrating glance.

"To a certain extent, yes, I do. She could have died out there alone on the streets, from hunger or exposure, or she could have been seriously injured in some way. Or taken by the wrong kind of person, someone who might have abused her, hurt her."

A shadow crossed Amos's face, his mouth tightened; there was a long, reflective pause before he finally said, "The last would have been the worst, in my opinion. If you're dead, you're free . . . certainly from further harm. Injured, you're in hospital hopefully, or being looked after somewhere safe. On the other hand, if you're grabbed by the wrong people, forget it." He shook his head, and there was a sudden sorrow on his face. "Those kind are *unscrupulous*. They're the ones who sell children to brothels and to white slave traders, who ship them abroad to be resold like so many cattle. Boys as well as girls. Sold to brothels, where they are in bondage for the rest of their lives." Amos paused, his eyes weary, his face pale. He sighed; then he noticed that Will was watching him closely.

Amos continued more slowly. "Then there are those criminals who run gangs of children; they teach *them* how to be criminals, to steal in the streets and on the ferries crossing the Thames. . . . The children are trained to be pickpockets, and they, too, are doomed to a life of crime and degradation."

Will sat back, staring at Amos, a man whom he had come to like, respect, and trust. After a moment, he remarked, "There's a whole world out there that few people are aware of. Especially people like me." He grimaced and added, "We're not all that well informed, are we?"

"That's true, sir. And you know, it takes all sorts to make a world," Amos answered. "Some of the worst types reside in Whitechapel, Limehouse, Southwark, and the environs. On the other hand, there are innumerable good, upstanding, law-abiding citizens living there as well. Rose could have ended up being taken in by good people. However, more than likely they would have been very poor, and she would have been an extra mouth to feed. It would have made it tough on them, and she would have been a burden."

"Rose had a narrow escape. I understand what you've been saying," Will murmured quietly. "And I do have a bit of knowledge from my sister. She has told me a little about those awful places—the rookeries, in particular. They sound vile."

"They're foul. Unspeakable broken-down tenements surrounded by dark alleys and cul-de-sacs, underground tunnels, dead-end yards. The rookeries are enormous slums. It's a violent world in there. Not even the police go in unless they have to, and they never go in alone or even in twos and threes. They enter as a large posse so that they can protect each other."

Leaning forward, Will now said, "You've painted quite a terrible picture. What I don't understand is why they're not torn down."

"And where would they *go,* the poor who live there? Answer me that."

"I don't know, but what you've described is something inhuman." Will shook his head vehemently, his eyes bleak, anger flickering there. "Here we are, you and I, sitting in this beautiful house, living in the most influential and biggest capital city in the entire world. *London.* Center of a great Empire, the greatest there has ever been. We are a prosperous, innovative, industrious nation. We are influential around the world. Money is plentiful. London, in fact, the whole country, is booming. And we are a kindly, humane race by nature. So, *you* tell *me* why the rookeries exist."

"I wish I could. I've often asked myself that, and I've come up with no real answers. There are people who try to help, such as Dr. Barnardo, who started the homes for waifs and strays. He has been most successful. Other openhanded wealthy people, women in particular, have done much to alleviate terrible situations, and then there's the home Lady Fenella and her aunt started for destitute women. Mind you, I understand what you're saying. . . . Why doesn't the government do something? Am I right?"

"Exactly. It makes me feel sickened and ashamed, and

now I truly understand why my sister has wanted to work with Lady Fenella and has given her money for Haddon House." He smiled. "By helping those much less fortunate, she has found the child she dreamed about. As for Rose, she must have a guardian angel watching over her."

"And she has a few angels here," Amos pointed out, some of the tension leaving him. He went on, with a sudden warmth, "Not only Lady Fenella, Mrs. Forth and Mr. Forth, but also Hugh Codrill. He has arranged everything in the most proper and legal way. Your sister and her husband have nothing to worry about, from what I understand. No one can take Rose from them now. She's their child, and she will have a good life."

I want you to do something," Margot Grant said, glancing at John Summers. "We must retaliate. I know they are responsible for Aubrey's death. *Jean, cheri, s'il vous plaît . . .*"

Reining in his black stallion, John stared back at Margot, who also reined in her horse. She gazed into his face, a face that she had come to love, and whispered, "I have a terrible foreboding . . . *les choses mauvaises . . .*" She left her sentence unfinished.

There was a moment's silence. The two of them had been riding along Rotten Row in Hyde Park for the past half hour, and now, under the spreading branches of the trees, they rested their horses. It was warm on this May Saturday, a beautiful spring day.

John let out a small sigh and murmured, "How can I possibly retaliate? I've nothing to go on. I can hardly accuse Edward Deravenel of murdering Aubrey Masters. The police say he died an accidental death, it's not even suicide. They've dismissed the idea of murder. I must admit, I'm torn, Margot darling . . . part of me thinks that Aubrey died because of his own carelessness, his strange eating habits. Yet another part tells me it has been a most *convenient* death for Edward Deravenel and his clique within the company. So yes, I'm suspicious, like you, but I must be careful what I do, for your sake as well as mine."

Margot nodded and suddenly smiled at him. Her face became radiant in the sunlight filtering through the leafy branches, and his breath caught in his throat for a moment. How beautiful she was this morning; her black hair was pulled back in a chignon, and she wore a jaunty royal blue bowler hat with a tiny spotted veil. The crisp white linen jabot brought a touch of femininity to her tailored royal blue riding jacket, which she wore with a long matching skirt and boots. Her black eyes were luminous in her pale, oval face, and she beguiled him as always. Margot held a fatal attraction for him, and there were times when he asked himself why he had allowed himself to become so involved with her. For besotted he was. Like father, like son, he thought, and pushed those implications away from him.

Resting her gloved hand on his arm, Margot said, "I know you think Edward Deravenel is a pleasant young man with little in his head except chasing women. But I think you misjudge him, John." Shaking her head, her eyes piercing his, she added, "I see him differently. Very much so. He is clever. And he uses his lighthearted personality to conceal his ruthlessness."

"You've said that before, my dear, and I must say I do see it. I'm not dismissing Deravenel as empty-headed, not at all."

"What *I* have *seen* is the way he has charmed his colleagues at Deravenels, at least those who have always had a leaning toward the Deravenels of Yorkshire. Such as Alfredo Oliveri and Rob Aspen. They appear to hang on his words. And *what* of Oliveri? You promoted him to be head of the Mining Division, and this, too, worries me. He has too much power now."

John laughed. "Oliveri is doing an excellent job," he answered crisply, although he was himself more than ever suspicious of Oliveri's true loyalties. Changing the subject adroitly, he asked, "How is Henry? You have kept him in the country for quite a while now."

"You were the one who told me not to bring him to the office. Said that he was looking frail and ill. So yes, he is resting in the country." Her black eyes suddenly danced, and she smiled invitingly. "Perhaps we can have lunch together. . . . I can prepare a *pique-nique.*"

"What about your staff?" he asked, raising a brow eloquently.

"I have given them the day off . . . the weekend off, in all truth, John."

"I see," he murmured and could not keep the smile off his face. "So, we have a whole weekend at our disposal?"

"Mais oui." Glancing around and seeing no one in sight, she leaned in to him and kissed his cheek, whispered in his ear what she planned for that afternoon.

He did not respond, merely stared at her.

They set off at a walk, continuing down Rotten Row. Margot's brain was filled with so many thoughts. But the most important was how to persuade John Summers to take revenge against Edward Deravenel. She was convinced he and his colleagues were behind the death of Aubrey Masters.

The Saturday lunch at Neville's house had become something of a ritual. Whenever they were all in London, the six men met there to review their progress and enjoy a pleasant meal together.

Now they stood in the handsome library, savoring an aperitif before going into the dining room. Edward Deravenel, as always, loomed over them, looking taller than ever, and even more handsome, if that were possible. He was talking earnestly to his cousin Johnny, who was listening attentively.

Edward had embarked on a discussion about libraries and books, and was confiding that one day, when he had a house, and money, he planned to have a library of his own.

"Like this one, perhaps?" Johnny asked, a brow lifting. "Except for the one at Ravenscar, I don't know of any other that is more beautiful, or better in any way."

"That's true," Edward agreed and then turned at the sound of Neville's voice. His cousin had closed the library door and was asking them to come and sit down near the fireplace.

They all did so at once, curious to know what Neville was going to say. For it was quite obvious he intended to speak; he took up a stance in front of the fireplace, without a fire today because of the mild weather.

"I am happy to announce that we are almost ready to attack the Grants and their gang, and to bring them down," he said. "After sixty years of ruling the roost at Deravenels, they will be hounded out of office."

"I do sincerely hope God is listening to you, Neville," Edward remarked, staring hard at his cousin. "Because whilst I believe we should strike them soon, I do want *us* to win."

"Oh, we will win," Neville assured him with a bright, confident smile. "Finnister has everything ready." Neville glanced questioningly at the private investigator, who nodded and stood up.

"I have now finished all of my work. The records from the asylums have been studied by numerous doctors, and all of them believe the records do indicate that Henry Grant is suffering from dementia. There is no problem regarding my two colleagues, the thespians, who have already ingratiated themselves with Beaufield, Cliff, and Dever. They *can* be blackmailed, I'm positive of that. Many of my other operatives have been spreading rumors about the Grants, rumors that have taken hold. Yes, we are ready." Amos sat down and smiled as the others applauded him. "Thank you," he acknowledged.

Neville said, "I think you have something to say now, Oliveri, do you not?"

"I certainly do," Alfredo answered and rose. "Over the

last few weeks I have kept you all informed about my old friend David Westmouth and the situation in India. I have received much documentation from him, which reveals the massive theft and skimming at our mines there. Westmouth is already en route to England, and he is bringing more evidence with him."

"When will he arrive?" Edward asked, leaning forward.

"Within the next ten days," Alfredo answered. "And as you know, Beaufield, Cliff, and Dever are implicated in some of the stealing in India, aside from their scurrilous behavior which Amos discovered."

"So they are doubly condemned," Edward murmured. "I have good news to report as well, in that I have discovered I have many friends within the company these days. We can rely on their support."

"Let us proceed in to lunch, gentlemen," Neville invited with a wide smile. "I think we can celebrate in anticipation of our success. Because I know we cannot fail."

thirty-five

Vicky glanced at herself in the dressing table mirror, adjusted her hat slightly, and then left her bedroom. As she climbed the staircase to the third floor, now known as the nursery floor, she reminded herself not to forget the envelope Stephen had given her before leaving this morning. It was a bank draft for Haddon House, a gift from them to Fenella in appreciation of all she had done in Rose's adoption.

As Vicky went into the playroom, Rose jumped off the chair and ran across the floor, her little face shining with happiness. Bending down, Vicky hugged her, then taking her hand, she led her back to the table where she had been drawing with a crayon in a drawing book.

"Where yer goin'?" the child asked, a troubled look in her clear blue eyes at the sight of Vicky all dressed up.

"To see Lady Fenella," Vicky replied. "I am going to have lunch with her."

"Me come?" Rose asked eagerly, instantly smiling. "Fenella nice leidy."

"Yes, she is, and she loves you, Rose, but it's not possible today. I will take you to see her very soon. Please don't worry, darling, I won't be gone for very long."

Rose nodded her understanding, but her body had tensed, and that apprehensive expression Vicky had come to know so well now flickered on her face. She always became upset and worried when Vicky went out.

"I promise I will be back in time to have tea with you," Vicky said, smiling reassuringly and squeezing the child's hand. "Frances will look after you." A frown brought Vicky's eyebrows together in a jagged line as she scrutinized the child. She was suddenly concerned. "You *do* like Frances, don't you?"

"Yeah." Rose leaned back in the chair and bit her lip, then asked in a low tone, "I live 'ere wiv yer fer ever?"

"Of course you will! I keep telling you that this is now your home, and it always will be, Rose. *Forever.* Until you're grown up at any rate, and then you can do whatever you wish." Leaning across the table, she added, "Don't you remember, darling, I told you that Stephen and I have adopted you?"

"Wot's it mean?" Rose asked, her eyes growing huge in her face.

"It means that *you* are *our* little girl. You belong to us, and we belong to you, and nobody can take you away from us. We are your parents." When she saw that Rose did not quite understand what this meant, she explained, "We are . . . your mother and father."

A wide smile spread across the child's face. "Yer me muvver?"

"Now I am, yes, yes, *I am.* But I wouldn't want you to ever forget your first mother . . . *Mam.*"

Sliding off the chair, Rose ran across the floor to her bedroom and went inside. When she came to the bedside chest, she opened the top drawer and took out the photograph and the prayer book which had been amongst her treasures in the cloth bag.

Vicky had followed her and now stood watching from the doorway, wondering what this was all about.

A split second later Rose came back to her, pointed to the woman in the photograph, and said, "Mam . . .'ere's Mam."

And then she offered Vicky the prayer book. "Mam . . . she gimme it. Mam put summfink in it fer me wiv 'er pen."

Vicky experienced a rush of excitement on hearing these words, and she held herself very still as she opened the prayer book and looked again at the inscription. Out loud she read, "To Grace from Mother."

Rose was smiling and nodding. "Yeah. Mam put it in."

"So this is *your* book? Not Mam's book?"

"Yeah."

"Then your name must be . . . *Grace.*"

"Yeah, yeah."

"*You* are Grace?"

"Yeah, I jest tells yer that. *Me.*" She patted her chest. "Me is Grace."

S everal hours later Vicky was recounting the story of the prayer book to Fenella and Lily. The three women were lunching together in Fenella's summer dining room, which opened onto the garden of her house in Mayfair. White wallpaper patterned with green ivy leaves, a plethora of flowering plants, and white-painted furniture made the room an extension of the garden. The overall effect was charming, light, and airy.

"I wonder why she never told us her name was Grace before now?" Fenella murmured, frowning.

"I can't know for certain, obviously," Vicky answered, "but I do have several thoughts. When we first questioned her about her name, she told us her mother called her liddle rosebud, and I think that's the name that stayed in her mind after her mother died. Assuming she *is* dead, of course. I have a feeling that the name Grace is associated with her past. Another time, another place, not London at all."

"Why do you say that?" Lily asked at once.

"Because I am fairly certain she and her mother lived near the sea. When Stephen and I took her to Stonehurst a couple of weeks ago, she was so happy when we went to

Romney Marsh. The first thing she did when we were drawing close to the beach was to sit down, take off her shoes and her stockings. She wanted to go paddling, she announced. When I questioned her about this, she *glowed* as she told me she had done that with Mam. She also wanted to look for seashells, became excited when she found a strand of seaweed. All in all, it was a very happy weekend for her. Another thought of mine is that she must have been in shock when her mother died and she was thrown out onto the streets. It's perfectly obvious she was *still* in shock when Amos found her."

Vicky paused, took a sip of water, and went on. "Fenella, I'm positive your friend Dr. Juno Newman would agree with me. Shock causes terrible problems for adults, never mind children. I'm sure it's worse for them. *Liddle rosebud* is what she's clung to because it is associated in her mind with her *mother* and *now,* rather than the *past.*"

"So where do you think she and her mother lived by the sea?" Lily asked, putting down her soup spoon, staring at Vicky.

"I'm sure they lived near the sea in the north, more than likely Yorkshire," Vicky responded, her voice full of confidence.

"Because she uses the name Mam, rather than Mum or Mother?" Fenella raised a brow quizzically.

"Yes, you're right."

"But you've told me she has such a Cockney accent," Lily reminded Vicky.

"Not all of the time, I've noticed," Vicky swiftly replied. "Sometimes she says *yes* instead of *yeah, isn't* instead of *ain't,* and so on. She was full of tension when Amos found her in the cart and brought her to Haddon House, as you well know, Fenella. Stephen thinks that she has begun to relax, to feel safe with us, and that she's changing in the way she speaks."

"That makes sense," Fenella said. "But I am still curious."

"Well, she says *thank you,* rather than *fank,* and the Cockney *f* is being replaced with *th* in certain words. But the shock aside, she's grieving for her mother, I'm sure. I've found her crying at different times, and when I ask her what's wrong, she just says '*Mam,*' in a desperate little voice and comes into my arms for comfort."

"Oh, that poor child," Lily exclaimed. "I would like to know who the fiend is that threw her out on the streets of Whitechapel. I'd have him horsewhipped."

"So would I," Fenella agreed, then shook her head. "It's odd, isn't it, Vicky, that we all thought the prayer book belonged to her mother and that it was her mother who was called Grace."

"Yes, but Rose was so specific this morning, very sure when she said it was her prayer book, that her mother had given it to her, and that she was Grace."

"What shall we call her?" Fenella now wondered, looking across at Vicky, then at Lily. "Rose or Grace?"

"I prefer to call her by what is obviously her real name . . . Grace," Vicky said. "But I could ask *her,* and we can always attach the name Rose anyway."

"So she would be Grace Rose Forth," Lily said, smiling. "That sounds rather nice. Anyway, I can't wait to meet her. I'm so sorry I haven't been well enough to come for tea as you've suggested several times, Vicky darling."

"You *are* feeling better, aren't you?" Vicky peered at her dearest friend. "There's nothing wrong with your pregnancy, is there, Lily?"

"No, I'm in good health really, it's just the ghastly morning sickness sometimes, it gets me down." She smiled. "Ned fusses so much about me. Frankly, I'm glad he's gone to Ravenscar with Will."

"They're going to stay up there all this week, through Whitsuntide," Vicky said. "Will has really been looking forward to it." A sudden smile illuminated her face, and she continued, "I rather think that there is a new lady in his life, and that she lives in Yorkshire."

"Oh, who is it, do tell us," Lily cajoled, her eyes filled with interest.

"I would if I knew, but I don't have a name, not yet at least. However, he seems very happy, and I've never seen my brother looking so well, so handsome."

"As usual, Ned hasn't said a word to me about it," Lily pointed out. "He never discusses anyone's business. Very discreet, my Ned."

Fenella laughed. "That may be so, but I do think most men gossip as much as women."

She rang the bell for the butler as she spoke, and within minutes the soup bowls had been removed and the fish served.

The three friends chatted enthusiastically about various matters during lunch, but the most important topic they addressed was improving Haddon House. Their aim was to find ways to better help those women less fortunate than they.

thirty-six

The two women who walked down the steps of the tall house in Curzon Street after lunch with their friend were good-looking, fashionable, and elegantly dressed. Because of their stunning appearance, many heads, especially those of the opposite sex, turned as the women glided across the pavement to the open carriage waiting in the street.

Vicky was dressed in a silver-gray silk taffeta dress with a tight waist and long, flowing skirt, topped by a matching jacket trimmed with pale green rickrack. On her head she wore a cartwheel hat of gray leghorn, which had pale green and gray osprey feathers fastened to the wide brim.

Lily was in her favorite pale blue. Her loose-fitting silk dress had a matching capelet that fell to her hips and helped to conceal her condition. Her hat was an unusual tricorn shape made of pale blue silk, with white ostrich plumes attached at one side, and she wore it with great panache, as stylish as she always was.

The driver of the carriage, Lily's favorite landau, helped her in first, and Vicky followed. The two women sat together in the low-slung carriage with its low half doors, spreading out their gowns and making themselves comfortable.

The landau was open to the world, its double, soft, folding tops at the front and back folded down on this beautiful

May afternoon. One of the reasons Lily loved this luxury carriage, which was only ever used in the city, was that its low shell showed off the occupants. It was often referred to as a women's carriage since their clothes were displayed to great advantage.

Once Robin, the driver, had climbed up onto his bench just above the two horses, Lily said, "We are taking Mrs. Forth home to Kensington, but let us drive through Hyde Park, it's such lovely weather."

"Righto, ma'am," Robin responded, made a clicking sound with his tongue, and set off up Curzon Street making for Park Lane.

Lily turned to Vicky and said, "Perhaps I'll come in for tea. If that's all right?"

"Oh, Lily, darling, that's wonderful!" Vicky exclaimed. "You know how much I've wanted you to meet Rose. . . . Goodness me, I'll have to get used to calling her Grace, won't I?"

Laughing, Lily nodded. "Yes, I think you will. On the other hand, she might wish to remain Rose, it's such a pretty name." Lily eyed her best friend carefully, dropped her voice, and added, "I'm so glad you and Stephen adopted her . . . you might even become pregnant now. That often happens, you know."

Vicky smiled but made no comment.

"It was very generous of you both to give Fenella a thousand pounds for Haddon House, she was thrilled," Lily murmured.

"We wanted to help, and she can make good use of the money, as you're well aware. You've been generous to her yourself these last three years, Lily."

"It's an important, worthy cause, and I have so many good things in my life. I *have* to give back, I just can't be any other way. When I think of those poor women and the straits they're in, I go cold inside."

"I do, too. Their plight makes me wonder what Grace's

mother went through. She was obviously living with some man who mistreated her."

"I agree, and I'm coming round to your idea that Grace and her mother did come from the north."

"Look, Fenella spotted the child's use of the word *Mam* for *Mother* immediately, because she comes from Yorkshire. As you well know, their family seat is just outside Ripon, and I was also instantly aware of it because I've spent so much time at Ravenscar with Will and the Deravenels."

"Yes, I know, and I suppose she must have picked up the Cockney accent in the last couple of years, don't you think?"

"It's more than likely—" Vicky broke off, turned to Lily, and said, "Doesn't Hyde Park look pretty today? I can't wait to drive through it."

"I knew you'd enjoy it." Leaning forward slightly, Lily said to the driver, "Where are you going to enter the park, Robin?"

"At the top of Park Lane, Mrs. Overton. I thought you'd get to see a bit more of it that way."

"Thank you, that's a splendid idea."

The two women went on chatting about Grace Rose, as Lily had suddenly started to call her, and also touched on the child she herself was carrying. "I'm glad I have purchased the house near you in Kent, Vicky. It will be a lovely, comfortable home for me and the baby, and if Ned wants to come and stay sometimes, he can. But as I've told him many times, there's no pressure."

"I know he wants to be involved."

"Did he tell you that, Vicky?" Lily asked, her eyes sparkling, her face eager.

"No, he didn't, but I can see how much he cares for you. He cossets you, is very solicitous of your well-being, Lily. I've been surprised, actually, because I always thought he would just . . . abandon you, let you get on with it all by yourself."

Lily laughed out loud. "As a matter of fact, so did I! And

I didn't care. I wasn't worried about myself, or the baby. As you know, I'm perfectly safe because of my late husbands. But I can't say I'm not glad Ned's happy about the baby. Obviously he means to be part of our lives. And before you remind me yet again, I know he won't marry me, he can't, and I don't want him to." Eyeing Vicky, Lily now murmured, "You think of him as the great womanizer, don't you?"

"Yes, don't you?" Vicky gave her an intent look, frowning slightly.

"Of course I do. He's always been a womanizer, and he always will be," Lily answered. "Women are his drug, he's addicted to them." Suddenly her trilling laughter broke out again, and leaning closer to her dearest friend, she whispered, "He once told me that he had been seduced by a young married woman when he was *thirteen,* and that he'd never looked back."

Vicky couldn't help but join in Lily's laughter, and eventually, as she calmed herself, she said, "Well, one cannot say that he's not *honest.*"

"Always, and too honest sometimes," Lily shot back.

The two women fell silent, and shortly after this the carriage entered Hyde Park, the dappled gray horses trotting forward at an easy, gentle pace. The trees were in bloom, green bowers filled with sunlight above their heads, and many of the shrubs and bushes were alive with color. It was May, and spring was truly full blown in this year of 1904.

Lily felt exceptionally happy this afternoon. The morning sickness seemed to have subsided in the last couple of days. Ned had been particularly attentive before going to Yorkshire.

It seemed to her that all was well with the world. Although she had not told Vicky or anyone else, Lily had purchased a lovely and rather compact house in South Audley Street and fully intended to live in it part of the time, leaving the baby in the country with the nurse and the other staff. It had struck her quite recently that she did not really want to give up her social life in London.

Glancing around, she now noticed a number of children playing on the grass. Some were rolling hoops, others were throwing balls to each other, and they all seemed to be so happy and carefree. There was nothing like the frolicking of children to cheer the spirits.

A few women were taking an afternoon stroll, walking along in pairs; there were several nannies out, pushing large perambulators; and she spotted several courting couples, moving slowly under the trees.

There was not much traffic in the park today, only a couple of carriages in the distance. How tranquil it was, this little green haven in the middle of the largest and most important city in the world.

"Good Lord!" Vicky exclaimed shrilly. "What's going on ahead of us? Look at the rider on that big charcoal stallion. Oh my God, he can't control the horse! It seems to be having some sort of a fit. Look now, Lily. Look how he is rearing up on his hind legs."

"I can't see!" Lily craned her neck, shuddered involuntarily, and cried to her driver, "Robin! Please pay attention to that horse up ahead. There's something wrong with it. Oh my God, it's bolted. It's heading this way, with the rider clinging on for dear life!"

Vicky was keeping her eyes pinned on the rider and the horse, her heart in her mouth. The horse was coming toward them, hell-bent for leather, throwing its head backward, snorting, its nostrils flaring. There was foam on its wide mouth; it bared its big white teeth. The rider seemed panicked, and as he drew closer to their carriage, Vicky noticed that he was handsome in a fleshy way, with dark eyes and hair, and a long scar on one cheek. He looked foreign to her. He stared at her for a brief moment through hard, knowing eyes. He glanced longer at Lily, and malevolently so, Vicky thought. She felt herself recoil, shivering.

"Robin, try to calm the grays!" Vicky shouted.

"Stop moving! Stop!" Lily screamed. "For God's sake stop the carriage moving, Robin. There's going to be an accident."

"I can't curb them, Mrs. Overton," Robin shouted back over his shoulder, every muscle straining as he pulled on the reins.

Everyone had seen the horse and rider, and children were running under the trees, away from the main avenue which cut through the park.

Suddenly the horse and rider were closer, now a few feet away from the landau. The great horse reared up on its back legs, snorting and tossing its head again. The grays instantly reacted, stamping their feet. And then they bolted.

They were moving too fast now, Lily understood that at once. Robin was pulling on the reins, but the horses and the landau had taken off at high speed. The animals had been totally panicked by the stallion.

It seemed to Vicky that everything happened very fast. Lily was shouting orders, as was she; Robin was doing his best to bring the grays to a halt, but with no success. Suddenly the horses increased their pace. Vicky and Lily both clung to the sides of the carriage. And then it happened. The landau tipped over.

Vicky felt herself being thrown sideways out of her seat. She screamed. A moment later she was lying on the grass along the avenue, stunned.

Lily had tried to grab hold of Vicky with no success and had been thrown out of the carriage as well; she was now sprawled on the ground, and a portion of the landau was covering her lower body.

People were hurrying to them.

Robin, bathed in perspiration, his face stricken, was trying to reach Lily.

Groaning and swallowing, Vicky opened her eyes and immediately saw horses' hooves. She recoiled at once, crying out, thinking it was the wild stallion.

"It's Mrs. Forth, isn't it? Stephen Forth's wife?" a cultured voice was asking her.

Vicky raised her eyes, saw a man dressed in proper English riding clothes; he was mounted on a roan, looking down at her with worried eyes.

She nodded and whispered, "Yes."

"My name is Horace Bainbridge. Stephen and I belong to the same club. Do you think you're hurt, Mrs. Forth? You must be."

"I don't know," Vicky responded, her voice raspy. "My leg hurts. It could be broken." Glancing toward Lily, she went on urgently, "*Please.* Go and help my friend, help her driver. He's trying to lift the carriage off her body."

"Certainly I will, at once. And I shall telephone your husband at the bank. Ah, I see policemen coming. I shall tell them ambulances are required."

"Thank you," Vicky whispered.

The man called Horace Bainbridge had trotted off; she could see him talking to the police. Now he was coming back to help Robin.

Vicky began to drag herself across the grass to Lily. As she drew closer, her throat tightened; dread flooded through her. Finally she reached her friend, took hold of her hand and held it tightly.

She could see Lily better now. The images hurt her eyes: the blue tricorn hat lying on the ground, the white ostrich feathers fluttering in the breeze . . . Lily's white face, oh, so very white. And the blood . . . so much blood . . . staining the pale blue silk . . .

thirty-seven

RAVENSCAR

Edward sat in a corner of the library, immersed in *Our Mutual Friend,* one of the novels by Charles Dickens which he had not read before. It had been published in 1865 and was one of the author's last books. Edward found it fascinating, even though the rowdiness from the other side of the library was beginning to annoy him.

Suddenly he sat up straighter and banged the book down on the small occasional table. "Stop it, George! You're being intolerable," he exclaimed, glaring at his brother.

"It's not me making the racket, it's Richard!" George cried, glaring back.

"Why are you always so ridiculous, George? And such a little liar. Of course it's not Richard, it's *your* voice I hear. Do you think I'm deaf? Or that I cannot distinguish the difference in your voices?"

George's bravado fled; he sat back in the chair looking sulky. For a moment he hated his older brother.

Richard said, "It's all right, Ned, I don't mind that he shouts a lot, although I do care that George says I don't know how to play chess."

"I don't blame you, Little Fish. And you certainly *can* play, and very well. After all, I taught you, and you've beaten me many times."

Will began to laugh. "You all sound just like my brothers. Goodness me, I might well be at home at this very moment."

"But you *are* at home," Ned shot back, laughing. "My home is your home, and it always will be wherever I am in this world."

At this moment Jessup came in, carrying a tray with a coffeepot on it and cups and saucers. After placing it at the end of the long magazine table, he looked across at Edward and asked, "I was wondering if you and Mr. Hasling would like a digestive with your coffee, Mr. Edward? Perhaps a Cognac?"

"I think I would, thank you, Jessup. How about you, Will?" He glanced at his friend, his geniality restored.

"Why not? And thank you very much."

George said, "I'd like a brandy, Jessup."

"Not on your life!" Edward said swiftly. "Just bring the two Cognacs please, Jessup."

The butler nodded and hurried out.

"When *can* I have a Cognac after dinner then?" George asked, suddenly belligerent, a tone which Edward well recognized.

"Not for a very, very long time," he shot back. "When you're grown up, and not until then, rest assured of that."

George did not respond; he just lolled in the chair. Moody and put out, he retreated into himself, as he did when he felt thwarted.

Richard, aware of the tension in the room, said in a placating voice, "It was kind of Uncle Neville to invite us to Thorpe Manor for lunch on Whitsunday, wasn't it, Ned?"

"Indeed it was. I'm looking forward to it, and I'm sure you are, too. You'll see Anne, and you, George, will see Isabel—" Edward broke off as the butler appeared in the doorway.

"Yes, Jessup, what is it?" he asked.

"A telephone call, sir, for Mr. Hasling."

Will put down the *Illustrated London News* he was reading and rose, glancing at Ned, shrugging to indicate his baf-flement. He said, "Please excuse me, Ned. I wonder who it can be calling at this hour."

A moment later Will was picking up the receiver in the Long Hall. "Will Hasling here."

"Hello, Will, it's Stephen."

"Stephen!" he exclaimed, surprised to hear from his brother-in-law. "Is everything all right?"

There was a moment's hesitation at the other end of the line, and then Stephen answered in a tightly controlled voice, "I'm afraid not. There's been a dreadful accident, Will. Vicky and Lily were involved. They were injured today—"

"Oh my God, no!" Will cut in and clutched the receiver tighter. "What happened? Tell me what happened. Are they seriously hurt?"

Stephen's voice shook as he explained what had occurred in Hyde Park that afternoon, and Will sat down heavily on the wooden hall chair, his heart sinking.

After he had hung up the telephone, Will sat for a moment or two, endeavoring to compose himself. Finally he rose a little shakily, and as he turned around, he saw Ned coming out of the library.

"You were so long on the telephone, Will, I began to think something was amiss—" Ned broke off when he saw his friend's face, and he exclaimed, "You're as white as a sheet!" He hurried forward, took hold of his friend's arm, saw the distress reflected in his eyes, felt Will's entire body trembling. "What is it? Please tell me."

Will nodded, then swallowed. "Let's go somewhere private, I need to speak to you alone."

"The Morning Room," Edward answered and guided his friend across the hall. He hoped the news wasn't something to do with his father's health.

Once inside the Morning Room, Will sat down in a chair and indicated that Edward should sit opposite.

He did so and asked again, "Tell me what's upsetting you, Will, *please.*"

"It's Vicky," Will began and took a deep breath, tried to steady himself. "And Lily. They were in an accident this afternoon, and—"

"Oh my God! Are they badly hurt?" Edward demanded, leaning forward, pinning his eyes on Will.

"Vicky has a broken leg and a broken rib, and her face is very badly bruised," Will began and realized that his voice was shaking. He swallowed and went on. "Lily has a broken shoulder and two fractured ribs—"

"Thank God they're both alive!" Edward interjected, relief rushing through him. "Broken bones do eventually mend."

"Ned, Lily has . . . a concussion . . ." Will paused, shook his head, and added in a voice that was almost inaudible, "I'm so sorry . . ." He shook his head once more, whispered hoarsely, "She lost . . . the baby, Ned."

"Oh, no, no," Ned muttered in a tone not much more than a whisper and closed his eyes. After a few moments, he opened them and stared at Will, sounding stunned as he said, "She so much wanted the child, and so did I, you know. I really did." He brought his hands to his face and wept.

Will rose, went to Ned, and bending down, put his arm around him. "I'm so sorry, so very, very sorry."

Ned clasped his friend's hand, held it for a moment, and then he sat up straighter, looked into Will's eyes. "Lily . . . and Vicky . . . they *are* going to be all right, aren't they? You're not holding anything back, are you, Will?"

"No, not really," Will answered, his voice cracking. "Lily . . . well . . . actually, she's in a coma."

Edward said nothing, just gaped at Will, and tears brimmed once again in his eyes but remained unshed. His mouth was trembling as he asked, "People do come out of comas, Will, don't they? She will, won't she?"

"Stephen was very hopeful, very positive. And they are now in the best of hands. Stephen has had them moved to the

Masterson Private Clinic in Harley Street, and they are getting the very best of medical care."

"I must go to London tomorrow, first thing," Ned announced softly, taking out his handkerchief, wiping his tear-streaked face.

"I know you must. So must I. We should catch the first train leaving York. At the crack of dawn."

"I'm so sorry about Vicky, Will. She's not in a coma as well, is she? Or injured more than you're saying?"

"No. Vicky sustained the injuries I mentioned, and that's all."

"What kind of an accident was it? You haven't said anything about that."

"I know, but I wanted to inform you of their injuries first, and explain Lily's condition, and—" Will stopped abruptly; he couldn't say it again, he couldn't mention the loss of the baby.

Edward seemed to understand this without being told, and he murmured, "I always thought the baby would be a girl, I don't know why, but I did . . ." His sentence trailed off, and he leaned back in the chair, staring at his closest friend, frowning. His bright blue eyes were red-rimmed. "Tell me how it happened, won't you?"

"Vicky and Lily lunched with Fenella today. At her house in Curzon Street. After lunching, they went for a drive through Hyde Park . . . because it was such a lovely day, and Lily was taking Vicky home to Kensington. Apparently a huge charcoal stallion went berserk on the main thoroughfare, and the rider was unable to control it. It galloped forward, caused Lily's calm little grays to become so frightened they bolted. They were going very fast, and the landau overturned." Will shook his head, his distress apparent. "Stephen says that this style of carriage has a high center of gravity, so when it's moving at great speed, it's prone to roll over."

"And that's what happened, isn't it?" Edward said in a

low, worried voice. "Christ Almighty! Lily and Vicky are very lucky they weren't killed outright." ˙

"I know," Will agreed. "Fortunately the police were on the scene within minutes, and an ambulance was sent for. Lily and Vicky were taken to the hospital at Hyde Park Corner, but later Stephen had them moved to the private clinic."

Edward took a deep breath, then blew out the air and shook his head vehemently. "I've seen some really wild riders in the park lately, especially when I've been on Rotten Row. A lot of them don't seem to be very good equestrians. And another thing, Will. What sort of man is it that cannot control his horse? I ask you that."

Will was silent, thinking of the things he was holding back.

Almost as if reading his friend's mind, Edward asked, "You have told me *all* of it, haven't you? Is there anything else I should know?"

When Will did not respond, Edward probed. "*Is* there something else? Please don't keep me in the dark. This is all too serious. And don't do my thinking for me either, especially if it's about Lily and her condition."

"There is something, yes, Ned, but it's not about Lily's condition," Will finally responded. "It's about Vicky actually, however, not her injuries. What it's about is . . . Well, she has a theory, Ned, about the accident."

"A theory?" Edward repeated and frowned.

"She's not sure it was an accident, she thinks it might have been deliberate."

"*Deliberate?* How could it have been deliberate? You said the horse went out of control—" Edward paused and fixed his eyes on Will, giving him a shrewd look. "We're both pretty damned good equestrians, you and I, and I suppose we could do a lot of things to a horse to make it run wild. And if we gave it certain medications, we could engender excitement, agitation in it, now, couldn't we?"

"This is exactly what Stephen said. Any good rider who

knows horses can manipulate one, especially if the animal has been doctored with something beforehand."

"Is Vicky suggesting that Lily . . . was a target?"

"Yes, I'm afraid so."

"She thinks it's the Grant faction?"

"That's what she's suggesting, Ned. When Stephen told me this, I asked him why she would think such a thing. He answered that Vicky hadn't liked the look of the man on the horse. She described him as dark-haired, with dark eyes, 'hard, knowing eyes' was the way she put it. And that he had a long scar on one cheek. She also thought he looked foreign."

"A hired hand?"

"That's the general idea. . . . She said that the rider had looked at her for a long moment but stared even harder at Lily. Vicky explained there was a malevolence about him that she couldn't quite define, and that it had made her recoil."

A terrible coldness settled over Edward. He suddenly knew that Vicky was right. He leaned forward, pinned his eyes on Will. "But *how* would they know Lily would be driving through the park? Answer me that."

"I think it's a relatively easy thing to figure out, Ned," Will answered. "Let's say Lily was being followed on a permanent basis, as we know you are. When she left Belsize Park Gardens this morning, she would have been spotted immediately in her landau and tailed. She goes to Curzon Street, to Lady Fenella Fayne's house. Vicky, who lives in Kensington, arrives in a hansom cab, which is dismissed. When Lily leaves after lunch, she takes Vicky in the carriage with her. A clever private investigator could have easily worked that out in advance. He would have anticipated that Lily would take Vicky home, drive with her through the park to Kensington. The rider could have been stationed somewhere along the route during the ladies' luncheon, ready to make a move if they appeared. If they didn't, well, nothing lost."

"A staged event, is that what you mean?"

"Yes," Will said, "and women are so *predictable,* you know. Most would want to drive through Hyde Park on a beautiful day, and a true lady, with manners bred in the bone, would always take her best friend home. *If* someone did cause the accident, they were relying on predictable behavior."

In the still of the night, when the din of the evening had passed, Edward lay in his bed, unable to sleep. He was fully aware that as long as Lily was in danger, sleep would elude him.

The accident had driven everything else out of his mind; all he could think of was his darling Lily, her condition, and the loss of the child she'd been carrying. He felt the pain of this most acutely, and he knew only too well how stricken she would be. Not long ago she had explained how much she wanted to have the baby. "I know that I can't have *you,* Ned, at least not forever. One day you will leave me, to go and start a whole new life . . . and that's one of the reasons I want our child . . . so that I can have a part of you with me for as long as I live." He had realized that night how much she truly loved him; tonight he understood, finally, how much he loved her.

His mind ran on. Would she come out of the coma? If she did, would her mind be impaired in any way? Would her physical injuries leave her damaged? On and on . . . He tossed and turned, restless, full of anxieties.

New demons began to creep into his head as he suddenly focused on Vicky's injuries and *her* well-being. And he began to struggle with her suspicions about the accident. Edward trusted Vicky's judgment, had always admired her, considered her to be rock solid, just like her brother, Will. If she suspected foul play, then so did he. How could he ascertain whether the Grant faction had been behind this ghastly occurrence?

When the clock in the corridor outside his room began to

strike four, Edward finally flung back the bedclothes and got up. He went into his adjoining bathroom, shaved and bathed; in the bedroom, he dressed in his traveling clothes; then he went downstairs. He had packed a few things last night, and his small suitcase was in the vestibule just off the Long Hall; next to it stood Will's luggage.

Edward walked along the corridor to the kitchen, Mrs. Latham's private domain. But of course she was not there, not at four-thirty in the morning. He ran the tap at the sink, filled a glass with cold water, and carried it back to his father's office.

Once seated at the desk, he took a piece of writing paper and began a letter to his mother. Mostly he thanked her for her concern of the night before, her heartfelt sympathy. She was a great lady, Cecily Deravenel, to the nth degree; she had shown him nothing but compassion, love, and understanding in his grief, and when he had confided that Lily had miscarried his child in the accident, his mother had wept.

When he came to the end of the letter, he told her he would remain in London until Lily was out of danger and well on the way to recovery. Only then would he contemplate returning to Ravenscar, most probably in July or August, to spend time with the family.

He had just sealed the letter when the telephone on the desk began to ring, and he picked it up at once. "Ravenscar," he said, "Edward Deravenel here."

"Oh, Ned, it's you . . . er . . . er . . . actually I expected Jessup to answer, it's Stephen."

"Good morning, Stephen. Do you wish to speak to Will? Or is it me you're looking for?"

There was a painful silence, and somehow, deep in his soul, Edward knew what Stephen was about to say to him. Instinctively, he braced himself.

"I'm so sorry to call at this hour. . . . However, Will said you would be leaving at dawn for London, and I didn't want to miss you. Ned . . . I have the worst news . . ." He could not continue.

Edward said, "Is it about . . . Lily?"

"Yes," Stephen whispered.

"She's dead, isn't she?"

"I'm so sorry, so very sorry, Ned."

"Thank you for calling," Edward answered, his voice husky, and hung up, unable to speak another word.

He sat staring out into the office, a room which he had always loved but which now seemed so alien to him. Blinded by tears, he pushed himself to his feet and rushed out, knocking over a small table in his haste, not even bothering to stand it up. Unlocking the French doors, he went down the steps cut through the hanging gardens, and he did not stop until he came to the ancient stronghold on the promontory overlooking the North Sea.

As he went into the circular ruin which had once been a watchtower the light changed, and dawn suddenly broke. A pure, crystalline light silvered the edge of the horizon, spread upward to illuminate the skies with radiance. "Lily! Lily!" Edward cried, lifting his eyes to the sky. Then leaning against the stone wall, he wept for her and for their baby until there were no tears left in him.

As he straightened and wiped his face with his hands, an icy coldness settled over him, and his heart turned to steel. He stood there looking out to sea and cursed the Grants. Those bloody bastards . . . they had killed his father and his brother, his uncle and his cousin, and now his woman and his child.

"I swear to God I shall not rest until I have destroyed the Grants of Lancaster," he screamed into the wind. Then he turned and strode toward the chapel, to say a prayer for Lily and the child he had never known.

thirty-eight

LONDON

I'm all right, really I am," Vicky said, looking up at Fenella. "I'm perfectly comfortable."

"I just want to put another pillow behind your back," her friend answered. "I had a broken rib myself once, and I felt much better sitting up than lying down."

"It's true," Vicky replied. "I didn't realize you were something of a Florence Nightingale! And thank you for the flowers. They're lovely, and you're spoiling me, Fenella."

Her friend merely smiled and seated herself in the chair next to the large sofa in Vicky's downstairs parlor, where Vicky was spending most of her time. Her leg, because of a break in the shinbone, was in a plaster of Paris cast, and she found it difficult to climb the steep stairs to the upper floors.

Before she could stop herself, Fenella leaned forward and straightened the colorful crocheted wool afghan which covered Vicky's legs. Finally leaning back in the chair, she asked, "How is Edward Deravenel? Have you seen him again?"

"Yes, he came for tea yesterday, with Will. He's taking it hard. Not that you would know it, actually. He's very self-controlled, but I know how much he is hurting inside. He loved Lily. The accident, the loss of their child and her death . . . well, all I can say is that he is *devastated.*"

"I'm not surprised, Vicky. I've known him for years and

I've always liked him. So many people dismiss him as an empty-headed, amiable young man who spends his time chasing the ladies, but I'm acquainted with a different Edward. Also, my father has a lot of time for him, thinks he's quite brilliant, in so many ways. Much brighter and more focused and ambitious than his father ever was, according to Papa."

"Will would only agree with you," Vicky murmured and fell silent. After a few seconds, she continued in a worried voice, "I'm afraid Will is rather angry with me. He said I shouldn't have told you about my suspicions regarding the accident, and you shouldn't have told Mark Ledbetter."

Fenella frowned. "But why on earth shouldn't you tell me? We're old friends, close friends! I mentioned it in passing to Mark because he's with Scotland Yard. It occurred to me that he might be able to find that incompetent rider, who wasn't all *that* incompetent after all, was he? If he did set out to cause an accident. Surely you want some sort of justice, don't you, Vicky?"

"That's just it, *the Scotland Yard part*. Will says Edward doesn't want Scotland Yard poking around in Deravenel business."

"I see," Fenella replied. "I'm sorry if I've caused problems, Vicky, but I'm afraid it's too late. Mark said he would come this morning around eleven o'clock to have coffee with us. He wanted to ask you a few questions."

Vicky sighed and bit her lip. "Then I shall answer them, Fenella, there's nothing else I can do. But I do hope Mark's investigation dies a natural death. . . . That's what Will and Edward hope, too."

No sooner had these words left her mouth than the doorbell rang, and Vicky glanced through the open door of the parlor, saw the housekeeper, Mrs. Dixon, hurrying to answer it. Glancing at the clock on the white marble mantelpiece, she said, "If this is Mark, he's a little early."

As Chief Inspector Mark Ledbetter came into the parlor,

Fenella went to greet him. "You are so very prompt. Always," she said, as he bent to kiss her on the cheek.

Mark smiled. "Only by a few minutes," he murmured and went across the room, leaned over, took Vicky's hand, and kissed it with a small show of old-fashioned gallantry. "Good morning, Vicky. I do hope you're feeling a trifle more comfortable."

"Yes, I am, thank you, Mark. And good morning." Vicky looked up at him and added, "Why don't you sit in the chair near the fireplace? It's very comfortable."

"Of course," he agreed.

Fenella said, "Mrs. Dixon will be bringing coffee in a few minutes, Mark, unless you would prefer tea."

"Coffee's fine, thank you very much," he answered, leaning back in the armchair. Glancing over at Vicky, he sounded sympathetic as he said, "It was quite an ordeal you had on Monday, and I was saddened to hear of Mrs. Overton's death. Such a terrible tragedy. I'm so sorry."

Vicky nodded, and unexpectedly her eyes filled with tears. This happened a lot lately; she blinked them away.

Fenella, deciding to jump in and try to diffuse the situation, said, "Mark, I'm afraid Vicky is now beginning to think she might have been overly imaginative in her theories about the incident. Not that Vicky is given to flights of fancy, mind you, she's really very down-to-earth. Nevertheless, she's rather sorry I troubled you."

"I've always been a firm believer in women's intuition, Fenella, you should know that by now. And you, Vicky, were an eyewitness to an occurrence that does leave me wondering. It sounds quite bizarre."

"It does, and it was," Vicky responded. "Everything happened so suddenly, so quickly. . . . I'm sure there's never been an accident quite like that before, especially in Hyde Park."

Mark nodded his agreement and went on in a conversational tone. "Why don't you tell me what happened on Monday morning, from the moment you left this house and went to Fenella's in Curzon Street to later, when the landau entered the park?"

"All right," Vicky agreed, and she carefully took him through her activities that day.

Mark listened attentively, and when she had finished he said, "Could you please describe the man again, the rider on the charcoal stallion?"

"He was dark-haired, had dark eyes. I thought they were hard, knowing, perhaps even cruel. There was a . . . malevolence about him, the way he looked at me and at Lily. And he had the appearance of a foreigner."

"What makes you say that?" Mark asked, his eyes not leaving her face.

"I'm not sure, but it did strike me that he wasn't English." Vicky stared off into the distance, narrowing her eyes, endeavoring to remember. Then turning back to Mark, she said, "His skin was a little . . . *swarthy,* I think that's the best word to use. Then the long scar down one cheek gave him a piratical look. He just wasn't . . . *normal* in his appearance, not the kind of rider one would expect to see in Hyde Park on a spring afternoon."

"What about his clothes?" Mark probed. "Were they the sort of togs an Englishman would wear for riding?"

"No . . ." Vicky paused, sounding hesitant. "I remember thinking how English and properly dressed Horace Bainbridge was; he's the man who knows Stephen and came to speak to me after the carriage overturned. I remember thinking that he was wearing proper riding clothes . . . I may have been making a comparison. The dark-haired man wore a burgundy jacket; the cut and the tailoring were off." She nodded her head. "Yes, now that I really am focusing, I realize the jacket was more European in style, and he had on strange trousers, not riding breeches. Actually, Mark, I do believe they were the trousers of a suit . . . yes, they matched the jacket. He must have pushed them into his riding boots."

Mark reached into the inside pocket of his jacket, brought

out a folded piece of paper, walked across to Vicky, and handed it to her. "Is this the man, do you think?"

Opening the paper, Vicky stared at the sketch on it and caught her breath. "Why yes, Mark, it is! How did you get this?"

At this moment Mrs. Dixon and Elsie, the parlor maid, came into the room, each carrying a silver tray. "Excuse me, madam," the housekeeper said to Vicky with a small smile and hurried to a console table under the window. She placed the tray holding the coffeepot and cups and saucers on one end of the table and made room for the tray Elsie was carrying. Coffee was poured, cream and sugar offered, and Elsie then took the plate of biscuits around. Within seconds the two women had departed.

Mark took a sip of his coffee, then began to explain. "Last night a dead body was found in the East End, down near the docks in Limehouse. The man had a gunshot wound to his head, and it certainly looks as if he was murdered. From the angle of the wound, it could not have been self-inflicted. When this murder was brought to my attention early this morning, it struck me that the description fitted the one Fenella had passed on to me. I had one of my men make the sketch, and I later went to the morgue to view the victim and look at his clothes. Although all the labels had been cut out, the clothing did appear to be European-made." Mark nodded and, pursing his lips, added, "And as you've probably guessed, the jacket and trousers were both cut from burgundy-colored cloth. But even without taking the clothes into consideration, the long scar on one cheek was enough to identify him as the rider who caused the accident. At least to me."

"There's no question in my mind either," Vicky said in a firm tone. "This is the man. Most definitely."

Mark finished his coffee, stood up, walked across to the console table, put the cup and saucer on the tray. Returning to the fireplace, he stood with his back to it, his expression reflective. Finally, he said, "Maybe this foreign-looking fellow was merely a poor rider, and therefore got into trouble with a disturbed horse and panicked. Perhaps it was, pure and simple, a terrible accident that led to an enormous tragedy." He looked from Fenella to Vicky, focused on the latter. "That *could* be true, couldn't it?"

"Yes," she agreed.

"On the other hand, what if it wasn't? Let's just suppose it was all staged. Why would anyone target you and Lily Overton, Vicky? *Who* would want to do either of you harm? And real harm at that."

Vicky swallowed, steadying herself, and remembered the written words which had been given to her last night by Edward. Words she had memorized, following Will's most explicit instructions. Slowly, she began, "I don't think anyone wished to harm me, no, not at all. If there was a target it was Lily." Now she paused, as Will had instructed her to do, and waited for Mark's next question.

"Why would someone wish to harm Lily?" he asked.

Edward had predicted that Mark would focus on Lily now, and she was ready with her answer. "My brother, Will Hasling, has felt for a long time that Edward Deravenel has an enemy, or indeed *enemies,* who wish to cause him harm. Some months ago, Edward was himself attacked and badly beaten up. So much so he was in hospital. I know from Will that it was an Inspector Laidlaw who looked into the attack. No culprit was ever found, nor does my brother, or Edward, know why anyone would wish to hurt him, or who those enemies might be. It's all a bit of a mystery."

"So you're saying that Lily Overton was a target because of her friendship with Edward Deravenel?" Mark sounded puzzled.

"I am," Vicky answered. "Unless, of course, I'm being a little imaginative about the whole thing. It could have been accidental, as we agreed a moment ago."

"I understand what you mean. On the other hand, perhaps

you're not imagining anything. After all, the rider is now a murder victim. If he *was* hired, they certainly got rid of him awfully quickly. The accident was Monday, he died last night, which was Wednesday. The only genuine witness to a staged killing, the killer himself, has been rendered unavailable, and most rapidly, wouldn't you say? All very convenient."

Vicky simply nodded, since she had been instructed to say nothing more.

Fenella glanced at Mark and asked, "So what's the next step?"

"We will endeavor to put a name to the body, and obviously we must attempt to find the person who shot the man. I hope we'll be lucky and come up with something." Mark shrugged. "However, some of these cases are hard to crack."

"It all sounds like a wild goose chase to me," Vicky pronounced in a strong tone, silently praying Mark Ledbetter would drop the case sooner rather than later. She hated the idea that she might have caused more heartache for Edward. Better to have the whole thing remain a mystery than have Mark digging into things which did not concern Scotland Yard.

thirty-nine

Lily Overton was buried on Friday afternoon. There were six pallbearers: Edward Deravenel, his cousins Neville and Johnny Watkins; his best friend, Will Hasling; Stephen Forth; and Amos Finnister.

Only a small number of Lily's friends had been formally invited to attend the funeral service and burial in Hampstead, and Vicky and Fenella had been quite unprepared for the number of people who were there. The church was full; all of Lily's friends and the people she had known had shown up to pay their respects.

There were a few gasps and whispers when the coffin was carried down the central nave by the pallbearers, all of them either unusually good-looking or distinguished in appearance.

Because Vicky was on crutches, she gave the eulogy in front of the three small steps which led up to the altar below the huge stained-glass window, positioned immediately behind the coffin. Fenella also spoke, as did Will, from the pulpit. All of them touched on Lily's generosity of spirit, her loving nature, the charities she had so generously supported, especially Haddon House.

At Edward's request, it was Johnny who read the Twenty-third Psalm, his voice wavering only slightly when he began with the words "The Lord is my shepherd, I shall not want."

It grew stronger with each line, and because he had a mellifluous voice, everyone listened attentively.

Edward sat staring at Lily's coffin at the bottom of the altar steps, covered in the white lilies he had sent. He was lost
in the deepest despair he had ever known, and he wondered
how he was going to go on.

As the vicar gave a brief sermon and hymns were sung,
prayers said, Edward asked himself why Lily had died so
tragically; she had been cut down at the prime of her life.
And then he thought of their unborn baby, and his heart
tightened within him. He was alone now that his darling Lily
was gone.

Later it was Will who took Edward's arm and led him back
to the coffin. As he hoisted it up on his shoulder with the other
five men and carried it out of the church, Edward thought of
John Summers and the Grants. Edward was convinced he
could place her death on their doorstep. He knew it deep in
his bones, and his bones never lied to him. How would he
avenge her death? There was only one way. Annihilate them.

Neville took Amos to one side and asked, "Did you get
any information out of Mark Ledbetter? Has he discovered anything?"

Amos drew closer and whispered, "It's more than likely
the rider was French. I got that from Paul Coleman, the police sergeant who works with the chief."

The two men were standing in a corner of Vicky's drawing room. All of those who had been invited to attend the funeral had come for refreshments after the burial.

Amos glanced around and said in the same low voice, "I
think we need to be in private, Mr. Watkins. Let me ask Mrs.
Forth if we can use another room."

Neville nodded and watched Amos pick his way through
the people who were sipping tea, nibbling on sandwiches,
and reminiscing about Lily Overton.

A few seconds later, Amos returned and said, "Mrs. Forth says we can go into the library." He ushered Neville across the hall. Once they were inside the library overlooking the large garden, Amos closed the door and strode over to join Neville near the French doors.

"To continue," he murmured. "Sergeant Coleman didn't have much more information to offer, at least that's what he said. However, I went down to Whitechapel last night and picked up a few things on my own. One of my contacts told me that a Corsican, who had once been in a circus troupe on the Continent, had been asking around about working with horses. My contact said the man had a deeply indented scar on one cheek, was dark-haired, and had black eyes."

"From the sound of it, that has to be the rider of the stallion," Neville ventured.

"The description certainly fits," Amos answered and continued. "Apparently the man's nickname was Nappo, short for Napoleon, because he came from Corsica, too. No one knew his real name, it seems. My chappie sent him up west, to Mayfair and environs, and he said that later he heard Nappo had secured a job driving a carriage for some fancy French family or, rather, a fancy French lady. My contact added, 'a real beauty she is, so I'm told.' "

Neville smiled a small, knowing smile, staring at Amos; he finally nodded his head. "A French lady, eh? Well, well, I can certainly think of one French lady who is a real beauty, and so can you."

"Yes, sir, I can. Margot Grant be the name."

"That does give us food for thought, doesn't it? Perhaps you can attempt to confirm that this Nappo worked for the Grants?"

"I'm already on it, Mr. Watkins."

"Very good. Was the incident in Hyde Park retaliation for Aubrey Masters's death, I wonder? What do *you* think?"

"More than likely."

"You told me a few weeks ago that I was being followed,

so why wouldn't Mrs. Overton have been followed as well? We're both closely connected to Edward, at least she *was,* I still am. And the Grant faction have a lot of money . . . they can afford to employ an army of private investigators, if they so choose."

At this moment the door of the library opened a crack and a small head of red-gold curls peeped around it. "Amos! Amos!" the child cried when she saw her beloved friend. As she flew across the floor to him, Amos bent down, and she came straight into his arms, hugged him tightly. He hugged her back, glanced up at Neville, and was surprised to see the most startled expression crossing his employer's face.

Releasing the child and straightening, Amos explained, "This is the little girl I found in Whitechapel, Mr. Watkins. Her name is Grace Rose, and she now lives here with the Forths."

Neville said in a kindly way, "Hello, Grace Rose."

The child gave a slightly wobbly curtsy. " 'Ello," she answered solemnly.

Suddenly, the door flew open, and Edward marched in, saying, "Vicky told me I would find you in here—" He broke off when he noticed the child standing near the French doors. She turned her head and, when she saw Edward, broke into smiles.

Cornflower blue eyes gazed into cornflower blue eyes and locked. It was Edward who finally blinked and looked away. A faint memory touched his mind. He tried to grasp it, but it was gone in a fraction of a second.

At last Edward took a step farther into the room and said gently, "Hello." The little girl simply smiled at him again but said nothing.

Amos said, "This is the child I found, Mr. Edward. Her name's Grace Rose."

"My goodness, here you are, Grace!" Vicky exclaimed as she came rushing into the library on the heels of Edward. "I've been looking all over for you."

"It's all right, Mrs. Forth," Amos murmured. "She's not really disturbing us."

"You're so kind, Amos," Vicky replied, taking hold of Grace's hand and leading her across the floor. "And I'm so sorry she intruded," she added, glancing from Neville to Edward, smiling, apologetically.

As the door closed behind them, Edward said, "I think we must make our moves against the Grants, Neville. I don't want to wait any longer. Surely we are now fully prepared to go to battle with them?"

"Indeed we are, Cousin." Neville smiled broadly. "And it shall be done. *Now.*"

M argot Grant stood staring down at the boy sleeping in the narrow bed. Dark lashes lay against his creamy skin, a small hand was resting under his cheek. *Her beloved Edouard.* Seven years old now, and the most important person in the world to her. He was her joy and her pride, an intelligent boy with a vivid imagination and such determination. There was no one like him, as far as she was concerned, especially in his personality and character. Henry twiddled his thumbs and did nothing; Edouard reached out eagerly to the world, wanting everything, knowing he could take it all, and he would, one day.

Edouard was the heir to Deravenels. She was going to make sure he inherited the mantle now worn by his father.

"Margot." The whisper of her name made her turn around.

John Summers stood in the doorway; he was staring at her longingly, and when she beckoned, he came into the bedroom immediately. Drawing to a standstill next to her, he put his arm around her waist and drew her closer, stared into her eyes. Against her hair he whispered, "I have to go back to London soon."

Margot nodded, then swung her gaze back to the child sleeping so soundly. "Isn't he the most beautiful thing?"

"After you, yes," John answered softly. It was on the tip of his tongue again, the question which always remained unasked. Was this boy his half brother? His father's son? He dared not ask her. Even if he did, certainly she would never tell him the truth. The boy must always be seen as Henry Grant's only child, and the heir apparent to Deravenels. John understood that necessity. He was the future of the Grant dynasty, young Edouard.

Leaning down, Margot touched the boy's cheek lightly and then turned away, and together she and John left the room on tiptoe.

Once in the corridor, John asked, "Where is Henry? I should say good-bye before I leave."

"He's dozing in his bedroom, as usual," Margot answered and took hold of John's arm, grasped it tightly. "Come with me for a moment, *cheri*. Let us take our leave of each other in the best way possible." A moment later she opened the door to a small sitting room and led him inside. Locking the door behind her, she stepped into her companion's waiting arms, kissed him deeply, and let her hand slide down his leg. She felt her senses swimming; her legs were suddenly weak, her heart pounded.

John pressed her hand against his crotch. "See what you do to me?" he whispered, and then he lifted her and carried her over to the sofa.

She lay back against the pillows, smiled up at him; he joined her, lifted the skirts of her loose summer dress, and slid his hand up a bare leg. There were no underclothes to hamper him, and after touching her intimately for a few minutes, making her gasp excitedly, he stood up, threw off his jacket and trousers. Lowering himself on top of her, he took her to him passionately. And she responded with her usual ardor, her desire for this man flaming through her; when they came to a climax together, she had to cover her mouth with her hand in order not to scream out with pleasure.

A short while later she went downstairs with him, and they shared a glass of wine on the terrace overlooking the lawns.

"I adore you, Margot," he said in a low, loving voice, touching his crystal goblet to hers. "And I'm sorry I must leave you here in the country. As always, business calls; matters at Deravenels must be attended to."

"I know. I know, *cheri,* and I thank you from the bottom of my heart for holding the company for my son."

He put his glass down on the wooden garden table and turned to face her. "Margot, there has been a new development. I haven't mentioned it because I wanted us both to enjoy our brief time together. However, I must inform you now that the mistress of Edward Deravenel died in a terrible accident earlier this week."

"Oh" was her only response.

John explained. "There's gossip floating . . . gossip that this wasn't an accident at all . . . that it was staged."

"How strange," she murmured and leaned back on her seat, seemed almost uninterested as she gazed into the distance.

John waited for a moment or two, expecting her to make some sort of comment, but she did not. He took a deep breath and jumped in with both feet. "Please tell me we didn't have anything to do with this, Margot. That you did not take matters into your hands."

"Oh no, *cheri,* I did not. Why would I?"

"You *were* behind the attack on Edward Deravenel."

"This woman Lily Overton . . . what did she mean to me? *Rien* . . . nothing. I think the suggestion that it was something created is ridiculous. Who can make a horse become crazed? *Ce n'est pas possible.*"

John gaped at her. He had not said a word about a horse going berserk; in fact, he had not given any details at all. Leaning forward, he picked up his glass and gulped down the last of the wine.

He began to shake inside. It took him a moment, but eventually he stilled the violent machinations revolving in his mind. He must not even *think* that they were involved.

Rising, he forced a smile onto his face, offered Margot his hand.

She took it. And he gently pulled her to her feet.

She said, "I will walk with you to your carriage. I'm so glad you came." She tucked her arm through his and went on. "I am so bored here in Ascot . . . and I miss you."

He made no response, merely nodded. He was too perturbed to say a single word to her.

forty

RAVENSCAR

"Do you think you can remember *everything*?" Neville asked quietly, looking across the small bridge table at Edward.

"Oh yes, Cousin. Please be assured of that. However, to make sure, I will commit some important bits to memory." Edward leaned forward, patted the pile of papers on the table between them. "I've already memorized certain salient points from my father's diary, if one can call it that. It's really a lot of notes, his odd thoughts about Deravenels, but useful nonetheless."

"And the company rules?"

Edward smiled faintly. "I have them down pat, thanks to my mother."

Leaning back in the leather wing chair, Neville asked, "Do you mind if I smoke a cigar, Ned?"

"Please do" was his cousin's laconic response.

Neville went through the process of clipping the end of the cigar, lighting it, striking several matches to do so, and puffing hard. Finally, it ignited, and he relaxed.

Although he had not shown it in any way, Neville was beginning to worry about his cousin. Since Lily's death, two weeks ago now, Edward had seemed depressed, withdrawn even, which was not like him at all. There was an aura of sadness around Ned, and it showed in his eyes, his expression. What struck Neville most forcibly was the quietness, almost a resignation, in the younger man.

As he glanced at him surreptitiously, Neville noticed the dark smudges under Edward's eyes, which were lackluster, and he appeared thinner in the face. He's not sleeping well, Neville decided, and he's grieving. But then why wouldn't he be? He had, after all, loved Lily; Neville had come to understand that. *Time.* He needs time to heal. But he's young, he'll spring back.

These thoughts brought a certain comfort to Neville, and he turned his mind to the board meeting which would be held in London in a few days. Ned would present his case against Henry Grant, and Neville was praying that he would win. *He had to win.*

For his part, Edward was focused on another meeting, one which had taken place last week. In the offices of Lily's solicitors, to be exact.

He had been meaning to tell Neville about this, yet he had not found the right time to do so. Deciding it was now, Edward announced, "Lily left me everything, Neville."

Neville sat up straighter and stared at his cousin through startled eyes. *"Everything,"* he repeated, incredulous.

"Yes."

"You mean she made you her heir?"

"That's correct."

Neville's light blue eyes narrowed. "Surely there will be some sort of trouble about this. Or is the will watertight?"

"It's watertight, but there is no problem, Neville. Lily was an only child, well . . . actually her brother died when he was a little boy, of meningitis. So she ended up being the only child of wealthy parents. There are no other relatives. Lily was alone, except for me. And Vicky, her best friend."

"I see." Neville puffed on his cigar for a moment and then murmured, "It's always been my understanding that her late husbands left her very well taken care of indeed. Isn't that so?"

"It is, and she had a very shrewd head on her. Lily made some excellent investments."

"It's a large estate?"

"Oh yes. Lily left me her house in Belsize Park Gardens, the house she recently bought in Kent, and another house she purchased about a month ago in South Audley Street. And—"

"Good Lord!" Neville exclaimed. "She has made you a wealthy man, Ned."

Edward sighed and pursed his lips. "She has. However, I'd much prefer to have her living and breathing and here in this room with us."

"Of course you would, I fully understand your feelings."

"She left most of her jewelry to Vicky," Ned went on, "except for a few things she bequeathed to Fenella, and some of her antiques to Vicky, other pieces to me. The rest of her furniture will go to Haddon House. Actually, Lily was rather generous to them, Neville, she also left money to Fenella's charity. And to several of her other favorite charities as well. The residue of her estate comes to me."

Neville sat back, his eyes focused on Edward. After a moment's reflection, he said slowly, "I imagine the residue is quite large."

"Yes," Ned murmured, "it is . . ." He decided to say no more.

Ever since he had returned to Ravenscar, Edward had found it hard to fall asleep. It was no different tonight. The moment he closed his eyes his mind had begun to work, numerous worrying thoughts jostling for prominence.

There was a full moon visible through the window, and it was coating everything in the room with a light layer of silver. Earlier he had opened the window, and in the past hour the weather had grown colder. It was always chilly at night here on the North Sea, even in summer, and Edward realized it must be bitter outside for the room to have grown this icy. The curtains were billowing like the sails of a ship.

Jumping out of bed, he went to close the casement, then walked over to the fireplace, threw another log onto the glowing embers. The log instantly flared, sparks flew up the chimney, and he knew that within minutes the room would be much warmer. Struggling into his woolen dressing gown and fastening the belt, he found his slippers, seated himself in a chair, pulled it closer to the hearth. His thoughts swirled in his head as he leaned forward to warm his hands.

A small smile flickered on his mouth and was almost instantly gone. It was the first time he had been even faintly amused since Lily's death . . . The look on Neville's face this afternoon had been quite priceless. Edward had known instantly that his cousin was flabbergasted about Lily's will, even if he had taken the news in stride.

Resting his head on the back of the chair, Edward closed his eyes and thought of Lily; her generosity to him had been astounding. He heard her solicitor's voice echoing in his mind as Mr. Jolliet had read from the will made three months before. "If a child, or children of mine do not survive me, and if I am not married, I do give and bequeath to my friend Edward Thomas Deravenel all of my worldly goods, as listed herein, and with the exception of . . ." And then Mr. Jolliet had read out the other bequests and the recipients.

Oh, Lily, Lily, if only you were here, Edward thought, his heart contracting. How I miss you, and how I wish I had told you just how much I cared for you. I did love you, Lily, I truly did, with all of my heart. His thoughts drifted; he fell down into himself.

Catastrophe lurks around every corner . . . life comes at you hard, to hit you in the face. Life is full of surprises, some of them good but most of them . . . catastrophic. That is what my mother asked me . . . has no one ever told you that life is catastrophic? Well, I know now that it is. That is the way it has always been, my cousin Johnny says, and what matters most is the way one handles catastro-

phes and heartaches, the pain of it all. He told me the othe *day that I cannot let Lily's death get me down. That I have* *keep my eyes focused on the goal: On Deravenels, he means* *And he is right, just as Neville is. I am glad it has now a* *come to a head. Glad that the board have accepted my re* *quest to bring a complaint against Henry Grant. I am we* *prepared for the board meeting. I have reread my father'* *notes, gone through all of the Deravenel papers, made m* *own notes, committed them to memory wherever necessary.*

Neville and I have met with Hugh Codrill, and he has re *viewed everything for us, all of the medical reports and analy* *ses Amos acquired. He has recommended a highly reputabl* *law firm, solicitors with whom we have met and who will ad* *vise me. No one can go to the meeting with me. Neville, Johnny* *and Will are not part of the company and therefore cannot b* *present. But I have Alfredo, Rob Aspen, and Christopher Green* *The three of them are board members, and they are on my side*

Alfredo explained to me that after I have presented m *case, the board will take a recess, discuss everything, and re* *turn to meet with me within two hours. At that time they wil* *tell me if I have a genuine case or not. If I don't, then noth* *ing more can happen. If they agree that I have due cause* *they will confer amongst themselves for several days. I wil* *be summoned to a second meeting, and they will pass judg* *ment. That is the procedure, and it has been in place for hun-* *dreds of years. Alfredo and Rob have helped me to keep my* *spirits up. They are strong, loyal, levelheaded.*

My cause is just. I must not lose. My father and my brother *died at the hands of the Grants, so did Uncle Rick and my* *cousin Thomas. And Lily and my unborn child. I keep saying* *to myself that I want revenge. But what I really want is justice* *for those who died. My cause is right. Henry Grant has given* *up his power to John Summers and his wife, Margot Grant.* *And over sixty years ago, his grandfather was the usurper.*

I am the true heir.

I aim to win.

• • •

A light tapping on the door brought Edward out of his reverie. Sitting up, he pushed himself to his feet and strode across the room.

Standing in the shadowy corridor was his youngest brother, shivering in his dressing gown, pale-faced, his slate-blue eyes grown almost black, genuine worry shadowing them.

"Good Lord, Little Fish! What are you doing here at this hour?" As he spoke, Edward grabbed Richard and pulled him into his arms, then swept him into the room.

"I'm worried," Richard murmured, his voice low.

"Come here, sit on my knee, and let's get ourselves warm. And you can tell me why a boy like you should be worried. After all, you have a mother and a big brother to look after you."

Climbing onto Edward's knee, Richard settled himself against his brother's broad chest and explained, "I'm not worried for me, I am worried for *you*. George told me that your friend died, your lady friend, that is, and that you were brokenhearted. Is that true, Ned, are you brokenhearted and devastated? That's what George says."

"And I wonder where Mr. Know-It-All-George gets *his* information. Not from me, I can assure you of that, Tiddler." Edward hugged his brother and then tilted the boy's face upward. "I'm going to be all right, my lad, and thank you for your concern. You mustn't worry about me any longer. Don't listen to George. I can look after myself, and I say again, I will be fine."

"Do you promise me that, Ned?"

"I *do* promise you that, Richard."

"I want you to know that I am here for you, if you need me," Richard announced, looking up at his brother adoringly. "I will always be here for you, as long as we both shall live. I want you to know that I will stand by you no matter what, especially when you have the fight with the man from

Deravenels." Richard frowned. "Who *is* the man you have to fight?"

"I have to fight Henry Grant and the men who are on his side within the company. His associates. But we are not going to . . . Well, it's not a physical fight, with our hands up, going at each other like in a boxing match. It's not that kind of fight at all."

"What is it then?" Richard asked.

Edward told him slowly, carefully explaining everything, and once Richard had nodded his understanding, Edward slid his brother off his knee and stood up. "Now, let's go down and raid Cook's larder. We'll have a midnight snack, and then you can share my bed if you wish, Little Fish."

His answer was the radiant smile on Richard's face.

forty-one

RIPON

Nan Watkins turned on her side sleepily, as always reaching out for Neville. He was not there; instantly she opened her eyes, saw the bedclothes thrown back, and her gaze flitted across to the windows in their bedroom.

Neville was standing at one of them, gazing out. Tall, erect, and very still, his stance suggested he was deep in thought. Nan knew he usually was when he stood there, often for an extremely long time.

There was a full moon tonight, and it made everything perfectly visible. His face, in profile, was vividly illuminated, and as she usually did, she thought how handsome her husband was. Her heart fluttered inside her. He was her whole life; without him she would be nothing. She genuinely loved her daughters, but her husband came first, he always had.

There had been other women before her, but none since their marriage. He had told her this countless times, but she would have known it even if he had not said a word. Neville was adoring of her, always sexually potent, and he spent most of his free time with her. There was also something else at play, his character.

Neville had never seen many women at the same time. He had always been attached to one, and only one. Yes, he had moved on frequently, yet he had remained faithful when in a relationship. In fact, in that respect he was the total opposite of his cousin Ned, who seemed able to handle several women at once.

Nan compressed her lips, remembering her conversation with Neville the other day. She now must correct her long-held assumption that Ned was the proverbial swordsman. According to Neville, Ned had been faithful to Lily Overton. Poor woman, Nan thought, dying like that. And she had been so young, in her thirties.

Long ago Nan had seen another accident with a landau, but fortunately no one had been killed. Her father had forever warned her that they could be dangerous carriages if driven at high speed, and her father had rarely been wrong.

Stretching her long legs, moving up in the bed, Nan settled against the headboard. It rattled slightly, and Neville swung around at once. When he saw her leaning against the mound of white pillows, he said softly, "Oh, darling, I awakened you."

"No you didn't," she responded and stared at him, realizing she desired him. She stretched out her arms, and he came to her, sat down on the bed, leaned into her. Putting her arms around his neck, she whispered against his hair, "I have such a hunger for you. . . . I long for you, and need you. Make love to me, Neville. . . . Perhaps tonight is the night to make that son and heir you crave."

"It is *you* I crave, my dearest heart."

Within seconds they lay naked in each other's arms.

He kissed her face, her eyelids, her neck, and swiftly moved his head down to her breasts, kissing them, smoothing his hand over them. Sliding down the bed, he now ran his hand over her flat stomach, down her thigh, until it came to rest between her legs. When he touched her most intimate part, she moaned softly and whispered, "Please, darling, please." And so he brought his tongue to her, kissing her womanhood until she shivered in ecstasy.

He took her to him swiftly, entering her with urgency,

plunging deep inside her until she cried out. "Now, Neville, now, oh, please, now." And when she began to shudder excessively, he threw off all his constraints and came with her when she climaxed.

Together they lay joined for a long time. He did not want to leave her, and she wanted him to stay where he was. He rested his head against her face, and they drifted in a gentle haze, simply enjoying the aftermath of their lovemaking.

Eventually Nan spoke. "You once said I am the only one now. Is that true?"

He smiled against her cheek. "Don't you trust me?"

"I do!" she cried and endeavored to sit up.

Neville held her, kept her body under his. "I know you do, and you can be certain there is no other woman for me, my Nan. Why should I want anyone else when I have you? These perfect breasts, your long, shapely legs, your slender, elegant body. And you do have such a lovely face. Not to mention *this* miraculous part of you." He slipped out of her, slid his fingers inside her, and within minutes brought her to ecstasy again.

"I think you might have made me pregnant tonight, darling," she said a short while later, staring at him.

Neville had rolled off her and was propped up next to her, sharing her pillow. "I hope so," he answered, "but it doesn't really matter in the long run, Nan. I can well manage without an heir."

"You're thinking of Richard, aren't you? He's becoming your surrogate son, isn't he? He's spending so much time here with you."

"Not really. . . . No, Nan, he isn't becoming my son. I just like the boy."

"And George? What of him?"

"George is rather strange, I must admit. An enigma to me. I sometimes think he might not be very trustworthy, do you know that?"

"But he's always so charming . . ." Her voice trailed off.

"Let us not mistake personality for character, my darling."

"You're worried about something, Neville, something important. I know you are. I saw it in your eyes over dinner. And then when I saw you standing at the window, I was sure you had things on your mind."

Pushing himself up on his elbow, looking down at her, Neville shook his dark head. "I cannot hide a thing from you, can I?"

"No, I don't suppose you can. I know you so well." She looked into his light turquoise eyes, saw his love for her shining there, but almost instantly those unique eyes darkened. "There *is* something wrong."

Neville sighed, continued to look into her face. He rarely burdened her with business, but somehow she always instinctively knew when to question him, like tonight. Sighing once again, he said in a low, concerned voice, "I'm worried about Edward and the board meeting at Deravenels in a few days. It might not go quite as well as we expected."

"Why is that?" Nan cried, her eyes full of alarm.

"The telephone call I took tonight was from Amos Finnister."

She nodded.

"He had hoped that two of his operatives would be able to persuade three board members from the Grant faction to resign, and—"

"Why would they do that?"

"Because Finnister had information about them that would be ruinous to them on all levels if made public. Unfortunately, they haven't responded in the way he wanted."

"And if they don't resign?"

"They will vote against Ned at the meeting, and he could lose his chance to bring his case against Grant to the board."

"What are you going to do?"

"I shall have to find some sort of weapon which will bring them around to our way of thinking. . . . Otherwise it will be a disaster."

forty-two

LONDON

Vicky finished pinning her hair on top of her head, arranged the curls at the front, and added the two tortoiseshell combs on either side at the back to hold everything in place. She stared at herself in her dressing table mirror for a moment, decided she was looking better for the first time since the incident in the park.

A brunette with hazel eyes and a creamy complexion, Vicky had a lovely face, which drew much of its quiet beauty from the calm and tranquillity which dwelt there.

Smoothing her hand over the high guipure lace collar of her cream blouse with its leg-o'-mutton sleeves, she clipped on pearl earrings, then, holding on to the dressing table, she levered herself up. Her leg was still in plaster, but she had learned to maneuver herself around the house, including mounting the stairs and descending them. She was rather proud of her newfound agility and skill despite the cast.

Glancing at the clock on the white marble mantelpiece, she realized she had an hour to waste before Nanny and Amos brought Grace back from Harrods, where they had gone to have lunch and do some special shopping. It was supposedly a secret from her, and she was amused that Grace and Nanny had managed to talk Amos into the expedition. She guessed the outing was to buy a small gift for her upcoming birthday.

Vicky left her bedroom and headed for the staircase. Holding on to the polished mahogany banister, she went up the steps carefully, lifting her long, cream-colored gabardine skirt so she wouldn't trip.

When she entered Grace's bedroom, she smiled to herself. The child had a penchant for neatness. Everything was exactly where it should be, and of course, there was her mother's photograph, propped up on the small bedside table. Vicky remembered how pleased she had been when Grace had placed it against the lamp, understanding the child finally felt safe here, knew no one would steal her mother's photograph.

Picking it up, Vicky carried it back into the playroom which adjoined the bedroom and seated herself at the circular table. The photograph needed a frame, and yesterday Stephen had gone to the silver shop they patronized and found one which was the right size and not overly ornate. Vicky took it out of the box, removed its wooden back covered in dark blue velvet, and attempted to fit the photograph in, then realized it was too bulky. The velvet-covered back would not sit correctly, and she was unable to fasten it down with the side clips.

Vicky took her spectacles out of her skirt pocket, opened the case, and put them on, examined the photograph. She realized for the first time that it was made of quite heavy stock and had a mount around it which framed the picture. The discolored mount was spotted here and there, and Vicky decided the spots had been made by water. No doubt it had been damaged when Grace had dragged the cloth bag around. Suddenly she noticed the faint lines on the mount, lines which had clearly been made by a frame.

She stared at the face of Mam, as she always thought of the woman, and nodded to herself. She had been very pretty indeed. Turning the photograph over, Vicky noticed that the brown paper backing was coming away at the edges. She decided the photo needed new backing and began to pull on one corner of the brown paper. It loosened but was not a easy to remove as she thought it would be. Suddenly she was afraid of damaging the photograph; Grace would be hysterical if anything happened to this one genuine memento of her mother, and to Vicky that was quite understandable.

Leaving the playroom, Vicky maneuvered herself down the stairs to her bedroom, found a file and a pair of nail scissors in her manicure case and went carefully back up to the playroom.

Sitting down at the table, she gently inserted the nail file and began to lift off the brown paper backing. Within ten minutes she had loosened one side and begun to work on the bottom.

The moment she pulled the backing off completely, Vicky saw the large piece of folded paper lying on the photograph; she knew instantly that the backing had been put there by Grace's mother, not the photographer.

For a moment she did not touch the piece of folded paper, simply stared at it. She was almost afraid of what might be written on it. *Coward,* she told herself and finally picked up the piece of paper and unfolded it.

Vicky had thought it would be a letter, but it wasn't, it was a birth certificate. However, inside the folds of the certificate, there was another piece of paper. She placed this on the table, far more anxious to read the birth certificate.

A woman's name, a name Vicky did not recognize, was written on the certificate, and the square where the father's name should have been written was blank. She's illegitimate, Vicky thought. Grace is illegitimate. Her eyes went to the top of the birth certificate, and she now read: "County of Yorkshire," and underneath: "Whitby," the name of the town. At least she now knew two more things about Grace: her mother's name and her place of birth. Anxious to know even more, she reached for the smaller piece of paper and opened it. A lock of red hair fell out; Vicky put this on the birth certificate almost absently, and looked down at the paper in her hand, reading swiftly.

"Oh my God!" Vicky exclaimed. "Oh my God!" she cried again, and her eyes unexpectedly filled with tears. She blinked them away and read the short note, once again, took the lock of hair, put it back inside the note, and folded it. To her surprise, Vicky discovered her hands were shaking as she replaced the note inside the birth certificate. Swiftly, she put both in her skirt pocket and sat back in the chair, too stunned to think straight.

It was the carriage clock on the mantelpiece chiming the half hour which brought Vicky out of her reverie. She blinked and sat up straighter, glancing at the clock. It occurred to her that she had only half an hour to put a new backing on the photograph and get it inside the silver frame before Amos, Nanny, and Grace returned.

She went to the bell at the side of the mantelpiece and pressed it. Within seconds Elsie, the parlor maid, was hurrying into the room. "Is there something you need, Mrs. Forth?"

"Elsie, please do me a favor. Bring me a roll of the brown wrapping paper, a pot of glue, and a pair of scissors. I want to tidy up this photograph before putting it in the new frame."

Elsie nodded. "Right away, mum." She dashed out.

Vicky sat gazing at the picture of Grace's mother, wondering whether to keep the discolored cream mount surrounding it. She made a decision and lifted it off. Printed in a type of scrolled handwriting was the name of the photographer, and underneath, the town: "Whitby." Without the discolored mount, the photographer's name was revealed. For the moment Vicky did not want anyone to know about Grace's background, so she put the mount back in place.

Once Elsie returned with the items she had requested, Vicky cut out a piece of the brown paper, glued it on the back of the photograph, and put the picture in the frame.

"Now it fits," she muttered as she replaced the wooden back covered in blue velvet. Turning it around and standing it up on the table, she nodded to herself, thinking how happy Grace would be when she saw her mother's portrait in the handsome silver frame.

forty-three

"Fer a rozzer yer not a bad chap," Albert Draper muttered, staring at Amos Finnister. "Even if yer bold as brass, askin' me agin abart Nappo. I told yer all I knows afore."

"First of all, Albert, I'm not a copper anymore. I'm a private detective," Amos explained, looking into Albert's eyes. "And you know it. Also—"

"Once a copper allus a copper," Albert cut in, grinning hugely.

"I concede you might have a point there, Bertie, but please help me. I must find out who this Nappo fellow worked for up west. It's worth quite a lot to me."

" 'Ow much?"

"Definitely a fiver . . . five pounds that is, not five shillings."

"Five quid! My Gawd! 'E must've done summfink awful, a real bleedin' 'orrible crime. I wus goin' ter arsk yer for ten bob. Changed me mind, though."

"Why did you do that? I'd always give it to you, Bertie. Anytime."

"Changed me mind 'cos I ain't no cadger, can't stand cadgers, Amos. Bad way ter make a livin', innit?"

"I suppose it is, and I know how proud you are. Come on, Bertie, you've got the goods on Nappo, so let's have it." Reaching into his pocket, Amos put some loose change on the counter and called out, "Two more pints of bitter, please."

The bartender of the Mucky Duck, as the Black Swan was known locally, called back, "Comin' right up."

Turning to Albert, Amos continued in a low voice, "Nappo was *bumped off* a few weeks ago; it wasn't suicide, you know that as well as I do. The Yard have come up with nothing, and I just need to know *who* it was he worked for up west."

Albert bit his lip, shook his head, looking worried.

Amos said, "Nappo caused a terrible accident in Hyde Park; a good woman was killed, another wonderful woman injured. Both of them have been involved in Haddon House. Hasn't your sister Gladys had a lot of help from them in the past . . . when that deadbeat husband of hers beat her up?"

"Beat 'er ter bleedin' pulp, 'e did, bleedin' bastard. If I ever gets me 'ands on 'im, I'll do 'im!" Bertie hissed, keeping his voice low. "So them fancy bits wus 'elping Lady Fenella, a saint I calls *'er*. That wot yer sayin', Amos?"

"I am."

Bertie nodded, his mind made up after hearing the name Haddon House, and drew even closer to Amos. "Wot I've 'eard is this. . . . It's the Frenchie wus employin' Nappo as a driver of 'er carriage, so I 'ears from me mate, 'im as knew Nappo. *Margot*, that's 'er name. Can't think of 'er last name."

"*Grant*, Margot Grant," Amos said swiftly, his excitement obvious. "Is that the name?"

"It is! That's it!" Bertie exclaimed, grinning from ear to ear. "Tells me mate 'e fancied 'er, wanted ter get 'er up the apples and pears, would've paid a king's ransom ter do 'er," Bertie explained. "Oh, yeah, Nappo fancied 'er awright. Wishful thinkin', innit?"

"Only too true. Are you certain of the name?"

"I am that. Let me think a minit. . . . Grosvenor Street . . . no, not right . . . Upper, that's wot's missing. . . . Upper Grosvenor Street, up west, that's where Nappo worked and dreamed of feckin' the Frenchie woman."

Amos felt a rush of relief. He wanted to shout out with

glee but restrained himself. "A name, Bert? Surely your mate knew Nappo's actual name."

Albert began to chuckle. "Yer knows wot, Amos, 'is real name wus Napoleon, 't weren't a nickname, the bugger wus called Napoleon by 'is muvver."

"His last name?" Amos probed.

Grinning again, Bertie said, "Sure as 'ell 't weren't Bonaparte." The Cockney began to laugh.

Amos couldn't help laughing with him. He had always liked Albert Draper's wicked Cockney humor. "So, come on, lad, let's have it."

"Dupon, or Dupont." Albert emphasized the *t*, continued, "That wus the geezer's name. Or Dupond."

"Thank you, Albert." Amos put his hand in his pocket and brought out a small packet. "A fiver in there for you, and I appreciate your help."

After pocketing the envelope of money, Albert looked hard at Amos, his eyes narrowing. "They did for 'im, did they, them buggers up west?"

"In my opinion, yes."

"D'ya think Nappo got in 'er nickers? That why they did 'im?"

"No, I doubt very much that he got anywhere with her. They had him killed because he knew too much."

"Bloody 'ell!"

"Thanks again, Bertie, you've been a genuine help."

Albert nodded. "Ta fer me dosh, Amos, yer a good un."

Amos nodded, picked up his pint and drank half of it, put the glass back on the counter. "I've got to be going, and thanks again, Bertie."

"See ya, Amos."

Once he was in the street, Amos pulled out his pocket watch. It was almost seven o'clock. He had told the two actors he would meet them at the Mandarin Garden at half past seven, so he had to hurry.

As he strode along the wharves, he sniffed, grimacing, fully aware of the stink of the Thames on this warm June evening. It was the most beautiful river in the world to him, but it was also the dirtiest, and it was rank in warm weather.

Walking at a rapid pace, Amos focused his mind on the information Albert Draper had given him. He had known Albert for many years, since he had been on the beat here in Whitechapel, and he trusted him implicitly. He now had a name to give to Neville Watkins and, more important, a positive identification of Margot Grant as Nappo's employer. This tied her and possibly Henry Grant to the crime. At least he had done something right. The failure of the two actors to persuade Beaufield, Dever, and Cliff to resign was the most unhappy conclusion to that particular part of his work for Neville Watkins.

Charlie had told him that the actors were good, often played toffs in the theater, and that they would do a proper job. Those were Charlie's exact words, "a proper job," just before he had sailed off to New York. To the New World. To a new life.

Amos made it to the Chinese restaurant in record time, and as he was shown to his favorite table in an isolated corner, he asked the waiter for jasmine tea. He sat down, a bit out of breath, thirsty, and relieved to see he was the first to arrive.

But he did not have to wait long. Ten minutes later the two thespians appeared. Justin St. Marr, as he called himself, in reality Alfie Rains, and his boon companion, Harry Lansford, who was really Jimmy Smithers. Two good-looking Cockney lads, old friends of Charlie, talented actors by profession. Nice lads, Amos decided, looking across at them. But somewhere they had gone wrong on the job for him. He aimed to find out how.

"Good evening, chaps," Amos said cheerily.

"Good evening, Mr. Finnister," they said in unison,

speaking in their upper-class voices. They were staying in character for the moment.

"Care for refreshments?" Amos asked, raising a brow.

"The same as you, I think, jasmine tea, please," Justin replied in his plummy tone.

"I'll have tea also," Harry added, equally posh.

Once the order for the tea had been given, Amos leaned across the table and said in a low voice, "I've got a real problem, lads, and I certainly need you to help me solve it."

They both nodded, looked at him eagerly, wanting to please.

The waiter deposited the teapots and teacups, and hurried away.

Amos leaned forward once more. "I want you to tell me again what happened when you finally pulled the rabbit out of the hat so to speak, and told those chaps you would expose them to the world."

"They laughed," Justin answered. "They just didn't seem to care, did they, Harry?"

"Justin's right, Mr. Finnister, they were totally unconcerned, acted as though it didn't matter one iota."

"Think, lads, go back over it in your minds. Didn't they say anything about the board, their immediate superiors, the consequences?"

"No," Justin said, shaking his gorgeous head of blond hair, biting his lip.

Harry looked as though he was remembering something; his eyes narrowed as he stared out above Amos's head. "Well, there was *one* thing . . . something Jack Beaufield said, and it struck me as being, sort of, well, out of context."

"What did Beaufield say?" Amos demanded, his heart tightening in anticipation.

"He said there would be no more summers in France if they were thrown off the board, and all three seemed to think it was funny. But I didn't get it, no, not at all."

Oh, but I do, Amos thought, his heart leaping. They know

something about Summers and Margot, something explosive.
An affair? I do believe they think they've got him by the short
hairs. But we'll see about that, won't we? he thought.

Harry now asked in a puzzled voice, "You look pleased,
Mr. Finnister. Do you know what Beaufield was talking
about?"

"I'm not quite sure," Amos answered and then smiled.
"But I think my boss will, and he'll certainly know what to
do. Now, lads, the treat's on me. What would you like for
your supper? Have anything, anything at all." He lifted his
hand to summon the waiter. He felt light-headed with happiness. Perhaps he hadn't failed after all.

forty-four

I t was Tuesday, June 21, in the year 1904.

It might turn out to be an auspicious day, then again it might not. Certainly today *his* destiny would be sealed.

Edward Deravenel stood at the window in his office at Deravenels, looking down into the Strand, thinking about the ordeal which awaited him. In a short while he would go into the boardroom and face seventeen members of the board, who would either champion his cause or defeat him.

His cousin Neville, his companion in arms, his mentor, had told him it was up to him to convince them his was a just cause, a rightful cause.

"You are a *seducer*, Ned, not just of women but of . . . well, just about *everyone*," Neville had told him earlier this morning, over breakfast at the Charles Street house. "You can seduce *anybody* when you so wish. Do it today, Ned. Charm them, beguile them, make them want *you* to win, not Henry Grant. But remember, as you seduce them, you must do it with a cold heart. You must be ruthless."

"I know that," Edward had answered. "And your own motto is engraved on my heart. *Never display weakness, never show face.*"

Neville had nodded and smiled, patted him on the back, and added, "Be inscrutable. Reveal nothing of yourself. Bear those points in mind and you will succeed."

Last night they had had a long session with Amos over dinner, and the private detective had told them about two meetings he had recently had.

One had been with a contact in Whitechapel. This man had given him information about the perpetrator of the accident in Hyde Park. According to Amos, the Corsican had been employed by Margot Grant as one of her drivers: she was irrevocably tied to the accident, which was not an accident at all as far as Amos Finnister was concerned. "Premeditated" was the way he had put it. "Murder, in fact, to my way of thinking. The Corsican *did* set out to kill Mrs. Overton."

The private detective had then gone on to tell them about the actors Justin St. Marr and Harry Lansford, who had inveigled themselves into the tight-knit social circle where Beaufield, Cliff, and Dever were prime movers.

Each actor had tackled the men individually, first Beaufield, then Dever, finally Cliff. They had explained that they knew dangerous secrets and would reveal them to the world if each man did not resign from Deravenels.

The actors had believed they had succeeded in convincing them all to step down. "And then suddenly everything changed," Amos had said. "Dever and Cliff told Justin and Harry to go to hell. It was publish and be damned, that sort of attitude. My actors were a bit flummoxed, I don't mind telling you. They were even more taken aback when they ran into the toffs at White's, and the three men laughed in their faces. It was Beaufield who then said something about 'no more summers in France' if they were kicked off the Deravenels board."

"He was alluding to John Summers and Margot Grant. As you surmised, they must be meeting secretly. There is no doubt of a sexual liaison there," Neville remarked.

"No doubt whatsoever, sir. I got it from the horse's mouth—this morning. The butler at the Grant house in Upper Grosvenor Street is about to vacate his position and was happy to blab."

Edward had jumped into the discussion at this point and directed a question at Amos. "Do you think that Beaufield, Dever, and Cliff conferred and decided to brazen it out?"

"That is my conclusion, Mr. Edward. I thought at first they might have spotted my two thespians and realized they were impostors. But I've changed my mind. We know those fellows are in cahoots and have benefited from the Indian skimming situation. Therefore, I think they know everything there is to know about one another. Birds of a feather, and all that."

Neville had laughed. Then turning to Ned, he had pointed out, "But the other board members don't know a thing. And you, my dear Ned, are going to give them all the gory details. No holds barred."

When he had arrived home last night, Edward had made innumerable notes, committed everything to memory like an actor memorizing his lines. That was the way he had thought of it then, and now. When he walked into that boardroom, he had to dominate the way a leading actor dominated a stage. He had to persuade, convince, beguile, and conquer his audience. *He had to make them his.*

They're waiting for you," Alfredo Oliveri said from the doorway.

Startled, Edward swung around, and nodded, half smiled when he saw his colleague and friend. As he walked across the floor, he noticed Alfredo's pallor; his freckles always seemed more pronounced when he was pale like this, and worried.

Coming to a standstill, Ned put his hand on Alfredo's shoulder and said in a calm and steady voice, "Don't fret. I am fine, and it *will* be all right, I promise you. Now, who is in there?"

"Everyone we expected, except for Henry Grant, of course."

"I knew he wouldn't come. He can't. And they can't let

him. He's pitiful these days, at least so I hear. There *are* seventeen board members, then?"

"Correct."

"I'm glad you went onto the board automatically when you were promoted to Aubrey Masters's job. Who's there in *his* place?"

"A new member by the name of Peter Lister. He was appointed by vote, of course, but originally recommended by Martin Rollins. He's neutral, by the way, Rollins I mean. Nice chap, very honorable, has good judgment. He's been on the board for donkey's years, and sort of guides it really, in an unofficial way. He liked your father. He'll be fair, *just,* perhaps even sympathetic. But he may play devil's advocate."

"Good to know. Who are the other outside directors? Remind me again," Ned said.

"Victor Sheen," Alfredo answered. "Also neutral, in my opinion. Matthew Reynolds and Paul Loomis, they're a bit wishy-washy, I've noticed. Don't carry much weight."

"Let's go then. Let's get it over with." Edward moved toward the desk, picked up a pile of folders, and went to the door.

Alfredo reached out, held him back, and said, "It *will* go exactly the way I explained. The procedure is quite simple. Martin Rollins will ask you to present your case. And you will do that. The board members will ask you questions; they may ask if you can produce evidence. There's just one thing I want you to remember. We're there to help you, if you need us. Me, Rob Aspen, Christopher Green, and Frank Lane. If you should need one of us, just look at us, or say our names. We'll jump right in with corroborating evidence if that's what you need. We're your backup."

Edward nodded. "I remember everything you've told me, and thank you. Thank you for being here for me today."

Together they walked down the corridor. Neither of them spoke, both lost in their thoughts.

Alfredo was praying that Ned would not see red and explode, as he occasionally could. Edward was keeping himself perfectly steady and calm. He was truly coldhearted, convinced that he must be ruthless in order to win.

When Edward walked into the boardroom a few moments after Oliveri, all conversation ceased. Edward glanced around, saw only one empty seat at the far end of the table. He walked down to it and stood behind the chair. "Good morning, gentlemen. For those who do not know me, I am Edward Deravenel."

There were mumbled good mornings, and Martin Rollins said, "Please take the seat in front of you. It was kept for you."

"Thank you, but I prefer to stand," Edward answered and placed the folders he was holding on the mahogany conference table.

Rollins nodded and announced, "Let us begin the proceedings. Mr. Deravenel, it is our understanding that you have a grievance with Deravenels and wish to present a case against an individual. Is that correct?"

"Yes, it is, sir. I wish to present a case against Henry Grant, chairman of Deravenels." Edward was going to do more than that, but for the moment he kept quiet.

"Mr. Grant is unable to attend today, due to an illness," Rollins said. "However, you may proceed, since we do have a full board present with the exception of Mr. Grant."

"Henry Grant is chairman of this company, but he is not the person running it," Edward began in an icy voice. "And, therefore, I believe he should be removed from the company. Because he is not running Deravenels on a day-to-day basis, he must be retired, as of today. The man running Deravenels is John Summers, and he has no right to be managing director. He is not a Deravenel by birth, and according to ancient company rules, only a Deravenel can be the head of Deravenels."

For a moment there was a flutter of asides, mumblings and Rollins exclaimed, "Gentlemen, silence please." Frowning, he focused down the length of the table on Edward. "I am vaguely familiar with this rule, but it has never been brought up before. Mr. Summers has been in charge for a number of years."

"Mr. Summers was supposedly assisting Henry Grant, but Henry Grant was and is an absentee landlord, as my father, Richard Deravenel, called him. And why was he an absentee landlord?" Edward paused dramatically, let his eyes roam around the table. No one spoke. Some met his gaze, others did not.

Edward continued in that steely voice. "I shall tell you why he was never here, and relegated his job to John Summers. He was in two different mental asylums over these many years. You see, Mr. Grant is suffering from dementia. He is not merely a pious and religious fellow, devoted to God, as some of you characterize him. The man is mentally disturbed and therefore incapable of running this company. Or any other company for that matter."

No one spoke. Everyone looked at Edward. Some were stunned, others pleased, yet others filled with sudden fear.

"That is quite an accusation, Mr. Deravenel!" Rollins announced in a cold, clear voice. "A *dastardly* accusation if it is not true, and I doubt that it is."

"It is absolutely true!" Edward contradicted him, his voice louder, fierce, emphatic. "I have the evidence here." He glanced down at the pile of folders on the table in front of him and went on. "I have all the medical records from the two asylums where he was being treated. I have doctors' opinions from those *madhouses,* and I have opinions from a number of highly respected psychiatrists, including Mr. Rupert Haversley-Long, of Harley Street, a most respected doctor who has worked with Dr. Sigmund Freud. In his opinion, Mr. Grant has not been sane for years."

"And has this psychiatrist, Haversley-Long, examined Mr. Grant?" Rollins asked, a brow lifting skeptically.

"No. But he has studied innumerable medical records and

has spoken to the doctors who looked after Mr. Grant in the asylums."

Martin Rollins, a reasonable man, now fully understood that Edward spoke the truth. He looked saddened as he asked, "And you say you have these medical records and reports here with you today, Mr. Deravenel?"

"Yes, I do, sir." Edward gave the older man a bleak little smile and added, "*Copies,* of course. But they can be examined by the board members at their convenience. However, they have been reviewed by some members already."

"Is that so!" John Summers spluttered, glaring at Edward but holding his temper in check.

"Yes, it is," Edward answered, his tone quiet, even mild. He looked at Christopher Green and raised a brow. "I think Mr. Green might have a word to say to the board."

Green nodded and rose. Almost as tall as Edward, he knew his height was effective at times, especially at board meetings. "What Mr. Deravenel says is perfectly true, Mr. Rollins and fellow board members. The records I have studied do indeed show that Mr. Grant was treated in two different mental institutions over the years. In my opinion, he is not able to run this company. I concur with Mr. Deravenel."

"John Summers is doing a wonderful job," James Cliff cut in, in a loud voice. "If Henry Grant is considered incompetent because of ill health, then John Summers can continue as before. He's a good man!"

"Hear, hear," some board members cried.

"Oh no, not hear, hear at all!" Edward exclaimed, his voice rising. "I do not believe Mr. Summers has been a good caretaker of Deravenels. But this point aside for the moment, he is not a Deravenel, he is not even *remotely* related to the Deravenels. He is, in fact, a second cousin once removed of Henry Grant. He has no right to the job."

"And who *do* you think should run Deravenels?" Jack Beaufield asked with a sneer.

You will regret asking that, you bastard, Edward thought,

staring back at the questioner coldly. He was remembering
that Beaufield was more than likely involved in the deaths of
his father, young Edmund, and Neville's kin. A murderer.

"I am the true heir to Deravenels," Ned finally said.
"More so than Henry Grant ever was. Over sixty years ago
now, Henry Grant's grandfather stole the company. The
company did poorly under him, although his father did a
magnificent job. But, and it is a big *but,* the Grants should
never have been at the helm of this company in the first
place. Through the laws of primogeniture, as we know those
laws today, I am the rightful heir as a true and direct descen-
dant of Guy de Ravenel, through my father, Richard Deravenel, who was the true heir before me."

There was a silence in the room. Several men shifted in
their seats. Beaufield glanced around, expecting someone to
denounce Edward Deravenel's claim, but no one did.

Beaufield said, sarcastically, "You're just a young pup.
Only nineteen. Why do you think *you* could run this company? Now tell me that, lad."

Edward did not rise to the bait. He merely smiled at Beaufield and answered quietly, "My age has nothing to do with
anything, certainly not my ability. Let us not forget that
William Pitt the Younger became Prime Minister of this great
country of ours when he was only twenty-four."

Alfredo Oliveri, Rob Aspen, and Frank Lane all clapped,
laughing.

"Just so," Rollins murmured. "But what about experience, Mr. Deravenel? Surely that counts for something."

"Yes, indeed it does, Mr. Rollins. For the last six months
I have been working at Deravenels and learning about every
division. I have had some wonderful teachers in Mr. Oliveri,
Mr. Aspen, Mr. Green, and Mr. Lane. I know a lot about our
Mining Division, the vineyards in France, the quarries in
Carrara, and our northern companies in Yorkshire. I have
learned about our cloth manufacturing mills in Bradford, our
ready-made clothing companies in Leeds, our coal mines in

Sheffield." Edward paused, smiled at Rollins, and then cast his glance over to the men he had just mentioned. "I think you may wish to talk to my colleagues later, get their opinions about me."

Rollins nodded, looking impressed and rather beguiled by the young man who stood so proudly at the far end of the room. Finally, he said, "So your case is against Henry Grant, chairman of Deravenels? Whom you say is no longer capable of running the company. And you are suggesting yourself as his replacement. In fact, you are asking for the removal from the company of Mr. Grant *and* Mr. Summers."

"I am indeed," Edward answered simply.

"Over my dead body!" Summers shouted, jumping up and waving his fist at Edward. "You young pup! How dare you come in here and propose such a thing. You are the one who is out of his mind, not Henry Grant. You should be ashamed."

"And you, Mr. Summers, are an enemy of Deravenels! You are a cheat, a liar, and an adulterer. You are the man who should be *ashamed.* You are the lover of Margot Grant, the wife of Henry Grant. It is you who has cuckolded him."

Not one man in the room moved. Nor did anyone speak. They did not dare. Martin Rollins looked as if he had gone into shock.

Summers still stood, his face purple with embarrassment and rage. He, too, had lost his voice.

Finally he said, "Only a lad of your age would make such an *empty* accusation." But as he spoke, Summers knew that he had met his true adversary. Edward Deravenel was ruthless and formidable, not to mention ambitious. Summers began to tremble inside, knowing that all was lost. Yet he remained standing, deciding to brazen it out. Fool though he was about Margot Grant, he had a certain courage.

"I do not make empty accusations, Mr. Summers," Edward responded in a low and dangerous voice. "I have evidence that you have been having an affair with Mrs. Grant for some time now. And I have that evidence in these folders here." He motioned to them. His eyes did not leave John Summers's face. "A Mr. Clarence Turnbull, butler to Mrs. Grant, has given a sworn statement revealing your sexual liaison with her."

Summers sat down heavily. He was a ruined man.

Edward looked directly at Rollins and continued. "I bring specific charges against Jack Beaufield, James Cliff, and Philip Dever. These three men have stolen vast amounts of money by skimming off the top at our diamond mines in India. And stealing diamonds. Aubrey Masters, now deceased, was also involved."

"Mr. Deravenel! These are very serious charges indeed," Rollins cried, wondering what was coming next.

"I have the evidence here. Mr. Oliveri and Mr. Aspen, who work in the Mining Division, came across this crime some months ago. Mr. Oliveri hired Mr. David Westmouth, an expert in diamond mining, in India, and Mr. Westmouth has given us all the evidence we need. Charges can be brought against these three men immediately. Mr. Westmouth is now in London."

Cliff cried, "Just try it, laddie!"

"Oh, I will indeed, Mr. Cliff. And at the same time, perhaps you should make arrangements for your illegitimate child to be taken care of properly. And your mistress. I'm sure Mrs. Cliff won't be doing that."

"*You bastard,*" Cliff shouted, looking not only irate but dangerous. "I'll bloody well get you for this, you bastard!"

"I doubt it," Edward answered softly. "You won't be able to do very much from behind bars. As for you, Mr. Beaufield, this is not the first time your hand has been in the till, and you will soon have other charges brought against you by your previous employers. And you, Mr. Dever, will no doubt be in the divorce courts as well as the criminal courts once your wife discovers you have a lover. A male lover at that."

Dever did not answer. He jumped up and almost ran out

of the boardroom. A frightened Beaufield followed him, and then Cliff hurried to join them. Only Summers remained, flabbergasted. Then he, too, made for the door.

Rollins cleared his throat and began carefully. "Mr. Deravenel, you have implied terrible things about these men who have long served Deravenels—"

"Served themselves," Edward interrupted.

Rollins ignored this comment. "I just hope you really do have the evidence to uphold your accusations. Otherwise you are going to be in serious trouble, sir."

"I can assure you that I have the evidence of everything I have just accused these men of . . . *absolute proof*. And various other board members know that I am speaking the truth, Mr. Rollins. You see, they have helped me to gather the evidence. It is they who have served Deravenels well."

Rollins nodded. "Thank you, Mr. Deravenel. You are excused. I would like you to pass me the documents you have for our perusal. We shall see you again shortly."

"And thank you, Mr. Rollins, for allowing me to bring the case and, I hope, to serve this company well."

All of the board members were silent; most were aghast at the unexpected downfall of men they had long known and respected.

Edward rose, walked the length of the table, and gave the pile of folders to Martin Rollins. Then he slipped out of the room, closing the door after him softly. Justice for my family, justice for Lily and the baby, he thought as he walked back to his office.

Exactly one week later, on Tuesday, June 28, 1904, Edward Deravenel was appointed managing director of Deravenels. The position of chairman was left open. It would never be filled during Edward's lifetime. He was the sole ruler of Deravenels, his domain.

Later in the company dining room, which had not been used for years, Edward sat down to a lavish repast with his mother and siblings. Also present were all of the Deravenels executives who had supported him in his fight to gain control of the company, as well as his comrade in arms, Neville; and Nan; his boon companions, Johnny Watkins and Will Hasling; and Amos Finnister, who had contributed so much. The rest of the board were also present. They had voted him in unanimously and were his admirers and adherents now, totally charmed by this charismatic man.

Earlier that morning Edward had given Neville, Johnny, Will, Amos, and Alfredo mementos of this day. They were round gold medallions on slender gold chains. On one side was the Deravenel family emblem of the white rose and a fetterlock, the rose enameled in white; on the other side was the sun in splendor, commemorating this happy day. Around the edges of the medallions on the side of the rose, was engraved the Deravenel family motto: *"Fidelity unto eternity."*

"I'll wear it till I die, and even after that," Johnny said, smiling wryly at Edward as he added, "And to think, from what Oliveri told me, you didn't even attempt to seduce the board."

"I didn't really get a chance, to be truthful," Edward confessed, grinning. "The only thing I could do, actually, was go in for the kill with the Grant faction."

"But it obviously worked," Will murmured, his hand on Edward's arm.

"Only too true," Neville interjected. "And I am very proud of you, Ned, very proud of you indeed."

Lifting his glass of champagne, Edward toasted them. "Here's to friends and friendship. May they last forever."

Margot Grant was speechless. She just stood there staring at John Summers, dumbfounded. After a few seconds, she said slowly, in a puzzled voice, "Are you telling me they ran out of the board meeting?"

"Yes, that is exactly what I'm saying. They did run, too, like scared rabbits. I was appalled."

"And what did you do?"

He sighed, admitted, "After a moment or two, I left myself; there wasn't much point staying. It was obvious Deravenel had taken the board by storm, and he did seem to have the facts about Cliff, Dever, and Beaufield. I'm afraid he was holding all of the cards."

"Oh, how stupid they were!" she cried and sat down on the sofa in front of the fireplace.

John moved across the room, draped himself against the fireplace, and stared at her.

She stared back, raising a curved black brow.

He said, "We might have lost this battle, but it is only a *battle*. We haven't lost the war."

"It sounds as if we have to me," she snapped, sitting up straighter. "What are we going to do?"

"At this moment, I don't know actually. I think we should go to Paris, you and I, take a break from all this business, have an intimate weekend together. *Chez toi.*"

Her face lit up.

"I can see the thought of being alone with me in your flat in Paris makes you happy," John said, a pleased expression in his eyes. "And the thought of it sends *my* head spinning. However, we must get back to business for a moment, Margot. Deravenel is sitting in my chair, the managing director's chair, and there's nothing that I can do about it. On the other hand, the Grants do own a huge number of shares in the company, and I think there has to be a Grant on the board, or there as a spokesman. I'm going to have to go back to the company rules, look a few things up."

"We can't let Edward Deravenel win, and—"

"He has, Margot, if only for the moment, of course."

She nodded. "You have to find a way to . . . unseat him."

"Indeed I will," John answered and sat down next to her on the sofa. "And what are we going to do with Henry whilst *we* are in Paris? He can't be left alone, you know."

"I understand that. He is perfectly happy at Ascot, and

Auberin, the butler there, knows how to take care of him. He will do so, following my instructions."

"That makes me feel easier." John stood. "I must go, I want to arm myself with enough facts so that I know what I'm talking about when the time comes."

part three

glittering temptations

edward and elizabeth

He pursued with no discrimination the married and the unmarried, the noble and the lowly: however, he took none by force.

DOMINIC MANCINI

She was of medium height, with a good figure, and she was beautiful, having long gilt-blonde hair and an alluring smile.

ALISON WEIR

Where Beauty and Beauty met,
Earth's still a-tremble there,
And winds are scented yet,
And memory-soft the air,
Bosoming, folding glints of light,
And shreds of shadowy laughter;
Not the tears that fill the years
After—after—

RUPERT BROOKE

forty-five

The spring supper dance was already under way at Lady Tillotson's splendid house in Berkeley Square. The strains of the orchestra playing music for the popular dance the Cakewalk came floating in from the magnificent ballroom, and there was a sense of gaiety in the air. It was a gaiety which seemed to prevail everywhere in London these days, with King Edward VII leading the way in this extraordinarily prosperous year of his reign, his sixth on the throne of England. London was the greatest capital in existence; the Empire ruled the world, and all was well under English skies.

In the beautiful drawing room which adjoined the ballroom, guests stood around or were sitting on gold-framed chairs, small sofas, and banquettes, sipping champagne and chatting. Tall, airy palms in heavy, cream-colored porcelain tubs were stationed in corners, and there were flowers everywhere: banks of lilies, peonies, roses, rhododendrons, and hydrangeas introduced rafts of pinks, cream and white, lilac, purple, and different reds, bringing vibrant color to the backdrop of the cream silk-covered walls and cream-and-gold painted woodwork. The air itself was filled with the delicate fragrance of the flowers and the more heady scents favored by the glamorous women who were present tonight, arrayed in all their finery.

Two glittering crystal chandeliers dropped from the ceiling at each end of the drawing room and were balanced by matching crystal wall sconces. The Waterford crystal pieces brought additional sparkle to the room and enabled the women to view one another's gowns with ease. And every woman was elegantly dressed in the latest styles, bought from the most famous fashion houses in Paris and London and worn with magnificent jewels. The men were equally elegant in their impeccably tailored black tails, starched white shirts, white bow ties, and matching white waistcoats.

Glancing around, the woman in black realized she was the only one wearing this dark color. Every other woman had chosen a pastel shade for her gown, so appropriate for spring. She did not care; she liked her choice, and it *was* appropriate for *her* at this moment in time.

She glanced to her left and saw her cousin Arthur Forrester heading in her direction, carrying a glass of champagne. "Thank you, Arthur," she said as he handed it to her and offered her a warm smile.

"Do you mind if I leave you alone for a few seconds?" he asked, as always scrupulously polite. "I'd like to smoke a cigar on the terrace with Woodstock and Hopkins, friends from my Eton days. Haven't seen those blighters for months."

"No, not at all," she murmured. "I'm sure Mama will descend on me at any moment."

He laughed with her and hurried off in the direction of the terrace. There was an eagerness in his eyes and a spring to his step.

Leaning back against the deep cream plush-velvet banquette, she glanced around, admiring some of the gowns, thinking that others were overdone, as was, indeed, much of the jewelry. Yet again, current fashion prevailed, and every woman wanted to ape Queen Alexandra, with her ornate chokers and dog collars of pearls and precious stones, the matching long strings of pearls and diamonds, all worn together. However, not every woman had a long, swanlike neck, as the Queen did. She smiled to herself, feeling pleased that she had kept her toilette simple tonight. It made her stand out, she thought, set her apart from every other woman present.

S he saw him the moment he arrived.

He caused quite a flurry as he hesitated in the entrance to the room, glancing around. People rushed to him, obviously wanted to welcome him, fete him, even. She wondered who he was.

He was very tall and broad-chested, and in the brilliant light of the room, his luxuriant hair looked silver. He was so handsome she was genuinely startled. She had never set eyes on a man quite like him.

With immense confidence he entered the room boldly, yet he moved lightly on his feet as he rushed, quite suddenly, toward a woman he obviously knew. She was a pretty brunette seated on the banquette opposite Elizabeth. Catching her breath, now that she had an even better view of him, Elizabeth realized he was indeed a big man. Yet there was no excess fat on him; he appeared athletic, very fit.

She was close enough to notice that everything about him was scrupulously clean, shining almost, and the silver hair was not silver at all; she could see that now. It was a burnished red-gold; he was very fair, his skin pink and white, and so *clean* looking. Like a freshly scrubbed schoolboy, was her unexpected thought.

He had seated himself next to the woman opposite; one arm stretched along the back of the banquette, rested between himself and the woman, and his right hand lay there, curled open slightly. He had beautiful hands, with long fingers.

To her amazement, Elizabeth suddenly knew she wanted those hands on her. Wanted him. Wanted every conceivable part of him. So intense was this feeling she felt her face becoming hot. How amazing . . . she was blushing. She hadn't blushed in years.

He must have dressed hastily; she noticed, suddenly, that the right cuff of his white dress shirt was open, hanging out of the sleeve of his superbly cut black evening suit jacket. He leaned in to the woman and kissed her on the cheek, almost absently, as an afterthought, it seemed to Elizabeth. He was talking to the woman earnestly, seemingly unaware of anyone else, even the others standing nearby, obviously wanting his attention.

"Elizabeth, what on earth's got into you?" her brother Anthony asked a trifle sharply, startling her, staring into her face as he bent toward her. "Gaping at that fellow like a common street girl! *Really,* darling."

Elizabeth stared back at her brother, who had so suddenly appeared at her side, and asked curiously, "Who *is* he? I don't know him."

Anthony was surprised to hear this. "You must be the only woman in London, if not indeed in the whole of England, who doesn't recognize *him.* That's Edward Deravenel, and please don't tell me you've never heard of him, because I certainly won't believe you. Others might, but not I. Everyone knows who Deravenel is, especially members of *your* sex."

"*That's* Edward Deravenel! Good heavens, Anthony, I thought he was a much older man! Certainly in his thirties, even early forties." She glanced across the room and went on. "Why, *he* looks to be in his twenties."

"Indeed he is, about twenty-three, something like that. But he's young."

"I've read about him in the newspapers. He gives very fancy parties, goes to all the best occasions given by others, and is quite the social animal, isn't he?" Not waiting for a response, she rushed on. "They say he's a genius in business. Is that true?"

"Don't really know, Lizzie darling."

"Anthony, please don't address me as Lizzie, you know I don't like it, and Mother *certainly* doesn't."

He ignored her comments. "Whether Deravenel is a genius or not doesn't really matter. He has very clever men working for him, and his cousin Neville Watkins by his side. Watkins is this country's greatest tycoon today, and some people say it's actually Watkins who runs Deravenels, and not our young friend over there."

"*Is* he a friend of yours?" Elizabeth asked swiftly, staring hard at her brother.

"Unfortunately not, an acquaintance, and merely a nodding acquaintance at that. We did do business some years ago with Deravenels, with the other branch of the family, the Grants, when they managed the company. Not since then, though, more's the pity." Turning his head, Anthony exclaimed, "Oh, darling, here's Agatha. I do believe I promised her this dance. Please excuse me, Lizzie." He winked at her mischievously, knowing how much she loathed any abbreviation of her name, this one most particularly.

"Of course, do run along with you, Anthony," she murmured in a slightly dismissive voice and sat back on the plush-velvet banquette. Now that she was alone again, she stole another look at Edward Deravenel.

At this precise moment he himself moved, drew away from the lovely brunette. He looked around, then glanced across the room.

His eyes met hers.

Her breath caught in her throat.

His eyes were the bluest she had ever seen, and startlingly so.

To her mortification, she felt herself blushing, not only because he had caught her watching him but because his eyes were suddenly, and unwaveringly, focused on her. Very slowly, a lazy, almost amused smile spread across his face.

For a moment Elizabeth couldn't look away, and then through the corner of her eye she saw her mother approaching, and she stood up, found herself heading rapidly toward the terrace. Within seconds she was opening the French doors and stepping outside. She looked about, saw that it was empty. Obviously, her cousin and his old school friends had gone for a walk in the garden below.

Although it was a pleasant April evening, it was, nonetheless, growing cooler, and she realized her error. But she wouldn't mind standing here for a moment. She was warm, and her face felt flushed when she touched it; moving closer to the balustrade, she placed her hands on the marble, liking the coolness.

She heard steps on the gravel footpath in the garden; voices drifted up to her, and she recognized Arthur's voice as he said, "He might have gone to Harrow, but why do we care? I think Churchill's a bloody good chap. He's done an excellent job as Undersecretary of State at the Colonial Office, and obviously Campbell-Bannerman has a lot of faith in him."

"I've heard that Campbell-Bannerman's not well," another voice said.

"Good Lord, Hopkins, where did you hear *that*?" Arthur demanded.

"*I* told him," Woodstock answered. "My father's close to the Prime Minister—he told him he'll probably step down next year."

"Good God!" Arthur exclaimed. There was a fractional pause before he went on. "If he does step down as Prime Minister, it'll be Asquith who succeeds him. There's nobody else."

"There'll be no election," Hopkins announced in a firm tone. "The Liberals swept to power last year, and they aim to stay. Churchill was lucky. When he crossed the floor of the House to join them, he knew what he was doing—"

"Hey, wait a minute! He crossed the floor because he was not happy with Tory policies," Arthur interjected, sounding annoyed as he hit back.

"There are some who say he's a traitor to the Tory Party and to his class," Hopkins muttered.

"I beg to differ," Arthur replied, lightening his voice. He laughed. "Come on, chaps, let's go back in and have a bit of the old bubbly, flirt with the ladies."

"I want to finish my cigar," Woodstock mumbled somewhat sulkily. "There's a bench over there, let's go and sit for a while."

Their voices drifted away, and Elizabeth leaned forward, looked out into the garden. Men and their politics, she thought, they drive me to distraction. But then again, politics were very much part of daily social life within the upper classes.

She sighed to herself. Hopkins was something of an argumentative chap; she rather agreed with Arthur. Churchill *was* a very promising politician. Her father had a lot of time for him, had always said he would go far.

forty-six

A few moments after the woman in black left the drawing room, Edward turned to Vicky and asked, "Do you know who that was? The young woman who was seated on the banquette at the other side of the room?"

Vicky shook her head. "I've no idea. I really didn't pay much attention, Ned darling. I was listening to you. However, just before you arrived I did notice a lovely blonde sitting down there." Vicky began to laugh merrily. "That's still your weakness, I gather. Blondes. You can't resist them, can you?"

"He certainly can't," her brother agreed, strolling toward them accompanied by Johnny Watkins. "I noticed the lady earlier myself. Rather striking. I've no idea who she is either," Will remarked.

"Ask our hostess, Ned," Johnny suggested, studying his cousin. "She wouldn't be here if she weren't somebody of importance. You know dear Maude, she's a terrible snob."

Ned laughed, stood up. "Please excuse me, Vicky. I can see Maude over there, talking to Lord Gosford. I think I should take your advice, Johnny, and inquire of our hostess who the lady in question is."

His cousin grinned, rolled his eyes theatrically.

"Come back quickly," Vicky said. "You promised me the next dance, Ned."

"Now *that* I certainly won't miss," he answered, smiling.

◆ ◆ ◆

Elizabeth had come to Maude Tillotson's dance because the renowned hostess was her mother's best friend. She had received one of the first invitations, and naturally er mother had pressed her to accept, along with her rother Anthony and their cousin Arthur Forrester.

She hadn't really wanted to attend in the first place; now he was frantically wondering how to escape. The dance eld no meaning for her, and she could not bear to be here. Edward Deravenel had unsettled her. I must leave, she decided, and right now.

"I hope I'm not intruding on your privacy, or any important momentary reflections," a mellifluous masculine voice said.

Elizabeth knew that it was *him* before she even looked ehind her. The curious thing was, she hadn't heard him approaching. She finally turned around and found herself tanding face-to-face with Edward Deravenel. Her throat vent dry, and she swallowed. He was larger than life, very close, so tall and distinguished. Charisma and masculinity eemed to radiate from him.

She leaned against the balustrade, relieved that it was here; she was shaking inside. Finally, growing conscious of he stillness surrounding them, her lack of response to him, he said hurriedly, "Oh no, you're not intruding at all. I simply came out . . . for a little air."

"It *was* warm inside." He paused, stared at her intently.

To Edward she was extraordinarily beautiful. Her face vas a perfect oval, with high cheekbones and a broad brow. Her eyes, large and set wide apart, were a light sky blue; she had wonderfully arched blond brows and a sensual mouth. Like that of most women who were fashionable, her hair was swept up on top of her head, piled high with a mass of curls at the front. But it was the color of her hair that captivated. Pure silver gilt, he thought, spun gold. She wasn't very tall, of medium height, but a cursory glance told me she had a lovely figure and high, firm breasts. Her dress, simple yet el-

egant, was made of black chiffon and lace, with a squar
neckline and slashed sleeves. The skirt floated around her i
the light breeze. The gown was in the new style, long, flow
ing, and full, without the once popular semibustle.

She cleared her throat softly.

He said swiftly, "I beg your pardon, how rude I'm being
staring at you in this way. Please forgive me. Actually, I hav
a feeling we've met before. We have, haven't we?" He knew
they hadn't; he would not have forgotten this beauty. But he
needed words to bridge the silence.

She was shaking her head. "No, we've never met, not ever
I would have remembered," she said, echoing his thought
without knowing that she did, and without any artifice.

"I am Edward Deravenel." He thrust out his hand.

She took it. For a moment, too long, in fact, he held her
hand tightly in his, and then he let go of it very quickly. Her
skin felt scorched.

At this moment she noticed the open cuff again.

"And you are?" he asked, raising a brow questioningly
his eyes searching.

"Elizabeth Wyland."

"I'm very pleased to meet you, very pleased indeed." He
bowed slightly, and as he did he noticed the gold wedding
ring on her finger. Straightening, he asked, "And you are no
doubt here with . . . Mr. Wyland?"

"Yes, my brother. That was the man I was talking to earlier."

Edward frowned, looked slightly perplexed.

She said quietly, "I'm a widow, Mr. Deravenel. I was mar
ried to Colonel Simon Gratton. He was in the British Army."

"Oh. I see." He seemed even more perplexed. "But you
did say Wyland?"

"Yes, I did, my maiden name." She shrugged lightly, dismissing this point. "My husband was wounded in the Boe
War, and when he came home to England from Africa i
1900, he was not the same man at all. The war killed hi

pirit, Mr. Deravenel. And he suffered from the aftereffects
of his wounds. Sadly for me, he died in 1904. My mother
said death was a relief for him, that his suffering was
over . . ."

"I am so very sorry. My condolences."

She inclined her head. "Thank you" was all she said.

"So here you are, Elizabeth!" Anthony exclaimed, walking
out onto the terrace. "I've been looking all over for you.
Mother would like to have a word with you, my dear."

Elizabeth merely nodded, then said, "This is Mr. Edward
Deravenel." Glancing at Edward, she added, "This is my
brother, Anthony Wyland."

The two men shook hands, and Edward said, "I'm not
certain, but I do believe we have met before, Wyland. Am I
not correct?"

"We have indeed, Deravenel. With my father."

Edward nodded politely, then turned to Elizabeth and
said, "Thank you for your courtesy." He flashed her a brilliant smile. "With your permission, I would like to call on
you in the near future, if I may."

"That would be very nice," she answered, then couldn't
resist saying, "Your right cuff is undone, did you know?"

He glanced down at it, smiled wryly. "Could you fasten it
for me?" He reached into his pocket, brought out a lapis-
lazuli cuff link that matched his shirt studs. "Here you are,"
he added, offering it to her.

She hesitated fractionally, then took it.

He shot his sleeve down so that she could insert the link
in the cuff. Her eyes on his sleeve, she murmured, "I receive
friends at four every afternoon."

When Edward returned to the drawing room a few
minutes later, Vicky was waiting for him. The orchestra was playing a waltz, and as he led her onto
the floor, she looked up at him and asked, "So who *was* the
beautiful blonde?"

"I never found out," he lied, although he did not know why. "Maude was leading Gosford off into the other drawing room, so I abandoned the quest." He laughed. "Got caught up with an old friend for a few minutes," he improvised, to explain his absence.

Vicky wasn't sure if she believed him, but she let the matter drop. It wasn't any of her business. She knew that Edward had not had a permanent relationship since Lily's death, just lots of women hanging around him.

Her brother, Will, called them "Ned's carnal relationships," and would laugh and say blithely, "Women are crazy about him. So much so, some chaps say he never has his trousers on. But I know differently. I'm with him at the office every day, and he works like a galley slave, believe you me."

Vicky knew this was true. Ned was a lot like his cousin Neville Watkins. Defying demons and driven by ambition, the two of them, she thought. She liked Neville, he was a man of his word and considerate. As for Edward, she loved him like another brother, but sometimes she had problems understanding him. Ned was a hard taskmaster with himself, yet he had, somehow, managed to acquire a reputation for being very much the ladies' man. But why not?

At almost twenty-three, Ned was determined to live the big life. And he was entitled; after all, he was young and single, and he had money, position, and background. Therefore he was in demand at all the dances, cotillions and balls, dinner parties, and every other kind of high-profile social event in London. Because of his wealth, success, and power, and that awesome charm of his, Ned was the most eligible young man in London these days. Since he was also stunning-looking and known to be a great lover, every woman wanted him. No wonder he was a little spoiled by women of all ages.

"Penny for your thoughts, sweet Vicky," Ned said, looking down at her. She had always been a favorite of his, and he went on gently, "You seem miles away. In New York, I've no doubt, with Stephen?" His bright blue eyes were questioning.

"That's right." She smiled up at him. "I miss Stephen so much, Ned, and so does little Grace Rose."

"When does he get back to London?"

"In about ten days, two weeks at the latest. Talking about that, I'm giving a party for Grace when he returns. I'd love you to come, Ned. With Fenella."

"Thank you, I will, and who else are you going to invite?"

"Amos, of course. Grace loves him."

"Good old Finnister, he's the salt of the earth. Splendid chap. I suppose my boon companion is coming, too."

"I haven't asked Will yet, but I'll mention it tonight. The only person other than you I actually did invite so far is Fenella. She's always shown such an interest in Grace."

"And done a great deal of detective work on her behalf," Ned pointed out, laughing. "Amazing how persistent Fenella was."

A little smile played around Vicky's mouth. "Yes, she was, and I for one am very glad. Now I really know who Grace is, and so much more than I did when I first found her birth certificate that day."

"How extraordinary that was, Vicky, just imagine if you hadn't decided to frame the old photograph of her mother you would never have known a thing about Grace. How odd life can be. Anyway, I must look for a gift. Tell me, what should I bring for her?"

"Goodness, I don't know. Let me think about it."

They finished the waltz in silence.

A short while later Edward found Will standing at the bar alone, drinking a glass of champagne. As he came to a stop next to his closest friend, Edward said, "You're looking glum. What's wrong?"

"I miss Kathleen rather more than I thought I would," Will said in a low voice. "I think I'm finally going to have to take that *fatal* step. Get married."

"I think you should," Edward answered swiftly, fully approving of Will's involvement with his cousin Kathleen Watkins, sister of Neville and Johnny. "She adores you, you know."

Will nodded and suddenly smiled. "That's good to know."

"Don't act daft, Hasling! You damn well know how she feels."

Will grinned, took a swallow of champagne, and asked, "And did you find out who the mysterious blonde is?"

"I did."

"And?" Will stared at Edward, frowning. "Why the long face?"

"She's a Wyland."

"God, no!" Will leaned closer to Edward and said, sotto voce, "Her father used to be very close to the Grants, very close indeed, although I must admit I don't know where he stands today, now that the Grants are living in France. But surely you knew the Wylands did business with the Grants. And for years. They go back a long time."

"My father once told me that the Wylands had been involved with Deravenels for over a hundred years, so they do go back, far back. I met her brother; he seems like a pleasant chap."

"Nicest of the bunch, so I've heard."

"She's a stunning woman, Will. I was captivated. I have to see her again. . . . By the way, she's a widow."

"Oh, Christ, no! Why is it that you always fall head over heels for blondes who are widows? It's uncanny. Come to think of it, she's probably older than you."

"Probably."

"Make it a short run, Ned, short and sweet, and then say farewell. She's from the enemy camp. Don't *you* forget that."

Edward gave him an odd look but made no further comment.

forty-seven

'm so very sorry, Elinor, but I really must be getting back to the office," Edward said, smiling at the woman seated opposite him.

"I understand, darling, but I am so disappointed," she murmured. "I thought we could spend the afternoon here. . . . We are alone, you know. As I told you, my housekeeper is off today. We could be . . . *together*."

"I had planned to be here with you, but something came up at the office this morning, and it needs my immediate attention. I have a meeting at three."

Elinor Burton nodded. "I realize you have a huge business empire to run. I don't know how you do it."

"Not alone, I can tell you that," he replied with a smile, standing up. "Thank you for lunch, it was delicious."

"All prepared by Fortnum and Mason." She laughed, also rose, and together they went out to the entrance foyer of her small house in Belgravia. "When will I see you again?" she asked.

"I'll try to come down to the country next week. I'll let you know." He pulled her toward him, held her tightly in his arms, then kissed her passionately on the mouth. She clung to him, responding enthusiastically.

After a moment, they stood apart, and she said, "You shouldn't have done that, Ned. It was far too tantalizing."

He merely laughed, gazing down at her, thinking how lovely she looked today, with her shining blond hair and hazel eyes that were golden in a certain light. "Oh, Elinor, you are a true beauty," he murmured, meaning it, and took hold of her again, suddenly aroused.

Elinor held him at bay, laughed lightly. "Oh, darling Ned, you're incorrigible. But not *now.* I will not be blamed for interfering with your business."

"Sanity usually reigns when I'm with *you.*" Flashing her his brightest smile, he let himself out of the house, and within minutes his mind was focused on business.

And then he stopped, thinking of Elinor. He had not been very nice to her today, and she really was the loveliest of women, sweet and gentle, and almost Madonna-like in her appearance. Turning around, he walked back to the front door and lifted the brass knocker.

Surprise filled her eyes as she opened the door and saw him. "Edward!" she exclaimed, staring. "Did you forget something?"

He smiled at her. "Yes, I forgot for a moment how much I care about you, darling. Can I come in for a short while?"

"Of course," she answered, opening the door wider. "But I'm confused. You said you had an important meeting to attend."

"I do," he said, turning to her in the entrance foyer. "But it's only one-fifteen; we had a very early lunch, you know. Noon . . . a little bit too early for me. Never mind, let's go upstairs, as you wanted to before." He took her in his arms and kissed her, and led her up to the next floor. She did not protest.

She was wearing a loose, navy blue silk dress with a dropped waistline, and she turned to him when they were in her bedroom and asked, "Could you unbutton me, please, Ned?"

He laughed as he started on the buttons, kissing the back

of her neck and her lovely blond hair as he did so. The dress fell to the floor; she stepped over it, turned to him, and smiled.

"How lovely you are, my sweet," he whispered, touching her cheek. There was something truly innocent about her face, and in her eyes there was nothing but peacefulness, and love for him. He had wanted her from the moment he met her, attracted by her innocence and simplicity. Of course she had fended him off, being a very proper widow, and virtuous; he had exercised every ounce of his charm. And eventually she had succumbed and given herself to him most wholeheartedly.

"What are you thinking about?" she asked, staring up into his eyes.

"I was thinking how your reluctance to start an affair with me actually made me want you all the more. In any other woman I might have thought the reluctance was a ruse, but I knew you were sincere."

"Oh yes, I was, Ned, but I'm glad now that we are together. You are so important to me. Let us go to bed, so I can show you how important."

Elinor was always ready for him, and after kissing her and smoothing his hands over her long, slender body, he knew she was growing more and more hot, agitated even, so he took her to him swiftly, entering her with great ease. She was truly ready, opening herself up to him like a flower, and the heat of her body aroused him further. He was unable to hold back. Against her neck he whispered, "Now, Nell, now, come to me." And she did so, clinging to him, her body trembling with joy under his.

As they lay together later, talking softly, she suddenly said, "You will come to the country this weekend, won't you?"

"I will. Where else would I want to be but with you?" he answered, knowing full well that he would visit her at her country cottage. He was not going to treat her lightly.

• • •

E dward had been in his office at Deravenels for only half an hour when Will knocked on the door and came in. "There you are. It's almost three, so let's go to the boardroom. Oliveri and Aspen will join us in a few minutes. How was lunch?"

"Pleasant. Marsden is a nice chap, but I don't think we'll be able to do any business with him."

"Where did you lunch? At White's?"

"No, *his* club. The Reform. But it was very quick, he was in a hurry," Ned answered, glad that he had indeed met Marsden at his club for a drink before rushing over to Elinor's pied-à-terre for their private luncheon. It gave him an alibi. The affair with her was a secret; they both wanted it that way, at least for the moment.

"By the way," Will went on, "Neville has finalized the plans for the Paris trip, to meet with Louis Charpentier. He telephoned a short while ago and said he'll have all the details later. But he's going in a few days."

"Very good. Shall we go into the boardroom?"

Ever since Edward had become managing director of Deravenels, Will had worked as his personal assistant. But he was also in charge of a pet project of Edward's, one which they were about to discuss.

Within seconds Oliveri and Aspen joined them and sat down at the conference table. After greetings had been exchanged, Edward said, "Well, tell me the big news."

"It's not *big* news," Alfredo answered. "But our contacts in Persia have confirmed that the company called Onpeg is definitely still there, continuing to drill for oil. At Masjid-i-Sulaiman."

"That's in southwest Persia," Rob explained.

"But they haven't struck oil yet, have they?" Edward asked, frowning. He glanced at Will as he spoke. "Nothing much has changed, has it?"

"Several other companies are out there, drilling in other

parts of Persia, and I think we ought to do what you've always wanted to do—send a team of our own to look around," Will said.

"Then let's plan it," Edward agreed, always sure of his visionary ability in business. It had served him well for the last three years. He had brought Deravenels back, had ensured its future and rectified much of the damage done by the Grant mismanagement. He was aiming to make the company more important than it had ever been.

"So," he went on, "who's to go? What about you, Oliveri? Do you want to hop out there to the desert sands of Persia?"

"If you want me to, I will." Alfredo grinned. "You know I love adventure."

"I'll go, too, if you think I can be useful," Rob interjected.

"I'm game. Persia appeals to me," Will announced.

"Oh no, not you, Will. I'm afraid you'll have to stay put. Now, chaps, let's discuss this further," Edward said. "Make the proper plans. I believe oil is going to be the big commodity of the future. And we must be in on its discovery. We need our own oil fields, they're vital . . ."

U nder no circumstances are you to allow him to climb into your bed," Jocelyn Wyland said, giving her daughter Elizabeth a hard and cautionary stare. "He has something of a reputation, you know, as a womanizer. And if you become intimate with him, that's it. You will soon be discarded."

"Mother, I've no intention of becoming intimate with Edward Deravenel! How could you think such a thing?" Elizabeth looked at her askance.

"Because if I were your age I'd take him into my bed at the drop of a hat!"

"Mother! *Really.*"

Jocelyn smiled. "I know I'm contradicting myself, but he is quite extraordinary and, I will add, irresistible to most women. Why should *you* be any different?"

"I'm not, and you're correct, Mother, but I'm not a fool. I'm hardly going to sleep with him now, when I want to marry him. That's my aim. Nothing less than marriage will do for *me*."

Jocelyn beamed at her eldest daughter. "I'm delighted to know that you have the right attitude about this. After all, sex is sex, and it can be most enjoyable. With the right man. But we are playing for bigger stakes here, Elizabeth. Let's not forget you're a widow with two young sons, and not much of an income from Simon's estate. Your father and I will continue to support you in the way you should be supported. However, I have big hopes for you."

"I know that, Mother, and I won't let you down. I know how to keep a check on . . . my emotions."

"You're a great beauty, and most men would do anything to possess you, my dear. But only the one who puts a wedding band on your left hand will do."

Elizabeth nodded, got up, walked across the small sitting room of her house in Cadogan Square, and stood looking out into the leafy square, thinking of Edward Deravenel. She wanted him desperately. After a moment she said, "I haven't seen him a lot, you know. Only twice . . . he came for tea."

"Hasn't he invited you anywhere, darling?" her mother asked, frowning slightly. "To the opera? A concert? Perhaps to dinner at the Ritz. That hotel's the most popular place with the denizens of society since it opened last year."

"No, he hasn't invited me out," Elizabeth said again.

"How peculiar. So how has he behaved when he's come for tea? What has he said? What happened?"

Elizabeth stared at her mother, wondering whether to tell her the truth. Opting for honesty, she said quietly, "He's talked to me affectionately, attempted to be amorous with me, kissed me on the cheek, the last time on the mouth, and he's tried to touch me . . . intimately. But I fended him off."

Jocelyn had always been able to talk openly with her eldest daughter, more than with any of her other children, and now she dropped her voice and asked, "Was he . . . *anxious*? Aroused?"

Elizabeth nodded. "Very much so, and the last time he was here he left angry because he was . . . rampant, raging to possess me."

"His frustration at not having his way with you got the better of him."

"I think so. He said I was a temptress, in a very annoyed voice."

Jocelyn burst out laughing. "Continue to tempt him, my darling, but don't let him get anywhere near you. Instinctively, I know the likes of him. A man who can't resist women soon moves on to fresher fields once he's picked the flowers in the field he's standing in."

Elizabeth laughed at this analogy, then confessed, "I'm head over heels in love with him, Mother."

"Keep yourself in check, Elizabeth. Save that love for after he's married you. Do you hear me?"

"Yes, I do. You have my promise."

"Has he made any attempt to see you again?"

"He sent a note this morning." Elizabeth glanced at the carriage clock on the mantelpiece. "He's coming this evening. Between six and seven."

"Has he invited you out to dinner tonight?"

"No, he said in the note that he would come for a drink."

"Perfect. And if he does want you to dine with him, say you cannot. I think I'd prefer you not to be seen in public with him at this moment. He's the most eligible man in London, and I don't want people to think he's had his way with you and then dropped you . . . that is, if nothing comes of this . . ."

"I understand."

"I trust you do, darling. Your future depends on your chastity at this time."

forty-eight

Thorpe Manor was one of the loveliest houses in Yorkshire. Beautifully proportioned, with a flowing front facade, many windows, and two towers with cream domes and shining spires, it was a perfect example of late Elizabethan architecture. The house was built of local pale pink stone, the window and door surrounds were outlined in cream limestone, and the whole was soft and gentle.

The house was set in a vast parkland of sweeping green lawns and great spreading oak and sycamore trees, flower gardens, walled rose gardens, and several ornamental lakes. Swans floated on the surface of the lakes, and peacocks strutted proudly on the terraces and lawns. The manor house had been in the Watkins family for centuries, gifted to Neville by his father when he married Nan. It had been their country home ever since.

Today the house was a hive of activity. The staff bustled everywhere; florists were filling urns and vases with roses and other flowers; chefs were preparing delicious food in the kitchen; caterers were arranging small gold chairs around the circular tables on the long terrace, straightening rose-pink organdy cloths and adding napkins.

In a few hours Kathleen Watkins, sister of Neville, would be married to Will Hasling in the private chapel on the estate. And afterward the family and guests would mingle at the reception, a garden party. It was a glorious June Saturday, a perfect day for a wedding.

Will stood in his bedroom, staring at Edward worriedly. "Are you sure my cravat is correctly arranged?" he asked. "Do I look all right, Ned?"

"Never better, old chap. In fact, if I were a woman, I'd marry you in a shot," Ned joked, grinning at his best friend.

"Oh, do be serious!" Will exclaimed, looking exasperated.

"All right, I'll be serious. *You've never looked better,*" Ned reassured him. "Tall, handsome, and Savile Row perfect down to the glassy toes of your shoes. Do stop being the proverbial nervous bridegroom and stand still so that I can attach your boutonniere."

Once the white rose was in place on Will's jacket, Edward handed another white rose to him and said, "Now it's your turn to affix mine." Both men were elegantly attired in morning suits—impeccably tailored black frock coats, striped trousers, and white waistcoats. Their cravats were of soft dove gray silk, each held in place with a pearl stickpin.

Stepping away from Ned, Will eyed his friend and joked, "And *I* would marry *you* at the drop of a hat, if I were a woman."

The two friends laughed together, and then Ned said, "Do you feel a bit constrained? Having Neville in Paris when you're on your honeymoon there?"

Will shrugged, looked unconcerned. "Not really. Actually, Kathleen and I will only be there for a couple of days before going on to the Côte d'Azur. Anyway, I doubt that we'll see Neville. He's going to be in meetings with Louis Charpentier the few days he's in Paris."

"Yes, that's true; actually, he'll be finalizing the deal to take over the Charpentier silk mills in Lyon."

Hearing the lack of interest in Edward's voice, Will glanced at him swiftly. "*You* don't sound very enthusiastic."

"I'm not. I couldn't care less, Will. I know Charpentier has a big business empire in France, and Neville craves it for us, but Deravenels is pretty solid these days. I don't think we need the Charpentier French holdings, not really. I'm more interested in *oil*. I'm glad we sent that team of geologists to Persia with Oliveri and Aspen. I hope we can stake a claim out there, I really do. In fact, I'm fanatical about it."

"You've always said oil is the future, and I concur. After the honeymoon, maybe *we* ought to go out to Persia, Ned, take a look round, you and I."

"Maybe. Although I have my hands full at the moment, as you well know. I have those Americans coming next month. They want to sell us their cotton plantations outright, and I've a mind to buy them. It makes great sense to me."

There was a light tap on the door, and Johnny Watkins walked in, looking as elegant as Ned and Will in his morning suit. "Ah, there you are," he said to Ned, "and *you* have the tray of white roses, I see. I need one, old chap, and so do the other ushers. And Neville."

"There's plenty here, and there's even one for Richard, Johnny. I don't want my Little Fish to feel left out."

"And George, what about *him*?" Will asked, throwing Ned a cautionary look. "We don't want a temper tantrum to-day of all days."

"Only too true. There is a rose for George," Ned answered quietly. George was an irritant these days; he worried Ned.

Ned attached the white rose to the lapel of Johnny's jacket and went on, "I hope you're wearing your other white rose. You are, aren't you?"

Johnny smiled at him, his gray eyes sparkling. "I'll never take it off, Ned. I told you, I'll wear it till the day I die, and even after." Picking up the small silver tray, Johnny now headed toward the bedroom door, explaining, "I must go downstairs and rally the troops."

Will watched Johnny go, and then, swinging to Ned, he said in a low voice, "Has Johnny asked you about the blonde you spotted at Maude Tillotson's dance?"

"No. Why?" Ned's eyes narrowed slightly.

"Because he *did* ask *me,* quite recently. He wanted to know if you'd found out who she was, and I actually lied to him, Ned." Will shook his head. "God knows why I did that. . . . I just felt I'd better not say she was a Wyland. I know Neville has always been suspicious of the family, because of their long-held friendship with the Grants."

"Thanks for being protective of me, Will, I appreciate it. But actually, I haven't seen her again. I mean, after the last time I had drinks with her at her house. She wasn't very . . . *cooperative,* shall we say? Not at all willing to share her favors with me, so I backed off. Too much trouble . . . a widow with two young sons."

"I'll say!"

There was another tap on the door, and Vicky looked in, smiling. "I've been sent to fetch the bridegroom and his best man." As she spoke, she came into the room, looking beautiful in a pale blue gown. She was a matron of honor with Fenella Fayne. "Let me correct myself, chaps. I volunteered, so I could give you each a kiss." She walked across to her brother and added, "And I want to wish you much happiness, Will darling, and all the luck in the world."

L ike her brothers, Kathleen Watkins had a strong resemblance to her aunt, Cecily Deravenel. She was a lovely-looking young woman, with a cloud of russet hair, large, pellucid gray eyes, and a slender, aristocratic face, finely boned.

As she walked down the aisle of the small chapel on the arm of her brother Neville, she felt as though her life was just beginning. She had been in love with Will for years, since she was sixteen, and now her dream was about to come true. When she left the chapel, she would be his wife. He would be her husband. Her happiness soared.

Will, waiting at the altar for Kathleen, thought she had never looked lovelier. As she walked toward him on her brother's arm, all his nervousness fled. He suddenly felt utterly calm inside. He knew he was doing the right thing, marrying this special young woman. He felt Ned squeeze his arm, looked at him quickly, and nodded. "I'm all right," Will whispered, answering the questioning look in Ned's eyes.

As for Edward Deravenel, the best man, he was relaxed and at ease with himself. He was happy for Will, knowing how much his friend had wanted to be married. He was lucky he had found the right person, someone who loved him so much in return.

Here she came now, his cousin Kathleen, a vision in white satin and white lace. There was the glint of pearls and orange blossoms in the small coronet on her head, and the tulle veil itself was like a great cumulus cloud around her face, soft, enfolding. She carried a magnificent bouquet of white roses, freesias, gardenias, and orchids, and as she drew closer, he caught a fleeting whiff of their mingled perfumes.

Behind her came her two matrons of honor, Vicky and Fenella, and behind them the bridesmaids: his sister Margaret; Neville's daughter, Isabel and Anne, and last, the flower girl, Grace Rose. All of the attendants were wearing pale blue silk, and the little girls, in particular, looked adorable, Ned thought.

In the background the organ played, and a lone soprano voice suddenly rang out:

O perfect Love, all human thought transcending,
lowly we kneel in prayer before thy throne,
that theirs may be the love which knows no ending,
whom thou for evermore dost join in one.

Neville and Kathleen finally came to a standstill in front of the altar. The organ music faded away, and the Watkins family priest was in place before the bride and Neville.

Ned felt in his pocket for the wedding rings. They were there. *Safe.* He relaxed once more.

And the ceremony began.

• • •

Satin and lace. Flower petals and confetti. Laughter and tears. Happiness and joy to overflowing. Champagne in crystal flutes. Sunlight shimmering. Shady seats under leafy trees. Music in the air. Mozart and Brahms. English country airs. Popular songs. Glamorous people. Beautiful clothes. Jewelry glittering.

People talking, laughing, moving . . . all around him. The garden party was a success, Ned already knew that. But he wanted to move away from the lawn, up onto the terrace, to sit down, to reflect for a moment. His mind was so full . . .

He walked fast, moving through the crowd, climbing the broad stone steps to the smaller terrace, which had been decorated with comfortable white wicker chairs and love seats. As he sank down into one of the wicker chairs, he saw his mother coming toward the terrace, and he waved. A moment later, he noticed Vicky, holding Grace Rose's hand, and they too were wandering across the lawn heading in his direction.

As his mother came up the steps, he stood, waiting for her, a wide smile on his face.

"How beautiful Kathleen looked," Cecily said. "Such a lovely ceremony, Ned, wasn't it?"

"It was indeed, Mother."

Suddenly Grace Rose was running toward them, and as she came to a standstill, Ned crouched down. "Hello, Grace Rose, you were the perfect flower girl," he murmured.

"Was I really, Uncle Ned?" she asked, smiling prettily.

"Oh yes, indeed!"

Turning to Vicky, Grace cried, "Mumma, did you hear that? Hear what Uncle Ned said?"

"I did, my darling. Now come along, we must go inside for a moment." Vicky smiled at Cecily and said, "Hello, Mrs. Deravenel. It's such a happy day, isn't it?"

"It is indeed, Vicky, my dear." Cecily glanced at the child. "And your name is Grace Rose, is it?"

"Yes," Grace said, bobbing a small curtsy.

"Well, hello, Grace Rose," Cecily murmured and smiled.

"Hello," Grace answered shyly, and then she put her hand in Vicky's and the two of them left.

Cecily watched them go into the house, and then she turned to Edward and asked, "Is that Vicky's child, Ned? She called her Mumma."

"Thereby hangs a long tale," he answered. "Sit down, and I'll tell you."

After Edward recounted the story of how Amos had found Grace on the streets and brought her to Haddon House, he told his mother about the birth certificate in the photograph frame, and the note.

Cecily sat up straighter in the wicker chair, and frowned. "So Vicky found out who the child's parents were. How amazing!"

"She discovered who the mother was. The father's name was not on the birth certificate."

"*Illegitimate*. Grace Rose is illegitimate then." Cecily frowned. "And what did the note reveal, Ned?"

"The name of the father."

"And who is the father?"

"Actually, Mother, I am."

forty-nine

Cecily sat staring at him. She was perfectly still, her face devoid of expression. And she did not say a word.

Finally, Edward spoke. "You don't appear to be surprised, Mother."

"I am; then, yet again, I am not. The moment I set eyes on that child walking down the aisle in the chapel, I was struck by her resemblance to you. At that moment I didn't know who she was. When I saw her with Vicky on the terrace, saw how you were so gentle and sweet with her, I assumed . . ." Cecily sighed, shook her head. "Forgive me, Ned, but I thought you and Vicky had had an affair, and that Grace Rose was the result."

"*Mother.* How could you think such a thing? Vicky's a married woman!"

"When has that ever stopped you?"

"My God!" Ned shook his head. "I must have the most dreadful reputation."

"Well, I don't know that I would use that word. From what *I* hear, most men envy you, and most women would . . . Well, let's leave it at that. The less said about women and their sex lives, the better."

Edward couldn't help chuckling. After a moment, he said, "There's no one like *you*, Mama. No one at all."

"So who is, or was, the mother of Grace Rose? I'm assuming the child was correct when she said her mother was dead."

"She is dead, yes. At least so I believe. Fenella thinks so, too, but actually I'm jumping ahead. Let me explain something. . . . Grace's mother was Tabitha James. She was the wife of the choirmaster at a church in Scarborough. I met her when—" Edward paused, compressed his mouth, then said vaguely, "When I was very young, we became . . . involved, but she was afraid we'd be caught, and she disappeared from my life. Then I ran into her again one day. In Whitby. She was widowed by this time and had gone to live there with her husband's spinster sister. Toby James had left her . . . destitute."

"And you picked up with her again, is that what you're about to tell me?"

Edward gave his mother a direct look and nodded. "Yes, I did."

Cecily frowned, shaking her head, and then said slowly, "But Ned, you must have been very *young*."

He bit his lip and didn't answer for a moment, then took a deep breath, blew out air. "When Tabitha lived in Scarborough, when I first met her, I was thirteen. . . . *She* seduced *me* when I was thirteen. When I saw her in Whitby, I was fourteen."

Although she was appalled to hear how young Ned had been when he had come to know a woman intimately, Cecily realized that her eldest son was not like most men. First of all, he was tall and had been extremely well developed as a boy of thirteen. He had appeared much older than his true years, not only in his looks but also in his demeanor. Ned had always been rather grown-up for his age, more sophisticated than other boys.

Leaning forward, Cecily now put her hand on Edward's arm, and her gaze was full of understanding. "How old were you when Grace Rose was born?" she asked softly.

"I must have been fifteen, Mother. I did endeavor to stand

by Tabitha as best I could." A faint smile flickered, and he said in a subdued voice, "There wasn't too much I could do . . . about giving her money. I didn't have any. But I would ask Cook for a picnic every time I rode over to see Tabitha, which was often. So I did provide food for her during her pregnancy."

Cecily closed her eyes convulsively, asking herself why children never came to their parents when they had problems, whatever those problems were. But she knew the answer. They were afraid to confide. And rightly so. If Ned had told her and Richard of the predicament he was in, he would have been sent away to boarding school instead of being tutored at Ravenscar. So he had struggled on his own, done his best.

"Are you all right, Mother?" he asked, looking at her worriedly.

"Yes, Ned, I am," she murmured and opened her eyes.

He searched her face. "I tried to be responsible, you know."

She nodded. "Then the baby was born . . . and what happened?"

"If you remember, I had bronchitis when I was fifteen and was quite ill for some weeks. When I finally got better, I rode over to Whitby. Tabitha was gone. In fact, other people lived in the cottage. I made inquiries. Apparently the sister-in-law had died and Tabitha had gone to London. That was all I knew."

"I see. You must have been upset."

"I was. Yes. But I told myself that Tabitha was in her twenties and capable. I thought she had probably gone to stay with a friend. She once told me she had a school friend who lived in Chelsea."

"And so you got on with your life, I presume." Cecily raised a brow quizzically.

"There wasn't anything else I could do," Ned replied.

"And then one day you met your child. With Vicky. Am I correct?"

"You are. I was struck at once by Grace Rose's looks, and so was Will. But we never actually discussed it."

"Not even Vicky? Didn't she spot the resemblance?"

"I think she did, Mother, but the circumstances were so strange; the way Finnister had found the child in a cart in Whitechapel threw everyone off. So *I* believe. How could that child be *mine*? Vicky thought Grace's coloring was just a peculiar coincidence. She told me that later."

"Once the birth certificate had been found, and the note, of course everything was out in the open. Is that the way it was?" Cecily stared at her son again.

"Let's just say six people knew. Vicky, Stephen, Fenella, Finnister, and Will. And me. You see, Tabitha had named me as the father in the note, asking that I be contacted. There was a lock of my hair inside the note."

"And your address? Was that not given?" Cecily wondered aloud.

"Just Ravenscar."

"But no one ever removed the brown paper from the photograph until Vicky did."

"You are correct, Mother. Actually, I didn't know much myself. I told Vicky that Tabitha had gone to London and disappeared from my life."

"You mentioned Fenella a short while ago. How did she come into play?"

"Fenella knows Whitby rather well, as it turns out. Although she grew up in Tanfield, she and her brother were taken to Whitby every summer by their nanny when they were children. For their seaside holidays. She was going up to Yorkshire to stay with her father just after the note was found, so she decided to do a bit of detective work. She went over to Whitby, talked to Tabitha's former neighbors, as well as the local tradespeople, and she found out two things. First, Tabitha James wasn't who she said she was; by that I mean she was seemingly the only daughter of a titled family and had run off with her music teacher, Toby James. Fenella was also given a name: Sophie Fox-Lannigan. This woman was seemingly the old school friend of Tabitha's who lived in Chelsea."

"Goodness me! Who would ever have thought that Fenella would be such a clever detective and go to all that trouble?" Cecily was impressed.

"You don't *really* mean that, Mother, if you think about it. Of course Fenella would want to help. And just think of the way she runs Haddon House. That's who she is, you know, a very caring person."

"That's true. She's also very inquisitive. Fortunately." Cecily threw Edward a knowing look and continued. "And I suppose Fenella went to see this lady, Sophie Fox-Lannigan, to ascertain what *she* knew."

"She did indeed look up Mrs. Fox-Lannigan. Tabitha's old friend still lived in Chelsea. Unfortunately, she didn't know too much. She told Fenella that Tabitha had stayed with her and her husband for a few months, and had then gone off with a man she'd met through friends of the Fox-Lannigans. He was a former guards officer, and a gambler, by the name of Cedric Crawford."

"And Fenella found him. Is that what you're about to tell me?"

"No, I'm not. Mrs. Fox-Lannigan told Fenella that Tabitha had ended up living with Crawford in Whitechapel in a terrible hovel of a place. Mrs. Fox-Lannigan had gone to see her a few times, taking money and food, and begging her to leave this man. But Tabitha seemed fearful of Crawford and wouldn't budge. Sophie was so troubled she kept going back, and one day when she went to see Tabitha, she had disappeared. All of them had. *Gone.* Just like that, without a trace."

"What a dreadful way for poor Tabitha to end up. She was never found, I suppose?"

"No. And obviously Crawford had flown the coop. Probably after Tabitha died. The child originally said to Amos

Finnister that the man had killed her mother. But we have no proof of that."

"This man Crawford pushed Grace Rose out onto the streets once her mother was gone, of that I'm positive."

"More than likely he did," Ned agreed.

"Who was she really? Tabitha?"

"She was the daughter of the Earl of Brockhaven, and therefore had a title in her own right. Before she married Toby James, she was Lady Tabitha Brockhaven."

"Has anyone been in contact with her family?"

"There is no family left, Mother. The Earl and Countess had no sons; Tabitha was the only child. Now the Earl and Countess are dead, the title is extinct. They were a rather impoverished family, according to Mrs. Fox-Lannigan."

"I see. How sad. . . . What terrible lives people do have." Cecily shook her head sorrowfully. "We all of us suffer such hardships at times, and in such different ways."

Edward, at this precise moment, thought of the word *catastrophe* and instantly pushed it away. He looked off into the distance, and then, turning back to his mother, he murmured, "That's more or less the whole story . . . except for one thing. Sophie Fox-Lannigan had a small trunk belonging to Tabitha. Once Tabitha and Grace had disappeared, she simply put it in the attics of her house, loath to throw it out. She mentioned this trunk to Fenella, who instantly remembered a key in Grace's cloth bag."

Cecily nodded. "I know what you're going to tell me . . the key in the bag fit the trunk."

"It did."

"And what did the trunk contain?"

"Notes from me to Tabitha. Letters from her father, begging her to come home, letters that said all was forgiven. A few bits of jewelry, not worth very much. Odds and ends that Vicky will give to Grace Rose when she's old enough to have them."

"And what does the child know, Ned? Does she know you are her real father?"

"No, no, not at all! I would never do that to Stephen and Vicky. They adore the child. We discussed it at length, and I was the one who asked them to allow things to remain exactly as they were. No big revelations. I did say I would like to be part of Grace Rose's life . . . but only as Uncle Ned. Also, you should know that now I am head of Deravenels, and have money, I have created a trust for Grace Rose. However, she mustn't know anything about my being her natural father. It's the best way, Mother, really it is. No one gets hurt."

"I absolutely agree with you, Ned. You have done the right thing. And despite what some people might think, you always do. In your own way." Cecily gave him a loving smile that had a hint of pride in it and said, "And so Grace Rose is . . . *seven* years old. Am I right?"

"Yes, you are. She was four when Finnister found her, but because she's tall, like I am, Vicky was always convinced that she was five, perhaps older. Naturally, the birth certificate confirms her age."

"Thank you for telling me the story. Now perhaps we should go take part in the wedding tea." As they went down the steps together, Cecily told her son, "I'd like to see Grace Rose again, Ned. A little later. Just to talk to her for a short while."

"I think that's a good idea, Mother. You should get to know her."

They made their way to the larger terrace, where the two families and guests were starting to gather and looking for their seats.

Neville came striding toward Ned and his mother, exclaiming, "There you both are! We wondered what had happened to you."

"Just catching up," Cecily remarked, wondering suddenly how much her nephew knew. Everything, she decided. Ned will have told him everything. He always does.

"You look perfectly beautiful, Aunt Cecily," Neville said

as he led his aunt toward her place at the family table. "This delphinium blue suits you enormously."

"Why thank you, Neville, and I must congratulate you and Nan. You are giving the most beautiful wedding I have been to in a very, very long time. It's superb, and the idea of a garden party was inspired."

A few minutes later Neville drew Edward aside and said in a low, confiding tone, "Are you sure you don't want to come with me on Monday to Paris to meet with Louis?"

Oh, so it's Louis now, Edward thought but said, "Thanks, but no thanks, Neville. It's your deal, and I think you should be the one to follow it through."

"Very well. And consider it done," Neville answered with a bright smile, placing a hand on Edward's shoulder. "We make the best team, you and I."

After all of the wedding speeches had been made and toasts drunk, the dancing began in the Great Hall. Many of the guests flocked inside, while others walked around the gardens, enjoying the beautiful evening.

It was at this moment that Cecily went in search of Vicky. She found her sitting at one end of the Great Hall with her husband.

"Vicky darling, may I have a word with you?" Cecily asked as Vicky looked up.

"But of course, Mrs. Deravenel. Excuse me for a moment, Stephen."

He had risen when Cecily had come to a stop in front of them, and now he smiled at her. "It's a lovely day, isn't it Mrs. Deravenel?"

"It is, Stephen, and a lovely wedding. I'm glad our families are joined."

Taking hold of Vicky's arm, Cecily quickly led her to the far end of the hall and out into a courtyard that opened off it "Vicky, I know everything," she began, wanting to get to the point at once. "Ned told me everything about Grace Rose. Just now, this afternoon."

"I always thought that you, more than anyone else, would notice the extraordinary resemblance between Ned and the child."

"I did. But I thought it might just be a coincidence."

Vicky smiled, nodded. "Coincidence plays such an important part in our lives, doesn't it? And sometimes lives are built entirely on *ifs.* . . . *If* Fenella hadn't opened Haddon House, Amos Finnister wouldn't have known where to take Grace. And *if* he hadn't worked for Neville, he wouldn't have known *me.* And on and on."

"Yes, indeed, it's amazing at times. Could we go and find Grace Rose? I would love to look at her again, Vicky, just hold her . . ." Cecily's voice trailed off.

"Yes, yes, let us go and find her!" Vicky exclaimed. Cecily Deravenel had had so many losses in the last few years, Vicky wanted her to have a moment of joy now.

They hurried back to the center of the Great Hall, where people were dancing. Music filled the air, and the sound of voices and of laughter swirled around them. The evening was just getting started. Supper would be served at eight.

Grace spotted Vicky first and came running to her. The child's beautiful face was full of smiles. She came to a stop and said, "I've been dancing with Richard . . . he swirled me around and around, Mumma. It was fun."

Vicky laughed. "You remember this lady, don't you, Grace? You met her earlier with Uncle Ned."

Grace nodded and offered Cecily a small, shy smile.

Cecily bent down, took hold of Grace's hand. "I forgot to tell you something, Grace Rose. . . . I am Uncle Ned's mother, and I want you to call me Aunt Cecily. Will you do that?"

The child nodded. "I love Uncle Ned! He's my friend."

"Can *I* be your friend?" Cecily asked.

"Oh yes," Grace Rose answered solemnly, staring at Cecily.

And then suddenly, much to Cecily's surprise, and Vicky's, too, Grace moved closer to Cecily, put her plump little arms around her neck, and nuzzled her cheek as if they were old friends.

Cecily held the little girl tightly in her arms and thought: This is my grandchild, my first grandchild, and I can never claim her as mine. But I can surely love Grace Rose. I can surely do that.

fifty

Whenever Cecily came to stay at Thorpe Manor, Neville and Nan gave her the room which had been hers when she was a child and a young woman, growing up here. This had been her father's favorite residence of all the houses he owned, perhaps because he himself had been born and grown up at the manor.

Philip Watkins had spent a great deal of time here in Ripon with his wife and children after he inherited the manor; the house had been in the Watkins family for centuries, and they were the squires in this little village in the Dales.

Cecily loved this old place, with its well-proportioned, airy rooms filled with light from the many leaded windows, the highly polished wood floors, the carved fireplaces, the nooks and crannies, eccentricities so frequently found in Tudor architecture.

The reception room Cecily liked the best was the Great Hall. Stretching almost the entire length of the house, it had a soaring brick fireplace and a unique carved overmantel, a beamed ceiling and tall mullioned windows.

Now, as she sat in the window seat in her bedroom, Cecily's thoughts went back to the evening which had ended only an hour ago: the dancing in the Great Hall, the elegant supper in the formal dining room, and the continuation of the dancing later. It had been an effortless evening, one full of music, merriment, and laughter, and Neville and Nan had been superb hosts. It seemed to Cecily that everyone had enjoyed themselves, and guests had stayed late.

Leaning her dark head against the window, she gazed out at the gardens. There was a full moon tonight, a June moon, and its radiant silvery light gave the garden a magical look.

She sighed. How often she had sat here as a young girl, dreaming of romance and marriage, of starting a family of her own. So long ago, at least so it seemed to her now.

Thoughts of her husband crept into her mind, but she instantly pushed them away. She could not bear that particular pain tonight, the pain of his loss, and the loss of her son Edmund, her brother, Rick, and her nephew Thomas. The bride's young brother who should have been here . . .

Cecily, always protective of herself, allowed these unhappy thoughts to slide away, fully aware of her responsibilities. There were still two young sons to take care of, George and Richard, and Meg, her darling Meg, eighteen now and beautiful.

She smiled as she thought of Meg as she was a few hours ago. How lovely she had looked, how happy she had been, dancing mostly with Edward. He had captured her for many dances, and the eighteen-year-old had been in her element with her brother, whirling around the Great Hall, light as air, her eyes sparkling.

Edward. The story of Grace Rose had captivated Cecily; she had been fascinated, touched, and appalled, all at the same time. Of course Edward had always been impulsive, yet also loyal to family and friends. But impulsive, yes. Easily tempted by women. Women threw themselves at him. They had done so even when he was only twelve and thirteen. She had noticed it, as had his father; they had endeavored to ignore it. Too much temptation had always been put in Ned's way.

Well, Tabitha James had enticed him into her arms when he was thirteen; although, in fairness, Cecily believed Tabith